WAITING FOR A BRIGHT NEW FUTURE

A heartwarming and uplifting page-turner
about second chances

SALLY JENKINS

*To Caroline
Happy reading!
Sally Jkins*

Choc Lit
A Joffe Books company
www.choc-lit.com

This edition first published in Great Britain in 2023

© Sally Jenkins 2023

This book is a work of fiction. Names, characters, businesses, organizations, places and events are either the product of the author's imagination or are used fictitiously. Any resemblance to actual persons, living or dead, events or locales is entirely coincidental.
The spelling used is British English except where fidelity to the author's rendering of accent or dialect supersedes this. The right of Sally Jenkins to be identified as author of this work has been asserted in accordance with the Copyright, Designs and Patents Act 1988.

Cover art by Jarmila Takač

ISBN: 978-1-78189-645-7

CHAPTER ONE

"How's Eric?" Lillian from next door was manoeuvring her wheelie bin in only her nightclothes and bare feet, oblivious of the stony ground and early morning chill.

"Hanging in there."

"When he passes, come for me. You shouldn't be alone with . . . well, you know . . . before the undertaker."

"Thanks." Stuart felt a lump in his throat and, head down, concentrated on positioning his own bin. This was the kindest offer anyone had made him and warmed something deep inside. After caring for his father for twenty-five years, everyone, the professionals and his elder brothers alike, just assumed he could cope. They didn't understand what it was like to close the front door on the world and be the sole lifeline for an ailing man. He took a breath before smiling at the woman he used to call 'Aunty' as a child. "Thank you very much. I appreciate that."

Lillian smiled and then started rubbing her arms and picking her way carefully back up to the house, as though she'd suddenly become aware of the cold and her lack of shoes.

At lunchtime she knocked on his door and presented him with a steaming apple crumble and a jug of thick, yellow custard.

"Things are easier to tackle after a nice pudding," she said.

Stuart carried the laden tray into the kitchen and then gave her a bear hug of gratitude.

Later, Stuart's father asked him to set up a video call with his elder brothers, Robert and George. "It's about the will." Eric spoke hesitantly and didn't meet Stuart's eye. "I should've changed things as soon as you and Sandra were born. But things were a mess back then and too much got overlooked. You've had the worst of it all along. I'm sorry. I'll explain to Robert and George, and then we'll get Mr Finch to draft a new document."

The warmth created by Lillian's kindnesses was replaced by a cold, creeping fear. Stuart had sacrificed everything to look after his father while his brothers, twelve and fifteen years his senior, had married, had families and surged ahead in their careers. They were both comfortably retired with no need for Eric's money. But if Stuart wasn't in the will, he would be left with nothing.

* * *

Robert and George sat in their separate little boxes on the screen looking apprehensive.

"I don't want Stuart to lose his home when I'm gone." Eric's voice was too weak to be picked up clearly by the laptop microphone and Stuart had to repeat everything their father said for the benefit of his brothers. It was a slow process.

"He's going to give me a life interest in the house." Stuart paraphrased his father's words. "I can continue to live here as long as I like. If I want to sell the house and move, that's OK, but the house or its proceeds always remain part of the estate. When I die, the grandchildren will inherit equal shares of the house."

Robert leaped in with the first criticism. "So, George and I will never see any benefit from the will."

George was mouthing madly like a fairground goldfish. Eventually he found the button to free his voice. "Agreed. It's not fair that Stuart gets all the benefit."

"This isn't up for debate." Stuart could barely hear his father above his brothers' protests. "The new will is being drawn up and I'll be signing it tomorrow."

Stuart wanted to wave his arms in the air and shout, "Yes!" His father was finally treating him like a valued member of the family in front of his siblings. He'd still have to generate income to live off when his father died, but he wouldn't be homeless.

A few minutes later, he clicked the red 'End Meeting' button and his brothers' thunderous faces disappeared into the ether.

The best man won! Good job I'm not around to stake a claim as well. The future is looking brighter, Stuart Borefield. Perhaps you can dig out those old guide books? There might be a middle-aged Dutch lady waiting at the Eiffel Tower. Ha! You thought I'd forgotten about your one and only one-night stand, didn't you?

Sandra was increasingly voicing her opinion inside his head, just as she'd done when he was a child. Back then he'd clutched at her, desperate for a sibling ally. Even if that sibling had had to be imaginary. "If you'd lived, Sandra," he said, "none of this would've happened. I might have been a famous explorer. Or, at least, the head of a school geography department."

Damn right it wouldn't have happened. I'd have got things organised in a totally fair manner so that all of us could have a decent life, including Dad.

The next day, Stuart got up early. He wanted a ride before he woke his father and got his bedroom into an acceptable state for receiving the solicitor. Cycling would clear his head and chase away the tension. He needed to be absolutely on top of what his father was signing with no possibility of giving his brothers any wriggle room.

Attaboy, Bro!

Before leaving he listened at his father's door. Silence. He thought about peeping in but if the old man was awake, he'd delay Stuart and the ride would be scuppered.

It was spring and the early morning air tasted of positivity and brightness as Stuart breathed in great lungfuls of it.

The dawn chorus was well underway and cheered his heart. It was difficult to be downhearted when England's green and pleasant land was brimming with new beginnings and singing birds. Stuart loved the way that the seasons and the plants and the animals always started afresh at this time of year. Whatever was going on in his own life, nature continued in its own remarkable way.

Afterwards, red-cheeked with fresh air and buzzing with endorphins, he was in and out of the shower in record time before nudging open his father's door with a tray of sweetened, warmed Weetabix and a mug of tea.

"Breakfast, Dad! Then we need to get a move on. Mr Finch is coming for your autograph today."

Silence.

Stuart put the tray down on the chest of drawers and patted his father's hand. "Let me sit you up ready to eat."

No response. The muscles froze in Stuart's stomach. He looked at his father's chest. Nothing. The coldness in Stuart's torso spread to his heart, morphing into fear. Trembling, he leaned over and put his cheek next to the old man's nose and mouth. No breath. The coldness in Stuart's body threatened to buckle his legs.

"Dad! It's time to wake up!"

Stuart's voice bounced around the room but there was no response. Eric was dead. This day had been on the horizon for years, tied up in a confusing spaghetti of emotions. In his darkest moments Stuart had looked forward to it. And then immediately felt guilty and disgusted with himself for even contemplating it. Mostly he'd wished it further and further away. But never had he actually considered the practicalities of being faced with his father's dead body.

CHAPTER TWO

He thought fleetingly of calling 999, but any emergency had long since passed. Should he find an undertaker or did a doctor need to certify the death first? Whoever came, should he position his father ready in a respectable position? Dress him in his best suit? There was a new shirt in the cupboard plus the sombre tie Eric had worn at his wife's funeral forty-five years ago. Getting the fashion right suddenly seemed of enormous importance. He didn't want people to think less of his father now he was dead. He opened the wardrobe and pulled out suit trousers. Eric wouldn't want strangers seeing him in his pyjama bottoms.

The doorbell made him jump. Then he remembered: Mr Finch. He was early but he would know the procedure. Stuart almost jumped down the stairs.

Lillian was on the doorstep, not Mr Finch.

"Lillian." Seeing her kind, open face and grown-up appearance, he fought to stop himself using the 'Aunty' prefix of his childhood. "My father just died."

Lillian's face froze, whatever else she'd been about to say forgotten as she processed Stuart's announcement. Then her sensible adultness took over. "Just? You were able to be with him. Thanks be to God. That must have been such a comfort to both of you."

"No." The word came out as a shameful mumble. He'd been warned his father didn't have long. He shouldn't have gone out. Every minute should have been spent at his father's bedside, just in case. "I don't know when he died. I found him." It seemed hours ago that he'd prepared that cereal and tea, now sitting congealed and cold next to his father. He looked at his watch; shockingly, only a few minutes had passed since the radio news headlines had accompanied his heating milk for the Weetabix. "A few minutes ago." A lump, that he hadn't known was in his throat, broke. The rest of his words were distorted by sobs. "I don't know what to do next."

"Do nothing, for a while."

Lillian guided him into the kitchen. She instructed him to make mugs of strong, hot tea and to find some biscuits. Then she went upstairs.

A couple of minutes later she was back with the still-laden breakfast tray. As Stuart poured the tea, his hands were shaking and he felt pathetically grateful to this old lady for stepping out of her own growing confusion to help him.

"Poor old Eric. But, I think his passing was peaceful." She patted Stuart on the shoulder. "And he's back with your mum now. No need to worry about either of them."

What about me? Sandra demanded inside his head. *Do I no longer feature on the list of this family's significant dead people?*

"Let's talk about this later," he whispered to her.

"Sorry? What did you say?" Lillian turned from emptying the Weetabix sludge into the pages of yesterday's *The Times* to make it into a parcel for the bin.

"What should I do next?"

"*We.* What should *we* do next? I'm not leaving you to deal with this alone. First you call the surgery. We should get a doctor out here."

The rest of the day had a dreamlike quality. At times, things happened in slow motion and then things collided together at speed. Mr Finch arrived and was despatched back to his office with a promise to get in touch after the funeral. It was late afternoon before the undertaker took Eric away, leaving Stuart shell-shocked.

"Come and eat with me and Jayne," Lillian suggested. "It's not a time for being alone. And you might want to talk to Jayne about that unsigned will? She's a legal secretary, you know. I overheard you and that solicitor talking."

"Robert and George!" It was impossible that he could've forgotten to tell his brothers about the death of their father. "I'll phone them now."

"And then you'll come round to eat? Jayne's moving back in with me. That's what I came to tell you this morning. She's under the impression I'm going doolally — but we both know that's not true, don't we?"

"Right. No. I need to catch my thoughts." He was too dazed to be sociable or to focus on any one thing.

Lillian patted his shoulder and left.

The house was more silent than it had ever been. Did life and hope have a sound even when none was audible? Did death suck that sound away leaving a vacuum?

He phoned Robert first.

"When did it happen?" His brother cut straight to the facts.

Stuart hesitated. He didn't want criticism for not checking his father before the bike ride, or for forgetting to call his brothers until ten minutes ago. "Earlier. I had to deal with the doctor and the undertaker. And the solicitor came."

"He didn't sign the new will?" Robert's voice reached towards hope.

"No. He didn't sign." Suddenly Stuart wanted to get off the phone. Circumstances were closing in. The darkness of being homeless. "Can you let George know?" He put the phone down without waiting for a response.

Everything would be OK. If he thought it enough times, it would be true. His brothers knew what their father had intended with the will. They would respect the old man's wishes. His brothers were decent and fair. Without that belief, he may as well start hoarding cardboard now against the concrete coldness of the railway arches.

I'd start that hoarding if I were you. Our big brothers have low stocks of the milk of human kindness.

CHAPTER THREE

Robert and George arrived early on the day of the funeral with a full complement of Stuart's nephews. It must have been a three-line whip because hardly any of them had crossed their grandfather's threshold since childhood.

Robert's wife, Cindy, squeezed Stuart's hand. "This must be turning you upside down," she said quietly. "But at least now you can build a life of your own."

His other sister-in-law, Theresa, ran a finger over the windowsill and seemed surprised when it came up clean. George was directing the younger generation in the unpacking of hired wine glasses and Robert was on his mobile arranging his golf schedule for the following week.

Stuart gave Cindy a small smile and was surprised to see a tear in the corner of her eye.

Three black limousines arrived to carry the family behind the hearse. Stuart was allocated to the last of these cars, along with his two youngest nephews, dragged from university for the day and looking awkward in dark suits. Twisting in his seat, Stuart saw Jayne's car pull out immediately behind them and match the respectful walking speed of the cortège. Her mother, Lillian, was in the passenger seat, already dabbing at her eyes with a handkerchief.

Outside the chapel, the family stood awkwardly while the professional pallbearers readied themselves and the coffin. The six men respectfully raised the coffin to shoulder height and the family were given the nod to assemble behind. Like a flock of crows, with new shiny plumage, the procession made its way down the short aisle. The family took their seats in the reserved front rows and the coffin was placed on the catafalque.

Standing to sing 'Amazing Grace', Stuart focused on the coffin and his father within. As the music died away and they sat down again, his shoulders heaved with emotion. He pulled out a hanky to blow his nose and keep the tears at bay. Then he felt a reassuring pat on his shoulder from behind; it was Lillian. Her cheeks were damp too. Stuart turned back towards the coffin and thought about his father.

Sandra was in his head. *I think I'm about to find out what it's like to be a daddy's girl. Wish me luck!*

He smiled. His twin sister had died when she was seven days old and, even though she was rarely spoken about, his parents had never got over their grief.

A dozen people, plus the family, returned to the house for food and drink. All of them made a beeline towards Stuart to shake his hand and offer condolences. He dutifully introduced his brothers who'd played such a small part in their father's later life but, after half an hour of making small talk, it was a relief that these people preferred his more verbose siblings. Stuart slipped into the kitchen and poured himself a fresh cup of tea. He longed for everyone to go home so he could have the house and his thoughts to himself.

"Mind if I join you?"

Caught off guard, his brain failed to generate words. Jayne was smiling at him. He'd been vaguely aware of her sitting beside Lillian in the chapel but, before that, when had he last seen her at close quarters? They'd acknowledged each other with a raise of the hand on the rare occasion he'd been in the garden when she'd visited her mum, but, ever since that betrayal almost four decades ago, there'd been a mutual avoidance of conversation.

And now here she was, hovering across the kitchen table from him on the least convenient day possible. Her familiar smile and the smell of her perfume made him feel wobbly.

She sat down without waiting for his permission. "I'm sorry about your dad."

"He'd lived to a good age." The phrase was automatic.

"Even so, he'll leave a massive hole in your life. What will you do?"

Stuart shrugged. "I haven't properly thought. It's been a bit of a whirlwind. How are you? I heard you divorced . . ." In his eagerness to move the conversation away from himself, he hadn't considered the insensitivity of mentioning Jayne's failed marriage.

She gave a wry smile and put her hand on top of his. He remembered teenaged fumbling in the dark.

"Don't worry. It was a long time ago. I instigated it and I'm well over it."

She removed her hand and he was back in the present day. A boring middle-aged man in his fifties talking to the woman who had set all his senses alight when he was a teenager. A woman whose magnetism hadn't gone away. The slim teenager in jeans had become a slim woman in a white silky blouse and formal black jacket. The jacket was well cut and the blouse made from expensive-looking material, but neither looked brand new. The top two buttons of the blouse were open, revealing a gold pendant sitting on Jayne's collarbone. Her face had aged well and her short dark hair had only a sprinkling of grey around the fringe and over the crown. She was exerting a familiar pull on his senses and she still had that knack of looking right into his eyes and almost touching his soul. For a fleeting moment he wondered if he should ask her out, for old times' sake. No — too risky.

"Dinner? This time next week?" She took him by surprise.

"Oh. I don't know." He couldn't read her subtext. He'd make a fool of himself. People like him didn't go on dates. "My head's full of all this." He gestured to the rise and fall of conversation in the living-room.

He thought he saw a look of disappointment but it turned into a brisk smile. "I admire what you did for your dad."

Stuart shrugged. "It had to be done."

"Exactly. My mum cared for Gran and, in return, I've moved back in to care for Mum. What goes around comes around."

"It can't always work like that. Neither of us has children."

"That's not our parents' fault."

Stuart's own lack of procreation was at least partly due to his father, but Stuart didn't correct her. Jayne stood up to leave and her posture reminded Stuart of a ballet dancer. He took his cue to show her out. On the doorstep she hesitated and then kissed him on the cheek. The sensation of her lips sent him back in time and when she turned away, his fingers felt the spot her lips had touched.

CHAPTER FOUR

Eric had specified there should be a formal will-reading in his solicitor's office. Stuart couldn't look at his brothers as they waited to be called into the law firm's boardroom. Instead, he stared at the varnished wooden floor of the waiting room. The dips between the individual planks were a darker shade of brown where the stain had gathered in larger amounts. He imagined himself disappearing down one of these cracks, unseen and unacknowledged. He had become an orphan in danger of losing his home and his role in society had vanished. If he was no longer his father's carer, who was he?

Mr Finch opened the boardroom door and gestured for them to come in. A young girl in a cerise trouser suit, followed with a tray of cups and a coffee pot. Mr Finch made pleasantries about the traffic and the weather until they were seated with coffee and the milk and sugar had been passed around.

"And so the will?" Robert prompted.

Stuart had done all the hills twice on his bike that morning, but tension still held his back and shoulders in the pain of an arm wrestle. His neck struggled for the strength to lift his head and look at the solicitor. The large boardroom table was made of a much darker wood than the floor in the reception area and the stain was more uniform. He raised his eyes.

Mr Finch glanced around at them. "Eric told me he'd discussed his new will with you all and the contents would come as no surprise."

"But he died before he could sign it!" The words shot from George's mouth.

"That is correct. But because we were all privy to your father's last wishes, it would be possible for us to enter into a Deed of Variation in order to execute that new will."

Energy returned to Stuart and he glanced around the table. His brothers would see this was a fair suggestion.

"All the beneficiaries need to be in agreement to allow me to do this," Mr Finch continued. "Are there any dissenters or do you agree with our moral obligation to uphold your father's wishes?"

George and Robert raised their hands.

"Are you dissenting or agreeing to the proposal?"

"Dissenting." The two men spoke in unison.

Stuart put his head in his hands.

And breathe.

When he looked up again, Mr Finch's sympathetic eyes met his.

"We're not completely heartless." George was talking quickly. "Robert and I have discussed this. We can't grant our younger brother a life interest in the house because that would mean our children won't get their grandfather's helping hand up the property ladder until it's too late. We don't want the money for ourselves, you understand, but to help the younger generation. It's hard being young and just starting out now."

Robert picked up the thread. "We're happy to allow Stuart to continue living in the house for twelve months from today, April the first. Then the house must be sold and the proceeds shared as per my father's original will. Stuart should be able to sort himself out with a job and somewhere to live within a year."

The room was closing in on him. Robert made it sound like Stuart's twenty-five-year absence from the classroom was no barrier to getting a new job. Even if some desperate inner-city school would take him, the prospect of attempting to control thirty cocky fourteen-year-olds with their own agenda terrified Stuart. He'd been living in virtual isolation for too long. And the whole exam system had changed. And the syllabus. And all that new technology. He couldn't do it. He wanted to curl up in a ball and roll away from the world.

Mr Finch spoke. "Stuart, what do you think of your brothers' offer? If you disagree with their suggestion, we could pursue legal action under the Inheritance (Provision for Family and Dependants) Act in order to activate the unsigned will. However, success is far from guaranteed and there will be financial costs to take into account. And you must also think about what such wrangling would do to your family unit."

He didn't have the money to pay legal bills. A fight would bleed him of the emotional energy he needed to grab something of life before it was too late. It wasn't fair that his brothers could walk all over him. After all that he'd sacrificed. His fists clenched in his lap.

And breathe.

The others around the table were staring at him, expecting an answer.

"Do you need time to think about it?" the solicitor asked.

Fight for what's yours (or actually ours) and add more wasted, bitter years to your life? Or break free and soar like a bird? Stuart stared out at the blue sky and imagined flying. Sandra was right; he wanted to live life like that, not mired in legal small print.

"Bugger them! I'm going to soar!"

There was a collective intake of breath. He thought he'd spoken to his sister in his head but he'd said the words aloud.

"Sorry. I meant to say that I accept the one-year grace period."

Robert and George smiled. Mr Finch looked satisfied that he didn't have to handle a messy dispute.

"Help yourselves to more coffee. I'll get a document drawn up to reflect this discussion for your signatures."

After they'd all signed and Mr Finch wielded his fountain pen as witness, Robert and George made a big display of pumping Stuart's hand and wishing him well for the next twelve months.

Then they were gone and Stuart was left with the anxious feeling that he'd made the wrong decision and a big, black pit of fear in his stomach.

CHAPTER FIVE

The house hung stale and heavy around him. Eric had offered little in the way of company but just knowing there was another living, breathing human in the house had made a difference. Stuart walked around each of the empty rooms. When you'd lived in a place for decades, you didn't notice it anymore. Now he considered it as an outsider might. An outsider who might judge Stuart himself by the place in which he lived. The wallpaper was grubby, especially in the stairwell. The carpet on the bottom step was worn thin. His father's old study had become a dumping ground for stuff that didn't have a proper home: the walking frame — obsolete since Eric became completely bedridden; two old desktop computers — kept to avoid hackers extracting bank details; a train set and boxes of Lego — Stuart had rescued these from the loft when his nephews were young, but the boys had turned their noses up and immersed themselves in gaming consoles that Stuart didn't understand.

You've let the place go, Stuart.

"I know, I know." His voice sounded odd in the empty house.

You've let it moulder away. If houses wore clothes, this one would be wearing an egg-stained tank top, shirt-sleeve garters and frayed braces. Please don't tell me you're going to live the rest of your life like the man that time forgot.

"Don't rub it in. I know I need to make changes."

I'm watching and waiting. Remember when you were a shiny new teacher with ideals about connecting with the teenagers in a way your teachers never had? You had a mullet haircut and never dropped into that corduroy, geography-teacher stereotype. Let's see a return of that confidence, please.

"I'm trying. Rome wasn't built in a day."

Sandra hadn't spoken to him with such regularity in decades and now, suddenly, she was a constant presence in the wings of his mind. It was probably a bad sign on a mental-health barometer, but very welcome in the vacuum that was his new life.

The conversations with his dead sister had started when he was small. For a long time, he'd never questioned the photo of two tiny babies on the sideboard, one dressed in pink and one dressed in blue. Then one day his parents had argued, not noticing him behind the settee with his train set.

"It would've been different if Sandra had lived instead of Stuart." His mother's voice had been a mix of anger and upset. "At least then I'd have someone to fight my corner. Someone who might understand the tedium of washer-loads of football kit and the work made by mud constantly being trodden in and out."

"I wanted Sandra to live as well! Not to become an assistant housekeeper to you but to add some gentleness and a balancing influence to the house."

"Which I can't provide because I'm too busy clearing up after you lot. I wanted a third child like a hole in the head but I'm left with all the extra work."

The conversation confused Stuart and he waited until the next day to ask his mother about Sandra. They were walking to school, his legs taking two steps to keep up with each of her urgent strides. She stopped abruptly when he asked the question. Stuart's own momentum carried him forward until his movement was sharply arrested by his mother's arm.

"Sandra?" she repeated, as though she had never heard the name before.

"I heard you and Dad saying you wanted her instead of me." He hadn't meant to say that but the hurt had stopped him going to sleep the previous night and now it came tumbling out. "You don't like me because I'm not a girl."

His mother crouched down, held his shoulders and looked him in the eye. "Daddy and I love you very much, Stuart." Her voice sounded like she *wanted* to make it loving, but she didn't do it quite convincingly enough.

He wanted to believe her but a strange feeling made him not trust his mother's words for the first time ever. "What about Sandra?"

"Sandra was your twin sister." Now his mother spoke almost in a whisper and he had to lean towards her to hear. "You were both born at the same time but she died when she was a week old."

Stuart was big enough to understand death. "Is she buried in the garden like Goliath? Is she in heaven? Can I talk to her, like you said I can still stroke Goliath in my imagination?"

"Yes, you can talk to her in your imagination. I would like you to do that." Then his mother had given him a bigger than usual hug and spoken quietly into his hair. "It will keep her memory alive."

After that he and Sandra had started conversing in his head. Sometimes the conversation felt so real that Stuart said the words aloud. His mother was always pleased when he reported back on the conversations; she would sit him on her knee and hold him close, eager to hear everything Sandra had said.

So, what's your plan? Sandra said to him now. *Where do you go from here? You're going to be kicked out of this dowdy museum by your own family. You've got no job. The future's not exactly bright, is it?*

"I know, I know. Don't get sharp with me." The last thing he needed was the voice in his head turning against him as well.

The task labelled 'Get Life in Order' floated like a huge, unassailable Zeppelin in his mind. It was easier to focus on the domestic minutiae around its edges. He got the health authority to collect all the loaned medical equipment including the walking frame, the special riser still fitted to the high armchair that Dad hadn't sat in for years, the hoist and the commode that had preceded the bedpan. He watched their joint daily life disappear into an unmarked white van. His father's death had left so many empty spaces. The cloying atmosphere of illness and decay was absent; the sickbed routine had been usurped by unfilled hours and his role in life had been kicked from under him. Stuart was Humpty Dumpty waiting to be put together again.

"He's in a better place, love." Lillian appeared as the two men with the van gave him the thumbs-up and reversed onto the road. She'd forgotten to put her shoes on again. "Concentrate on yourself now. It's Easter next weekend; you can smell spring in the air. Create a new start for yourself."

Then the old lady touched his arm. "I've got fruit scones in the oven and I've used those sultanas that are soaked in brandy for Christmas cakes. They were on offer in the supermarket because they're nearly out of date. Come and help me eat a couple. I love it when the butter melts into them."

Stuart didn't need much tempting to put thoughts of his future on hold for another hour or two. "That would be lovely. And while we're at it, I'll help you find your shoes."

Lillian glanced down and seemed surprised to find she had nothing on her feet.

* * *

The cycling club held a long-distance Audax ride every Easter Saturday. It was ten years since Stuart had been able to leave his father for that length of time to take part. One hundred kilometres in a day — did he still have the stamina? He wavered between fear and confidence. The old quote about only regretting the things that you didn't do, rather than the things you did, came into his mind. He remembered the idealistic young man with the mullet haircut. Before his confidence failed, he went on the website and signed up.

The night before the ride he panicked. It was a solo event. What if something on the bike failed? He had no one to phone for help. What if he got lost? He'd never bothered with a GPS because Dad's needs meant he never rode outside the locality and his map reading was rusty. At three a.m. he got up and walked around the house. With Dad gone, his responsibilities had disappeared but he felt, more than ever, that the weight of the world was on his shoulders. He decided not to do the ride. It was silly to court pressure when there were so many other changes going on in his life. Perversely, the decision not to ride increased the tension between his shoulder blades and prodded Sandra to say her piece.

One week of life was all I got. One lousy week. And I was too tiny to make the most of it. I never graduated out of that plastic hospital fish tank. But I do know that you were beside me the whole time. The warmth of your body and the sound of your snuffly breathing probably kept me going for longer than if I'd been a singleton. So, I owe you one. I'm going to kick your arse until you successfully integrate back into society. I don't want a brother who neighbours describe as a recluse or who scares the kids in the park because he sits there in a big, smelly coat, handfeeding the pigeons and squirrels, or who lies dead in his house for months before a postman notices the smell. Stuart Borefield, it is your duty to live life for the both of us and you will start tomorrow with this cycling thingy.

She was right. She was definitely right, but that didn't make it easy. He had to move forward one challenge at a time. One hundred kilometres on no sleep was not a good idea.

He walked back upstairs. There was an orange glow from outside the landing window. He paused. As a teenager, when he'd still been plucking up the courage to ask Jayne out, he'd discovered if he stood on the top step and angled his head properly, he could see into next door's garden and sometimes he'd see Jayne out there. That was the signal for him to go nonchalantly into their own garden and pretend to fiddle noisily with a plant by the side of the fence until Jayne noticed him and came over for a chat.

It was dark now and there was no one in the garden, just a pool of orange light sprawled on the paving stones beneath the kitchen window. Maybe Lillian couldn't sleep either. Knowing that someone else was awake was comforting and Stuart's shoulders eased down from their rigid position. He got back into bed and must have slept because the alarm clock shocked him awake a couple of hours later.

He poured milk, stirred oats and made porridge in the microwave. He brewed strong coffee to give himself a mule-kick start to the day, and added two spoonfuls of sugar, and then he created a track of golden syrup around the edge of the porridge. He tried and failed to add the discrete markings of eyes and curved mouth to form a smiley face. Instead, it was a criss-cross of lines where he'd failed to stop the flow of the heavy syrup between markings. Stuart smiled at the bowl anyway. Then, as the caffeine and sweetness began to shoot energy through his body, he felt the first stirrings of excitement at the day ahead. He fetched sandwiches from the fridge and filled his large plastic drinks bottle with water. According to the map there were three cafés and a couple of pubs en route, where further food and drink could be purchased.

Positivity buoyed him up as he queued in the church hall to have his name ticked off the starters' list. A few riders he knew by sight patted him on the back and wished him well. Someone else said they hoped to see him at the first café stop for a catch-up. The feeling of camaraderie swept away his lack of sleep.

As the event started, they rode two abreast but gradually everyone found their own speed; some were naturally faster and disappeared from view, while the more social animals, who preferred chat over physical challenge, gradually slid to the back of the bunch. Stuart settled somewhere in between. His legs found a rhythm, his mind calmed, emptied, and he became aware only of his own regular movements, the birdsong and the patchwork of green, yellow and brown fields alongside the road. He crested a hill and gazed over the valley below, a rainbow arched itself across the sky. Richard Of York Gave Battle In Vain.

The old mnemonic was swiftly followed by memories of his mother. Whenever they'd seen a rainbow, she would sigh with contentment and tell him the sight of a rainbow meant that everything would be all right. Problems would take flight and solutions appear with ease. Now the sight of the rainbow made his heart rise with hope for his future.

He freewheeled down the other side and spotted a huddle of cyclists outside a café. He ordered coffee and a hunk of bread pudding, and joined their banter. A stream ran close to their table and, during lulls in the conversation, the sound of its pure, bell-like trickle over the rocks helped ease the tension in his muscles.

The day continued fine, friendly and fun. Towards the last few miles his legs started to protest. It was years since he'd ridden this distance and he should've worked up to it more slowly. He deliberately slowed his pace, aware from the map that the largest hill of the route had been saved until last. To stand any chance of making it to the top he needed to conserve energy. A multitude of Lycra overtook him and the Mexican wave of encouragement transformed into a new tide of determination within him.

As the hill came into sight, he pedalled harder to build up momentum. His legs had already propelled him almost one hundred kilometres and were heavy with fatigue. The muscles in his thighs trembled. He tightened his grip on the handle bars. He kept pushing down with his feet as the road rose beneath him. Every few turns of the wheels he changed down a gear until there was nowhere left to go with the lever. He forced leaden muscles against pedals the weight of elephants. His speed was virtually nil and he began to wobble. Stuart wasn't a quitter. He continued the battle, trying to raise himself off the saddle into a standing position to generate increased downward force into the pedals. His balance faltered in the absence of forward propulsion. With no time to remove feet from pedals, the bike went over and Stuart's left shoulder banged onto the kerb, just as a minibus of youths sailed past on his right-hand side. They jeered at him through open windows and then disappeared over the top of the hill.

For a few seconds he lay awkwardly, feet still attached to the bike and shoulder throbbing. He'd tipped over like a five-year-old attempting to lose his stabilisers. He needed to get up before he was seen. Ignoring the argument from his shoulder, Stuart reached forward, unclipped himself from the pedals and then gingerly stood. Very slowly he stretched out both arms, in front of him and then above his head. He raised and lowered each of his shoulders in turn. His left side was painful but mobile. Diagnosis: his pride had taken the biggest hit. He pushed the bike the short distance to the top of the hill, his calves making it known that he'd never have beaten this gradient on two wheels. No cyclists went past, no witnesses to confront over his failure. He remounted and went at speed downhill towards the church hall and the finish. Inside there were pats on the back and words of praise. Stuart held himself tense to avoid wincing when people caught his left shoulder.

"Brilliant stuff for someone who doesn't usually ride that distance!"

"Can't wait to see you tackle something longer."

"Good to have you back on the longer distances."

Stuart hadn't expected to feel emotional but the liberal praise and easy friendship swept through parts of him that had been empty for years. He blinked hard, suddenly realising what he'd been missing. Then his conscience got the better of him; he couldn't start this new life as a fake. "That last hill beat me. I came off and walked the last hundred yards to the top." He grimaced and gave his shoulder a rub.

"Are you OK?" One of the women looked concerned.

"It's fine, really." The sharpness of the pain had genuinely dulled to an ache. Maybe it was the distraction of people and the emotion of finishing or perhaps, alone at the brow of the hill, everything had seemed worse than it actually was, like when sleep failed in the early hours of the morning.

Two of the older male riders exchanged looks and then one of them spoke. "We walked that bit too."

"I came off there last year," someone else said. "I was determined the bugger wasn't going to beat me. It did."

Stuart left the church hall on a high. He'd set himself a challenge. He'd wobbled last night but had still gone on and completed it. And he'd enjoyed the process. The ache in his shoulder felt like a badge of honour, or even a medal. He remembered the rainbow and suddenly felt his life was going in the right direction. Stuart Borefield had a bright new future.

He smiled inwardly.

Attaboy! You're a brother to be proud of.

When he got home there was a message on the answering machine in Robert's lawyer voice. The meagre contents of their father's bank accounts would no longer be available for Stuart's living expenses. As a gesture of goodwill, Robert and George would subsidise him for one month, on condition that receipts were produced. After that he was on his own. The contents of their mother's jewellery box had been noted on the day of the funeral and would be collected next time his brothers were in the area.

The black Zeppelin inflated further, blotting out the shiny feeling his cycling success had created.

The next morning, he sat at the kitchen table trying to brainstorm a way forward. An income was needed, and fast. Lillian walked past the window and knocked on the door. Stuart didn't want to make small talk, but the old lady had already seen he was in.

"Happy Easter!" She held up a large foil-wrapped chocolate egg, suspended in a gaudy red-and-yellow open-fronted cardboard box.

"Thank you. But there was no need."

"Nonsense, there was every need. You are a boy who needs cheering up." She gave him a hug and a kiss. "Even middle-aged men are entitled to some indulgent, brightly coloured fun. Chocolate always makes the world feel better. Now, tell me what happened at the will-reading."

Stuart hesitated. Broadcasting family business felt disloyal. But Lillian had always been almost family.

"We need a plan," Lillian said when he'd finished.

His spirits rose a little. A problem shared and all that.

"You and Jayne, you're both like homeless cats. She's moved back in with me now, you know. She says it's to keep an eye on me, she thinks I'm going doolally, which is complete nonsense of course. I can function as well as the next person. Between you and me, she's moved back because her flat is so tiny. A studio she calls it, with everything in the same room. A bedsit I call it. It's all she could afford after the divorce. He was a gambler, you know."

"I didn't know that."

"She tried to make it work as long as she could but his debts meant they were always living hand to mouth. It didn't suit my Jayne; she likes nice things. I don't mean she's extravagant but she saves up to buy quality."

Stuart remembered the gold pendant sitting on the bare skin of Jayne's collarbone at the funeral. "She's lucky to have you to take her in." He wished he'd been brave enough to accept Jayne's invitation to dinner. That's what someone with a bright new future would have done.

"By pooling my pension and her salary and only having one roof over our heads we'll both be a bit better off. That's what she says anyway. Now banks are all on computers, I don't keep an eye on the money like I used to. I could cope with that little book that you took to the building society but now . . ."

Lillian's face fell. Behind that capable facade she hid her own worries and confusion.

"Chocolate." Stuart broke open the egg and placed the pieces between them on the foil wrapper.

"You and she are at a crossroads. As an old woman who loves her only daughter and is very fond of the boy who grew up next door, it would give me peace if you got together." Lillian put a lump of egg in her mouth. Her next words were mangled by the chocolate. "Do you still hold a candle for Jayne?"

Yes. No. Was there a right answer? When Jayne had touched his hand at the funeral and kissed his cheek, there'd definitely been a connection. But he'd been a monk for twenty-five years; it was impossible to know anything except that he didn't want to be on his own for ever. He made a show of chewing a piece of egg before speaking. "It was a long time ago. People change."

"My Jayne hasn't changed. She's still got her head screwed on properly. I told you she was a legal secretary? She might be able to get you a proper share of the house — after all, it's what your dad wanted. That was the plan I came to tell you about."

A better man might pick up the cudgel and prepare for battle. There was no doubt a guaranteed roof over his head would rapidly shrink that black Zeppelin. But getting there would eat into the mental reserves also needed to propel himself out of the shadows of merely existing into a brightness of being. He didn't have the stamina for both. And maybe, if his brothers put up a fight, which they would, the house would have to be sold anyway to meet the legal bills. But he couldn't throw Lillian's whole plan back in her face — he had to pick up at least part of it. And it would be very nice to see Jayne again.

"I can't cope with fighting the will. But perhaps Jayne might like a catch-up for old times' sake. Have you got her mobile number?"

Lillian's face broke into a grin and from her pocket she handed him a piece of paper with the number already prepared. "She does yoga. That's how she stays slim and walks so lovely. I did it too when I was younger."

Stuart smiled at the old lady's attempts to sell the charms of her only daughter.

As Lillian stood to leave, Stuart remembered the light he'd seen in the early hours the previous day.

"Were you struggling to sleep?"

A shutter dropped over Lillian's face. "Something like that."

This closing down of a subject was out of character for the lady who'd known him since childhood and Stuart felt a pang of anxiety. That, and the often-missing shoes, made him think there might be some grounds for Jayne to be worrying that her mother was going 'doolally'.

CHAPTER SIX

Stuart kept Jayne's number under his jar of change on the worktop, trying to work up the confidence to do something with it.

You're making a mountain out of a molehill. It's not a date. Just two friends meeting for a chat.

It *was* a mountain. Sandra didn't understand. He hadn't socialised properly for decades. He had no job. Soon his home would be gone. In their previous life, Jayne had had little patience with time-wasting drifters. As soon as she got the full picture about Stuart Borefield's current life, she would run a mile. He wasn't strong enough to take a second rejection by her.

Lillian has been good to you. You owe it to her at least to make that call.

"I will do it when I have a plan! Go away and let me think."

First on the list was a job. He searched online for 'How to get back into teaching geography after twenty-five years'. The Geographical Association's website indicated that there'd been a lot of changes in the classroom and recommended prospective returners should visit a Geography Quality Mark school as well as catching up on the revised geography National Curriculum and the GCSE and A-level specifications, plus returners might also need to update their geography subject knowledge to teach some of the new content. And then there would be all the hassle of finding a vacancy. His meagre confidence shrivelled further at the enormity of all these tasks after the years spent in relative solitude with his father. And even if facing a room of thirty teenagers didn't make his knees quake, getting back into the classroom wasn't going to be a quick process.

Stuart needed to start generating an income now. He needed to cast his net wider. His only other 'work' experience was in caring. But despite all that time at his father's bedside, he had no proof of his competence at that. Twenty-five years and not even a certificate. Even so, it still seemed more likely to produce a fast positive result than returning to teaching — that might be something for later, when he felt like a proper human being again.

He searched the internet for local care agencies. It wasn't difficult to find a vacancy nearby that he could apply for:

Experience is not essential for this role. We provide specialised induction training plus ongoing support, training and guidance.

Stuart composed a letter of application, attached his meagre CV and emailed it. He was invited for an interview that same afternoon. This was both good and bad; there was no time to lose his nerve but also no time to source a proper interview outfit, decide where he wanted to be in five years' time and concoct a textbook reason for why he suddenly wanted to be a carer so late in life.

"Male carers are particularly in demand," Veronica, the manager of the Primo Care Agency explained. "Caring is seen, unfairly, as a menial job that leads nowhere. And, therefore, most men won't even consider it. But most agency owners, like me, started off making house calls and worked our way up. Caring is generous with its job satisfaction and the routes upwards are there if you want them."

Stuart nodded.

"So, you cared for your father. Tell me more about that."

It was the first time Stuart had gone into detail about everything he'd had to do for his father with anyone. His brothers had always looked as though they were about to throw up if he'd so much as mentioned a bedpan. The doctor and district nurse had never had the time to listen; they'd only been interested if something had been wrong. He told Veronica about giving his father a shave every other day. He'd tried to encourage his dad to do it himself using an electric shaver but Eric had liked a wet shave and hadn't been able to manage it with the tremor in his hand. Next, Stuart moved on to the bed-bath routine, glancing at Veronica to see if her eyes were glazing over yet. Stuart was enjoying himself. For years, this major part of his life had been a taboo subject and now, finally, it merited attention. Detailed attention. He imagined this might be how it felt on a therapist's couch, able to suddenly vocalise everything that had been building inside but couldn't be adequately shared with anyone else. He could've talked for hours but Veronica interrupted him.

"I'm impressed. Your father was a lucky man."

Stuart tried to shrug modestly. He'd forgotten about his left shoulder and had to hide the wince of pain.

"I assume you have a car and are entitled to work in the UK?"

Stuart nodded and put his passport on the table as proof. The document had never been out of the country but he'd renewed it every ten years in a gesture of hope.

"I'll need to get an enhanced DBS check done. As soon as that's in place we'll arrange a start date. There's an elderly gentleman on our books for whom you'd be brilliant. He funds his care privately and is happy to pay for double-length visits because he wants companionship as well as care. He gets on OK with our ladies, but I think having another man to talk to would make all the difference."

Even sitting down, Stuart felt as though he was growing in height. His shoulders went back and, without being bidden, his lips curved into a smile.

"What do you think? Will that suit you?"

Stuart realised she wanted an answer and he couldn't just bask in the glow of being wanted.

"Perfect." There was a pleasant vision of satisfactory if not extravagant financial independence in his mind. Then Sandra walked all over it.

Don't be so easily pleased. You are a marketable commodity. Don't undersell yourself. If you don't reach for the moon, you won't even get a single star. Remember when you had the courage to apply for Head of Geography even though you'd only been in post a few years? That ambition must still be inside you somewhere.

He didn't get Head of Geography, but it had been important to be seen to be ambitious, ready for future opportunities. Now, sitting in front of Veronica, it wasn't easy to rediscover the flame that had once burned so brightly. "How long will the DBS check take? I'd like to start as soon as possible."

That's not what I meant. Ask about the money.

"Usually only a couple of days, which gives us time to get you kitted out with our polo shirts and aprons." She pointed to the Primo care logo stitched just beneath the left shoulder of her pale blue top. "Plus I need to show you the app we have for recording the notes about each visit. It means relatives can access the notes remotely."

Stuart nodded and then swallowed hard. "Obviously, I need to know about the money."

"Obviously." Veronica smiled at him. "I would have to start you on minimum wage and take it from there."

Stuart started to nod but Sandra's demanding voice wouldn't leave his head.

Ask her for more. Male carers are in demand and she's got a client with money lined up for you.

"I . . . given my experience . . . and I'm a man . . . perhaps you could offer a bit more?"

Veronica frowned. "You are asking me to break the equal-pay legislation."

Shit! Now Sandra's interfering was going to cost him the job before he'd even started. Assertiveness and ambition weren't good. He needed to go with the flow for a while until he was used to being back in the real world.

"Sorry. I didn't realise."

Veronica stood up and proffered her hand. "Let's shake on minimum wage and if you perform well and want more responsibility, you'll progress up the ladder like anyone else."

Stuart shook on the deal.

Make sure she sticks to her side of the bargain. You don't have enough time left to be walked all over.

"Go away," Stuart muttered under his breath once he was outside Veronica's office.

* * *

Back home, he looked at Jayne's number underneath the change jar. Was there such a thing as a meeting between a single man and a single woman that wasn't a date? Lillian would have mentioned leaving the number and primed Jayne for it being a date. Did *he* want it to be a date? He remembered that kiss on his cheek at the funeral. He picked up the piece of paper then put it down again, placing the jar firmly on top. Lillian had said that Jayne liked nice things; she wouldn't be interested in a low-earning care worker. She'd want someone more ambitious, someone with money and a place in society. She wouldn't make the mistake of choosing another waster to share her life after her experience with Carl.

He went to close the curtains just as a brand-new Audi pulled up at the kerb next door. The man who got out was casually dressed in an open-neck shirt and pullover. This was a man who would have the money to buy Jayne nice things. He should look away. This was none of his business. But the man had RIVAL stamped all over him. Within seconds, Jayne was at the man's side, giving a wave of her hand to an invisible Lillian. Stuart moved behind the edge of the curtain.

The man kissed her. On the cheek. But it was a still a kiss. Jayne was smiling. The car's taillights became bright in the growing dusk and Stuart closed the curtains. He was shaking when he sat down. A stupid overreaction.

Relieved that she's not sitting at home waiting for your invitation? Sandra injected the best of her sarcasm into the words.

Stuart waved his arms to make her go away. It was too soon to get romantically involved with anyone. He'd only make a hash of it. But his brain wouldn't stop wondering what it would be like to have someone to share his empty future. A companion to change the horizon from bleak grey to sunshine.

They could travel and his pristine passport would become battered. They'd go for long walks, enjoy the theatre and . . . His thoughts paused over the possible physicality of a relationship. He didn't know the rules for mature people rediscovering dating. Jayne, and the vast majority of women entering a second or third long-term relationship, would be far more experienced than he.

Would they find him boring? Should he reveal his inexperience or try to bluff his way through it? Suddenly it was all too daunting. He hovered with Jayne's phone number over the kitchen pedal bin. Had second thoughts and put it back under the change jar.

* * *

It was the beginning of May when, after his induction training, Stuart made his first call on William Rutherford. Frightened of being late, he arrived ten minutes early and sat in his car wondering whether to wait until the appointed time. His stomach was churning with apprehension and had accepted only one slice of toast for breakfast. Being paid to be somewhere at a particular time to carry out a particular role felt like an enormous responsibility, one which he wanted to carry out to the absolute best of his ability. He waited five minutes and then got out of the car. There was a key safe beside the front door and Stuart had been entrusted with the number because William couldn't reach the hallway.

He fumbled with the keypad and turned the dial. Nothing. He tried again, focusing hard on the slightly blurry figures. Nothing. Finally, he pulled his reading glasses from his jacket pocket and realised the '3' was actually an '8'.

"Hello, Mr Rutherford!"

There was a grunt in response and Stuart followed the noise into a back sitting-room overlooking the garden.

"So you're the man. They told me they were sending a man."

"I'm Stuart. Pleased to meet you."

The old man took Stuart's hand in a grip far weaker than the strength in his voice. He was sitting in a high orthopaedic chair at the side of an unmade bed, dressed in navy paisley pyjamas. Wispy grey hair stuck out at odd angles from his scalp and he looked in need of a shave. His face, like his body, was too thin.

"Which do you want first, cup of tea and breakfast or washing and dressing?" Veronica had advised him that a cheery nature, positive conversation and the ability to keep distaste hidden, whatever the task, were the absolute essential qualities she looked for in all her staff. Apparently the clients were quick to complain if they got a sourpuss.

"Remember," Veronica had said, "you will probably be the only person that client sees or speaks to all day. Make your visit count in more ways than simply giving them something to eat. Give them some conversation and brightness to help carry them through the day."

Stuart grinned at Mr Rutherford, waiting for his answer. Apparently it was important to give the clients choice wherever possible, to give the illusion they had some control over what was happening to them.

"You don't need to speak so loudly and you don't need to sound so jolly." The voice was tetchy and the old man's frown deeply etched. "I'm not deaf and artificial jolliness comes across as condescending. I'm a lonely, useless, friendless old man who can't look after himself. Don't treat me like a child."

The smile that Stuart had tried to make cheery slid from his face and he fumbled for a positive answer. Naively, he'd expected clients to welcome him with open arms. This wasn't the shiny new job and start of a new life that he'd expected.

"I'm sorry things aren't so good for you at the moment." Stuart removed his jacket. "I'll just hang this up and we'll get started." He escaped into the hallway where he'd noticed a row of hooks and paused longer than necessary.

He deserves a kick in the balls. Are you going to do it, or shall I?

"Not now, Sandra. Have some empathy."

I never got a proper chance at living, so empathy is an unknown quality.

"I can't talk about this now. I'm at work."

Ooh! Hark at you, the man with the new career and full of your own self-importance all of a sudden.

"Not now."

"Are you on the phone reporting my rudeness?" The old man's voice travelled through the slightly open back-room door. "I don't like people who can't say things to my face."

Stuart rushed back into the room, hoping his face hadn't flushed. Mr Rutherford's expression reminded him of the headmaster at the school where he'd taught and he automatically started to grovel.

"I wasn't on the phone. Just mumbling to myself. It's a bad habit that kicks in when I've got a lot to remember. First day in a new job — there's lots going round in my head."

"I hope they haven't sent me a madman. If I wanted to be among mad people I'd have gone into that home like my daughter wanted. But who wants to sit in a circle around a television at full volume all day?" He paused, as though to refuel his voice with bitterness. "If you're working for me, I demand absolute transparency in everything. No forced happiness. If you're having a bad time, I want to know about it. Knowing that other people have problems makes me feel better — it makes me less of an odd one out, if you see what I mean?"

Stuart nodded. This was nothing like what he'd expected and he needed to get the visit back on track. Mr Rutherford was paying for a full hour but already ten minutes had gone and Stuart hadn't yet provided any sort of care.

"Shall we start by washing and dressing you?"

"I think I'd better use the commode first." Mr Rutherford gestured towards what looked like a simple chair. Stuart's father had had something similar before the bedpan. "Given enough time, I can manage by myself but since you're here, I'm paying you and the clock is ticking, you can give me a hand."

"Absolutely." Stuart looked down at the old man's feet to check that they weren't crossed or in the wrong position for standing. "Just lean forward slightly before you start to stand."

"I know, I know. I'm not a novice."

When the transfer from chair to commode was complete, Stuart stepped back.

"I don't want an audience. Would you?" Mr Rutherford made a waving gesture with his right hand. "Go get that breakfast ready that you were mithering about. And make sure the porridge is properly hot. Some of those women that come serve it lukewarm. When I complain they mutter about health and safety and burns. You better not be one of those namby-pambies as well."

Stuart went into the kitchen and took deep breaths to calm himself before pouring milk, weighing oats and turning the dial on the microwave. This was all much harder than he'd expected. Then William called for him to come back. Stuart pulled on gloves, ready to wipe the old man and wash the commode.

"Do you watch soap operas?" William demanded.

"No."

The microwave pinged faintly in the kitchen.

"Do you have a girlfriend or wife who watches them?"

"No." Stuart fetched clean underwear from the drawer indicated by his client.

"Good. I can't abide those women who come in gossiping about who's sleeping with who and speculating what might happen next. It's as though they believe it's all real! If some people put as much energy into their real lives as they do into their television viewing, they'd be happier and more fulfilled."

"Everyone's entitled to a bit of relaxation at the end of the day and surely watching the soaps is no worse than escaping into a novel?"

William merely grunted in response.

With the old man clean and comfortable, he went to retrieve the porridge. It would have cooked and now cooled to an edible temperature.

William took a mouthful and shook his head. "I warned you and you didn't listen. Please don't make me ring the agency with a complaint on your first day. I want it hotter."

The prospect of Vanessa sacking him after his first-ever client visit was dire. Stuart had to do whatever it took to make William happy. He pushed the dish back in the microwave and watched it through the glass until it was on the verge of boiling over. Then he took it out and gave it a stir.

"And don't forget a healthy dollop of golden syrup this time."

Stuart did as he was told and placed the bowl on the tray on William's knee. William loaded his spoon and put it in his mouth.

"Agh!" The spoon went flying, the tray tipped and hot porridge landed in Mr Rutherford's lap. "Are you taking the piss or deliberately trying to scald me?" The words came out staccato-like as he waved one hand like a fan in front of his mouth and the other one tried to push the hot porridge mess off his lap. "Who on earth gives an old man porridge at boiling point? Get me water. Veronica's sent a dumbo with no common sense."

For a second Stuart froze, horrified at the damage he'd inflicted on an infirm pensioner, then he raced for water and a damp cloth.

"Sorry! Sorry! I didn't realise exactly how hot it was." Stuart didn't stop trembling until he was sure there was no sign of scalding on the skin beneath the sticky trousers and William had calmed down. They both agreed on toast as a suitable porridge replacement.

Later, after two cups of tea and when Stuart had voluntarily extended his visit by an extra hour in order to clear everything up, Mr Rutherford began to thaw a little.

"I won't phone the agency to complain this time because I think there's a chance we might get along better than I do with the ladies," he said. "What do you think?"

After the stress of the previous ninety minutes and the fear of possibly losing his job on his first day, the words were music to Stuart's ears. "I think we're made of the same stuff. Let's drink to a long and mutually beneficial partnership." Stuart crossed the fingers of his left hand behind his back and, with his other hand, clinked his own mug of tea against Mr Rutherford's.

He felt good as he drove home. Perhaps he wasn't completely out of the woods with Mr Rutherford yet, but he'd dealt with a difficult situation and succeeded. Looking after the old man was going to help fill the empty spaces in his life. Not in an exciting explosion of freedom but enough to be getting on with for the time being. Best to take things slowly. He'd already asked Veronica if she had any other clients for him but she'd said it was mostly women on her books and she needed to sound them out personally before sending a man to them.

In his kitchen, Jayne's phone number stared at him from under the change jar again. The man with the bright shiny Audi grinned at him. Stuart dithered.

CHAPTER SEVEN

The more Stuart thought about calling Jayne, the less confidence he had to do it.

It's obvious that you want this to be a date and not some platonic rubbish. Oh dear, you are going to have to up your game to stop Audi man getting in the way. I'm going to enjoy watching! There was glee in his sister's voice.

Do you remember when you asked Jayne out the first time round? The number of 'accidental' meetings you engineered at her front gate. Then I pointed out that she wasn't without other admirers and you were in there like a shot. A little bit of competition is good for sharpening reflexes.

Stuart ignored his sister's amusement. He and Jayne had been good together. They'd made each other laugh over stuff no one else found funny, like how a tin of Carnation evaporated milk could be full when you opened it and not evaporated at all. Or the way their chemistry teacher gave a barely discernible hop every five steps he took down the corridor. It was years since Stuart had felt that invisible connection to somebody and the yearning to have it again was growing.

But the Jayne he remembered wouldn't settle for second best and Audi man proved she still had ambition. Before Stuart made any move towards Jayne, he had to ground the

Zeppelin completely. He still wouldn't measure up to Audi man but would be doing his best under the circumstances. The next stage of his plan was to make use of the space in this house while he still could by getting a lodger to supplement his meagre income.

There was a local Facebook group, offering recommendations of tradesmen, stuff for sale and local news. It was to this group that Stuart now went to post his request for a lodger. He'd drafted the post the previous evening so he could re-read it with fresh eyes today before submitting. He wanted his words to be clear and honest so there was no hassle with a tenant who didn't fit the bill. Now he looked again at the description of what he was offering/wanted:

> *Single, working person wanted for a double room in a three-bedroomed house close to town centre. House will be shared with one other resident. Shared bathroom, kitchen and living area. Must be clean, tidy and quiet. Room available for the next eleven months only, at a weekly rent of £150.*

The advert seemed to cover all bases. Told them exactly what was on offer, for how long and at what cost. He closed his eyes and tried to think if he should add anything else.

Remove the word 'quiet'. Take life as it comes. Hope for somebody noisy to kick you out of your comfort zone.

"And keep me up all night with loud music? I don't think so."

Like me, you're going to be a long time dead and that old Mr Rutherford is hardly going to set your life on fire, is he?

Perhaps Sandra was right. He crossed his fingers, deleted the word 'quiet' and pressed 'post'. For a few minutes he kept refreshing the page but there was no deluge of applicants.

He needed the passive income generated by a lodger. His wages from the agency wouldn't stretch to all the bills. The house was tired. It lacked a posh shower and sleek built-in wardrobes. The carpets were worn. No one would find living here an attractive prospect. Better to get some regular money than nothing at all and have to go crawling to his brothers, who would likely say 'no'. After two hours of social media silence, Stuart amended the advert to one hundred pounds per week to include all bills.

Five minutes later he had a direct message from a lady wanting to view the room. They arranged an appointment for the next day, after his morning call on Mr Rutherford.

This time Stuart ensured the porridge was hot but not burning by tasting it first. The old man was grumpily satisfied. But still he managed to squeeze an extra thirty minutes out of the visit by insisting that Stuart be a sounding board for his morning cryptic crossword.

That meant the lady interested in the room was standing on his doorstep when he arrived home. Fifteen minutes early. Curvy, with Platinum-blonde bobbed hair, a zebra-striped fake-fur bomber jacket, purple leggings and high heels. He recognised at once that her multicolours made her an unsuitable lodger for a grey man. As he got nearer, Stuart realised she was quite small because, even with the heels, she was still half a head below his five foot eight inches. She offered her hand to him in greeting.

"I'm Florence. I've come about the room."

Stuart was slow to react and Florence's hand hovered awkwardly in mid-air.

"I've got the wrong house, haven't I?" Her hand went from mid-air to her scarlet lips. "I am so sorry. This is typical of me. My friends call me frantic Florence because I'm so disorganised and everything's a frantic panic. But you don't need to know all that. I'm talking too much. I always do that when I'm nervous and especially when I've made a mistake like this. I really am sorry."

Florence hitched the strap of her bag further onto her shoulder and started to walk back down the drive, the gravel making a meal of her heels. The fake fur wasn't long enough to cover her bottom. Stuart's eyes followed it. After a few seconds he mentally slapped his cheeks and Sandra insisted on her two pennies' worth.

Don't ogle! It's rude. Has it been so long since you got the hots for anyone? And why have you sent her away?

Stuart felt his cheeks redden. He could not disagree that he found Florence's curves attractive even if her dress sense portrayed a personality that wouldn't sit at all well in his house. "I didn't send her away," he muttered. "She wasn't what I was expecting and I couldn't react quickly enough."

Then call her back. She looks fun. You need someone like her to brighten up your dull little life. It's not as if you've got to marry her. It's only for eleven months and you can put a lock on your bedroom door if you're scared.

"Go away and stop goading me!"

The purple bottom was now out of sight and Stuart went inside.

Fifteen minutes later the doorbell rang.

"Me again! This is totally confusing. I haven't got my reading glasses with me so I can't see it properly. Can you help?" She was holding up her phone to show the messages they'd exchanged arranging the viewing. "You are the right house, aren't you?"

CHAPTER EIGHT

Florence squinted again at her phone, deep lines of concentration scoring her forehead. With her eyes looking downward, Stuart got the full benefit of the mauve paint on her eyelids. Her perfume was distinctive but not unpleasant. He'd behaved badly towards her. It was wrong to judge a book by its cover. He shouldn't have let her go thinking she'd made a mistake; everyone deserved a chance.

"My father died. I'm sorry. I'm a bit disorganised. My brain is struggling to keep up with the outside world."

"That's really sad." She adopted a genuinely mournful expression. "If the room's no longer available or now's not a good time, I . . ."

"Now's a great time. Come in." He stood back to let her through the front door.

"Shall I take my shoes off?"

Stuart thought about the shabby carpets that wouldn't look any worse if a steam-roller drove over them. Then he thought about the unnatural angle forced on Florence's feet by the little shiny red boots. It reminded him of the ancient Chinese practice of binding girls' feet and condemning them to a lifetime of hobbling to keep up with men, rather than allowing them to stride out on an equal basis.

"Yes, please."

She sat down on the bottom stair, undid zips and eased her feet that were clad in yellow socks out of their prison. She flexed her toes and gave them a rub. "That feels better."

"I'll give you the tour."

He took her through the house. He pointed out the things that would make living there attractive, such as use of the efficient washer-dryer he'd had to buy to cope with the amount of clean sheets and pyjamas that Eric had needed, and the high-speed internet that had allowed him and his father to each stream different programs on catch-up.

Florence was making enthusiastic comments when suddenly Stuart got cold feet. He hadn't anticipated a lodger like this. Florence was coming across as someone who'd like to socialise and chat. Stuart had envisaged more of an introvert like himself. Someone who'd prefer to keep out of the way. Stuart was too old to bend his routines to fit around another person.

"So, which is the room you're letting out?" she asked.

He'd spent the last few days returning his father's sick room into something resembling a pleasant, if faded, bedroom.

"In here. The décor is a bit old and there might not be enough wardrobe space for," he hesitated and then continued quickly, "a fashion-conscious lady. And there's no TV."

"This would suit me. And when I'm in, I can watch TV downstairs with you, can't I?"

She gave him a broad smile. For some reason he'd expected her teeth to be artificially bright but they were closer to the shade of his own, off-white with a tendency to slightly yellow. Combining this with the lines on her face that refused to play hide and seek, Stuart decided she must be about the same age as him, or possibly slightly younger.

"This is the bathroom. You'd have to share it with me. It's not one of those modern showers."

"No problem."

When they were back downstairs in the kitchen, Florence said, "I like it. When can I move in?"

"Don't you need to think about it? Perhaps view some more properties?" He'd expected her to murmur something about letting him know and then, if she did decide to take it, he could tell her someone else had got in before her.

"There's nothing else in the area that I can afford. I'm leaving my husband. He doesn't know yet, obviously. Money will be tight." The cheery volume of her voice dropped and she looked at the rings on her left hand.

This was happening too quickly. Even if Florence didn't need time to think about the house, he needed time to think about her. He didn't want someone with emotional baggage. He didn't want someone to watch television with. He just wanted help with the bills plus he'd naively envisaged chatting with a range of people and then choosing the most suitable person. Florence was too full-on and too sudden.

He wanted to tell her that he'd made a mistake in his post and it should've been £150 a week. He wanted to be honest and say that they wouldn't be compatible housemates. But either of those things would've felt like kicking her in the teeth when she was already down.

This is what I love about you, bro. You're always on the side of the underdog. Reminds me of that time the neighbours opposite put in a planning application for an extension to make life easier for their disabled daughter. Everyone started waving their NIMBY flags but you talked them round. You were brilliant. And you will be brilliant again.

An extension on a house across the road and an unsuitable person inside your own house were two completely different things.

Stuart played for time. "What do you do for a living?" Perhaps he could say 'no' on the basis that she wasn't earning.

"I'm a singer in a tribute band." Her eyes suddenly sparkled up at him and she spoke with enthusiasm. "You remember the Blackberries?"

Stuart's knowledge of any pop music beyond the eighties was nil but the Blackberries had been big in his student days. They'd played the sort of music that had had everyone rushing to the dancefloor. Even now their hits still got regular airings on Radio 2. They'd comprised a male drummer, male guitarist and two female singers who'd worn high-heeled boots and figure-hugging stage outfits.

"My era," he said.

"And mine. Our audience is full of middle-aged boppers. It's really rewarding to stand on stage and watch people squeeze along the rows and into the gangways so that they've got room to dance. Sometimes I feel like we're providing a social service for all these people who've become uptight with age, worry and responsibility. At our concerts they can let their hair down and have a really good time."

Stuart was surprised at Florence's insight into the human psyche. Maybe she wasn't as shallow as he'd first assumed.

"We're called Double Berry Black. We play all the local venues, up to a fifty-mile radius. I'll get you free tickets to come along."

Any sort of pop concert would be the last place he'd think of going. Yet when he was at university, gyrating his hips and raising his arms in the air had been second nature — after a few pints. He got a sudden longing for those days when anything had seemed possible. When the future had stretched interminably in front of him and only success had crossed his mind.

"Can I move in tomorrow?"

CHAPTER NINE

That night Stuart didn't sleep. He was trying to invent a diplomatic way of stopping Florence moving in. A pop singer was too far from his own life experience. It would become evident very quickly that they weren't suited and he needed a way out. But there was none, unless he used underhand tricks to make life in his house extremely uncomfortable for her.

In the early hours he got up and made cocoa. As he went past the landing window, he again spotted a pool of orange light spilling onto Lillian's patio. Perhaps she struggled with insomnia. He'd read somewhere that happened to old people. Stuart knelt on the carpet with his milky drink and watched the light.

A figure came out of the house and stood in the pale orange glow. It was Lillian in a long, light-coloured nightdress but no dressing gown. Stuart shivered for her; it was May but still cold outside at night. Lillian walked from the patio onto the lawn. She was no longer in the spotlight but still easily visible. As she prowled about the grass, slightly stooped with age, she looked ethereal. Stuart imagined her as an old, wise, tribal elder. He finished his drink and Lillian stepped back onto the patio. She wore no shoes. He took his mug back down to the kitchen and when he returned past the window, she was gone and the light was out.

It felt far too early when the alarm shocked him awake and Stuart's fingers felt automatically for the snooze button. Then he remembered he was a working man now with a breakfast visit to Mr Rutherford to fit in before the Sunday club ride. A small part of him cursed replacing one responsibility with another that equally curtailed his movements. But Veronica had promised him every other Sunday off.

* * *

With the old man fed and watered, Stuart arrived at the meet point just in time. He relished the way he was feeling more included in the group. Since his father's death, several people with whom he'd had little connection before had made a point of shaking his hand and offering their condolences. This had led onto longer, more general conversations and the beginnings of friendships.

As the bikes made easy work of a long, flat stretch of road, the club's programme manager found his way to Stuart's side. "Can I add you to our rota of ride leaders? It works out about once every twelve weeks or so."

Hearing the words brought a rush of pleasure that he was both wanted and thought capable.

"Yes. Great. If you can manage to make it one of my Sundays off?"

"No problem. I do the rota twelve months in advance so no one can complain they don't have enough notice. Somebody's dropping out at the end of the year so you won't actually need to do anything until January. OK?"

"Wonderful."

Over a mug of tea and a piece of bread pudding in the café, Stuart's name and contact details were added to a sheet of paper and he officially became a part of the Sunday Ride-Leaders' Rota. He cycled home with a smile on his face, barely noticing the usual fatigue in his legs following the long ride.

He'd only just got dressed from the shower when Florence pulled up in a metallic-orange, fifteen-year-old Fiat Panda. The roof was badly faded and the bonnet mottled. Stuart helped carry her stuff inside. There was one suitcase, sporting a tattered airport label for a flight to Palma. There were numerous carrier bags overflowing with shoes, electric hair gadgets and a heavy one containing pans.

"They're my best ones," Florence said when she saw Stuart looking at them. "Jim will only burn them and there's no reason why he should get to keep all the household stuff. If you promise to be careful, you can borrow them."

Once everything was upstairs, her room looked like a junk shop after it had been picked over on sale day.

"I'll leave you to it then," he said.

"Do me a favour." She tossed the car key at him. "Lock the car for me. It's not worth much but I can't afford for it to go AWOL. Don't want to disappoint my fans by not turning up to gigs on time." She winked at him.

Stuart stuck the key in the driver's door and heard the clunk as all the other doors synchronised. To be sure he tried each of the doors.

"New car?" Jayne pointed a remote at her own car, a six-year-old Mini with immaculate paintwork, and then opened the driver's door.

She'd caught him by surprise and he had no conversation prepared. Suddenly he was a teenager again. He smiled and tried to look casually indifferent. Then he realised she was waiting for an answer.

"No." Stuart hesitated. There was going to be no way of keeping Florence a secret. "It belongs to my new lodger."

"Oh."

There was an awkward silence that Stuart felt he should fill. "It seemed a waste having empty rooms when other people have nothing."

He didn't want to admit he needed the money, although Lillian had probably told her daughter everything. He wished Jayne would get in her own car. Her expression was wavering from friendly to blank and back again. He thought about her phone number lodged under the change jar waiting for him to feel confident enough to rival Audi man. That time was unlikely to come.

"You're making money out of the house while you still can. A good move — that's one in the eye for your ungrateful brothers." She smiled broadly at him.

Suddenly everything was all right again and she was on his side. A sudden rush of kinship between them made him consider asking her out right now, face to face. Dinner. Tomorrow. At the Italian down the road. Nice and convenient so they could walk and both have a glass of wine. Or two. The memories of meandering home together as teenagers flashed through his mind. Kissing and whispering in the passageway just before they reached their houses. Leaving it until the very last minute to let go of each other, so Jayne could rush up to her front door before her 11 p.m. curfew. His toes curled and his body warmed as he remembered.

"Jayne?" he began.

"Yes?" Her smile was still bright, hopeful. This was his opportunity.

"Hi!" Florence walked between them, right up to the small fence that marked the border between the two properties. "I'm Florence. I just moved in today."

Jayne made no effort to hide her surprise. Stuart wanted to dematerialise. Florence was still wearing the purple leggings and tight yellow top from the previous day. On her feet she had huge slippers with dogs' heads on the front. For some reason she'd clamped her artificially blonde hair in place with plastic pink hair-slides that looked as though they belonged to a toddler.

Jayne straightened her black jacket and put a hand on the neckline of her silky blouse. Even though it was Sunday, she looked like a legal secretary.

"I'm Jayne."

It was the first time that Stuart had seen Jayne looking even a little flustered.

"Pleased to meet you, Jayne." Florence held out her hand. "Are you and Stuart . . . an item?" Florence inclined her head towards him.

Stuart wished for an earthquake, a bolt of lightning, or even a sudden rainstorm.

Jayne caught his eye. Her conspiratorial expression warmed his cheeks and increased the feeling of connection between them. She spoke slowly. "No. We're not."

"Shame — you'd be good together. Anyone could tell that, just by looking at the way you communicate. There's a sort of body language between you."

"I have to be off." Jayne stepped neatly into her car and shut the door.

She gave him a wave and a grin as she pulled off the drive.

Stuart tried nonchalantly to return her smile and hand gesture while struggling to suppress his frustration and anger at Florence.

"Why are you looking at me like that? I only stated the obvious. Can I have the car key, please? I think I left my lady shaver in the boot."

Back inside, Florence warmed to the topic of Jayne. "It's obvious you both fancy each other. And you've got her phone number safe." She pointed to the change jar.

The benefits of a lodger were rapidly diminishing. "It's private," was all he could manage in his own defence.

"Private or not, don't let life pass you by. Move in on her."

I agree with our colourful new friend. We rarely regret what we did do, only what we didn't.

CHAPTER TEN

The next morning, Stuart was up before Florence for his early morning call to Mr Rutherford. It was a few minutes before seven when he went out to the car. From the corner of his eye, he caught a movement near the hedge on the far side of Lillian's garden. He leaned over the fence to get a better look. It was probably a cat choosing its toilet or a fox scavenging for food. The shape was difficult to see in the shadow of the high hedge but as it shuffled backwards onto the lawn, Stuart saw that it was no animal. It was Lillian. In her crouched position she wobbled, lost her balance and then sat down hard on the lawn.

"Lillian!" Stuart hurried down his drive and up the next one.

She was wearing a dark cardigan over a long pale nightdress patterned with faded pink rosebuds. She was missing her glasses and her expression was vulnerable and lost. Mud sat between her bare toes.

"Here — take my hand." She grabbed his outstretched hand and he slowly pulled her to standing. "What are you doing outside so early?"

"I lost my wedding ring. I thought it had dropped off when I was gardening. But it's not there." Tears began to roll down her cheeks. "It's all I had left of him."

Stuart felt awkward. This confused, vulnerable version of Lillian was a stranger to him. She brought her left hand to her face and wiped it across the bottom of her runny nose, leaving a dirty, brown streak. There was a gold band on her fourth finger.

"The ring is on your finger."

She raised her hand and stared at the gold as though she didn't believe it. "I don't know how it got back on there." She pulled at the ring but age had made her knuckles too large to let it pass.

As Stuart guided Lillian around the side of the house to the back door, Jayne appeared. She'd obviously dressed hurriedly in grey joggers and a sweatshirt and her hair was still tousled from sleep. She looked less 'confident legal secretary' and more 'approachable human being'. The sort of person with whom he could imagine reconciling differences and building a relationship. But with Lillian clutching at his hand like a small child, he couldn't dwell on that possibility now.

"Mum! I heard voices. What on earth?" Jayne looked from Lillian to Stuart and back again. Her eyes were anguished and there was concern in her voice.

He had to bow out now, otherwise he'd be late for Mr Rutherford. "Just a bit of confusion," he said lightly. "Lillian thought she'd lost her wedding ring but it was on her finger all the time. I've done it myself — thought I'd lost something and then looked everywhere except the most obvious place."

"Oh." Jayne was searching his face for some further explanation that he didn't have.

He wanted to stay and help but there wasn't time. Stuart gave a little shrug and gestured at his car. "I'm late for work."

* * *

"I thought you weren't coming." Mr Rutherford's voice was impatient. "I nearly pressed this stupid button round my neck — I didn't want to die of thirst and wet myself before someone decided to send a replacement."

William had already manoeuvred himself into the high chair at the side of the bed.

Stuart took his coat off. "You should stay put until I arrive, Mr Rutherford, even if I'm late. One false move and you'd be marooned on the floor. Or worse, dead."

"Would that be so bad? I'm waiting to be summoned to the pearly gates. I can't remember the last time I did anything productive or for the good of someone else. The purpose went from my life a long time ago. If I could bribe St Peter to get to the front of the queue, I would."

What was the correct response to a comment like that? Stuart wanted to overcompensate, crack a joke and make out that all would be well. But that was papering over a hole that would tear wide open again as soon as Stuart left. The old man needed something tangible to keep him going. But giving someone a purpose to stay alive wasn't as easy as offering a butter mint to suck.

"You'll probably be surprised to hear this, Mr Rutherford, but at the moment your purpose is to stay right here and keep me in a job. I need the money. I need the diversion from my own circumstances and I need the company. Sensible male conversation that I can't get at home. Besides, jumping the queue just isn't British."

The old man put his head on one side as though considering the veracity of this. "If you want me to believe that you haven't just dumped a load of bullshit to make me feel better, you'd better elaborate on your personal circumstances. I'm not some old dear whose mind is shrinking. My mind is as sharp as it was when I was a GP."

Stuart knew he was in danger of making himself look pathetic in front of the old man.

"I'm waiting. And don't make something up — I can spot a liar by his body language."

Stuart told his tale as he assisted Mr Rutherford onto the commode. It was easier to talk while he was doing. He helped the old man to wash and dress. While he was soaping legs and then rolling on socks, he didn't have to look the old man in the eye and see his pity, or his sympathy, or his eye-rolling at the situation that Stuart had allowed to happen.

"So there you have it: your money, plus Florence's rent, is just about keeping me solvent until my home is pulled from under me. Then, who knows? Destitution or will a bright new world open itself up to me? Is that enough purpose to keep you alive?"

Mr Rutherford nodded in a satisfied kind of way. "Call me William. I think we can be friends. We need each other, if you see what I mean."

"William." Stuart smiled. He liked being called a friend. He didn't want to be an impersonal body who rushed in and out with rubber gloves and a brusque manner. That wasn't job satisfaction. Job satisfaction was the warm sensation he had right now.

"How do you actually feel about losing your home? You give an impression of extreme sangfroid, but you can't be genuinely so indifferent about it."

This was a scab Stuart had been trying to leave unpicked. If he gave his mind free rein in that direction, his anger boiled and the true ugliness of his personality fought to break free. "I'm not indifferent. Inside I'm bitter and twisted. Sometimes I hate my father and brothers."

"But you choose not to fight it."

"I've wasted enough years of my life on a family that doesn't care." He wondered if William could hear the tightness in his voice. "I've chosen to move past that and be my own man." The words came out stronger than he felt. "Besides, all the fighting in the world will be wasted if the house has to be sold to pay the legal bills. I have no capital."

William nodded as though he was satisfied. Stuart went to make breakfast.

"Tell me some news from the outside world," William demanded once he had a mug of tea and a bowl of porridge, at a safe but hot temperature, on the tray in front of him. "Give my mind something to chew on."

Stuart began to recount the day's headlines from the news bulletin he'd heard in the car on the way over.

"Not politics and stuff. As new friends we shouldn't discuss that — our relationship isn't yet strong enough to weather different points of view." William scraped the last of the porridge from around the edge of the bowl. "You said your new lodger was a woman. Tell me more about her — do you think you and her might, you know, get together?"

"No." He didn't even have to consider the question. "We're poles apart. I'm thinking perhaps I should get rid of her."

"Tell me more."

William was easy to talk to and Stuart realised that the old man did truly have a purpose in helping him at this present moment. Just talking was helping him organise his thoughts.

"I like her," William said. "She sounds the sort of colourful character who'd brighten anyone's life. Don't get rid of her. I want her to brighten my life through your stories. We all get stuck in a rut and she's going to drag you out of yours. Grasp that opportunity while you can. Infirmity brings us all down before we're ready."

The old man was looking happier and sounding more positive than when Stuart had arrived. The pair had never met, but Florence was influencing William for the better. Stuart took the breakfast things into the kitchen to wash up and he made a flask of tea in case William wanted another drink before Stuart's lunchtime visit.

William's my sort of man. Sandra spoke her mind as he stood at the sink. *We're on the same wavelength about Florence. She's like a rainbow coming into your grey world. You get rid of her at your own risk.*

"All right, all right, message received clearly and understood."

"Did you say something, Stuart?" William called from the adjacent room.

"No!" Stuart shouted, checking there was enough stuff in the fridge for making William's lunch when he returned. "Just having a mutter to myself."

"First sign of madness, that is," William said as Stuart put his coat on, "talking to yourself. You want to watch it or they'll be carting you off and then where would I be? We need each other, remember?"

CHAPTER ELEVEN

Florence had been living with Stuart for a fortnight. It hadn't been an easy two weeks. The house had been devoid of a woman's presence for over forty years and this new one wasn't slow at making her mark.

Stuart had bitten his tongue at the tights, washed in the bathroom sink and hung over the shower screen to dry. One evening there'd been a pair of knickers there too. Stuart had averted his eyes and decided no one would notice if he went a day or two without showering.

Radio 2 had now become a thing in the kitchen. Stuart preferred the constant talking from Radio 4. There was something comforting in a human voice keeping him abreast of world events. He hated going about his day in ignorance of the detail behind the headlines. He tried to explain this to Florence the first time she filled her bowl to overflowing with Frosties and milk, changed the radio station and sat down opposite him.

"Nonsense," she said. "We've both got plenty of problems of our own without wallowing in those of people on the other side of the world."

"It's our duty to be aware of how badly others are being treated, so that we can do something about it."

"We can't do anything except give money to charity and hope they spend it the right way. Money that neither of us can currently afford. When I didn't want to eat my tea, my mother made me think about the poor starving children in Africa. That was supposed to encourage me to eat my sprouts. It had no effect, except that one day, I tipped my cabbage and carrots into an envelope and asked her to post it so the poor starving children could eat my vegetables. She never mentioned those children again. And she never posted the envelope."

"But if we don't know what the government is doing, how can we decide who to vote for when election time comes?"

"That's easily solved. Don't vote. I never have. Keep life simple."

Florence had shocked him in many ways since she'd moved in but this statement was something Stuart couldn't live with. Not voting was irresponsible. It equated to letting strangers decide your future. And, in a turn-up for the books from a girl who wouldn't hear a word against Florence, Sandra was there supporting him before he'd begun to articulate his thoughts on the matter.

Tell her, Stuart. Tell her those suffragettes did what they did for a reason. She must be educated about Emmeline Pankhurst and the others. Her opinion is criminal. As someone who's never had a chance at proper living, I abhor those who refuse to take any responsibility for the society in which they live.

"Florence," Stuart began. "Over a hundred years ago women fought long and hard so that people like you could have a say in how our country is governed."

Florence shrugged and started swaying her shoulders in time with a tune that had just begun. It felt like trying to engage with the stubborn teenagers in his class thirty years ago.

He took a breath. "While you're living in this house, I will be obliged to add you to the electoral register. The council send out a form in the summer and we'll have to put your details on there."

"That doesn't mean I actually have to vote."

"Correct, and unfortunately you've just missed the local elections. But there's plenty of time for me to persuade you of your responsibility as a citizen before the next election."

Florence appeared to consider his statement. "I'm happy to make a bargain over this. I will put my name on that bit of paper and consider voting. But only if I can get you dancing."

"Dancing?" A streak of fear ran through him. "What kind of dancing?" Dancing as a student, in the dark, in the middle of a drunken crowd when everyone had had a few beers was good. But not now. Not with a virtual stranger; a woman he hardly knew. He was too old and set in his ways to consider any sort of dancing. Dancing was not in his plans for a bright new future.

At that moment an old Blackberries hit started on the radio.

"This sort of dancing!" Florence was on her feet, twirling around the kitchen floor and singing along to the music, drowning out the recording.

Suddenly she and her clothes didn't look too colourful or too garish. Singing and dancing, Florence looked completely natural. Movement and music came to her as easily as skulking in the shadows came to Stuart. He was mesmerised by the way the supple movements of her torso reflected the rise and fall in the volume of the song, the way the rhythm from the radio reflected in the rhythm of her limbs and by the way the expression on her face shone with absolute happiness.

Stuart was envious. He didn't want to sing and dance, but he wanted that happiness. He wanted to feel it inside him and he wanted others to recognise it in him. But this was one of those wishes that began in your head as a small boy on December the first. You wished with all your heart for Santa to bring the biggest train set in the toy shop window on Christmas Eve. You told Santa in his town centre grotto, with Mum sitting beside you. On Christmas morning, you knew immediately the box was too small. It was a train set but on a very small scale. Mum and Dad were looking at you hopefully, as though they had a vested interest in the outcome of the presents Santa brought. Robert and George made the condescending *oohs* and *aahs* of older brothers. Everyone wanted this tiny railway set to be good enough for you. And you had to pretend it was.

"Do you like it?" Mum asked, kneeling beside you.

"Yes, thank you to Santa."

There was a collective release of breath in the room and the day continued, but with a large lump of disappointment already filling your stomach before Christmas dinner appeared. If Stuart tried to reach for Florence's brand of happiness, disappointment was bound to follow, just like it had when he'd tried to reach for the train set.

"Join me!" Florence paused and held out both hands towards him.

He wanted to follow her lead. He imagined himself with her confidence, her voice and her magical way of blending with the music and allowing it to enhance her. If he tried, he would fail and she would be a witness to it.

"It's your era. You said so yourself." Her feet were moving again. While that music played, she couldn't keep still. It was her job but it also enhanced and fulfilled her. "Have a go. It's joining in and letting go that matters. There's no one watching."

Incorrect, he thought to himself, *the best dancer that I've ever met is watching and I will have to face her every morning over toast and remember how I resembled a sack of potatoes when dancing in the kitchen.*

She came right up to him and took both his hands in hers.

A weird but not unpleasant feeling travelled up each arm. Florence's eyes looked suddenly surprised and he wondered if she was sharing the same addictive sensation. It was akin to the glow of whisky trickling down the throat and reaching a sweet spot within. The sort of glow you always wanted more of. But however much he had, it wouldn't give him dancing feet.

"No!" He spoke louder than he intended.

Florence stopped swaying and took a step back, an expression of shock and hurt on her face.

CHAPTER TWELVE

Florence switched the music to Radio 4 and walked out of the room. A bright candle flame had been extinguished, leaving only semi-darkness. Regret hung on the fringes of Stuart's mind.

He wondered about the electoral register — would she stay long enough to add her name to it? He was merely her landlord, not her educator nor her Henry Higgins. He couldn't expect her to go to a polling station if he wouldn't even dance in his own kitchen.

Later, Florence came downstairs in her stage outfit. This was bigger and brighter than her everyday clothes, but with the advantage that there were no colours battling furiously against each other. She stood in the kitchen doorway as Stuart stirred a pan of homemade carrot soup for his tea. In the overhead fluorescent light, her eyeshadow sparkled with metallic bronze glitter, her extra-wide belt glowed with the warmth of gold and the white catsuit looked like something from a washing-powder advert. All her curves were evident but covered tastefully while maintaining her attractiveness.

"I'm sorry," she said. "This is your house and I shouldn't have been so forceful about getting you to do something outside your comfort zone."

Stuart shrugged. It was obvious that Florence thought he was boring. Did it matter? Not a jot to anyone in the big outside world. But to Stuart, what his lodger thought was beginning to matter a lot.

"We're like chalk and cheese, us, aren't we?" she continued. "Probably no bad thing if a little bit of each of us rubs off on the other. But best not to force it, eh? I've survived all these years without voting and you've got this far without letting your hair down with a song and dance. Truce?"

Stuart held back from shaking her hand. Her words were a seed of disappointment. Agreeing to the truce felt like waving goodbye forever to his chance at the happiness he'd seen on her face. He didn't want to bang the door shut on that.

"I'd still like the chance to convince you of your electoral responsibilities."

She frowned and then grinned. "In that case I think we've got ourselves a deal. I'll listen to your persuasion but you have to sing and dance." She looked at her watch. "No time now but tomorrow it's a date!"

They shook hands.

"One more thing," Florence continued. "I was going to ask you earlier but with us falling out, the moment didn't come. I could do the cleaning for you. I've plenty of time during the day but you're in and out with your carer visits. And when you've cleaned up for other people you probably don't fancy getting stuck in here. What do you think?"

If this was a criticism of his standard of cleaning, Florence had more diplomacy than Stuart had given her credit for. "Is there something wrong? Tide mark round the bath? Dust on the skirting boards?"

"No, no. Nothing. I just thought it might help. A woman's touch and all that."

Offers of help in Stuart's life had been rare over the last few decades and he was touched that Florence had noticed how his backwards and forwards work with William left him with little free time. "Yes, it would help, thank you."

"Great." She held out her hand again.

Bewildered, Stuart took it — he'd never met a woman so keen on shaking hands before. Perhaps she was a Freemason.

"A thirty pound a week reduction in the rent should make us quits."

"What?"

"I did enough cleaning without pay when I was with my old man. Now I've left, I do everything on my own terms."

"But you didn't say."

"Stuart — please don't tell me that you expected me to pick your underpants off the floor for free?"

He didn't leave his underpants on the floor but he had assumed Florence had offered to help out of the goodness of her heart. Obviously, along with everything else, he'd lost the skill of reading people during his father's illness. "I don't—"

"I had you down as an honourable man."

"Of course, thirty pounds sounds fair." Doing the cleaning himself would be preferable to losing that amount of money each week but what else could he say without appearing to take advantage of her generous nature?

Florence gave him a double-thumbs-up sign and a broad grin before disappearing into the evening. The orange Panda sputtered for a second on the drive and then crunched over the gravel.

Stuart took the soup off the heat and sat down. Were all women so manipulative?

No, manipulative wasn't the right word, it made Florence sound evil and she wasn't that. Playing things to her advantage was probably a better description.

Able to twist a man around her little finger, is the phrase you're looking for. Sandra was in his head again. *And yes, given the right man, we are all capable of doing it.*

"Are you saying I'm gullible? After twenty-five years in almost solitary confinement, you'd be gullible too."

Not gullible. You wouldn't fall for the 'You are due a tax refund — give us your bank details' scam, you're just susceptible to the wiles of certain women. You agreed so quickly to Florence's suggestion because you want to please her and keep her sweet. That is definitely good because she is FUN and that is what you need in your life right now! If it costs you thirty pounds a week, who cares, it's only money.

"In less than a year I will be homeless. Thirty pounds multiplied up by many weeks is worth having."

At your age you've got to take your fun where you can find it. There was a time when you'd have a go at anything. Remember the geography field trips you took your sixth formers on? You always used to start the singing on the coach.

"That was to distract the girls who swore blind they always threw up on long journeys."

Who was the teacher who put his heart and soul into compering an evening talent show in the youth hostel?

"To stop the little idiots sneaking outside for a cigarette."

No matter the reason. Stuart Borefield wasn't always grey. We just have to find the felt tips and colour him in again.

If only it was that simple. Stuart sighed and warmed a bowl for his soup.

* * *

The next day Florence declared that she was going to the supermarket to stock up on cleaning materials and needed petty cash.

"Petty cash? I'm not a big shot business enterprise." Stuart handed over a twenty-pound note and said he was going cycling and expected the house to be pristine when he returned.

"Ooh! Hark at you!"

This time he gave her the double-thumbs-up sign and went to get changed.

She was cleaning the inside of the lounge windows when he returned, sweaty and red-faced from the hills. He felt her gaze travel up and down his body. Then she gave a little smile. It took all his willpower to stand his ground in his own house and not rush upstairs to change.

"I didn't know you meant proper cycling with Lycra and everything."

"Is there another kind of cycling that's not proper?"

"I had you down as a tweed-and-plus-fours man. Whatever plus fours are. But you suit this sort of cycling better." There was a note of appreciation in her voice. "You absolutely have the figure for Lycra. Give us a twirl."

It was embarrassing. Little girls in tutus gave twirls. He hesitated, about to refuse.

"You want to talk about elections — I need something in return."

Stuart always kept his word and he was supposed to be coming out of his shell and having fun. He shuffled his feet so that he turned 360 degrees. It didn't feel like fun. Florence stretched her arms out at shoulder height and smiled at him encouragingly. Feeling like a ballerina in drag, he copied her.

"I'll fetch the music," she said. "Let's make the most of you being sleek, flexible and fit. And I mean 'fit' in both senses of the word." She threw him a wink. "You'll make some lucky lady very happy."

Stuart was already hot from pedalling up the hills but now his face was burning and he could feel an increased dampness under his arms.

"This sounds like the Blackberries but actually it's us." She swiped something on her phone and a familiar beat filled the room. Florence's body began to reflect the rhythm. Stuart saw past her slippers, apron and jeans and sensed her real stage presence as she fell into sync with music. This time she didn't sing as she danced, but it was her voice coming out of the speaker. She held out her hands and called him over. "Time to keep your side of the bargain!"

His limbs moved like a wooden puppet with tangled strings. He'd discarded his cycling shoes in the porch and was now in stockinged feet, which made him feel vulnerable.

"Just mirror what I'm doing and dance like no one is watching."

He was a couple of seconds late with every move and by the time he'd grasped one pattern repetition, Florence had switched to a different arm wave, hip wiggle or sidestep. He was like an electric toy whose diminishing battery power was making his movements slow and uncoordinated.

"You're too uptight. Let your shoulders relax. You'll know when you're doing it right because the music will carry you."

Concentration was threatening to burst his brain. He wanted to give up, flop on the sofa and simply enjoy watching Florence's lithe movements. But giving up didn't move life towards that bright new future. Giving up meant more of the same greyness. He didn't want more of the same, he wanted a proper life. He wanted happiness.

His shoulders wouldn't weave like Florence's. His hips were made of concrete. His arms and legs were getting better at waving, kicking and generally being busy but they were headstrong and wouldn't be governed by the music.

The song ended and Florence swiped her phone before the next track could begin. "I really enjoyed that," she declared. "It's so much more fun when you've got a partner. That's why I love performing — everyone in the audience is your partner and we're all urging each other on to bigger and better things. You'll be good at this in no time — a lesson a day will chase your awkwardness away."

They sat down on the sofa next to each other.

"My water will be going cold." Florence pointed at the lime-green bucket by the window. The lurid colour made it obviously a new purchase and not one discovered under the kitchen sink.

There was a small gap between them, along the line of the two flat sofa cushions. If either of them moved, their thighs would meet. It would be embarrassing. Especially in his cycling Lycra. Stuart tensed his muscles and tried to lean imperceptibly in the opposite direction.

"I hope I'm paying you by results and not by the hour?" He gave what he hoped sounded like a light-hearted chuckle.

Florence frowned at him. "I hope that wasn't a dig. I'll be keeping the whole of this house to my usual standard."

He raised his hands in a gesture of surrender. "My jokes are obviously worse than my dancing. I don't know when those windows last saw a cloth. You're doing a fantastic job."

She smiled and patted his knee. The spark of electricity took him by surprise and he stood up quickly. "I'd better get in the shower."

"When I came back from the supermarket I met that woman next door, with her mother."

"Lillian and Jayne?"

Florence nodded. "The old lady seemed subdued. She walked up to the front door without speaking. The younger woman, Jayne, was full of questions, mostly about me and how long I was staying. She was a bit pushy, if you ask me. She even asked if we were 'having a relationship'." Florence added the air quotes. "But I put her straight on that one."

"You asked her the same question the day you moved in." Stuart spoke lightly but his mind was working. Jayne's question was a good sign, surely. He thought about the phone number underneath the change jar.

"But she was like a dog with a bone. Wouldn't let it go. Did we spend our evenings together, she asked. I told her I was out performing most nights and she seemed to relax a little. But she has definitely got designs on you."

Two women standing on the driveway discussing him and not even talking about how he was doing 'a good thing' by caring for his father. It was a weird, surreal happening.

"In retaliation I asked her about Audi man."

"What?"

"Three nights in a row he's dropped her home at the time I've got back from performing. In a big, posh black car. You need better antennae."

This wasn't good. Stuart had only seen the car once and had assumed the attraction of Audi man was on the wane. He struggled to keep an expression of neutral disinterest.

"Anyway, the good news is that she said she was going to finish it. Something about Audi man not getting on with the old lady. She described him as 'one of those men who lack human depth'. She was quite earnest about it all, as though she really wanted me to get the message."

Relief and fear. Stuart's heartbeat increased. The football had been passed back to him and he had another chance at the goal.

"Reading between the lines, I think what she really wanted, was to make sure that I passed the facts on to you. Ask her out." His lodger was looking at him triumphantly. "She'll say yes. I guarantee."

Florence obviously thought asking Jayne out was something he was capable of and something which would receive a positive response. But he still had to find the right words and an appropriate opportunity and brace himself for possible rejection . . . He couldn't explain this to Florence, so he ignored her last sentence and headed for a shower.

In the bathroom he peeled off his cycling gear and looked at himself naked in the full-length bathroom mirror.

How did today's women like their men? Rounded or curved? Cycling had kept him slim. Perhaps verging on skinny? Was skinny good or would he get the proverbial sand kicked in his face? He adopted a Mr Universe pose, arms at shoulder height and bent at the elbow, feet apart, knees softened and flexed his muscles. Not bad, and probably better than most men his age. His eyes travelled down his body and he wondered again about the question of sex. Would he be dreadful or was it like riding a bike?

Another voice burst into his head, making him jump.

You'll catch your death standing around naked like that! You did mend the lock on the bathroom door before Florence moved in, didn't you? Otherwise she'll be in here ravishing you.

Stuart grabbed the bath towel and wrapped it around himself. "Go away! You're my sister. You shouldn't be in here."

OK. OK. Don't get your knickers in a twist. I'd be useless at advising you anyway, never having had the opportunity for a sex life myself. But, given the chance, I think I might have been rather good at it.

"Too much information." Stuart closed his eyes, focused his mind on the darkness behind the lids and counted to twenty. When he opened his eyes and relaxed his thoughts, Sandra was gone. He dropped the towel, fiddled with the temperamental dial on the shower and stepped into the flow of hot water.

The decision about if, when and how to approach Jayne bounced around his head.

CHAPTER THIRTEEN

Stuart waited until Florence had left for that night's performance before taking Jayne's number from beneath the change jar. Without giving himself time to think or to kick the football out of play, he picked up the phone.

"Hello?"

"Jayne, it's Stuart, from next door."

"Stuart! I'm just going to move into the kitchen. Mum's got the telly on and I can't hear you properly."

The clever words that he'd been playing on a repeat loop inside his head since composing them in the shower disappeared like music on a mangled cassette tape. He fumbled in his head for a dynamic conversation opener. Nothing was available and he resorted to the mundane. "How's Lillian? Florence said she seemed subdued when she saw you earlier."

"Not good." Jayne's voice dropped. "Even with the TV on, I can't talk about that over the phone. But it would help to discuss it. Do you fancy going out for dinner tomorrow? I could book a table at the Italian for seven thirty?"

This was too easy — there'd been no need for a rehearsed but casual speech about how they should catch up for old times' sake. She'd even picked the same restaurant he was going to suggest but, unlike him, she'd probably eaten there;

Stuart had run his finger down the Eateries Directory page in the free paper.

"Sounds good." His heart was thumping but he tried to keep his voice nonchalant, as though going out for a meal with an attractive woman was a regular occurrence in his life. "Shall I call round for you at about quarter past?"

"I'll look forward to having some proper conversation for a change."

Stuart put the phone down and raised a triumphant arm. Something close to euphoria swirled within him. He closed the curtains against the darkening sky and dug out an old Blackberries cassette tape from his student days. He and Dad had never upgraded the 1980s hi-fi encased in smoked glass, which took up far too much space. It was hardly used and Stuart was amazed when it actually produced sound.

He had no muscle memory of the moves that Florence had shown him earlier but he tried to let his body feel the rhythm of the music, the ebb and flow of verse and chorus. His attempt at solo dancing probably looked moronic but was actually enjoyable. Stuart wondered if dancing only worked when you were feeling happy or, if the opposite were true and dancing could make you happy and confident. Had the latter happened to him this afternoon with Florence?

* * *

"Any plans for this evening?" Florence had chosen to perfect her stage makeup standing in the draught by the hall mirror, rather than using the one in the bathroom, her bedroom or the dressing room where the band were gigging tonight.

"Not particularly." If he mentioned Jayne, Florence would act like a teething puppy with a slipper.

"It's just that you're looking rather dapper."

Dapper. She made him sound like an old man. He'd showered and changed into what he'd thought was a semi-smart outfit of beige chinos and an open-necked blue shirt. Clothes that he rarely had occasion to wear. He'd checked his brown slip-on loafers were clean and placed by them by the door. Dapper. That wasn't the image he wanted to project. "What do you mean?"

She turned from the mirror, pursing her lips together before she spoke. "You've got a clean bib and tucker. Seems over the top for a bowl of soup alone in the kitchen."

"Dapper — do you mean old fashioned?" He tried to keep his voice light.

"Compared to a twenty-year-old on a hot date — yes, old fashioned. Compared to other fifty-something males nervously trying to impress — you're absolutely up to the minute fashion-wise."

Her words swiped a rug from beneath him and he landed flat on his back.

"Enjoy! And say hello to Jayne for me." Florence blew a kiss over her shoulder and was gone.

For a weird moment Stuart wondered if she'd bugged the telephone. Then he realised that parting shot was a wild guess, designed to wind him up. He slipped on his shoes and pulled together the jigsaw of his confidence, pushing 'dapper' from his head.

Jayne opened the door as soon as he knocked. She had her jacket on and handbag over her shoulder. "Bye, Mum!"

"Aren't you going to invite Stuart in so I can have a look at him?" Lillian's voice competed with the theme tune of a soap opera.

"You know what he looks like and we'll be late." She pulled the door shut behind her and smiled at him. "I am so looking forward to this."

It was the same smile that had peppered the excitement of his sixth-form years and stuck in his memory for nearly forty years. He felt a shiver of anticipation inside and smiled back at her. "Me too."

He wondered if he should hold her hand. Jayne hadn't made it clear whether this was an actual 'date' date or a 'just good friends' date. They walked side by side without touching.

"I saw little Miss Superstar going out. How do you two get on?"

"Fine. She can be a bit . . ." He stopped mid-sentence, surprised to find himself not wanting to be disloyal to his lodger.

"In your face?"

"Yes. But she means well."

"Not your type though?"

He glanced sideways at Jayne. "No."

Jayne nodded as though he'd given the right answer and switched the subject to a work colleague whose cat had a mystery illness and was costing a fortune in vet's bills.

"Pets are like children," Stuart said. "You can't put them to sleep just because they cost too much."

"I don't see the attraction in pets. Especially cats. Cats don't show loyalty — they're free spirits and always on the take."

Stuart was saved from shifting his views towards Jayne's by their arrival at the restaurant. When they'd ordered, he moved the conversation to the subject Jayne wanted to discuss.

"How's Lillian?"

Jayne took a breath and touched the gold pendant on her collarbone. "Not good. She wakes at all times of the night and goes outside. Sometimes I hear her and sometimes I don't. When I do, I bring her back inside and settle her down again but then I can't get back to sleep. There's all these worries going round in my head."

Stuart remembered the orange pools of light on the flagstones outside the kitchen window. But it didn't tally with the capable woman who'd been a rock the day his father died, or the fun 'aunty' who'd always remembered his childhood birthdays with a brightly wrapped non-educational gift.

"When Mum was looking after Gran, she didn't have to combine it with a full-time job as well. Some days I'm so tired I can only operate on autopilot. You must have noticed the change in Mum as well? She really worries me."

"Apart from that business with the ring and sometimes forgetting her shoes, she seems the same as usual to me," he said. "Insomnia's common."

"I took her to the doctors." Jayne paused as the waiter brought their starters and poured wine. "She wasn't happy about going but I said it's better we know what we're up against."

Stuart popped a mushroom into his mouth and immediately regretted choosing a dish with garlic in the name. If Jayne did see this evening as a date with a proper kiss at the end, the taste in his mouth had just ruled it out. If he qualified for a 'next time' he'd go for prawn cocktail.

"He thinks it might be the start of dementia. The level of confusion will vary but will probably become more frequent." Jayne brought her eyes up to meet his and there was a slight shake to her voice. "There's medication that may slow the progression but there are no guarantees. She's devastated. I'm devastated. She doesn't want anyone to know so, please, don't mention it to her or anybody else."

"No, of course not." Stuart wanted to touch Jayne, to offer comfort in more than words. But there was no hand resting on the table and attempting to do anything else would be awkward and cringe-worthy. "I want to help. You must tell me what I can do."

Jayne blew her nose and then took a breath as though steadying herself. He looked down and busied himself with his mushrooms.

"You are so lovely. Most men run a mile." She smiled at him again and, despite the laughter lines around her eyes giving her age away, he was back in an age when parents were a nuisance because of curfews and no-party rules. Back then, the possible reversal of the parent-child carer role had never crossed their minds.

"Really, I do want to help. I know how lonely caring can be. And how it wears you out, emotionally as well as physically."

"Thank you. I've been forced to tell a few people because of my absences from work and the reactions are beginning to teach me about that loneliness. You'd be surprised how many people turn away when you say the word 'dementia'."

Stuart wondered if this included Audi man. He couldn't find the nerve to ask her.

"Let's talk about something cheerier." She was looking at him with an expression that was suddenly too positive to be natural. "Hobbies?"

"Cycling?" The question mark in his voice came out accidentally. He wasn't sure the answer was good enough.

"Good one. For me it's yoga."

"I've never tried that." He didn't add that the slowness of yoga movements made them seem pointless to him.

"I started after the divorce. It's good for everything — back, core, flexibility and mindfulness. Helps me destress. You know when your head is full of all that stuff you don't want? Yoga, plus the meditation at the end of the class, help to empty it all out. I've needed it even more since I started worrying about Mum. I only get rid of the chatter in my head when I'm doing yoga."

"Hmmm." For Stuart there was no better cure for stress than fresh air and vigorous exercise. But each to their own.

They switched to 'holidays I would take if money was no problem.' Stuart described a 'gap year' in Australia. As he spoke, he realised the awful news about Lillian had vanquished his nerves and enabled him to talk to Jayne as if the years since they left school had never happened. Even in her fifties, she still wanted to backpack around India.

"I never did it. The lure of an engagement ring and the excitement of a big white wedding was a bigger attraction. Do you remember the royal wedding when we were eighteen, just before you went away? It stuck in my head as a fairy tale and probably made me hurry Carl up the aisle. I even tried to get a replica of Fergie's dress but Mum made me see sense and get something a little less bouffant and more fitting for a small church."

"You looked lovely. Dad showed me the photos when I was back from university."

"You were invited to come to the wedding with him."

"I know but . . ." The pain of watching the girl he loved marry another man would've been too great. He'd been in his final year and all that day he'd looked at his watch and imagined the service and the celebrations. He'd ended the night sitting under a table in the Students' Union bar, completely blotto. His friends had had to get him home and onto his bed. He'd stayed in his room the whole of the next day, incapacitated both by the hangover and thoughts of Jayne on honeymoon with someone else. He vowed never to fall in love again. The humiliation and pain weren't worth it. Given how his life had turned out, it hadn't been difficult to keep that promise.

"Marrying Carl was the wrong decision." She put a hand over his as he reached for his wine glass.

It made him jump first and then he relaxed into the pleasant sensation. His eyes met hers and he realised she was enjoying this as much as he was. Warmth spread through his body.

She spoke while holding his gaze. "Would you be willing for us to try again?"

Stuart hesitated. For years he'd hardened his heart towards her. Then she'd sought him out at the funeral. Lillian had produced her mobile number. Florence had been given the third degree. All this had melted the shell around his feelings, increased his confidence and made him believe a brighter future with Jayne at his side was possible. But the pain of that long-ago rejection was still vivid. He didn't know if he'd survive it a second time.

"You don't want to. I understand. This is embarrassing. Forget I ever said anything. Please." The words were gabbled and hope had slipped from her face.

Stuart couldn't bear the anguish that replaced it. She fiddled with her pendant.

"Yes. I would like us to try again."

Wow, bro! That's the most decisive you've been in years.

Stuart's heart was racing. Jayne's face was alight with pleasure and he had brought her that joy. She squeezed his hand and he telegraphed the same unspoken message back to her. He remembered the signals they'd sent to each other this way on the school bus, hands hidden beneath discarded blazers, and fizzed inside.

Jayne's lasagne was sizzling in its dish when it arrived. There was an accompanying aroma of cheese, tomato sauce and, most importantly, garlic. Later, after they'd discussed everything from favourite books through the funding of care in later life to house prices, Jayne waved away the pudding menu and Stuart didn't argue.

On the way home, they stopped, for old times' sake, in the passageway just short of both their houses. Stuart recognised the thumping of his heart from the very first time they'd stopped here. Back then, like now, it felt like he'd been handed the most precious opportunity, but this time he wouldn't let it slip through his fingers. Unbelievably, it seemed that Jayne felt the same way about him. They would be each other's bright new future.

Jayne moved closer, her head tipped upwards, towards him. Stuart had only a split second of nerves before kissing her.

CHAPTER FOURTEEN

"You've changed," William said brusquely the next morning. "I've never heard you whistle before and you've got bags under your eyes. You've pulled, haven't you?"

Stuart smiled and helped the old man from the chair to the commode. It felt as though he'd been grinning since the moment of that kiss.

"It's Florence, isn't it? It's not possible for a man and a woman to live together under the same roof without a bit of how's-your-father. I could've told you that if only you'd asked."

"It's not Florence. I've already told you, she's not my type. I'll leave you in private while I make the breakfast."

William's kitchen looked out over his back garden. The beds were overgrown and the lawn was just about kept in check by a man who arrived fortnightly with a mower in the boot of his car. Today, the depressing view carried a sheen of happiness. Today, everything carried a sheen of happiness. Today was the start of his bright new future. Jayne still found him attractive. Still liked him after all these years. The connection between them was still there. For the first time in decades, he felt confident about life.

What a turn-up for the books. Stuart and Jayne back together.

"What's that supposed to mean, Sandra?"

Nothing. Personally, I don't know what your attraction is, but that's sisters for you. Perhaps you've got some innate animal magnetism that I can't feel.

"If you haven't got anything positive to say, please don't speak."

Ooh! Are you trying to get rid of me? It doesn't work like that. I kept you company when our parents and big brothers were too busy to notice your existence. I was the one who walked beside you at our mother's funeral when Dad went to pieces. I was the one who held your hand when Carl came on the scene.

"I don't dispute any of that but right now I need the privacy and free will to conduct my own love affair."

No fear. I'm not coming into the bedroom with you. But after all these years, that will be a hurdle, won't it?

"Go away, Sandra. You're messing with my head."

Ooh! Look who's throwing their toys out of the pram. I'm going nowhere. Your life's just starting to get interesting. I don't want to miss the best bits.

Stuart gave himself a slap on both cheeks and went to clean up William.

"Talking to yourself again?"

"My sister gets on my wick." Stuart suddenly realised what he'd said and added quickly, "She always phones at awkward times."

"That your phone over there?"

Stuart snatched his mobile from the sideboard alongside William's door key. He'd deliberately taken his phone out of his pocket and left it there to remind himself to complete William's notes on the app before leaving and putting the key back in the safe.

"Want to talk about it?"

"Nothing to say. There was a cat in the garden. I was talking to it through the glass. Mouthing off about my sister. It's a stupid habit I've had since childhood and I rarely admit it to anyone."

William nodded at him, obviously not believing a word. Stuart heard Sandra's laughter in his head. The magic of last night with Jayne had dissipated like mist in a hot morning sun. Stuart gritted his teeth and opened a drawer to get clean underwear for his client.

William was obviously enjoying the diversion of Stuart's behaviour and wouldn't let it go. "I've never seen a cat have such an effect on a man through a barrier of glass. This may be a true case of the cat having got your tongue. The moggy's stolen the sunshine of your mood too."

Stuart kept himself half turned away from the old man; he wasn't going to be drawn any further.

"Now you're clean and dressed, I'll fetch the porridge through." He stripped off his gloves and went back into the kitchen.

* * *

"I'm going away for a few days." Florence was manoeuvring a suitcase down the stairs when he got home.

"Oh?" Stuart's mind was still on his anger with Sandra and William.

"Going to see my daughter down in London. And the grandkids."

Slowly Stuart's brain cranked into gear. "You're a grandma!"

"Yes. Child bride." Florence reached the bottom of the stairs and ferreted in her oversized handbag. "I have a grandson and a granddaughter." She produced a photograph on her phone and moved closer to Stuart so he could look. "Shayne and Eunice. And that's my daughter, Shirley, named after my singing idol, Shirley Bassey. And that's her partner, Jacob, standing behind. Only he's left her now."

"Lovely children." He hoped that was the right thing to say. "How's Shirley coping on her own?"

Unusually there was no immediate bouncy, witty remark from his lodger. For a few seconds Stuart thought she wasn't going to reply and wondered if he'd put his foot in it.

Florence took a breath. "To be honest, she's up and down. I'm worried about the kiddies. That's why I'm going to visit. It's a surprise — she doesn't know I'm coming."

"What about your gigs?"

"Our guitarist fell off a ladder and sprained both wrists so we're temporarily off the circuit. Don't worry, I'll still pay my rent."

The house would be his again! There would be no enforced jollity, no windows flung open to 'air' the place, no damp underwear, no dancing and no music. He could return to the warm cocoon of Radio 4 or silence, whichever he chose. Free will would return!

Florence's grin returned. "It leaves the coast clear for you to invite Jayne into your love nest."

It was true what they said about a woman's intuition. He hadn't told her anything about last night.

"Please could you run me to the station?" Florence's eyes widened slightly. Even if he'd wanted to, saying no to that expression would have been impossible. "It'll be nicer than getting a taxi."

Stuart carried her suitcase to the car. She sat in the front and fiddled with the radio until she found something she could sway along to.

"No need to park up," she said when the station came into sight. "I'll just hop out and grab my case from the boot."

He did park properly and he carried the suitcase onto the concourse for her. He stood there while she examined the departures board, bought a coffee and two chocolate bars.

"What happened to the diet?" he asked. Florence didn't need to diet, that was all in her head and voiced out loud to him when she caught herself at the wrong angle in the mirror.

"A train journey isn't a train journey unless there's something nice to eat. If you take an apple and a carrot — pouf! All the excitement is gone." She turned and looked down the length of the track. "This is mine, just pulling in." She had no free hands but stretched her neck up to kiss Stuart on the cheek. "Thanks for the lift." Then she tottered down the platform in her little red boots, the coffee balanced in the crook of her arm and the freed-up hand pulling the suitcase.

Dancing music sprang from the car stereo as soon as Stuart started the ignition. Without Florence swaying along next to him it sounded fake and over the top. He switched back to Radio 4, which was part way through a drama he couldn't follow. He turned the noise off and retreated inside his own head and the bright prospect of seeing Jayne again that evening.

Have you decided on the film, bro? And the snacks? And the clothes you're going to wear? It wouldn't do to appear on a second date in the same outfit you wore for the first.

"Stop making it into such a big deal. We're two old friends going to the cinema together."

How many 'old friends' linger in an alley for twenty minutes snogging? It was beautifully sweet but definitely more than just old friends.

* * *

"You remembered!" Jayne laughed and squeezed his hand when she saw the name of the film over the entrance to the small independent cinema.

"How could I forget? You were always talking about it. How many times did you see it?"

"Every time it did the rounds. When I went with you, it was my fourth time. And you bought me an ET cuddly toy for Christmas."

"I was too embarrassed to ask Dad for the money. I got that paper round especially to save up for it."

"You big softy! I was so stupid to let you go."

It was impossible to stop smiling with Jayne at his side again. This time round they bought coffee instead of coke and bypassed the popcorn, but the magic of sitting close together in the dark was exactly the same. Stuart draped his arm along the back of Jayne's seat in the same way he'd done as a teenager. Back then, the film had been halfway through before he'd had the courage to move his arm to Jayne's shoulders and it had been nearly time for the final credits before she'd turned her head towards him so that he could gamble on a kiss. This time they held hands from the beginning, occasionally gently squeezing fingers to reassure the other that they were more important than the film.

"That was really lovely." Jayne smiled at him as he killed the engine on the gravel drive in front of his garage. "Thank you."

He leaned over the handbrake and kissed her.

"I used to take ET to bed with me and wish it was you."

Things he wished he'd known at eighteen. He kissed her again and for a moment they sat quietly holding hands.

"You've adapted to having a lodger?" Jayne's voice was hesitant, as though she'd been working up to asking the question.

"She's . . ." Was there a right answer to this question? "She's brought me out of my comfort zone."

"Being a performer . . . she must be more glamorous and exciting than . . . ordinary people."

Stuart cottoned on immediately and was touched. He squeezed Jayne's hand and then tried and failed to find the right words. "I'm too old for excitement. It's not good for the heart. Ordinary people are much more my kind of thing."

"I like ordinary too." Jayne smiled and then suddenly she was pulling away from him and fumbling for her handbag in the car foot well. "Oh, no. Mum's outside in the cold."

Lillian had opened the front door and was coming towards them in her nightdress.

"Sorry. I've left her too long. Thank you for a lovely evening."

"No. Thank *you*."

Then she was gone.

CHAPTER FIFTEEN

Florence was away for four days. Initially, the house felt empty, devoid of the spirit that had kicked it so suddenly alive. Then Stuart relaxed. The need to double-think his movements had vanished. He didn't have to peep out of his bedroom and check the coast was clear before scuttling to the bathroom. He ate breakfast in his dressing gown and let the washing up accumulate instead of clearing up after every meal.

Most importantly, his home was now his castle again and, as Florence had pointed out, the stage was set for inviting Jayne round. His heart hammered and he had to take deep breaths. The restaurant had gone well and the kiss had gone even better. Finding a cinema showing *ET* had been a stroke of luck. They'd spoken every day, the conversation had continued to flow, mainly about what had happened to the mutual friends they'd been at school with. Jayne had kept in touch with people and Stuart hadn't.

What made him nervous was being alone here in the house with Jayne. She'd been inside at the wake but the other people, noise and hubbub had helped to disguise the dated décor and the bachelor feel that Florence kept highlighting to him. Jayne would look carefully at the mausoleum, furnished mostly with things chosen decades ago by his mother, and she would impose that same dull, dated personality on him. Florence had actually said that she'd taken one look at the house and expected him to be a boring old fart with no oomph but that, slowly and with her help, he was proving her wrong. Jayne might not be so forgiving. He couldn't cope with losing her again so soon.

On the third day of Florence's absence, Jayne was delving in the boot of her car when Stuart got back from his early visit to William.

"She's still away then?" Jayne stood up.

Stuart nodded. This was his unexpected cue to issue an invitation. Caught by surprise, his mind took a moment to compare preparing the house for Jayne versus formulating a different going-out kind of plan. He couldn't afford a restaurant again. But he didn't want the house to give her the impression he was a boring old fart. Damn Florence for highlighting his failings and making him self-conscious. Now Jayne was closing the boot and looking towards the house. He had to say something before she disappeared.

"Would you like to come round this evening? For a drink or something?"

Her eyes lit up. "I could bring a casserole. I'd invite you to ours, only Mum will be there. And, well, it wouldn't be the same, would it? Does seven thirty suit you?"

"Perfect." Stuart tried his best to keep his voice casual, as though this wasn't a big thing for him.

"See you later!" She gave him a bright wave.

It was too late to redecorate the house but there must be something he could do to make it look less like a middle-aged man's wallowing hole. How did people make their house attractive when they were trying to sell? He'd caught odd bits of infuriating make-over programs when looking for something more worthwhile to watch. It was time to go shopping.

Flowers went into the only two vases in the house, pink carnations on the mantelpiece in the lounge and orange chrysanthemums on the coffee table. Scarlet scatter cushions brightened up the brown Draylon sofa. An equally bright red cloth, sprigged with white daisies, went on the table to perform the double duty of adding colour and hiding scratches. And finally pleasant smells.

Baking bread would be best but there'd be no guaranteeing the results if he went down that path. Better to get the smells ready-made than risk creating an odour more like burned toast in a greasy spoon. Instead of air fresheners reminiscent of toilets, he'd gone for a couple of scented candles that promised transportation to a pine forest and all the pleasurable sensations of a country walk.

Two bottles of white wine went into the fridge. He wasn't a connoisseur and had chosen on the basis of price, not the cheapest but not too expensive.

At 7.15 he lit the candles and turned on the top oven to warm plates for Jayne's food. She hadn't mentioned pudding and so he'd put an Arctic roll in the freezer, just in case.

She arrived exactly on time. He watched as she crunched across the gravel carrying a casserole in hands covered with brightly striped oven gloves. A scarlet apron covered tan-coloured trousers and a short-sleeved cream top. Her short hair looked freshly groomed. She walked tall and, for a moment, Stuart wondered what she found attractive in him. He moved back from the window and waited for her to knock. He hovered on starting blocks in the kitchen, not wanting to appear too keen, eyes on the frosted glass in the top of the front door. The silhouette of Jayne's head was visible. No knock. No doorbell. He waited a bit longer. Nothing.

Then there was a muffled voice. "Stuart! Stuart!"

He walked down the hall and opened the door. Jayne pushed past him and raced for the kitchen.

"Thank God," she said as she put the dish down on top of the hob. She discarded the oven gloves on the floor and examined her hands. Then she turned on him. "You saw me from the lounge window! You could see I had my hands full. This dish is red hot; it's just come out of the oven. Why didn't you bloody well open the door?"

If he'd known she'd seen him . . . If he'd used his common sense and realised the dish must be hot and that she had no free hand with which to knock . . . If he hadn't been so self-centred about wanting to appear unexcited, as though having a woman round for dinner was an everyday occurrence . . . "Sorry. I didn't realise that you couldn't knock."

"I thought that would have been blindingly obvious to any fool peeking out from behind a curtain."

Stuart quashed the urge to grovel at her feet and plead for forgiveness. Instead he changed the subject.

"There's wine in the fridge. Shall I pour?"

"I'll do it." She took the bottle and rolled it back and forth between her hands. "That feels good."

"Did you burn your hands? I could take you to A and E?"

"They'll be OK." She was starting to calm down now. "They haven't blistered, just feel a little bit tender." She handed the bottle back to Stuart to be opened.

He'd forgotten to prepare for the cork but there was a corkscrew in the cutlery drawer somewhere. He found it and tried to plunge it through the foil covering the top of the bottle. When it met resistance, he pushed harder. This wasn't supposed to happen. Was it possible to get a dud cork that wouldn't take a corkscrew? This must look like complete masculine ineptitude. The heat rose in his cheeks. He didn't dare look at her.

"Stop." She touched his arm.

He looked up. Her anger was gone and she was grinning broadly.

"I'll do it." She took the bottle from him, peeled off the foil and unscrewed the top.

His brain was too slow to think of a witty response. Jayne was laughing; whether at him or with him, he couldn't tell. Either way, it was better than her earlier thunderous face. She poured them both a large glass.

"I think we need it," she said.

"Can we start the evening again, please?"

She nodded and raised her glass. "To the joy of getting to know one another all over again."

Stuart clinked his glass against hers and they both drank deeply. Jayne suggested they eat before the casserole cooled too much.

"I've got plates warming in the oven."

"Fantastic."

He made a theatrical show of putting on Jayne's oven gloves to retrieve the plates. Perhaps the wine gave him the courage. Florence floated through his mind. She would have appreciated his exaggerated performance. It would have made her laugh. It dawned on him that before Florence he would never have contemplated doing anything specifically to entertain people.

He put the plates on the table with the flourish of an extrovert waiter. "Ta da!"

Jayne touched one. "Cold." She wasn't laughing.

He looked at the dials on the oven and then closed his eyes. He managed to keep his mouth shut while he mentally cursed. "I turned the wrong dial on the oven. I am so sorry."

Jayne took over. She turned the oven on and put both the plates and the casserole inside. In the absence of an ice bucket, she put the wine back in the fridge. She checked that everything was ready on the dining table.

"Nice new cloth." There was a slight edge to her voice that Stuart struggled to read. "Cushions and flowers too. I see Florence is making her presence felt. She told me she was doing your cleaning."

Which was least bad — admitting that he'd made the colourful touches specifically for tonight or pretending that Florence had her feet well and truly under the table? He played it safe and stayed silent.

As they ate and drank, the atmosphere between them thawed again. By the time the casserole had gone and they were almost at the bottom of the bottle, it felt as though they'd travelled back in time nearly forty years to an era when they drank cider underage in the local pub and could make a bag of crisps and a couple of halves last all night. Stuart was enjoying himself.

A rare phenomenon for you, bro. Make the most of it.

Jayne put her hand over his. He twisted his palm upwards and gave a squeeze in return. He had a positive feeling that, despite the disastrous start to the evening, everything was going to be fine.

He opened the second bottle of wine, this time managing the screw-top with aplomb. Jayne talked about her anxiety over Lillian.

"Most of the time she's quite normal but I know she's going to deteriorate, it's just a question of how quickly. It's like my real mum is leaking away through an unstoppable hole. Sometimes, when she's gone to bed, I cry. I'm scared about coping with her on my own. I'm not as strong as you. Mum says you were magnificent with your dad."

There was a brief silence while Stuart remembered. He swirled the wine around in his glass and then looked up at Jayne. "Very little that I did was magnificent. Actually, probably nothing was magnificent."

"That's not what Mum said. She said you did everything for him."

"I did." He wanted to be honest with Jayne, even if it felt like admitting to a form of criminal neglect. "But a lot of the time I was short-tempered. Sometimes I cut corners. All of the time I was resentful."

Jayne's expression fell. "There's no hope for me then. I'm still the impatient fool I was in the sixth form. I don't relish the thought of wiping my mum's bum or attending Music for Memories at the community centre. Or spooning mush into a dribbling mouth."

"There are lots of good care homes around. I could help you choose."

"Mum would hate that. She'd much prefer being looked after at home by people she already knows. I owe that to her after what she did for Gran. Besides, she's my mum." There was a catch in Jayne's voice. "I can't just send her away like an unwanted parcel."

This time Stuart put his hand over Jayne's and gave it a squeeze. "Don't take on too much for too long, like I did. Compromise is needed. On both sides."

"But when the dementia properly takes hold, she won't understand the concept of compromise. All she'll see is my rejection." Jayne swallowed and blinked. "I don't want her left muttering in a corner by herself."

"It won't be like that." Stuart wanted to reassure her and take away the fear of what was to come. But he couldn't. He was lucky — he'd escaped the burden of dementia. Jayne was going to be hit with a double whammy. "Perhaps you could keep her at home but have carers coming in? It would be cheaper than a care home and keep Lillian where she's happy."

Jayne sighed and had a mouthful of wine before she spoke again. "This is when being an only child is difficult. It's all down to me."

"It's worse when you've got siblings muscling in on the decisions but shying away from taking any of the practical crap themselves."

"Mum said that Robert and George hardly showed their faces but managed to walk away with the house. You could fight it, you know?"

Stuart shrugged. "Time's short. I need to start living my life. I don't want to go back over all the injustices that have got me to this point."

"Maybe no siblings *is* better."

The wine had mellowed him and this pooling of concerns made him feel closer to Jayne. The years were rolling back. "I'm always here if you need help. Someone to bounce ideas off or even something practical."

"That is so kind of you." Her face brightened and Stuart saw a hint of the mischievous energy of eighteen-year-old Jayne. "Do you remember the round of post-A-level house parties?"

"David Bowie."
"'Let's Dance'."
"UB40."

"'Red Red Wine'." Stuart squeezed her hand again and suggested releasing the Arctic roll from the freezer.

Jayne shook her head and indicated they move to the settee. It was much later when Jayne eventually stood up to leave. They lingered over a kiss in Stuart's hallway.

"It's so much easier to conduct a relationship when you don't have to skulk around like teenagers," Jayne whispered. "And I wish I'd married you in the first place. You are far, far better for me than Carl."

There was a lump in his throat and he couldn't respond. He watched until Jayne was safely inside her own front door. Then he punched the air. "She wants me!"

CHAPTER SIXTEEN

The next morning, Stuart had barely returned from William's when there was a tapping at the kitchen door. Lillian was smiling and waving through the window.

"Jayne was actually humming this morning as she got ready for work and smiling like all her Christmases had come at once," the old lady said when Stuart let her in.

"Why?"

"Oh, Stuart. It's obvious. Something good happened between the two of you last night. Whatever you did, it worked. Jayne is in love."

"Really?" He'd intuited that she'd enjoyed herself. But the phrase 'in love' was a shock. "It was all a bit of a mess-up when she arrived and she didn't want pudding."

"Stop putting yourself down." Lillian pulled a chair out and sat down. "In ten years' time, you and Jayne will look back and laugh at whatever hiccups there were. This morning she is on cloud nine and I thought you should know. Now, are you putting that kettle on or do I have to do it myself? And I've brought us a piece of lemon drizzle each." She placed a foil-wrapped parcel on the table.

It was a relief to busy himself with the teapot and mugs while his heart hammered and he tamed the expression of joy that was being reflected back at him by the kitchen window.

"It's her birthday next month. You should do something special."

"Right." He paused. "What should I get her?"

"I can't tell you. It has to be something that could only come from you."

Stuart frowned. "You mean not chocolates and not flowers."

"Exactly. Anybody can buy those. You need something much more personal."

Oh dear. How good at original thinking are you, bro?

They drank tea and got sticky fingers from the moist lemon drizzle. A frown developed on Lillian's face. "I should buy something too. But the money's in the computer."

"In the computer?"

"Instead of a bank book. Jayne put it in the computer. It's only thin." Lillian made a gap between her thumb and forefinger to illustrate the depth of a laptop. "I'm not rich but I don't know how it all fits in there. Would it be one-hundred-pound notes?"

It took an act of will to control the curve of his lips.

"Can you get it out for me?"

"I can't do that but I can ask Jayne and then take you shopping."

"Don't say it's for her birthday!"

"No. That will be our secret."

Lillian left smiling and Stuart panicked about what to buy for Jayne. It took nerve to walk into any sort of ladies' shop and to buy online he needed to know exactly what he wanted. And the size. And decent presents cost decent money.

Originality is key, bro. Get her something no one else will think of.

"Perhaps Florence will help. She must know what women like."

No. This has to be all your own work. An idea will come to you if you let your subconscious do the work.

To busy his conscious mind, Stuart found his old OS maps of the area and started planning his first route as a ride leader. He'd be leading the slowest group and had been given the name of the café at which all the groups would converge. The route there and back was up to him. It was still months away but every time he thought of taking charge, he got a rush of nerves. It felt like a rite of passage he had to go through in order to properly belong. Thorough preparation was the only way to reduce his anxiety. Fail to prepare, prepare to fail. He'd learned that lesson in front of thirty fifteen-year-olds who'd had no interest in learning geography.

As he studied the network of lanes and contours, his worry over the birthday present subsided and he was left with only positive thoughts about the previous evening and the future.

Florence called him from the station in the afternoon to ask for a lift home. It was drizzling and murky, but Stuart whistled as he loaded her suitcase into the boot and she settled beside him. His mind was luxuriating in the memories of the evening before. It was like having his own internal sun that made the raindrops sparkle and the traffic jam became precious extra time to dwell on his good fortune.

"Have you had a personality transplant while I've been away?"

"What?" Stuart flashed his lights and let a couple of cars into the queue in front of him.

"Somebody's extracted all your boring old fart juices and replaced them with an overdose of the joys of spring."

"I'm just feeling happy."

"Jayne?"

"Yes, Jayne." There was no point in trying to hide it. He wanted the whole world to be happy with him.

"I like it when I'm right. The love of a good woman always increases a man's confidence. Have you . . . you know, yet?"

"We've only had three dates. I'm not a dirty old man." Stuart kept silent about his nerves in that area. The last time he and Jayne had had a physical relationship was as fumbling teenagers. Since then she'd had a lifetime of sex with one of the studs of the sixth form. Stuart had had virtually none. He didn't count the Dutch girl in Paris.

"Don't leave it too long. Like everything, it's a case of use it or lose it."

Stuart shuddered. Any hope of success was probably already lost.

Florence unlocked the front door and he followed with her bags. Even through his rose-tinted glasses, her purple bottom had lost its lively wiggle. The zebra fake fur was flattened and the red boots hampered her walk more than usual. She wore the same clothes she'd set off in but the overall impression was subdued rather than energetic. She unzipped the boots in the hallway, did her customary stretch, wriggle and massage of her toes and then slumped at the kitchen table. Something was wrong.

"How was the visit?" He put a mug of mule-kick coffee in front of her.

"No biscuits?"

He produced chocolate digestives from the place he'd hidden them at her request. She ate two before answering.

"Shayne and Eunice were in dirty clothes and the beds stank. It took me four loads of washing to change all the sheets, freshen the towels and make sure they each had a wardrobe of clean clothes. Shirley just sat and watched me as though I was mad. She was on a different planet to the rest of us. The kids had become shadows of their former selves, thin as rakes and too scared to say boo to a goose. The only food in the house was junk. Shayne asked me if I could leave him some cash so they could at least buy bread and milk after I'd gone. He said he'd hide it under his mattress to make sure his mother didn't get her hands on it."

Florence paused, both hands wrapped around her coffee mug as though trying to extract every last bit of comfort from its warmth. "I'm sure she's taking drugs again. She'd stayed clean since the kids were born. But she hasn't coped well since their father left."

"Drugs?" Drugs happened in an alien world of needles, white powder and squats on TV.

Florence nodded. "Sometimes when I was there, her pupils were huge and she'd get irritable at the slightest thing. Me being there was the biggest irritation because I wanted to know where she was going and what she was doing. We argued all the time. She accused me of being controlling and I accused her of child neglect." She blew her nose. "And, of course, the kids heard it all."

Stuart was upset on Florence's behalf. He wanted her happy shine back to match the novelty of his own good feelings. Her boundless energy had irritated him but it was far better than this.

"Did you report her? Aren't the children in danger?"

"How could I report my own daughter?" Florence's expression became hard and her voice snappy. "You can never understand because you don't have children. A mother does everything she can to protect her children. I failed to protect Shirley from drugs but I'm not going to let her be prosecuted and get a criminal record that will stop her getting a job and making a better life for my grandchildren." The words tumbled out as an aggressive rant.

"Sorry, I didn't think." Stuart offered another biscuit. She pushed the packet away and started pacing up and down the kitchen.

"So what happens now?" He spoke gently, trying to bring down her frustration and anger.

"She promised me she'd quit. She promised me she'd stop using the children's maintenance payments for drugs and look after the kiddies properly instead." There was a long pause and Florence stopped walking. "I don't know if I can trust her. Before I left, Eunice gave me a big hug and whispered, 'Don't leave us here, Grandma. Take us home with you or take us to Daddy's.' It broke my heart."

"Can you contact the children's father?"

"That would be betraying Shirley. I don't know what to do."

Her face was a picture of pain and without any forethought Stuart stood up and hugged his lodger.

As he let her go, she looked as shocked at his out-of-character action as he felt. "I needed that," she whispered. "Can you do it again?"

This time a sparky feeling travelled along his arms and into the very core of his being. Now his whole body was warm and tingling. Florence's expression, as they pulled away from each other, was one of wide-eyed amazement. He was sure she'd felt the exact same thing. Then she clutched him tightly, as though he were a lifebelt in a stormy sea and about to be dragged from her by a giant wave. They stood together for a few minutes. As Florence's emotional tension eased, Stuart relished the feeling of bringing comfort to this bright new person in his life. They'd known each other only a short time but Stuart was going to do his best to support her.

"I'll run you a hot bath," he said. "And how does spaghetti bolognaise sound for tea?"

She gave him a small smile. "Both those things sound lovely. And I'm sorry for dumping my troubles at your door. Especially when Jayne had you soaring so high."

He left Florence in a bathroom full of steam and the scent of bergamot. Before cooking, he had to make his late-afternoon visit to William. When he arrived, the old man put down the newspaper crossword.

"There's something different about you," he said.

"Different from earlier?" Stuart had been grateful that William had made none of his usual outspoken comments during his breakfast and lunchtime visits that day. William had been subdued, complaining that he'd slept badly and didn't want conversation. Stuart had gratefully retreated into a mental replay of the best bits of the previous evening with Jayne.

"You seem more alive. Brighter. More a part of the world than skulking timidly in your shell."

"I feel that way too." He felt sad for Florence but buoyed by the way she'd accepted his support.

"So what's happened?"

"Florence came back." Stuart paused. "And I saw Jayne again last night. It went well. Very well, in fact."

"That's good." The old man massaged his chin with his hand in the manner of the thinker.

"It's not all good."

"Oh?" The old man's eyes were alert.

CHAPTER SEVENTEEN

"Florence is upset. Very upset. It turns out her daughter's a drug addict and her grandchildren are suffering. She doesn't know what to do and I don't know how to help." Stuart explained his lodger's torn loyalties between safeguarding her grandchildren while not betraying her daughter. "It's like all her bounce has been extracted."

"A lose-lose situation, indeed." William studied the middle-distance, as though getting ready to make a pronouncement on the solution to the situation.

The room was silent for a minute and Stuart's own brightness subsided as he thought about Florence's dilemma.

"And Jayne?" The old man's sudden shift of topic took Stuart by surprise. "Is first love just as good second time around?"

Stuart's grin returned but he chose his words carefully. He didn't want to embarrass himself by confusing his romantic longings with the reality of their fledgling relationship. Lillian's 'in love' statement might have been an exaggeration. "We had a very pleasant evening and I think we may have a future together." He paused. "Second time around has the potential to be deeper. Better. Much better. More mutually supportive. Jayne's worried about how she'll care for her mother. I can be there for her and I like that."

"Two women at difficult times in their lives looking to you for support."

"I suppose so." He hadn't thought about it like that and suddenly felt a few inches taller.

"I like you, Stuart."

William's words took him by surprise. "Oh! Thanks."

"You're one of those rare people who genuinely want to help others."

This was embarrassing. "I'll put the kettle on and make you a sandwich. Cheese and pickle?"

Stuart escaped to the kitchen. He spread butter, sliced cheese and then took the meal into his client. He suddenly remembered William's lack of energy earlier in the day.

"You weren't well this morning. Shall I get the doctor to give you the once over?"

"It's nothing. The general malaise of old age." William was smiling but his brightness didn't look genuine.

"Are you sure?"

"I was a GP for thirty-five years. I'd know better than anyone if I was ill."

Stuart wasn't convinced but there was only so far he could go if his client wouldn't accept help.

William didn't speak again until Stuart was pulling his coat on. "You've got tomorrow afternoon off."

"Oh?"

"Don't worry, I'll still pay. I know how hard up you are. I've asked my daughter to call. There are things I need to discuss with her, alone. It's my birthday and I dropped a few hints that I'd like one of those posh afternoon teas with the sandwiches and scones and cakes. You can get them delivered these days. If we don't eat it all, I'll save you some."

"You still want me in the morning?"

"Absolutely. You can help me put on my best bib and tucker. I want Andrea to realise that I'm still compos mentis and able to make my own decisions."

When Stuart got home, Florence was wrapped in a fluffy pink dressing gown watching one of her soaps in the lounge.

Stuart got to work chopping an onion, frying mince and locating a tin of tomatoes at the back of the cupboard. He couldn't do anything practical to help Florence but he could provide a secure base to help her relax and plan her next move.

"I've spoken to Jacob, the children's father." Florence tried and failed to twist spaghetti around her fork. "He's come to an agreement with Shirley that he will have the children every weekend. That gives them two full days and nights of proper food and care. And he's told Shirley that if they look neglected in any way, he'll contact social services. We're hoping that will give the children some stability and encourage Shirley to buck her ideas up."

"Sounds like a good plan."

She looked up from her plate. There was a dribble of bolognaise sauce on her chin. Stuart pointed to his own chin. She got the message, caught the splodge with her finger and licked it. Then she grinned at Stuart.

"Feeling better?" he asked.

"A little. But you never stop worrying about your children, no matter how big they get."

Stuart's own mood rose in tandem with Florence's and he wanted to make her even more buoyant. An idea flashed through his mind. It was brilliant but she would think him odd and she might still be too miserable from her visit to Shirley.

Go for it! Sandra knew his thoughts. *It would be brilliant for both of you. Definitely fulfils the 'bright' part of 'bright new future'.*

CHAPTER EIGHTEEN

Stuart smiled at the rare vote of confidence from his sister.

"You look like the Cheshire cat." Florence was staring at him.

"It's nothing. Well, it is something. An idea that might cheer you up. Or you might think I'm stupid, but that's nothing new, is it?"

"And the idea is?" She was smiling at him encouragingly.

He took a breath. "Let's dance."

"Well, that is a turn-up for the books."

But she remained seated. He'd overstepped the mark. Misread the signs. "We don't have to." He spoke quickly. "I know you're still upset and it was insensitive of me to suggest it. There's the washing up and everything. I'll get on with that — you have charge of the remote control."

He stood up. She was right behind him and touched his arm. Her touch sent a spark around his body and he stepped away.

"I do want to dance and I know just the track." She fiddled with her phone and portable speaker. "Not the Blackberries this time."

Even Stuart recognised the tune that filled the kitchen.

"Do you know the actions?" Florence's body started moving to the beat that had made dance floors magnetic at millions of weddings and cross-generational parties.

He shook his head.

"You soon will. Basically our arms are forming the letters Y M C A."

It was impossible for a body not to move as the beat engulfed the kitchen and Florence became a part of the rhythm. There was no room for feeling self-conscious as he focused on replicating the movements of his partner's arms as his own limbs stretched above his head. Eventually he got the movements to flow.

As the song died out, Florence swiped something and it started again from the beginning, but louder this time. It was starting to get dark outside and Florence turned off the fluorescent light, leaving only the blinking red light on the cooker and the illumination from the setting sun. The pattern of movements was now embedded in his head. Stuart closed his eyes and let the music take him. He was nineteen years old again. But this time he was dancing without the prop of alcohol or the purpose of getting off with the girl he'd been eyeing-up all week or because he didn't want to be the only one leaning against the wall when all his mates were going for it. He'd started this dancing to help Florence but he was continuing for himself.

When the music stopped again there was a moment's silence. Then a sudden rap on glass.

Stuart jumped.

"Oh my God! There's a face at the window!" Florence was backing away towards the hall.

Stuart turned to look. It was an angry face with gesticulating arms and wild hair. Florence turned the light back on but that made it harder to see into the almost-darkness outside. Stuart was sure it was a woman. He turned the key on the inside of the kitchen door and opened it. Jayne charged in, wearing leggings and a cagoule. It had started to rain and her short hair stuck to her head, her eyes were wide and she was agitated.

Jayne looked from Florence, still in her dressing gown, to Stuart and back again. "Mum's gone missing and I don't know what to do." Her voice was anguished.

A tonne weight of guilt smacked across Stuart's shoulders. How could he have given himself up to music so loud that it blocked out the woman he was falling in love with?

"We'll help you look," Florence said immediately. "I'll get dressed."

Stuart put his arms around Jayne, ignoring the damp feel of her. For a moment she sobbed into his shoulder and then she lifted her head to speak in a halting voice. "It's my fault. I went to a yoga class on the way home from work. I have to miss so many of them now because of Mum. She might have panicked because I was later than usual. Perhaps she went looking for me?"

"You mustn't think like that." He held her close. "No one is to blame. And we'll find her."

For a couple of minutes, they were both silent and then Jayne spoke quietly. "Is there something between you and Florence? You looked very cosy together. I thought we'd agreed to—"

"Absolutely not. I promise. She's got problems with her daughter and I was just trying to cheer her up." He kissed Jayne on the lips.

"The dancing was your idea?" For a moment the upset on Jayne's face was wiped away by amazement.

"Yes."

"You are a dark horse, Stuart Borefield." She ran her fingers down the side of his cheek.

Stuart kissed her gently again.

"Come on, lovebirds." Florence bustled in. Stuart kept tight hold of Jayne's hand.

"How long has she been gone?" he asked as they stood beneath umbrellas on the pavement, looking up and down the street.

"Since lunchtime. Most of the time she's as right as rain. Only has momentary lapses. But not today. I went to work and phoned her about noon. She said she was meeting Nora, her friend, for lunch at the park café. That's why I went to yoga — I knew she'd had some company earlier in the day. When I got home at six thirty the house was empty but I thought she might have gone back to Nora's house. At seven I started to worry and phoned. Nora said Mum never turned up at the café. Nora tried phoning Mum at home but there was no answer. She assumed the lunch had slipped Mum's mind and she'd gone elsewhere."

"That poor lady, out in this downpour." Florence shivered and pulled the zip on her jacket higher.

"Have you called the police?"

Jayne shook her head. "I didn't know how soon you're allowed to call them."

"The park's too big for the three of us to search in darkness. We need dogs and a proper plan."

"Sniffer dogs! You don't think . . ."

"I don't think anything." Stuart put an arm around Jayne's wet shoulders. "Except that we need to find Lillian quickly. Let's go back inside and call the police."

Jayne was crying too much so Stuart called, emphasising Lillian's vulnerability. Within an hour, a team of officers was at the park. Stuart and Jayne tried to guess the route Lillian would have taken from home to the café and back. Florence waited in Lillian's house in case the old lady came back.

Nothing was found walking the main tarmacked paths but the undergrowth couldn't be tackled until first light when the dogs would be available. Jayne and Stuart went home to Lillian's. They sent Florence next door to bed.

When they'd dried off, Stuart made cocoa and tried to shoo Jayne upstairs to sleep while he sat by the phone.

"There's no way I can sleep knowing that Mum is wandering around out there," she protested. "You sleep. I'll sit by the phone."

In the end, they sat side by side on the settee, cupping mugs of hot sweet liquid. Anxiety made Stuart reach for biscuits but Jayne refused. Eventually she rested her head on his shoulder. He held her close. There was a faint whiff of coconut from her hair. It made him think of Bounty bars covered in chocolate.

"I'm so glad you're here," she said. "Carl was never supportive. He always moaned when I said Mum was coming round for her tea."

Stuart's heart grew full. "Lillian's always been good to me and my family. There's no way I'd abandon either of you."

They didn't talk much through the night. The silence was like a warm swaddling blanket. Stuart couldn't remember ever feeling this content. Perhaps being needed by another person was a basic human necessity. Jayne's breathing slowed and she was asleep. He wondered if he could move her from his shoulder to lying down on the sofa so she didn't get a crick in her neck. But he was frightened of wakening her and so they remained close together. Stuart risked raising a hand and gently stroking her hair. She shifted slightly towards him and, even with the worry about Lillian, his heart swelled and his spirits rose.

He thought about Jayne's birthday. He wanted to spoil her but a lack of money and a lack of ideas hung in his way. The last birthday they'd celebrated together had been Jayne's eighteenth and he'd had the same problems then. In the evening there'd been a house party. Jayne's parents had gone next door to eat fish and chips with his dad, leaving the house to the youngsters. But the best bit of the day had been earlier. He and Jayne had cycled up to the old quarry. He'd bought a four-pack of cider, a chocolate cake and a single candle. The cider had erupted when they'd tugged on the ring-pulls and they'd tried to catch the golden liquid in their mouths.

"It's like champagne!" Jayne's face had been alight with happiness.

He'd opened the boxed cake and stuck the candle in the top. Jayne had looked expectant and then he'd realised. "No matches." He'd made a big show of rubbing two sticks together and Jayne had held her stomach with laughter. Then she'd elaborately blown out a pretend flame and they'd broken the cake into pieces with their hands because Stuart had forgotten a knife and plates as well.

He looked down at Jayne's sleeping face and wondered if she remembered all the gorgeous details with the clarity he did. Eventually the natural light seeping in through the curtains woke her and she went for a shower. Stuart gathered cereal and bread for breakfast. He glanced at the clock and his heart lurched. He was expected at William's. It was the day of his daughter's visit. The old man wanted helping into his best clothes. If Stuart cried off at such short notice, Veronica would play hell. A carer's job could be a matter of life or death, or, at the very least, you were leaving someone in grave discomfort. And the person who would find William in that discomfort was his daughter, Andrea. Stuart could lose his job.

"Do you think Florence will mind the house and phone again while we go to the park?" Jayne had wet hair and reddened cheeks from the shower. Dressed in a fresh blouse and jeans she looked more composed than the night before but her voice still faltered over her next sentence. "I'd really like you with me today."

"I'm sure she will but . . ." He wanted to stay with her more than anything but his conscience was pulling him towards the duty of his job. The police would find Lillian without him but Jayne needed him here. The future of their relationship, his bright new future, might depend on what he said next. Even if he called Veronica now, it wouldn't be possible to send another carer for a few hours. He couldn't leave William to wet himself. "Mr Rutherford can't get himself to the toilet or make a drink." He looked at his watch. "I'll be gone two hours max. I can meet you at the park."

"I thought . . . never mind. It's just after the other night we . . ." Her voice was emotional and she turned away from him. "I can't eat any breakfast. My stomach's churning."

"I promise I'll be as quick as I can." He felt like a rat. An unreliable, slippery rat. One minute he was offering to help her and the next he was turning his back.

With love comes great responsibility. If it helps, I think you're making the right call, bro. Do you remember when you were kids, before the hormones kicked in? You both always made a point of giving each other your last Rolo. You were like kids in a TV advert.

"Not relevant now," he muttered under his breath. "This is a life-or-death situation. Go away."

Just a random memory I wanted to share.

Stuart ignored his sister and went over to Jayne. He put an arm around her shoulders and held her close. He felt her breath on his neck plus the shame of a traitor as he spoke quietly. "Me being here won't have any influence on whether or not Lillian's found. The police will be looking for her in a calm, logical way. We're too emotionally involved to do that."

"But *I* need you."

"I want to be here for you, believe me." If he had a normal job he would've phoned in and told them the truth. "But I have to see to William first. If the situation between William and Lillian was reversed, you wouldn't want her left to fend for herself. If I stay with you, I'm putting another old person at risk."

Jayne raised her tearstained face and looked at him. "I give in. But be as quick as you can."

He nodded and kissed her gently on the cheek.

"You're late!" William shouted as soon as Stuart stepped into the hallway.

"Sorry! I'll tell you why as we go along. Porridge or cornflakes today?"

"And you've forgotten."

"No, I haven't. Andrea's coming and it's best-bib-and-tucker day."

"It's my birthday!"

Stuart hit his forehead with the heel of his hand and cursed. "I'm sorry," he said and then he told William about Lillian and Jayne. "It's no excuse," he finished up. "But there's only so much stuff I can juggle around in my brain. After years of quiet living with Dad, it feels like I've been tossed into the middle of a car crash and am trying to separate the tangled wreckage with my bare hands."

"No matter. That poor lady out there in the dark and cold all night. I'll try and be as pliable as possible so that you can get off early. I'll eat while I'm still in my pyjamas, no point in risking a spill down my best shirt. And because it's my birthday, I'll have extra golden syrup, please."

Between them, they managed to reduce the one-hour call to only forty-five minutes.

"Enjoy the cakes." Stuart tidied his stuff away.

"The cakes will be lovely but I don't think Andrea will see eye to eye with me when I tell her what I've decided."

There was no time to follow up on that remark.

A police car was parked outside Lillian's house when he got back. The string of tension that had been teasing his shoulder blades all night pulled tight. He took a breath and prepared himself for the worst.

Florence opened the door before he reached it. She was smiling. The string turned to elastic and his shoulders eased back a little.

"She was in the shed! Jayne's about to run her to the hospital for a check-up." Florence pulled him to one side so that two uniformed police officers could leave. "Our shed."

Then Jayne appeared and touched him on the shoulder. "Will you drive us? I feel too frazzled to be safe."

Stuart nodded and within minutes was back in his car. Lillian sat in the back wrapped in a blanket, looking pale and tired. Jayne was next to him and looking equally exhausted.

"So tell me about it?" he asked, checking his mirrors as he slowly reversed over the gravel and back into the road.

"She was in your shed. You don't keep it locked." There was a faint accusatory tone in her voice.

"Why was she in there?"

"Don't talk about me as though I'm not here. It's quite simple. I forgot who I was supposed to be meeting. I thought it was your mother, Stuart. She and I used to take a flask of coffee and a plate of scones into your shed when we wanted a good gossip. You and Jayne played on the lawn and it was easy to keep an eye on you through the open door of the shed. As long as you had your own mini picnic of orange squash and biscuits you never bothered us and we spent hours putting the world to rights. I forgot I was meeting Nora in the park and went to the shed instead."

Jayne twisted around in her seat. "But Mum, Stuart's mother's been dead more than forty years. It was more than a simple slip of the memory."

"I drank coffee and ate all the scones. And I'm sorry, Stuart, but I had to have a wee so I went behind the shed. I came to no harm. I'm just tired."

At the hospital, a doctor confirmed Lillian's self-diagnosis and sent her home with strict instructions to rest and to double-check her calendar before leaving the house.

After Lillian had gone to lie down, Jayne made a cup of tea and sat opposite Stuart at the kitchen table. "Yesterday, when I saw you dancing with Florence . . . You were smiling . . . in a different way to how you smile with me. I don't have her glamour and there's Mum to think about and . . . well, if there's no future between us, I'd like you to tell me now . . . because I thought we . . ."

Stuart's heart tightened at the vulnerability in his girlfriend's expression. "Oh, Jayne! Florence and I are OK as landlord and lodger, but that's all." Landlord and lodger — words that were devoid of emotional connotation, but when he pictured himself and Florence dancing, they didn't fit. Confused Stuart pushed the thought away, took Jayne's hand and brought her up to a standing position. "It's you and I who have the connection. Florence doesn't come into it. It's us that have the shared past, the shared present and enough in common to create a shared future."

Her eyes lost some of their fear and she hugged him tightly.

Before he left, Stuart made a notice for each of Lillian's two external doors. In bold block capitals he printed:

BEFORE LEAVING THE HOUSE, CHECK THE CALENDAR. WHERE ARE YOU GOING?

"That is a genius idea." Jayne held him close again.

Stuart kissed her slowly. Helping people made you feel that you belonged to the real world. And when you loved someone, what else could you do but help?

CHAPTER NINETEEN

Stuart shouldn't have forgotten William's birthday within twenty-four hours of being told. That morning, there'd been no birthday cards at the house. Andrea would bring one but the old man never spoke of anyone else. William deserved better. Leaving Jayne to fuss over Lillian, Stuart bought a card from the corner shop, removed the price, signed his name and drove round to push it through the letterbox. The old man would still be enjoying afternoon tea with his daughter and she'd fetch it off the doormat for him.

He didn't want to be a distraction from the long-awaited visit so he parked some distance from the house. The two of them should be in the back room and wouldn't see him but, just in case, he took what cover he could from parked cars and overhanging hedges. He'd never have cut the mustard as a plain-clothes detective tailing a suspect.

William's gold-coloured letterbox was stiff. Stuart prised it open, wary that it might snap shut and deliver part of his forefinger along with the birthday card. His envelope landed on the mat with a faint splat. He caught a low undercurrent of conversation.

"Dad! You can't be serious." The sudden raised voice of a woman.

Indecipherable, quieter words, which must be William.

"This is definitely NOT what Mum would want!"

Stuart gently lowered the gold flap and left. If William wanted Stuart to know about the argument, he'd tell him in his own good time.

On his way home he called at the library. Since Eric's death, his visits here had got longer and more leisurely. Today, there was a man pinning something on the noticeboard.

"Mr Borefield! Geography."

Stuart focused on the man's face and slowly a GCSE group from thirty years earlier presented itself. "John Harrison?"

The man beamed. "You remembered me."

They shook hands and John pointed at the notice he'd just pinned up. "I'm the new president of the public speakers' club and we're recruiting. How do you fancy it? Being a teacher, you'd be a natural."

"No." Stuart stepped away. He had no wish to ridicule himself in front of an audience. Then he realised he ought to soften the blow. "I don't speak in public. I haven't taught in years."

"At least give it a try?" John looked over his shoulder, as if to check no one else was listening. "To be honest I need to grow the club for the sake of my CV. I've been made redundant and I'm hoping that making the club a success will help me stand out to employers."

The thought of addressing an audience made Stuart feel clammy. He didn't need to put himself through it. He had to focus on that bright new future, not things that were going to sap his self-worth. But he felt a kinship with John and his unemployment. "What happens at the speakers' club?"

John told him about prepared speeches, impromptu talks and learning to evaluate the speeches of others.

"We're friendly and all feedback is constructive."

Still it sent fear to Stuart's core.

"The confidence created by public speaking will creep into all areas of your life. Honestly — it's life-changing. We meet in a room at the Red Lion if you fancy a pint during the proceedings."

Bright new future, bro! Bright new future! This could be part of your toolkit for moving forward.

Stammering and blushing in front of an audience didn't equate to a bright new future. But Sandra's insistent voice wouldn't be pushed from his head and he couldn't crush the optimism on John's face.

"All right, I'll come but just the once." Saying yes was easier than saying no and having to argue with his sister.

* * *

The next morning, Stuart's card had appeared on William's sideboard alongside a huge one from Andrea, which proclaimed: *Best Dad in the World.* There was also a new pot plant with shiny green leaves. Stuart withered inside when William charged him with the responsibility of keeping it alive.

"Well, I can't get over there with a jug of water, can I? Andrea's particular; if she turns up and it's not in tip-top condition, I'll get it in the neck. She doesn't make allowances." Then the old man passed a giant unopened box of Belgian chocolates to Stuart. "My daughter is one for big gestures done very infrequently, without thinking what's actually wanted. It's all about how they make *her* feel. But she should've known better about the chocolates. A moment on the lips, a lifetime on the hips." The old man patted his thighs. "Especially when you're bedridden. Give them to your lodger. She'll burn the calories off in no time with all that singing and dancing. Wouldn't it be grand to go and watch her one day? Aren't you tempted?"

Stuart shook his head. He didn't have the nerve to go alone and he couldn't imagine Jayne in the working men's clubs where Double Berry Black played. "Aside from the chocolates, how was your birthday?"

The old man shrugged. "As expected. The grub was good. The conversation less so. I tried to get the leftovers for you but she was in a bit of a mood and whisked everything away with her." William didn't mention the argument and Stuart couldn't ask without admitting he'd eavesdropped.

On the way home Stuart had a clever idea. He would use the chocolates to bribe Florence to take notice of current events and politics. Each time she listened to the whole of the *World at One* on Radio 4, she would earn a chocolate. If she could verbally summarise the main points to him afterwards, she would get another.

"Don't treat me like a child. Or even worse, a dog. I haven't done book learning like you, but I'm not stupid," she said when he explained his bright new scheme. "This is like putting a star chart on the kitchen wall or making me go on my hind legs and beg." Then she stomped upstairs.

Put so bluntly, Stuart realised immediately that the bright idea had, in fact, been condescending. He tried to apologise but Florence wouldn't come out of her bedroom. "Now you really are being childish," he shouted through the barrier of the door and then abandoned her to go cycling.

The fresh air, hills and physical challenge improved his mood. And put things in perspective. Florence was his lodger, not his protégée. Not his responsibility. She was a temporary blip and would be gone in a matter of months. It didn't matter whether she did or did not engage with politics or the world around her. For the next nine months they could co-exist with their different outlooks on the world.

She met him in the hallway when he got back. "I'll do it. If you do it too."

He smiled at her.

Florence's expression was guarded. "This is simply an extension of our previous agreement about the dancing and the electoral roll. Neither of us is to become a performing animal, rewarded with titbits for bending to the other's will."

Later, Florence's music went back on and Stuart earned a chocolate for improved coordination in his movements to 'YMCA'.

"You have one, too." He offered her the open box.

"I haven't listened to the news."

"I don't like eating chocolate alone."

She chose a truffle dusted in cocoa powder. "That's good because I don't like watching you eat chocolate alone."

Stuart smiled as a liquid cherry filling spilled over his tongue. Florence grinned back as she licked cocoa from her fingers. Stuart tried to ignore how her unconsciously sensual action made him feel.

* * *

Excuses for avoiding the speakers' club meeting floated in Stuart's mind.

He asked Jayne what she thought he should do.

"Tell him you're sick or you've got to put an extra shift in at work. Or just tell him the truth. It's silly pushing yourself out of your comfort zone when we could have a very comfortable evening at home together."

But he'd spent over two decades of evenings at home.

Do it! You know you want to.

Sandra was right again. Even though the prospect was giving him the heebie-jeebies, he did want to give it a go. And he didn't want to let John down.

"You're mad," Jayne said when he told her his decision. "At our time of life we should be taking it easy, not searching out new challenges."

John welcomed him into the back room of the Red Lion and introduced him to a dozen people. Their names got lost in the fog of Stuart's nerves.

The first half of the meeting had Stuart in awe. There were three amazing speeches about beekeeping, morning routines and guide dogs for the blind. These were followed by feedback, which was heavy on praise but also gave points to work on for the future. There would be no future meetings for Stuart — he could never match up to those who had stood at the front of the room and just talked.

During the interval, Stuart was grabbed by someone called the Topics Chair. Apparently as a visitor to the club,

Stuart could choose his own subject, from a given list, for the impromptu part of the evening, rather than having it thrust upon him fifteen seconds before taking the stage.

"I'll give it a miss," Stuart said. "I'm only here to watch."

"It's important to have a go." The Topics Chair was insistent. "Even if you only speak for twenty seconds, you've made a start on your public speaking journey."

"No, I . . ."

Bright new futures don't come sailing towards cowards.

There could be no argument with Sandra in this public setting. He glanced at the list on the sheet of paper being offered to him. "Keeping fit. I'll talk about that."

Sandra gave him a little round of applause. Stuart prayed for the fire alarm to go off before his turn.

Twenty minutes later his name was called and he walked to the front of the room to polite clapping.

He looked at the audience and they looked back at him. He couldn't think of anything to say. He knew nothing about keep fit. It was a stupid subject to have chosen. John caught his eye from the back of the room and smiled encouragingly, the teacher and pupil roles reversed. All the faces in the audience were still staring at him, waiting for something foolish to trip from his lips. He'd known he wouldn't be able to do this and he couldn't. Jayne had been right. He threw an apologetic glance at John and returned to his seat.

He didn't even have the confidence to completely abandon the meeting and go home. His cheeks felt red hot when he touched them and there was a tremor in his hands.

The rest of the speakers passed in a blur.

"Do not let that experience put you off." John shook his hand at the end of the meeting. "We all freeze from time to time. You'll be better when you've had time to prepare what you're going to say in advance. We meet again in a month. I'll put you down for a short ice-breaker speech. Prepare five minutes on whatever you're passionate about."

"I don't think so. It's obviously not for me."

"Think about it," John urged. "You inspired me as a teacher and I want to do the same in return. At least think about it."

There seemed to be no way out of agreeing to consider a short, prepared speech for the next meeting. As soon as Stuart was back in the car the list of excuses that he could give John began forming in his mind.

Absolutely not! You should embrace this opportunity, bro.

He ignored his sister.

* * *

The contents of William's chocolate box diminished as Stuart learned the moves to one of the Blackberries hits, necessitating lots of leg-kicking and arm-waving. The *World at One* became their daily lunchtime listening. Sometimes, Stuart suspected that Florence wasn't properly concentrating, but she usually managed to answer any questions he asked her.

Despite still feeling like a wooden puppet put together by an amateur carpenter, Stuart was enjoying the energy Florence swept into his life. Then she upped the ante.

"You can choose three chocolates at once if you join in with the singing on any track," she said after another successful dance session, her face glowing with enthusiasm.

He refused. Point blank. One of the last things he'd done at the behest of his mother was audition for the church choir. They'd turned him down and his mother died soon after. He had no confidence in his singing. He would rather face that expectant audience at speakers' club than sing.

"Besides," he said. "The chocolates are nearly all gone."

Florence spoke regularly with Shirley's partner, Jacob, about her daughter and grandchildren. Apparently, Shirley was using less and there was some improvement in the state of the youngsters. When he put Eunice and Shayne on the phone to Florence at weekends, she always came away smiling.

Stuart, meanwhile, paid great attention to the calendar. Robert and George had given him twelve months and the time was flowing like sand through open fingers. In eight months, he'd have to wave goodbye to Florence, find a cheap hovel and more income. His earnings plus Florence's rent covered his current expenditure but that combination wouldn't work going forward when he would have to pay rent himself. And, although she knew the score, would Jayne really still want him when he was impecunious? And on top of all that, he had either a watertight excuse, or a speech to prepare.

CHAPTER TWENTY

The other date creeping closer on the calendar was Jayne's birthday. Stuart still had no idea what present he would buy. Whenever his mind was free to roam, the problem bubbled to the surface.

"What do women like for their birthdays?" He was cycling alongside one of the women on the Sunday club ride and he tried to phrase the question casually.

Jennifer glanced from the road to him and grinned inquisitively. "What sort of woman?"

"Fifties, a neighbour."

"Flowers, chocolates."

He frowned. "Something that looks like I've put thought in?"

"Just a neighbour, you say?" Jennifer's expression was teasing him.

Just then the quiet lane ended in a noisy T-junction with an A-road and all conversation stopped as the group concentrated on crossing the fast-moving traffic and picking up the lane on the other side. By then Jennifer had moved forward in the group and he was alongside Mike.

"I've finally decided to sell Mavis's bike," he said. "Every time I see it hanging in the garage is a fresh punch in the stomach. Grief is a funny thing, but, as my daughter keeps saying, it's time to move forward."

Stuart nodded and for a few minutes there was an easy silence between the two men as they freewheeled at speed downhill, generating a wind that would have grabbed any speech.

Stuart remembered Jayne's eighteenth again. He saw her teenage grin as they'd raced and she'd pulled slightly ahead of him. He remembered how carefree they'd been, abandoning their bikes as soon as they'd reached the quarry and falling into each other's arms. Was that feeling of weightlessness only for the young or could they find it again?

"I might be interested in the bike," he said as they slowed against the resistance of a gentler slope. "How much are you asking?"

Mike looked pleased. "I'd let you have it for free. Mavis would be glad it was going to a good home. But what would you be wanting with a ladies' bike?" Jennifer's earlier inquisitive look had transplanted itself to Mike.

"Let's just call her a friend."

Later Stuart drove to Mike's, folded down the backseats of his car and carefully loaded the bike in. The other man's mouth wobbled with emotion even though he was trying to control his expression.

"Cheers for this. It will be looked after, I promise." Stuart patted Mike's arm. "And I owe you a pint."

Late that evening, Jacob phoned unexpectedly on the landline. Florence was still out at a gig and Stuart took the call.

"I didn't try her mobile." Jacob's voice was strained. "I didn't want her to get the news when she was out somewhere. I wanted her to be at home and secure with you. She talks a lot about you."

The sentiment of the last sentence hardly registered with Stuart. "News? What news?" Not one of the children, please. That would destroy her. She doted on those children.

"Shirley has died of a drug overdose. It must have happened sometime over the weekend. I found her when I took the children back. Or rather Eunice did. She was first into the flat. I should've realised something was wrong when she didn't answer the door and I had to use my key."

It was as though something had happened to Stuart's own loved ones. He'd heard so much about this little family and how much they meant to Florence. "Oh my God. How are the children?"

"In bits. Shirley wasn't the world's best mum but she was the only mum they had. They loved her. They've finally cried themselves to sleep, which is why I'm ringing you so late."

Florence was going to be devastated. Stuart wanted the words she heard to be as gentle as possible. "Would you like me to tell her when she gets back?"

"That would be great." Stuart could sense Jacob's relief. "I didn't want to ask you to do such an awful job. Telling a mother her child is dead — it's a terrible thing to lay at anyone's door."

"It's OK. I'd rather she didn't hear it over the phone. But there'll be questions. She'll want to talk to you. Can she ring you back tonight? I can't imagine any of us sleeping much."

"Tonight's fine."

Stuart's hand shook as he put the phone down. How was he going to do this? It was late and the house had become chilly. He put the gas fire on in the lounge, turned off the overhead light and switched on the two standard lamps. They were part of his mother's homemaking legacy and rarely used because they weren't bright enough to read by and unnecessary when the main light was on. He wondered about alcohol and decided against it. Hot, sweet tea was the traditional remedy for everything. Perhaps biscuits. It was a shame he had none of Lillian's lemon drizzle cake — sugar was always good. He sat on the sofa and tried to rehearse in his head how he was going to break the news.

The sound of tyres on gravel made him jump. He got to the front door before she had time to put her key in the lock.

"You're up late."

"I'll make you some tea. You must be tired. Go and sit in the lounge."

She made no effort to move away from him. She frowned. "Why are you acting strangely? You should be in bed."

"Please, let me do this for you." In a second the words would tumble out of him, here in the hallway with her still in her coat and little red boots. He didn't want that.

"OK. OK."

When he carried the tray into the lounge, she was cosily on the sofa with her legs tucked under her, scrolling through her phone.

"Tea and Jaffa cakes."

"Is this a ruse to get me to watch some late-night political discussion? If it is, you need to buy more Belgian chocolates. Jaffa cakes don't cut the mustard." Her eyes were teasing him and she had that amazing, genuinely happy smile that he'd never seen on another living person. His words would snatch that from her. Possibly for ever.

"It's not politics."

"You've found some other way that you want to change me! You know the rules: I only bend in your direction, if you bend in mine. We find a happy place in the middle. Singing is my next challenge to you. We could practise a bit with a nursery rhyme. Jack and Jill went up the hill to fetch a pail of water." Her voice changed to a half-singing, half-chanting lilt.

When he didn't join in, she stopped abruptly and grabbed both his hands. "Something's wrong. It's the children, isn't it?"

"It's Shirley." Stuart tried to speak slowly and keep his tone calm. He had to be the strong one. "She's passed away. They think it's a drug overdose."

"Is this true?" The tips of her fingers were digging painfully into the backs of his hands, as though she was torturing him to get at the truth.

"Yes, it's true."

Florence dropped his hands, emitted a feral yowl and bent over clutching her stomach. "My baby. My beautiful baby." She rocked from side to side on the sofa, her shoulders heaving.

The pain of watching her distress was acute. Stuart put a hand on her back and stroked her but she was too far inside herself to notice. He wrapped his arms around her and tried to hold her but she shrugged him off and continued to rock in a dark place. He wondered if he should call a doctor and get something to calm her.

"Florence?"

She paused and raised her head slightly. The heavy stage makeup was streaked down her face. Stuart fetched the kitchen roll for her to blow her nose. "The tea will make things more manageable. There's plenty of sugar in it. Don't let it go cold." He picked up a mug to pass to her.

Florence wheeled her arms around like a windmill. "I don't want fucking tea! I want my daughter back!"

There was a crash as her flailing arms hit the drink that Stuart was offering. The cup caught the edge of the coffee table and smashed. A dark wet patch erupted on the brown carpet. Florence went back to rocking and Stuart watched the stain creep outwards. It was like watching the slow spread of misery from Shirley's sad death. So many ruined lives. So many affected by the ripples. Like him, like Jacob's new partner. Like the people Eunice and Shayne would meet as they travelled through life — the emotional baggage of losing their mum, however poor her maternal skills, would never leave them. Stuart could vouch for that.

He drank his tea, barely registering that it was now cold. He tried to hold Florence again. This time she didn't pull away. As the minutes crept by, she rocked less and eventually rested against him without moving. He passed her more kitchen roll.

"Thanks," she muttered. "I never asked about Eunice and Shayne. Who's looking after them?"

"They're with Jacob. Fast asleep."

"Did he find her or what?"

Stuart tried to move her hair back from her face so that he could read her expression better. The lines across her forehead and around her mouth and eyes were deeply etched and emphasised by her anguish, exhaustion and spoiled makeup.

"Jacob said you could call him anytime tonight. They found her when he took the children back and he'll fill you in on the details." He handed her the cordless landline. "Do you want to talk in private?"

"No. Stay, please. I need someone to hold my hand."

Florence spoke to Jacob for fifteen minutes. Stuart tried not to overtly listen but it was hard to do anything else. Florence's hand gripped his. At times it was painful. He said nothing and wondered if the imprints of her fingertips would still be visible on his skin the next day. Eventually Florence ended the call and he waited for her to speak.

"We decided to sleep on it and talk again in the morning."

Stuart nodded. "Can I get you anything now? Fresh tea?"

"Yes, please. And then I'm going to take my makeup off and have a shower. I can't get into bed like this." She gave a wan grin and pointed to the ruin of her face.

A few minutes later Stuart took fresh tea into her bedroom. She was in the pink fluffy robe dabbing at her face with cotton wool. The night after his mother died, Stuart had been lonely in bed. Everyone had urged him to be a brave, big boy and he'd lacked the courage to object and ask if he could sleep in the warmth of his father's bed. He also didn't have the guts to ask Florence if she'd like the comfort of someone beside her as she tried to sleep.

"I'll see you in the morning," he said.

CHAPTER TWENTY-ONE

Florence was already dressed and in the kitchen when Stuart went down at six thirty. He'd been hoping she'd sleep late so he could give her his full attention when he got back from William. There were dark shadows beneath her eyes.

"Jacob said he'll phone me when the children are otherwise occupied. I wanted to be ready for the call."

"I'm supposed to visit William . . ." The sentence tailed off. He remembered the anguish caused to Jayne when she perceived him as putting the old man before her. But there was nothing between him and Florence. No unspoken promise of commitment. He braced himself regardless. He was learning that women were nothing if not unpredictable.

"You get off." Florence blew her nose but didn't seem to be reproaching him. "You were brilliant last night. But the world doesn't stop, does it? I don't want that old man to suffer on my account."

He hoped the relief didn't show on his face. "I'll be back as soon as I can."

She waved him away.

As Stuart pulled up outside William's house, he felt powered by adrenaline. It was imperative that he be back at Florence's side as soon as possible. He fumbled the numbered buttons in the key safe and was forced to take a breath and proceed more calmly.

William immediately grasped the need for speed but in Stuart's eyes the old man ate, drank and moved in slow motion. He wanted to wind him up or put in new batteries to make him go faster. But William's limbs continued to bend with difficulty as they were manoeuvred into armholes and trouser legs. In contrast, the minute hand on William's wall clock went at speed, emphasising the length of time Florence was spending alone with her grief and anxiety.

"I'm sorry," William said for the twentieth time. "For Florence's loss and my inability to get out of first gear."

"Really, it's no problem." Stuart typed his notes while William ate porridge.

"You go." William stopped eating and balanced his spoon on the edge of the dish. "It plays havoc with my digestion if I eat too fast and I can manage to feed myself without your beady eyes urging me on."

For a second Stuart tussled with the guilt of abandoning his client and friend against the regret at leaving Florence at home alone with her grief. Florence won but he'd make it up to William later. "Thank you. I really do appreciate this."

"Another day we'll get your bright new future sorted. I think its path is becoming clearer."

Already in the hall, Stuart barely registered the old man's words. All that could wait.

When he got home, Florence once again had her bag packed. She'd covered her tiredness with makeup and wore a loose beige blouse made of silky material instead of one of her trademark bright close-fitting tops. Her trousers were black and tailored, not clinging; they were more the classy sort that Jayne would choose. In front of him was an ordinary grandma, not the fun, feisty Florence.

"You look more . . ."

"Respectable?"

"Less bold."

"That's the idea. I've got two motherless kiddies who need some loving. They don't need a self-centred, star-struck bit of mutton dressed up as lamb. I'll be going with Jacob to talk to teachers and social workers; the last thing we want is the children snatched into care because of a dodgy granny who, if you half close your eyes, looks like she might be on the game."

This new, sedate Florence looked like any of the middle-aged women who wandered round the supermarket or gathered in the windows of coffee shops. From nowhere came the sudden realisation that he preferred his lodger bright and bubbly, even garish, breezing into the house and bringing bounce and life into the place.

"Station?" Stuart asked, dangling his keys.

"Please. But give me a hug first." She looked calm but when he looked closely, her eyes were too bright and there was a small tear on her right cheek.

She clutched at him like she'd never let go. He held her tight, not wanting to let her go. Eventually she pulled away.

"None of this will be easy," she said. "And of course Jim will be there."

"Jim?"

"My husband."

He'd forgotten she was still married.

Or maybe you've got selective amnesia, bro.

"Shall I come with you?" The words came out before his brain had processed them. "To support you?"

Florence looked shocked. Then her face broke into a smile. "I like you, Stuart, because you are open and honest. You're not like other men."

She took both his hands in hers and when she looked into his eyes, he felt like he was the only person in the world that mattered to her. "I can't think of anyone else I'd rather have at my side right now. But it wouldn't work. Jim would be pissed off. Jacob would be weighing up your influence on his children. I'd be worrying about whether or not you were OK. There'd be nowhere for you to sleep. Besides, what about William? And Jayne?"

Florence was far more sensible than the 'frantic Florence' she'd first described herself as.

"Station, then?"

When she'd gone, the house was flat. Flat used to be normal. Now the flatness was obvious and unwelcome. He lingered so much on his lunchtime and teatime visits to William that the old man almost had to throw him out. It didn't make sense that the flatness in the house was affecting him so badly.

He went out to the garage and surveyed Mavis's old bike. He felt and inspected the tyres, looked carefully at the brakes and chain, and ran his fingers over the paintwork. The bike was obviously well used but in immaculate condition. Mike was known for his bike maintenance skills and Stuart guessed he'd given it a full service before even thinking about selling it. There was nothing for him to do except determine how to engineer time away from Lillian for Jayne. Since her mother had gone missing, she'd become hyper-protective of her.

He ate scrambled eggs on toast for his tea followed by a chopped banana doused in honey yoghurt. The crossword didn't hold the appeal of pre-Florence days. The people talking on Radio 4 were saying things of no consequence. His mind wouldn't focus enough to decide which excuse to give to John prior to the next speakers' club meeting. The drizzle outside the window looked like the drizzle in his mind. It came to him slowly that, since Florence had arrived, he'd learned to prefer people to his own thoughts. He picked up the phone and dialled next door.

"7-6-9-3-2-5?" Lillian had that old person's habit of announcing herself with her phone number.

"It's Stuart, is Jayne there?" His voice came out hesitant and anxious. Stuart still couldn't quite believe that he'd been given a second chance with his first love.

You think she might suddenly realise that you don't measure up to Audi man? Man up! You are offering her something more valuable than a shiny car. Be confident in your own attractions.

Stuart hated Sandra's impression of a cryptic crossword but there was no chance to answer back; Lillian was speaking.

"Yes, she's here! And I am so glad you two have become friends. It makes an old lady very happy." Then she lowered her voice. "Did I tell you it's her birthday soon? I know it's soon because I made her write it on the calendar in a different colour pen so it stands out. She's such a good girl, she deserves a lovely day."

"Mum!" Jayne's muffled voice held a hint of reprimand.

"Here she is, I'll hand you over."

"I'm sorry, Stuart. She's becoming something of an embarrassment."

"No problem. Do you fancy coming round? If you're busy or Lillian needs you, no worries."

"I'll be there in ten minutes. Mum's settling down to watch *Vera*. There's something about that detective woman or the Northumberland countryside that calms her and keeps her in one place. We'll have a couple of hours."

As soon as Jayne arrived, Stuart told her about the death of Florence's daughter.

"A drug overdose!"

He nodded. The events of the last twenty-four hours were still whirling around his mind like so much discarded litter outside a chip shop.

"So, this daughter, she was a junkie?" Jayne's expression said she was trying to make sense of a situation far removed from her own experience. "Like you see on the TV — stick thin, hollow-eyed, sprawled on a dirty mattress in a squat?"

"Probably not as bad as that." His instinct was to stand up for Florence's family. "She had two children with her most of the week so she must have been functioning. And Florence went to stay with her a while back; she wouldn't have done that if it was just a mattress in a hovel."

"It makes you think, doesn't it?"

"How do you mean?"

"The impression of ourselves that we give to others might not be the whole truth." Jayne paused. "In comparison to Florence, I'm boring. But at least I don't have a secret like that."

"You are not boring!"

She ignored him. "Do you know that Florence is clean?"

"What?"

"This is going to sound awful." She took his hand. "I'm not deliberately trying to be nasty or kick a woman when she's down, but Florence can be very hyper. Is it natural that a middle-aged woman has so much bounce and spends so much time whirling like a dervish? And she's always urging you to join in — that could be an attempt to normalise her actions."

This was something Stuart had never even considered. "Florence doesn't do drugs."

"I'm only saying this because I care about you." Jayne took a breath. "But what goes on in her bedroom or when she's out doing those gigs? Take it from me, most middle-aged women don't have Florence's energy."

Stuart felt his fists curl tightly in response to Jayne's words. He made an effort to loosen them and put them behind his back. "She doesn't do drugs." He repeated his words slowly and firmly.

"OK. OK. I'm sorry." Jayne held her hands up in surrender. "I jumped in at the deep end but it had to be said."

The words elephant and paddling pool come to mind. Stuart ignored his sister and concentrated on what Jayne was saying.

"I raised the question because I care about you. And it's the legal secretary in me. If, and I realise now it's a big if. *If* Florence was involved in drugs in your house, you wouldn't come out of it squeaky clean." She moved towards him and took his hands. "Please can we start this evening again? I overreacted and I'm sorry. Very sorry."

Stuart's defences relaxed. They'd successfully negotiated their first disagreement and everything was going to be OK. He pulled his girlfriend into a hug. "Yes, please, let's turn the clock back fifteen minutes."

She smiled at him and kissed him slowly on the lips. His toes curled and he pulled her closer. They spent the rest of the evening snuggled on the sofa.

"I overreacted because I was scared." Jayne had her head resting on his shoulder, making Stuart feel protective.

"Scared?"

"Scared of Florence's alien world touching ours and spoiling it. And I don't just mean the drugs thing. I mean her whole glamorous performing lifestyle. I can't compete with that. I can't offer you anything out of the ordinary. You want a bright new future but I don't understand what that means for you. I can only offer a dull new future. I like being me. Eventually I want to retire and enjoy a slower pace of life, perhaps with the odd sunshine holiday if finances allow. I don't want new experiences and challenges. I've had enough of that over the years. But I really would like to share my future with you. Will that be good enough?"

"Being with you is more than good enough. I never thought I'd get this second chance." Stuart pulled her closer. "You don't need to compete with Florence. Nothing is going to spoil what we've got."

"University did. We promised to wait for each other and didn't."

Stuart fell back through the decades to their hurried farewell on the gravel drive while his father waited in the car laden with boxes and suitcases. "I . . ."

She interrupted him before he could remind her that she'd been the one at fault. "You were swept into a world completely unknown to me with parties, concerts, halls of residence, freedom. I was sure you'd never keep your promise in the midst of all that temptation."

"I . . ."

Jayne put a finger over his lips. "I didn't want to waste three years of my youth waiting to get dumped or cheated on by you. That's why I started seeing Carl."

"But I . . ."

"Now I know I was wrong."

"Absolutely, you were wrong and nothing will ever come between us again."

It was Stuart's turn to kiss Jayne. Her admission of the insecurity she'd felt back then and was still feeling now clarified a whole lot of things and evened up their partnership.

When Jayne looked at her watch, *Vera* was coming to an end.

"I've really enjoyed having a break from Mum this evening. Thank you. And sorry about . . . earlier."

"The enjoyment was mutual."

"There is something I want to ask you. A big favour." She paused. "There's a yoga retreat coming up. I go every year to destress and reflect on life. It's just one night." Another pause. "But this time I'm scared to leave Mum. I know I have to tailor my life to suit hers but I need this break. Since she went missing, I've not been to yoga. Now I understand why people bang on about the need for respite care and Mum's not even that bad. Yet." Another pause. "Would you mind sleeping over at Mum's? If she wakes in the night, she sometimes loses it."

"No problem." It felt good to be wanted and appreciated.

"Thank you." She kissed him again.

On the way to bed he noticed the door to Florence's room was ajar. He hesitated and then pushed it fully open.

Every drawer in the chest was open and clothes were spilling out. The duvet was in a scrunched heap as though Florence had just leaped out of it. The wardrobe door was propped open by a shoebox and a pile of high heels were visible under the bed. Florence had obviously packed in a hurry. He wondered if she'd phone while she was away or if the alien world she was visiting would swallow her whole.

CHAPTER TWENTY-TWO

Florence stayed away for a fortnight. She phoned twice but from the sparsity of information she offered, these calls were for reassurance that Stuart was OK, rather than looking for support herself. He mentioned staying overnight with Lillian so Jayne could go away.

"And you're OK with that?"

"Of course I am. Jayne deserves a break."

"Sometimes I think you're too good for this world. I bet Audi man didn't do babysitting."

"Audi man didn't grow up with Lillian as an honorary aunty."

"No one deserves that bright future more than you, Stuart Borefield. Make sure it doesn't pass you by while you're looking the other way."

Florence's reaction surprised him. Wouldn't any man do whatever it took to help the woman he loved?

* * *

William had appeared preoccupied since his birthday, prying less into Stuart's personal life and offering little conversation during the washing, toileting and eating routines.

"Do you need to see a doctor?" Stuart asked again.

"What? No. I'm fine. Just thinking things through. Did you manage to get that jam mark off my best jacket? I need it tomorrow."

"Going for a job interview, are we?" Stuart tried to lighten the atmosphere, thinking how Florence twirling around the room would soon brighten the old man up.

"Ha ha." William was still capable of a sarcastic tone. "No, the solicitor's coming. I'm putting my affairs in order before the Grim Reaper stakes his claim. After what happened with your father's will, I'm not leaving any loose ends or misunderstandings. When I'm standing on my cloud in heaven, I want to be able to look down and think I did the right thing by all concerned."

"A wise move." And then Stuart attempted another joke. "Seeing how you enjoy the company of that stray moggie that sits on the window sill, I bet the cats' home is going to be in for a bumper windfall. I hope you've told Andrea?"

"Andrea knows my intentions and isn't fully in favour." William made no acknowledgement of Stuart's attempt at humour. "But, in this life, you reap what you sow."

Stuart felt a sudden kinship for the unknown Andrea. Maybe she would react differently to him. He hadn't made a fuss. He hadn't challenged the will. He hadn't pleaded with his brothers. He hadn't done any of this because he wanted to reach for his bright new future unhindered by a bitter family feud or long legal proceedings that would eat into any final payout. But now he wondered whether not fighting had been the right decision? Having money would have generated far more options for his future. And it would be nice to be able to treat Jayne occasionally. She deserved nice things.

I raise my hands in apology, bro. I might have directed you towards that possibly wrong decision. My naivety about real life has a tendency to push me into the over-idealistic corner.

Stuart battled not to respond aloud to his sister's first-ever apology. He swallowed hard and let her continue.

We're both older and wiser now that we've seen something of the outside world. But note, I said possibly *wrong decision. A lack of money means you have to push yourself out there instead of hiding at home. Bright new futures don't come looking for you. Think of all those billionaire recluses. You wouldn't want to be one of those, would you?*

Now wasn't the time to get into an argument with his sister about the quality of her advice. He pushed her away and cast his mind back to the overheard argument between Andrea and William. She must have been trying to argue her case as a beneficiary. He hoped she could put her hurt feelings to one side and visit her dad again so that regret didn't travel with her forever. William supported an overseas charity that carried out cataract operations on the poor. Perhaps Andrea's share of the money was being reduced in favour of helping people on the other side of the world to see again. Was short-changing your family to benefit strangers overseas the right thing to do? Stuart had no idea.

* * *

The Saturday that Jayne went away, Stuart took an overnight bag next door and ate his evening meal with Lillian. She was pleased to see him and produced a strawberry jelly she'd made especially for the occasion. He had to force an enthusiastic smile as she spooned the half-set slop into his dish.

Lillian frowned at the consistency. "I forgot how long it needed to set. I only thought of the idea this afternoon."

"Doesn't matter." Stuart brought a spoonful up to his lips. "It will taste just as good."

"Wait! Ice cream. I got it out of the freezer earlier so I didn't forget." As she said the words, Lillian seemed to realise this had been the wrong thing to do.

Stuart accepted two spoonfuls of melted raspberry ripple into his jelly. The taste was sweet but the consistency meant the dessert needed careful handling to avoid a jelly-fall down the front of his T-shirt.

Afterwards he washed up and Lillian dried.

"It's lovely to see more of you, Stuart. It's kind of you to stay with me. Jayne worries about leaving me on my own. Usually I'm all right but sometimes I forget things."

"Don't we all?"

"But sometimes it's dangerous. Like when I forgot about meeting Nora."

Stuart placed the last cup on the draining-board, tipped the water from the bowl and dried his hands. Then he touched Lillian lightly on the arm. "Don't worry about any of it. I'm happy to help when I can."

"And when you and Jayne get married, you'll always be here to help."

"Get married?" His heart lurched.

"Jayne's been so happy since you two got back together. She floats through the days with a smile on her face instead of dragging her feet around like she used to." Lillian sat down. "But in the times when my brain clears, I'm not sure it's the right thing. Getting married, I mean." She twiddled with the bottom of her cardigan. "In my perfect world, you'd be here with me and Jayne every day. But it's so soon after your dad. It's taking advantage of your good nature."

"It's not taking advantage. I've got nothing else to do. And I like you."

Lillian's frown turned into a smile of relief.

"But we've not reached the getting married stage."

She frowned again. "You think you haven't but neither of you are spring chickens and I'm definitely not."

"You take charge of the remote while I make a pot of tea." He put his hand on the small of her back and tried to guide her out of the kitchen.

"Don't fob me off. I'm only doolally some of the time. Right now I'm sane and you know I'm talking sense. It's something to be considered."

A gold star for Stuart! You definitely score more highly than Audi man with the old lady. But what do you do next?

Stuart ignored his sister and focused on distracting Lillian. "Chocolate digestive or bourbon cream?"

The old lady took a detour to the biscuit tin and loaded a plate with enough chocolate biscuit variations to feed an army, counting under her breath as she arranged them.

He wondered if he should tell Jayne about the conversation. Probably not. He needed to get his own mind clear on the getting married thing first.

"Have a biscuit." Lillian thrust the plate under his nose. "And think about what I've said. And no, Jayne doesn't know my opinion on this matter. And yes, I will have forgotten this conversation by tomorrow, which is why I had to say it now."

The quietness of the house when he returned home the next day and the nagging knowledge that the next speakers' meeting was looming forced Stuart to focus his mind. Lying about why he couldn't attend, even over the phone when no one could see his body language, didn't come naturally to him. And lying to a former pupil didn't feel right, especially when he'd been given a space on the evening's program and would therefore be creating a gap if he didn't attend.

If he wrote the speech down and then read it out, word for word, perhaps he'd be able to cope with all those eyes staring at him. He'd be looking down at the paper so he wouldn't even have to see the audience. Then he'd tell the John the truth — that he had no need to speak in public and therefore wouldn't be coming again.

Speak about something he was passionate about, John had said. Cycling was the only thing that got him fired up. He decided on the history of cycling and started researching the old bone-shaker bikes and penny-farthings. He needed a lot of content to fill five minutes.

* * *

When he got the call to collect Florence from the station, Stuart was elated. He pulled into the car park far too early and paced up and down the platform, right down to the end where the noticeboard gave the Samaritans' telephone number. He peered down the line, looking for a sign that the train was approaching.

According to the loudspeaker announcement, the train was nine carriages long. When it pulled in, Stuart scanned its length but the passengers were disgorged in such numbers that it was impossible to identify any individual. Then he spotted the distinctive zebra-patterned fake-fur jacket. He trotted towards her, glad she'd dropped the respectable grandma persona for the real Florence. He waved. She waved. Then Stuart hesitated. She kept turning to a man immediately behind her, as if explaining the way and encouraging him. Something cold inside him said this was Jim, Florence's husband.

CHAPTER TWENTY-THREE

They got within speaking distance. Florence had two pet carriers, one in each hand. Her handbag was slung across her chest like a giant, schoolgirl peggy-purse. The man had Florence's suitcase. She turned to him. "Thank you so much, I never would've managed without you."

"No problem. I hope things sort themselves out." He gave a little mock salute and followed the crowd towards the exit sign.

She put the pet carriers down and gave Stuart a peck on the cheek. "He was so kind. Jacob put me on the train but I was worried how I'd manage at this end. That man, I didn't even ask his name — that's bad of me — was interested in Slowcoach and Tibby and he was getting off here, so it all worked a treat."

"Slowcoach and Tibby?"

"The children's pets." She pointed to the containers now on the floor at her feet. "A tortoise and a cat. You can work out which is which. Jacob's new partner is allergic to cats and, well, the children are bored of Slowcoach — he doesn't really do much. He's just another thing to look after in the chaos down there."

She picked up the containers again and Stuart took the suitcase. He led the way to the car, trying to grasp this new situation. As a child he'd had a goldfish for three months, then he'd found it floating on top of the bowl and his father had flushed it down the toilet. He and his mother had had a little cry, and then that had been that as far as pets were concerned.

"What are you going to do with them?"

"Nothing. They won't be any bother. You don't have to do anything. After what the children have been through, I can't get rid of their pets. They have to know they're safe and happy here."

"The cat smells."

"It was scared and weed. But there's plenty of newspaper in there to absorb it. Don't worry about the car."

When they got home, Florence went in search of a cardboard box that could be made into a temporary bed for Slowcoach in the garage. Tibby refused to come out of the carrier until Florence opened one of Stuart's tins of salmon. Then she ate the whole tin before crouching down and doing her business in the corner of the kitchen by the door.

It was a battle not to say anything critical. Florence was constantly on the defensive about the animals. "She only pooed there because we were too slow to open the door for her to go outside. What she really needs is a cat flap." She looked at him expectantly.

"That means cutting a hole in the door." Florence's longed-for return was clouded by all these new demands.

"Yes." She nodded encouragingly. "And I'll pay for the flap."

"It's not actually my house."

"What your brothers don't know won't harm them. And a cat flap isn't a big red flag for making house prices fall."

The grey, white and black tabby strolled over to Stuart on white paws and circled his legs. Then it rubbed itself against his shins. It purred, as if adding its own persuasion to Florence's.

"She likes you."

Without thinking, Stuart bent and stroked the top of the cat's head. The animal stretched its head further towards him.

"She loves being tickled under her chin. Shirley used to do that." Florence's voice trembled over her daughter's name.

Stuart transferred his hand from the top of Tibby's head to the white fur beneath her chin. The cat responded by arching her neck backwards and increasing the vibrancy of her purring. This act of pleasing the cat pleased Stuart.

"There'll be a YouTube video about how to fit a cat flap," Florence offered, "and I could be your carpenter's mate."

"OK." He straightened up and stretched his back. "You buy what we need and I'll have a go."

Florence left immediately in the faded orange Panda and Stuart went to see what tools might be lurking in the garage from when his dad had been active around the house.

Fitting the flap wasn't straightforward. According to the internet, the first task was to measure the height of the cat's stomach from the ground. Tibby was sound asleep on the sofa. Stuart prodded her awake. At first she ignored him, but at the second prod she raised a paw and revealed her claws. Stuart wouldn't be beaten by a cat. He picked up the ruler and used it to gently poke her again, hoping to encourage her into a standing position. Both front paws caught hold of the ruler and Tibby's eyes flashed malevolently. Then she stood up and proceeded to show him what she thought by sharpening her claws on the sofa cushions.

"No!" The cat had morphed from a cute thing in need of love and comfort into a vicious, self-centred creature.

Tibby threw him a look of disdain and jumped down to the floor. Stuart grabbed her by the collar and positioned the ruler vertically beneath her. She mewed loudly and refused to stand still but he got some kind of measurement. Five inches, he scribbled on a bit of paper.

Next step was to mark this height in the centre of the door and position the template supplied with the cat flap according to the mark. Then he needed to drill a hole in each corner of the template to mark the outline of the required opening.

He found an electric drill behind some old tins of paint. He guessed it was simply a case of plugging in and hoping it would work. There was a socket in the garage he could test it with. He plugged it in. Nothing. He flicked the switch on the socket to turn the power on. Nothing. He fiddled with the drill, being careful at all times to keep the sharp end pointed away from him. Nothing.

He skipped to the next step of the instructions, wondering if he could somehow manage without the four drilled holes. The next stage called for a jigsaw. He didn't know what a jigsaw was in terms of DIY. But he memorised the picture on the laptop screen and went delving around in the old cardboard boxes on the garage shelves. There were a couple of ordinary saws but nothing that resembled a jigsaw.

"I can't do it."

Florence was in the middle of the kitchen floor with a mop. The smell of cat poo had been replaced by the strong scent of artificial lemons.

"You're a man."

"What's that got to do with it? We aren't born with a set of tools in our hands."

Florence sniggered. Stuart realised what he'd said. The innuendo hung embarrassingly between them. Then Florence's attempt to neutralise her face went too far the other way and her countenance changed into that of a solemn vicar. Stuart grinned.

"Jim will do it!" Her face glowed with the customary Florence enthusiasm. "It's for the grandkids and he dotes on them. He was brilliant with them while we were down there."

Jim with Florence in London. He looked at her and wondered.

She is still a married lady. She's allowed to go places with her husband.

Stuart turned to the kitchen sink. He needed to get Sandra out of his head before he could look at Florence again.

"My concern is him trying to win her back, when the best thing for both of them would be to stay as far apart as possible." He mentally sparred with his sister, being acutely aware that he must not speak aloud. "She doesn't need any more emotional aggro right now."

Florence is streetwise. She can look after herself. Concentrate on your life. Are you sure that you don't have personal reasons for not wanting Jim to win Florence back?

Stuart took a deep breath and gave himself a slap on both cheeks. Then he turned back to Florence with what he hoped didn't look like a fixed smile.

"How did you and Jim get on? You know, considering you're actually separated."

"He was only there for five days, he couldn't get any more time off work." She paused. Stuart felt as though she was examining his face to see what affect her words were having. "Actually, I was glad he was there. We talked a lot about our memories of Shirley growing up and the good times we had together. We both had a little cry. Well, actually I cried a lot more than him but that's me — my feelings won't stay hidden."

"Do you think you two might get back together?" He adopted a light tone and an 'I don't care what you do' expression. Stuart would miss her rent money and skill with a duster and her singing and her positivity and . . . He quashed the feelings before they could take on a proper shape.

"No. I'm still me and Jim's still Jim. We're two jigsaw pieces that only fit together under force. And even under force, if you look carefully there's a ridge between us."

"Right."

"But he'll come and fix the flap right now if I call him."

Stuart was about to suggest Tibby and Slowcoach went to live at Jim's house instead but then realised that would mean Florence visiting her husband in order to check on the animals. That wouldn't be good for her.

"Yeah, fine. Call him." Now Stuart was torn between wanting to be absent when Jim came but also wanting to get the measure of the man who felt, inexplicably, like an opponent. A comparison wouldn't come out in Stuart's favour. "I think I'll have an hour on my bike before it gets dark."

He pulled on the Lycra in double quick time and was away before Jim arrived. This would be a good opportunity to start checking out the route he was planning for his first group ride as leader in January. It was silly to be worrying about it this far in advance but the thought of a dozen people looking to him for leadership made him wobble inside. 'Fail to Prepare, Prepare to Fail' ran around his head again.

As he pushed on the pedals to beat the gradients, he imagined the man Florence was married to. Taller than Stuart, broader shoulders, less grey hair, confident in his own skin, an experienced man of the world, excellent at DIY. Fighting the hill was like proving something about himself in comparison to Jim.

By the time he'd reached the summit his pace had slowed considerably, giving time to survey the countryside: the cornucopia of green shading, the meandering gentleness of a river, bright yellow patches of rape fields and the softer golds of cereal crops. This view always lifted his spirits and readjusted, at least temporarily, his perspective on life. Then he flew down the other side and onto steady flat pedalling, the release of the summit being replaced, unbidden, by the spectre of Jim.

My, you're getting your knickers in a twist. Sandra butted into his mind. *What's with the inferiority complex?*

On the flat he had enough breath to speak out loud. The wind snatched at his words but the act of speaking helped sort out his emotions. "It's that confidence thing again. After all that time alone with Dad, how do I come across to other people? Is it wrong for me to want to appear an equal to anyone else? If I had more confidence, perhaps I'd have challenged the will and wouldn't be in a mess now."

Stop comparing and play to your own strengths.

If he had any strengths, he would. He crouched low over the handlebars and pedalled as hard as he could to generate the momentum to get him up the next hill. He stopped at the top to make a note on the map, wondering whether the gradient might be too much for the slower riders. Perhaps he should find a flatter way around. Longer but flatter might actually be quicker for the less experienced in the group.

When he got home, the cat flap was in and Jim was gone.

"Here, hold that dish of food just inside the flap and shout for Tibby. She's in the garden and I want to get a photo of her coming through the cat flap to send to the children."

Still in his Lycra, Stuart did as he was told, holding the flap open so the horrific smell of the cat food went outside. "Tibby! Tibby!" he called.

Florence was crouched just behind him with her phone at the ready.

Tibby shot through the hole, tipping the dish from Stuart's hand. Taken by surprise, Stuart sat down heavily on the floor, knocking over the crouched Florence. They ended up in heap together with Tibby climbing over them to get to the spilled food.

"I think she knows how to use it," Florence said, her breath warm on the back of Stuart's neck.

For almost a full minute, neither of them chose to move. Stuart recognised the same joyful sparks as when he'd comforted his housemate following her previous London visit, when Shirley was still alive.

Then Florence's hands electrified his chest and his shoulders as she used him as a prop to get herself upright. "I'll get the mop out again." She pointed to the scraps of food that had flown too far from the dish and Tibby had chosen to ignore. Her face was flushed and her voice wavery.

Shellshocked at their bodies' reaction to the accidental collision, Stuart sat on the floor for a moment longer and then gave himself a shake.

CHAPTER TWENTY-FOUR

The following day was Sunday and Florence announced she was going back home to talk to Jim. There was much to sort out about the children's welfare and Shirley's meagre estate. Jacob would join them via video call while his partner took the children to the park.

The opportunity of an empty house for the day was too good to miss and Stuart skipped the club ride to invite Jayne for lunch. He felt an urge to see her, a need to validate his feelings for her.

That's sweet, bro. It's true — absence really does make the heart grow fonder.

Stuart ignored her and called his girlfriend.

"Lunch would be lovely. Mum said you were brilliant while I was away. Thank you so much for that."

"No problem."

"I'll have to bring her, if that's OK? I've got one session a week at the day centre for her but the rest of the time she's alone during the day when I'm at work. I can't leave her at the weekend as well."

Not perfect. But he agreed and crossed his fingers Lillian wouldn't bring up the subject of marriage again. Stuart took them out to the patio to meet Slowcoach who was enjoying a lettuce leaf in the sunshine.

"You say the children's father was South African and the tortoise came over with him years ago?" Jayne asked.

Stuart nodded as he made sure the garden chairs were free of dirt before they sat down.

"Can I have a look at its shell?"

"What?"

"I once read that tortoises were used to smuggle diamonds between Angola and South Africa, but not all the tortoises reached their destinations. There may be some, possibly adopted as pets, who are still carrying their diamond cargo." Jayne knelt down by Slowcoach and ran her fingers around the edge of his shell. Slowcoach sensed her touch, stopped chewing on the leaf and turned his head towards her. Tortoises didn't have the facial equipment to communicate dislike by expression, but Stuart got the message that Slowcoach wasn't enthusiastic about having his dinner disturbed.

"Where do they put the diamonds?" Lillian was taking an interest now. "I hope it's not cruel to the animal."

Jayne was kneeling as low as she could, bent over with her head sideways and her left ear almost touching the floor. Her voice came out slightly muffled. "They stuck the diamonds on top of the shell and then they got another tortoise shell, just a little bigger, to place over the top. The second shell hid the diamonds and was supposed to fit well so that, to the untrained eye, it looked like the tortoise had just the usual single shell."

Stuart was sceptical. "I doubt very much that Jacob's family was into diamond smuggling."

"You didn't know Florence's family was involved in drugs." Jayne glanced up. "But the fact that they weren't involved is the whole point. If they knew about the diamonds, they would've already taken them. But if Slowcoach somehow strayed out of the grasp of the smugglers, as some of them did when they were released near the border to cross into South Africa alone and as nature intended, then the diamonds might still be there under its shell."

"And how can we tell whether there are diamonds under the shell?" Stuart pictured the joy on Florence's face when he announced that her family had suddenly become rich.

"I think we'd have to remove the shell."

"Wouldn't that kill it?" Lillian was following the conversation, moving her head between the two of them as though she was at a tennis match. "Wouldn't it be kinder to just wait for it to die?"

"Tortoises live for ever and we have no idea how old this one is, do we?"

Stuart was uncomfortable about the direction in which Jayne was heading. It wasn't his tortoise and he didn't think Florence would agree to anything that might make Slowcoach suffer, even if it could transform her own life and the lives of her grandchildren. "Lunch is ready." He directed the two ladies back inside and away from Slowcoach.

"I can smell cat wee," Jayne said as Stuart passed round carrots, peas and cauliflower in his mother's favourite flowered china tureens. "Has a stray started using the patio as a toilet? You can get a spray to deter them."

Stuart sniffed, but smelled only roast potatoes and gravy. His nose had already got used to the animal. He paused, trying to frame his words positively. "The cat belongs to Florence's grandchildren. She's looking after it until everything gets sorted. She's called Tibby."

On cue, Tibby wandered in from the patio, tail held high. She went under the table and then positioned herself next to Jayne's chair and made little mewling noises.

"The poor thing's hungry." Lillian chopped up all of her remaining chicken, put it on her side plate, added a drop of gravy and then, with obvious effort and a groan, she bent and put the plate at her feet.

Tibby moved like lightning.

"Mum! You shouldn't do that."

"It does no harm."

"That's not what you used to say when I was a little girl giving treats to the dog down the road."

"Says she who's willing to remove a tortoise's home from its back!"

Stuart winced at the barbed comment and hoped it was the dementia talking.

"I suggested nothing of the sort." Jayne's cheeks had flushed.

He tried to send Jayne a supportive message by widening his eyes meaningfully. Being bad-mouthed by the person for whom you'd put your life on hold was soul-destroying. They finished the meal in an awkward silence. Then Stuart gathered up the plates and Lillian insisted on helping with the washing up. Stuart tried to say that he'd do it later but Jayne kept repeating that it should be left for Florence because she was being paid to do the cleaning.

"It's not right to expect the girl to clear up after us when she's had none of the pleasure and has just lost her daughter." Lillian stood at the ready with a tea towel.

Stuart agreed, but kept his mouth shut. Jayne was obviously under stress from her mother's attitude. They did the washing up between them and afterwards Jayne suggested they make the most of the afternoon sunshine in the park.

"It's nearly the end of August. Autumn will be here before we know it."

Stuart found it difficult to tame his long, fast stride to match Lillian's elderly meandering as she stopped to admire plants and sit on benches. She needed no help walking, just a little extra time. When her mother was engrossed in reading the 'In Memoriam' plaques around the edge of the bandstand, Jayne took Stuart's hand and squeezed. The gesture warmed him and he turned to look at her.

"I'm sorry," she said quietly, "about Mum having to be with us today. And she's started putting me down whenever possible. You know I wouldn't hurt the tortoise. I was just interested."

Stuart squeezed her hand in return. "It's a common habit in older people with nothing else to think about. I got it from Dad. And Veronica talked about it before I started working with William. Whatever Lillian says about you, it's water off a duck's back to me."

Jayne leaned forward and kissed him. It was longer and held more passion than the kisses they'd shared before. Their adult relationship was developing differently to when they'd been hormone-engorged teenagers. Jayne was bringing the baggage of a long but ultimately unhappy marriage plus a mother she couldn't abandon. He was bringing naivety about the workings of adult romantic relationships and years of sitting on the side-lines watching life go by without him. Together they could make this work. The basis of their second-time-around partnership was becoming firm, concrete compared to the fickle feathers of their teenage years. Stuart savoured the unspoken mutual feelings behind this kiss.

When their lips separated, their hands remained joined and it took Stuart a couple of seconds to reorientate himself.

"Tell me about the retreat," he said. "How did you get on?"

"It was like stepping into a bubble of relaxation for twenty-four hours. Fruit and veg smoothies instead of the endless cups of tea that Mum wants. A choice of classes and guided meditations. Healthy meals and proper conversation at the dining table." She gazed into the middle-distance. "If I'm perfectly honest, I wanted to stay there forever. And then as soon as I got home, the weight of Mum and all the related issues landed back on my shoulders. I love her but I don't know whether I can cope with what is to come."

Stuart squeezed her hand. "I'll help you work it out."

Lillian had finished reading the plaques and was watching them with a smile on her lips.

"You two were always meant for each other. I tried to tell Jayne to wait for you when you went off to university. But, as usual, she wouldn't listen. All her friends were getting engaged and married and she wanted to do the same."

"Mum!"

Stuart squeezed her hand again. "We've talked about that, Lillian, and I understand what happened back then."

Lillian grunted and then led the way around the lake in her slow, steady pace. Stuart and Jayne followed, still holding hands.

The next step would be to take Jayne to bed. His heart missed a beat. How could he tell if Jayne wanted that as much as he did? As a teenager she'd had no inhibition about pointedly telling him she was on the pill. But that was in an atmosphere of curiosity, of not wanting to get left behind, of not wanting to be the only one who hadn't 'done it'. The only barrier back then had been finding a suitable place.

In the end he'd been able to take advantage of his father's regular Rotary nights and had taken Jayne back to his own bedroom. His dad had soon worked out what was going on but had diplomatically said nothing. He'd simply left a packet of condoms on Stuart's bed with a note telling him to pin that same note to his bedroom door when more supplies were needed. Jayne's pill confession meant Stuart didn't have to go through that embarrassment and he screwed the note up and threw it away. They'd both been virgins and, initially, teenage lust and excitement had been the driver for him. But gradually the physicality had come to mean something on an emotional level and he'd believed they were joined for the long term.

"Cup of tea?" Lillian was standing outside the park café. "My treat."

They sat at a table next to the window, overlooking the lake.

"What do you think happens to ducks when they get old?" Lillian said. "Do you think they need care? Or do they just drop dead and sink to the bottom? I've never seen a dead duck."

There was a silence as the burden of ageing, care and death hung in the air around them.

"I guess nature finds a way." Stuart reached across the table and patted Lillian's arm. "But you're not to worry. Jayne and I are here for you."

Jayne flashed him a grateful smile. He couldn't stop a grin spreading across his face.

"If you two are going to get married, do it sooner rather than later. I want to walk my daughter down the aisle!"

CHAPTER TWENTY-FIVE

Fortuitously, Lillian's weekly session at the day centre coincided with Jayne's birthday. Stuart found another of Veronica's carers who was willing to stand in for his lunchtime shift with William and he persuaded Jayne to take the day off work, instructing her to wear leggings or something similar plus trainers. She arrived on his doorstep buzzing with excitement.

"I can't wait to know what this is all about," she said as he led her into the kitchen and made coffee for them both. "Are we going walking?"

"No." He handed her an envelope.

"Curiouser and curiouser!" Instead of a traditional birthday card, Stuart had made a large cardboard ticket entitling the bearer to a *Mystery Trip with Lunch included*.

Twenty minutes later he opened the garage door and gestured inside. Mavis's bike was polished and ready with a gift-wrapped parcel balanced on the saddle. He thought he saw the beginning of a frown on his girlfriend's forehead but it disappeared before he could be sure. His heart sank a little. Jayne unwrapped the present to reveal a bright pink bike helmet. Then she looked at him hesitantly.

"Put it on. I'll adjust the strap for you." He fitted Jayne's helmet correctly, put on his own and shut the garage door behind them. "Ready?"

"No. Wait. This is lovely and everything." She paused and Stuart felt more excitement seep away. "I can't do this. I haven't been on a bike since we were together before. Since I was eighteen."

"You never forget."

"It's the traffic. I can't suddenly go off cycling in all the traffic. And my muscles aren't used to it. I won't be able to keep up."

He hadn't considered any of these obvious practicalities. His eye had been on the romance of recreating something that had been perfect nearly forty years ago. But still, he so wanted to do this cycling thing. He wanted her to remember how they had been and how they could be again. Cycling could become the shared interest that would bind them together. But Jayne was right. She needed to practise and build up to it.

"Let's take the car. If I take the wheels off I'll get both bikes in the back with the seat folded down."

"I'm sorry." Jayne took the helmet off and fingered her hair back into place. "Were you thinking of the quarry and my eighteenth?"

He nodded.

"Come here, you big softie." She held out her arms and pulled him close. Maybe the day could still turn out perfect.

He parked on the rough ground adjacent to the quarry and reassembled both bikes. It was a remote spot with few visitors, which was why they'd liked it as teenagers. Set amongst crags, it was filled with deathly cold, dangerous water. When the sun caught the dimpled surface it looked inviting, but people drowned there. Occasionally, for pure pleasure, black-suited divers tipped themselves into the depths from a small rowing boat, always in pairs. Perhaps for them, supermarket trolleys, rusty bicycles and old quarry machinery equated to a sort of treasure.

Stuart followed as Jayne wobbled her away along the footpath that circled the huge hole in the landscape. When they arrived back at the car she was smiling with achievement.

"Let's go round again," she said.

This time she was more confident and went a little faster. There was hope that with some gentle coaching she'd eventually be able to join him in 'proper' cycling.

Jayne gently laid her bike on the grass and reached her arms and body towards the sky. It was a pleasure to watch her; there was no trace of the poor posture that plagued most desk workers. Then she gave her legs a shake. "My muscles need a stretch after that." She placed her hands on the floor and raised her bottom into the air. It looked like a triangle with her hands, feet and bum creating the three corners, her leggings and close-fitting T-shirt creating a smooth edge to her limbs and back.

Stuart got down onto his hands and knees, curious about what Jayne got out of yoga — to him it seemed so gentle as to be a complete waste of time. She gave him an upside-down grin. Gingerly, Stuart straightened his legs and raised his bum. He immediately felt a stretch down the backs of his legs even though he was on his toes, with his heels refusing to go anywhere near the floor. He groaned and lay flat out on the grass.

Jayne laughed and came down onto her knees. "I'll show you how to do cat cow — that's easier." Still on all fours, she showed him how to alternately flex and round his back. This was more achievable. "Well done. Now we could—"

"Picnic time," he announced before she could suggest any more contortions and opened his panniers.

"Ooh! Chocolate cake and cider. My favourite."

"Plus candle. Minus matches and knife. But, because we are grown-ups, I also have a flask of tea and sandwiches."

As they ate, the few clouds that were hovering were scattered by the breeze and the full heat of the sun came through. They made pillows with their fleeces and laid back, eyes closed and holding hands. Their fingertips transmitted a constant Morse message of affection and contentment. It was a moment that should last forever.

"I didn't think I'd ever get this feeling again," Jayne whispered. "There's so few people who you can happily be silent with. I'm so glad you came back into my life, Stuart."

He squeezed her hand. "Likewise." He lifted her hand to his lips and kissed it.

"Coming out here without Mum is absolute luxury. Sometimes it feels like we're joined at the hip. I can't do anything without making sure Mum is being cared for or won't be left alone too long. Does that sound mean?"

"It doesn't sound mean at all. I've been there and done that. Don't beat yourself up for how you're feeling. Just enjoy today for what it is."

They were quiet again in the warmth of the sun until the muffled sound of Jayne's phone became urgent. With a grunt she sat up and fumbled in her pockets.

"Yes . . . no, not a problem. I'll be there in forty-five minutes."

Stuart sat up and waited for the explanation.

"It's Mum. She's agitated." Jayne's face was anxious and apologetic all at once. "They say she's suddenly realised it's my birthday and is insisting she needs to be with me. Nothing they can do is calming her down. Do you mind if we go?"

"It's fine. I'll sort the bikes out and get them loaded." It wasn't fine, everything had been going so well. But he hid his frustration as he bent over the bikes to remove their wheels and load them into the back of the car.

Jayne flapped around alternately apologising and expressing anxiety about Lillian.

"Pack the picnic stuff away." He didn't like the way she was hovering over him, as though she thought her close proximity could speed him up.

"There'll be other days out, I promise." She'd obviously sensed his disquiet but who was to say that those other days wouldn't be rudely interrupted as well?

He tried to stop his thoughts. He was being unfair. Lillian couldn't help getting old and Jayne loved her mother. It was just frustrating that, after all the years with Dad, he couldn't have a small window of freedom before starting over again with responsibilities.

As he put out his hand to release the handbrake, Jayne took hold of it and squeezed. "We will work out a way round all of this. We can still have romance. It might just need a bit of patience and pre-planning."

Stuart smiled at her. This wasn't Jayne's fault. It was circumstances. And, where there was a will, there was a way around or through circumstances. Together they'd find that way. "Let's not leave Lillian in a tizzy any longer."

"Mum's right. You are a good man, Stuart."

* * *

The next morning Lillian knocked on the door. She was apologising and handing him a plastic container of homemade ginger biscuits before she was even over the threshold.

"It's like there's two of me," she said. "One's an inconsiderate spoilt brat and the other's the normal me who has to put sticking plaster on the wounds caused by the brat. Hence the biscuits — a peace offering."

"Don't worry about it. There was no problem, honestly."

"There was." Her voice was tight and she busied herself with his kettle and teapot so he couldn't see her expression. Eventually she had no option but to turn round and bring two mugs to the table. Her face was desolate. "I ruined Jayne's birthday. And you'd gone to so much trouble."

"It doesn't matter. I misjudged it anyway. I don't think cycling's her thing."

"That's not the point. This morning, when she told me all that you'd done, her face and voice were bubbling. She was pleased that you cared so much. I wish I hadn't made you cut it short. I am so selfish."

"It really doesn't matter."

"It wouldn't matter if it was a one-off. But it's going to get worse. I can only talk about this when I'm feeling really in control. Like now. The minute the grey mist starts wrapping itself around my thoughts, I feel like a child demanding maternal affection, or in my case, Jayne's attention."

"Lillian, you don't have to tell me anything unless it's making you feel better."

The old lady took a biscuit, dunked it in her tea and ate it in silence before she spoke again. "Jayne wants to look after me at home as I deteriorate. Something to do with the fact that I looked after her gran and therefore she owes it to me. When that grey mist is anywhere around, I want her to do that too. I feel vulnerable and I want to stay with everything that I know, in my own house with my own things, with my daughter and the people I've known a long time . . ." she paused ". . . like you."

It was painful to hear the old lady try to make sense of what was happening to her. It must be even worse to be the person giving life to these words.

"When that grey mist lifts," she continued. "It feels like the dawn of a sunny day on holiday but with clouds on the horizon. I feel like me but I know that if I stay in my own home with Jayne caring for me, it will ruin her life and that of anyone she chooses to share it with." She stopped talking again and looked at him meaningfully. "In my slightly misty days, I appear normal, but inside I'm fighting to find the right thoughts. At those times I've probably asked you to help Jayne look after me. Now, with my head clear, I want to clarify exactly what I mean. I want you to help Jayne find a way to have me *cared for* either at home with carers or in a home. I want her to be free to live her life. Understand?"

Lillian's last word came out as a stern command. Stuart nodded. Understanding was one thing but persuading Jayne, without it looking as though he was doing so for selfish reasons, was another. "I understand but Jayne *wants* to care for you. She loves you. If I try to persuade her otherwise, it will look like my own selfishness talking, like I don't want to be involved in caring for you."

Lillian leaned across the table. "Who knew growing old was so difficult?"

CHAPTER TWENTY-SIX

The date of the next speakers' club meeting had crept up without Stuart noticing. Or maybe, subconsciously, he'd tried to wipe it from his mind. He drank his morning mule-kick coffee, looked at his pile of notes on the history of cycling and realised, with less than twelve hours until the meeting, he was about to see the truth of his Fail to Prepare, Prepare to Fail motto. Sick with apprehension, he typed up his script between visits to William. Phoning John at this late stage really would sound like he was making excuses and wouldn't help his ex-pupil demonstrate the success of the club on his CV.

He pulled into the Red Lion car park and took deep breaths. After this meeting he would tell John he couldn't come again. He took a seat on the back row. His fists were clenched, his armpits damp and his heartbeat had doubled in speed. No one else seemed to be going through the same anguish. His name was called. The walk to the gallows was painful. He positioned his notes on the sturdy wooden lectern, put on his glasses and started to read. He tried to pretend it was a school assembly but an audience of judgemental adults was far worse than disinterested teenagers.

His hands gripped the frame of wood surrounding his notes as though someone might snatch the whole contraption away from him and leave him exposed to the rows of staring faces. Stuart was aware that he was reading too quickly and not making eye contact.

He got halfway through before he ran out of breath and had to gasp like a surfacing diver. The fresh intake of air tickled his throat and suddenly he was coughing. He coughed and coughed until he almost retched. Someone pushed a glass of water at him and led him to a chair. His coughing was the only sound in the room and the meeting didn't resume until he'd got himself under control. Stuart wanted to die of shame.

"Well done, Stuart."

He looked round in surprise. It was the end of the meeting and he was trying to leave without speaking to anyone when John ambushed him.

"I loved your choice of language and the way you took us on a logical journey through time. That was a good speech structure. I'm really looking forward to hearing you speak again."

It was praise that Stuart didn't deserve or want, and he knew it was only to ensure he came back again to swell the club's numbers. A little seed of defiance started to glow in his chest. He'd tried to help John out. Twice. It was negatively affecting his own self-esteem and therefore he wouldn't do it again.

"Just a couple of points for improvement. Try to speak more slowly and practise talking around bullet points rather than reading from a script," John continued. "The additional benefit to that is you don't need as much material and you're less likely to trigger a coughing fit. I'll stick you on the programme again for the next meeting."

You did well, bro! He thinks you can do better. He wants to hear you speak again. Are we coming next month?

Stuart ignored Sandra, that seed of defiance had grown and he felt suddenly buoyed. His heart calmed and his hands stopped shaking. He wasn't going to be pushed into things that he had tried and discovered weren't for him.

"No, John. I won't be coming again. I don't enjoy public speaking and I have no need to practise the skill for my career or anything else. Thank you for the experience and I wish you well with the club and your job hunting." He held his hand out to his former pupil. "No hard feelings?"

John looked disappointed but he shook his hand. "No hard feelings. But if you ever change your mind . . ."

"I won't."

Wow, bro! You stood up for yourself. When was the last time that happened? You might not be a great orator but you've certainly grown in confidence.

* * *

Robert and George gave Stuart twenty-four hours' notice that they were coming to inspect the house.

"It's what landlords do. It's to protect you as well as us. It means when you move out there's no nasty surprises and we don't ask you to fix any damage done when Dad was still alive," Robert explained on the phone. "And you muttered something at the funeral about getting a lodger to help with the bills. At the time we were too emotional to think it through. We've thought now and we are disallowing lodgers. A lodger means additional wear and tear plus problems when we want them out so we can sell."

"Oh!" Implications were crashing around in Stuart's head like a busy day at the dodgems.

"We'll be there about ten tomorrow."

Florence was having a late, slow breakfast in the kitchen in her pink fluffy dressing gown. Her gig the previous evening had been further away than usual and she hadn't got back until the early hours. Stuart was tired too. He found it hard to sleep when he knew she was still out, consequently William had found his carer subdued this morning.

"Would you be able to make yourself scarce tomorrow?"

"Jayne again?" Mischief danced across her eyes.

"An inspection visit by my brothers. And they won't allow me to have a lodger."

"Oh!" Her expression switched to panic. "I don't want to ask Jim. It will give him too much satisfaction."

"I'm not throwing you out." He paused, surprised by how strongly he felt about not throwing her out. A few months ago he would've bowed immediately to his brothers' request but he'd changed since then. He wouldn't be trampled anymore. However, his transformation didn't stretch as far as having the guts to actually admit to having a lodger. "But I don't want them to find out about you."

Florence grasped the situation and glanced at her watch. "OK. We leave at six for tonight's gig. Until then I will clean this house until it sparkles and pack my stuff so that it can go in the loft — or will they look in there too?"

It was more likely that his brothers would investigate the loft for forgotten treasures rather than rootle through drawers and wardrobes in the spare room. "No need to pack, just clear away all visible evidence from the surfaces and strip your bed in the morning."

They both worked hard for the rest of the day, Stuart with the lawn mower, shears and spade, and Florence with a duster and mop. He wondered how she had the energy to put on a bright, professional face and perform when he was absolutely shattered.

"The audience gives me energy," she said, checking her makeup in the hall mirror before leaving. "Applause and hearing people singing along to our big numbers is pure adrenaline. There's nothing to beat it. That's why people love doing karaoke in pubs. I'm going to get you doing that one day, you're already part way there. I heard you humming over the cooking the other day."

"If I ever do karaoke, you'll have to do something very major, like putting yourself up as a candidate for the local council."

"As if they'd elect an empty air-head like me." With that she was gone.

The next day Florence was up at seven, looking as though she could do with another couple of hours sleep. Stuart was on his way out to see to William.

"I'll be gone before you get back," she said. "Make sure you open all the windows so there's no lingering smells of my perfume or Tibby's accidents. I'll take her with me and put Slowcoach in his box in the garden."

Despite Tibby's mastery of the cat flap, she still had a tendency to prefer dark corners of the house as her toilet. Florence put it down to some trauma from her life with Shirley and Stuart didn't have the heart to refuse the cat a home for Florence's sake. His lodger still had very many down days when she dwelt on her bad mothering and why Shirley had ended up as she had.

When Robert and George arrived with their wives, they sat in the kitchen with coffee and biscuits.

"We're not trying to push you out early," Robert said. "We promised you a year and a year is what you'll get. But we want to be able to hit the ground running with estate agents and house viewings. We don't want any last minute, nasty surprises."

"It's a bit chilly in here," Theresa interrupted, "with all the windows open. Do you mind if I close them?" She was already on her feet and reaching over the sink to pull the biggest one closed.

Cindy glanced at Stuart. There was no choice but to nod his agreement and Cindy, the taller of his two sisters-in-law, stretched to close the smaller, higher windows.

After a couple of minutes Theresa frowned and flared her nostrils. "Can I smell cat wee?"

Stuart's brain raced to find an excuse. "There's been a stray hanging around. Big fat ginger thing. If I'm out in the garden and forget to close the door it's straight in here."

"You'll have to do something about that," George said. "Those sorts of smells get deep into the carpet and are a bugger to get rid of."

"Let's start the tour." Robert stood up. "Upstairs first."

He took the lead with Stuart bringing up the rear. As they went past the hall mirror, Stuart was the only one who noticed the folded piece of paper tucked just behind one corner of the glass. He snatched it out and unfolded it.

So sorry, I hope you see this note in time to do something about it. When I tried to get Tibby into the basket she scarpered under my bed and I couldn't get her out. Perhaps you can say she's a stray that's jumped in through an open window? I closed the bedroom door to keep her in there — don't want you having to search the house for her. Florence XX

She'd drawn a cat smiley face alongside the kisses. Kisses? He smiled. And then he realised Florence would put those on a note to anyone.

"I've never really looked properly before," Theresa was saying, "but this bathroom is out of the ark. And that airing cupboard takes up so much space."

"*In need of modernisation* in estate-agent speak," George said.

"It'll fetch far less than properties in the area that don't have 'old person lived here' stamped all over them." Robert opened the small, mirrored cabinet.

Stuart's brain panicked and went into recall mode. Had Florence ever put anything in there? He was pretty sure not. Despite his protestations, she liked to litter the side of the bath and the windowsill with her lotions and potions so they were all, 'where I want them, when I want them'.

The cabinet was closed without comment.

"Two toothbrushes?" Theresa pointed at the glass that served as a toothbrush holder. "Have you got a lady friend staying over? My, you're a dark horse, Stuart." She winked at him and gave a sly grin.

Now he dithered. Should he let them think he was sleeping with someone or should he pretend they were both his?

"More power to your elbow, eh?" Robert gave him a nudge that missed its target and hit him painfully in the chest.

"You seem to forget that Stuart is entitled to a private life." Cindy was gesturing them all out of the bathroom. "Give him some privacy."

They gave Stuart's room only a cursory glance and then moved to their father's old room. The door was closed and no one stepped forward to open it. Stuart hoped they might give it a miss. He prayed that Tibby was still under the bed and would stay there.

"It's got to be done." Theresa stepped forward and put a hand on the door knob.

"I distributed his better clothes to charity shops and binned the rest." He wanted to prepare them for the room looking different. "And of course all the medical equipment got taken away. It's like a normal bedroom now."

There was a vague shuffling of feet as though no one wanted to go into this room associated with sickness and death. Then Theresa opened the door and strode in.

"Oh!"

Everyone followed her gaze towards the bed. It was stripped apart from a plain white, padded mattress protector and a black, grey and white tabby cat.

"Shoo!" Theresa said sharply.

"It's a rum do if a stray cat is getting all the way upstairs and through a closed door."

"That's what you get if you leave windows open."

"I thought you said the stray was a ginger tom."

Tibby was looking at Stuart, as though waiting for him to issue an explanation that would put the world to rights and stop these people staring at him.

"It is. This must be another one. Perhaps the ginger one told its friends to come." He tried to make it sound like a joke, but it came out like something a child would say. Then Stuart caught sight of the pink fluffy dressing gown hanging behind the door.

CHAPTER TWENTY-SEVEN

Stuart moved and leaned against the door so it opened flush with the wall, hiding the dressing gown.

Robert clapped his hands sharply in Tibby's direction.

"Out!" George shouted at the cat.

Tibby got the message. She stood up, stretched her forelegs and jumped off the bed. Then the cat paused and looked around at her audience. Robert bent and clapped loudly again next to Tibby's ear. "That will teach it not to come in again."

Tibby hissed but stood her ground.

"It's made our house stink and it's no right to be here." George made a move towards her.

Stuart could feel the cat's confusion and fear. He pushed past his brothers and picked her up. "It's OK, I'll put her outside."

"And you need to put measures in place to make sure it doesn't come back."

Tibby was starting to struggle in Stuart's arms. He whispered in her ear to calm her. "Hey, Tibs, relax. No one's going to hurt you while I'm here."

"Did you just call that cat, Tibs?" Theresa was closer to him than he'd realised.

Stuart closed his eyes and allowed his eyeballs to roll heavenward.

"It's not a stray, is it? It's your cat." His sister-in-law sounded triumphant. "I thought it looked too comfortable and at home on the bed."

Tibby added claws to her wriggling-to-escape movement. Taken by surprise, Stuart dropped her and she raced ahead of them down the stairs and into the kitchen. She pawed at the large box Stuart had put against the back door to hide the cat flap. There was no point pretending anymore. He pulled the box to one side and Tibby clattered through the flap. Stuart remained next to the grey plastic cat door and faced his brothers. He tried to make himself tall. He thought of Florence and her motherless grandchildren. In his imagination they were pale little waifs with ridiculously low life chances. He had to shield their pet from harm. He took a breath and tried to puff out his chest. If he could attempt to speak in front of a full audience at speakers' club, he could speak up for himself now.

"We can't allow you to keep pets or carry out unauthorised enhancements." Robert emphasised the last word as though Stuart had built a huge conservatory without planning permission. "The cat must go."

"You have seven days," George added. "And we will be checking up on you."

Stuart took another breath. This was a crossroads in how he let himself be treated by the rest of his family. He could tell Florence to find a new home for Tibby and break her heart and the hearts of her grandchildren. Or, he could stand up for his rights to live in this house in any manner he chose.

He'd never before stood up to Robert and George. They were years older than him, they had life experience; as he'd come up to each stage in life, they'd both been through it before and therefore had always known better. His father had always backed up his elder sons on this. It was taken as read in the family that George and Robert knew best and would make the decisions.

"We're going above and beyond by letting you have a rent-free year here." Robert's voice broke into his dithering. "That agreement does not allow pets."

Cindy was looking uncomfortable. Stuart held out half a hope that she might stand up for him but she glanced at Robert and then remained silent. Theresa was nodding in agreement at everything the two men said.

"That agreement makes no *mention* of pets." Stuart tried to keep his voice as level as Robert's and spoke slowly. As far as he could remember, the agreement also contained no mention of lodgers but he wasn't going to bring Florence out into the open unless forced. "Allowed or disallowed."

The men exchanged a shrug. The lack of an immediate response gave Stuart the confidence to continue arguing his position.

"I don't think the agreement mentioned *inspection* visits either. So you are only here because I've given you permission. My patience has run out and therefore it's time for you to leave." He moved towards his brothers, making flapping gestures with his hands to shoo them into the hall and in the direction of the front door.

Robert started to move and then stopped, turning to face his youngest brother. "You are getting away with this on a technicality. As you well know, that agreement was drawn up in a rush and therefore doesn't contain all the clauses of a usual rental agreement. But you do have a responsibility to leave this house in excellent condition."

Stuart raised his hands. "Oh! I'd totally overlooked the excellent décor, wonderful bathroom and up-to-the-minute kitchen."

Robert narrowed his eyes. "Don't kill me with sarcasm, kiddo."

Cindy's eyes sought his, saying, *I'm sorry*.

George said, "I think the worm is trying to turn."

Stuart's fists clenched — he wanted to lash out at his brothers. But they were gone. As their cars revved over the gravel he thumped, hard, on the inside of the front door until his fists hurt.

* * *

"He was spot on, wasn't he, your big brother?" Florence beamed at him. "The worm is turning and I'm so proud of you! And Tibby's proud of you for not buckling under pressure and making her homeless."

Stuart held back from admitting that he'd stood up for himself more for the sakes of Florence and her grandchildren than Tibby herself. "It didn't help my cool composure when I spotted your dressing gown behind the door."

"Ah! But you proved yourself on that score too. Now, I can't sit here all evening massaging your burgeoning ego. My public beckons."

Triumphing over his brothers had left Stuart buzzing and feeling he could move mountains. He spotted Slowcoach making his way across the lawn. If there were diamonds, and if there was a safe way of retrieving those diamonds, that would elevate him further in Florence's eyes. He brought the tortoise inside, fetched his father's old magnifying glass and tried to spot if there was an extra ridge along the edge of Slowcoach's shell, indicating a false layer. Nothing. He ran his finger around the edge of the shell, trying to find a place where a second shell might not fit quite so snugly and a gap could be felt. Nothing. He wondered if the diamonds would show up on an x-ray or ultrasound. Sure that a solution would come to him, he spread newspaper over the lounge floor and contemplated Slowcoach. He searched the internet. Nothing about diamond smuggling using tortoises. He wondered if Jayne had been winding him up and he'd fallen straight into a gullibility hole. He didn't think she'd do something like that but he wasn't yet brilliant at reading people. The day's confidence began to leak away.

It doesn't take much, does it? One little setback and you start to feel unworthy again. Man up! You've ousted Audi man, so why would she wind you up?

"Virtually the whole of my adult life has been spent in a siding and now I'm trying to play with the express trains on their terms. Terms they've been practising and nuancing for years. Is it surprising my confidence ebbs and flows?"

All the more reason why you have to be single-minded and focused.

His sister was right. If he let doubts take over his mind, he'd never build himself a future.

Phone Jayne and check the veracity of the diamond story. Imagine the embarrassment if it isn't true and you turn up at the vet's asking for an x-ray, or, even worse, try to remove the shell yourself. Florence will not be pleased.

He phoned Jayne, ready to laugh it off if she'd been winding him up.

"Of course it's true!" Her excitement cascaded through the words. "Perhaps we could keep a diamond or two before telling Florence? Think what a difference that would make to our future together."

"No. We don't do anything without Florence's full knowledge."

"Relax! I was joking." There was a pause. "I'd come round and help you but Mum's in one of her anxious moods tonight. She's frightened about the future. Her future, my future, our future. She's pulling me down but I can't leave her."

"Would it help if I came to you?"

"I don't think so. Not unless you want to try a bit of meditation after I've settled Mum?" There was a note of hope in Jayne's voice. "I've just downloaded an app which teaches mindfulness and meditation. I'm hoping it will shut down all those chattering worry voices in my head. A bit like on the yoga retreat."

Stuart took a breath. He hated turning her down but all that sort of stuff made no sense at all to him. He'd had too many years of living inside his own head.

"If I can master it, I might try it on Mum," Jayne continued.

Stuart made what he hoped was an encouraging noise.

"Speak tomorrow."

He continued to watch Slowcoach late into the night. He looked at him from all angles, trying to detect something in the animal's gait that might indicate an ill-fitting shell or uneven distribution of weight. He tapped gently on various parts of the shell, trying to decipher, from the sound, anything unusual. He asked the tortoise out loud if he'd packed his own shell and did it contain any prohibited substances. The slow blink of the black eyes said, *that's for me to know and you to find out*.

He was sitting in the semi-darkness of just one standard lamp when Florence's key turned in the lock. In the hall she hummed quietly to herself.

"Oh!" She put her hand on her heart when he emerged from the gloom. "I thought you'd be in bed." She paused, peering over his shoulder. "Is that Slowcoach on the newspaper in there?"

Stuart nodded.

"Why is he in here? Is he ill?"

"No, there's something I need to tell you. Something that could change your future." He led her into the lounge and she sat down. "There might be diamonds under his shell."

"Diamonds?"

Stuart told her the story. "I think we should investigate further," he finished.

"No! You're talking about maiming or killing Slowcoach on the basis of some cock-and-bull story that might not be true."

"We could talk to the vet."

"Vets don't come cheap! And how would we convert these uncut diamonds to money without admitting they were smuggled? My family, and Jacob's in South Africa, would be investigated for criminal connections. We could end up in prison ourselves."

"There must be a way." He remembered Sandra's advice to stay focused if he wanted to achieve anything.

"No! And I'm not leaving Slowcoach with you."

She went out to the garage and fetched the tortoise's cardboard box, laid him gently on the straw and took him up to her bedroom. Her door closed with a thump.

* * *

The next morning, when Stuart got back from his breakfast visit to William, Florence was loading up the faded orange Panda.

"You can keep Tibby for the time being," she said. "Just until I get myself somewhere proper to live. But I've got Slowcoach. My rent's paid up until the end of the week, I haven't given you any notice so I won't be asking for that money back."

"Where are you going?"

"Somewhere life, in all its forms, is valued and they don't prise shells off tortoises." She slammed the car door and then rolled down the window to continue talking. "This won't just harm Slowcoach. It would tear my grandchildren's lives to shreds if Jacob was arrested for diamond smuggling. I can't let them lose two parents in quick succession." Then she revved the engine too much and scattered tiny pieces of gravel in her wake.

Stuart slumped on the sofa. It didn't make sense that Florence had left. She must realise that he would never pursue the diamond thing without her permission. He put his head in his hands. He felt inexplicably empty.

CHAPTER TWENTY-EIGHT

William spotted something was wrong straight away. "You've got a face like the little boy Santa forgot."

"Soup for lunch?" Stuart suggested lightly. "There's chicken or tomato in the cupboard. I'm no good at croutons but I could do you some toast to dip in?"

"Which woman is it that's causing you grief?"

"I'll make the soup decision for you. Chicken with thick buttered toast coming right up."

"When a man is wearing your expression, it's always woman trouble."

In the kitchen Stuart employed the tin opener aggressively and the soup responded in the same manner, spraying itself up the front of his T-shirt.

Less anger, more accomplished!

"Stop making up your own stupid sayings! It should be less haste, more speed."

Oooh! Somebody's got a beef on.

"No, I haven't." The soup was beginning to spit in the microwave and he'd forgotten to cover it with a plate. Now he'd have to wipe the thing out before he left.

Something has seesawed your equilibrium. Maybe you should try Jayne's meditation.

"There's nothing wrong with my equilibrium." He tried to take the bowl out of the microwave with his bare hands, burned the ends of his fingers and reached for the tea towel to use as an oven glove.

You've forgotten to press the toaster down.

Stuart left the soup and did the toast. Focus. Focus. Focus. Finally, Stuart got the tray of food in front of his client.

"Who were you talking to?"

"What?" Shit, now William was going to think he was a madman ready for a straitjacket.

"In the kitchen."

"Oh — on the mobile. I just had a call on my mobile."

"As usual, your mobile's over there on top of your jacket. It was there the whole time that you were in the kitchen."

"Eat the soup before it gets cold."

For the first few mouthfuls they sat in silence and then William started up again. "I've said it before: part of the service you provide is companionship and conversation. You're not supposed to stare at me as though you want to pick the bowl up and pour the soup down my throat, so you can go home and spend the rest of the day muttering to yourself behind closed doors."

Stuart pursed his lips, looked down at his hands and said nothing.

"I want you to answer me two things. Why are you so miserable and who were you talking to in the kitchen?"

Answering either of William's questions would show Stuart in his true colours: a loser and a madman. He didn't know why he was miserable. His finances were going to take a hit from Florence's departure but he could get another lodger. One that agreed to pay the full amount of rent rather than bartering with cleaning services. One that didn't require him to undergo a personality transplant in order to 'loosen up'. People lost lodgers all the time. It was a form of rejection, which was why it had made him feel down, but, in the grand scheme of his bright future, it was a minor, financial irritant not a grand finale.

"I'm still waiting?" William was wiping the last part of his toast around the soup bowl, soaking up the dregs of the light brown liquid.

"I'm not miserable. I've just got the hassle of finding a new lodger. Florence moved on." His voice stayed level. Nothing wrong with his equilibrium.

"Why?"

Mind your own business. "Circumstances. Things have been traumatic for her."

"Won't be easy for her to find somewhere else that's cheap and will take animals."

"She's left Tibby with me. Until she gets sorted."

The old man nodded slowly, weighing Stuart's words but not commenting.

"Battenberg and a cup of tea?" Stuart took the now clean bowl, anxious to move the meal on and get out of there.

"Please. And," he paused and gave Stuart a wink. "Why not leave a second piece of cake on the table here with my flask for this afternoon?"

"I shouldn't but I will." Stuart relaxed a little. The old man seemed happy with his explanation and had forgotten about his second question.

As he boiled the kettle and made tea for them both, plus some for later in William's flask, he thought up a football conversation opener to do with the change of manager at City, William's team.

"You didn't talk to yourself this time?" William was in there before Stuart could put the tea tray down and frame his own question.

"I don't talk to myself."

"So who do you talk to when sound comes out of your mouth but there's no one else in the room?"

To reveal my identity or not? That is the question.

Manners, and the small matter of being desperate to keep this job now that his rental income had gone, meant Stuart couldn't ignore William's question. His brain struggled. Sandra's voice had been with him ever since he questioned the photograph. His dead sister had kept him company through the long years of caring. Most of the time she'd been a comfort. Since Dad died, she'd changed, become cheekier, more sarcastic, more 'in your face', as they'd say on the TV. Like him, she used to be grey and reserved. Unlike him, she'd now become alive and colourful.

William was peeling the marzipan from around the edges of the cake and eating it separately. "It's the first sign of madness," he said, taking a small breather between marzipan and sponge. "Like growing hair on the back of your hands."

Stuart spread his right hand in front of him and looked down.

"That's the second sign." William broke off a pink square of sponge and ate it before speaking again. "You'll feel better with it off your chest."

The old man would probably drum him out of town but he'd asked for the truth and Stuart couldn't think of any other plausible explanation.

"My twin sister died a few days after birth. Her name was Sandra."

A proper name check, I like it. First time any family outsider has been told about me for years. This is almost my fifteen minutes of fame.

"When I was young there was always a photo of her on the mantelpiece. People would say, 'Such a shame about pretty little Sandra. I bet you would've loved to have a girl in the family after all these boys?' Mum and Dad would always agree and look sad. When pushed, even Robert and George would agree that a sweet little sister would've been better than a pesky kid brother who was always after their attention and wanting a sparring partner or a football opponent. Nobody ever thought about the effect this talk would have on me."

Stuart paused, waiting for some sympathetic reaction from the old man to let him off the hook of further explanation. William maintained a neutral but interested expression. Stuart was obliged to fill the silence.

"At first I didn't understand the connection between Sandra and me. Then, when I was about five, I asked Mum about the picture of the two babies, one in a pink babygrow and the other in blue. She explained that I was the baby in blue and that Sandra, in pink, was my twin sister. Sandra had been too good for this earth and now lived with the angels in heaven but everybody missed her and wished she was still here. The brains of small boys don't work well. I interpreted all of this to mean that I was second best. My parents had wanted a girl, not another boy. Sandra had been the good one, too good to live and therefore I was the bad one, left to live in a family that didn't really want me."

William's expression didn't change but he stopped his demolition of the Battenberg. One pink and one yellow square still remained on his plate, glued together with a thin layer of red jam.

"I tried to live my life well enough for two twins, a boy and a girl. That's probably why I ended up caring for Dad instead of pushing Robert and George to pay for professional carers. I had to prove my worth to the family."

"Whatever you did could never replace the only girl in the family, who was put on a pedestal, idolised by all and endowed with perfection." William had folded his arms and spoke slowly. He looked like an underweight but wise old sage with wispy hair.

And I thoroughly deserve those accolades. Do I not? Stuart ignored her.

"It was a long time before I became aware that was what I was doing. It was near the end of Dad's life. Lillian, next door said something to me, and a lightbulb went on. Shortly afterwards, Dad died and Sandra's personality changed."

"Your dead sister's personality changed? She's the one you talk to?"

"Yes and yes." It was getting increasingly difficult to put things into words. Stuart didn't fully understand what went on in the far corners of his mind. "She started off as an imaginary friend, like most children have, but mine had some foundation in reality. Unlike most children, my imaginary friend didn't go away. Plus, talking to Sandra was one thing

I could do to please my mother." Stuart paused. "And Sandra was a crutch to me when Mum died. Then, as a teenager she was my sounding board. Especially when girls were a mystery and I needed to work out how to ask a girl on a date or how to move in to kiss her. Then when I was caring for Dad, I was isolated. He was often asleep. Talking to Sandra was my way of coping and letting off steam. Some days she probably saved our father from physical violence."

"How did she change?"

Stuart became aware of a growing feeling of lightness as he talked. When said out loud, his secrets became less dark and less threatening. "She stopped being a goody-goody and became more combative. More argumentative. As though she's fed up with me and how I behave. She's trying to push me towards a brighter future. And she thinks she knows me better than I know myself. Which is annoying."

William appeared to contemplate this statement. Stuart's hour was almost up and he wanted to leave. He wanted to escape to the comfortable greyness at home. The argument with Florence, her departure this morning, baring his soul to William; he was exhausted.

"Have you finished with your mug and plate?" The quicker he got cleared away, the quicker he could sink back into his invisibility.

Only you'll never be able to do that again, will you? Not now you've had a tiny taste of what life in the outside world is all about. Now that Florence and Jayne have opened your eyes to what goes on beyond your own four walls. Now that you've started to stand up for yourself a little bit. Now that you've been put on the rota to lead club rides.

"Sandra exists only in your imagination."

"Yes."

"So, if Sandra's changed, doesn't that mean that, actually, it's you that's changed?"

Stuart frowned. Cold logic meant, yes, it must be him that had changed. But inside he still felt the same. He wasn't a burgeoning butterfly about to break into a beautiful flight. He was still a nondescript caterpillar shuffling along.

"There's no other explanation, is there?" William persisted. "Maybe through the Sandra of your mind, you can better articulate your desires." He popped the last pink square of Battenberg into his mouth and Stuart escaped.

* * *

At home Sandra was silent. Usually he only had to call her to mind and there she was. Now, without her, he was completely alone. He felt uneasy. He paced the house unable to settle, he looked at his watch and decided he could just catch the club's Retired Afternoon ride.

"Stuart! How's your girlfriend enjoying the bike?" Mike was grinning expectantly. "Mavis would be pleased to know it's gone to a good home."

"It's good. All good. She just needs a bit of practice with the traffic and that." It was a white lie. After Mike had given him the bike for free, he couldn't say that Jayne had shown no further interest in cycling.

"Bring her along to the Sunday ride one week."

"That's difficult. She's got her mother to consider."

"What a shame. Just as you find freedom, a different lock clicks closed."

Stuart was relieved to see the front of the group begin to move off and no further comment was necessary as they all followed, negotiated the roundabout onto the main road and settled into place. Everyone else on this ride was at least ten years older than him and the pace and terrain was sedate rather than physically challenging. They left town and followed B roads, riding past golden fields, muddy entrances to farms and through the shade provided by overhanging trees. Stuart's thoughts calmed as nature rather than urban clamour surrounded him. Eventually the road started to run parallel with a river. The slow steady speed meant there was time to admire the swans with their half-grown fluffy grey cygnets. Then the water disappeared and the verge was filled with smell of wild garlic. In the distance were the formal gardens of the local stately home. Stuart could just make out the shape of the lake and the clusters of ancient oaks.

He made a mental note to have another go at persuading Jayne back onto the bike. On these quiet roads she'd be able to find her cycling legs. And she'd enjoy the way fresh air generated an inner peace without any conscious effort to meditate or stand on your head or whatever mindfulness thing it was that Jayne swore by.

"Hare! To the right." The call rippled through the group and Stuart caught sight of a giant-sized rabbit lolloping across a field. At first it seemed intent on a destination in the far corner and then it swerved to retrace its path before changing course again and disappearing beneath a hedge. Stuart wondered at the creature's apparent indecision. He'd thought humans were the only ones unable to steer a direct course towards what was best for them.

At the end of the ride, Mike said that he'd tell Mavis her bike was being put to good use.

"How will you do that?"

"Her presence is still in the house. I feel it."

"Like a ghost?"

"No. Just a presence. I can talk to her. Ask her advice." Mike's eyes dropped to his handlebars. "Now I sound like a madman."

"No, you don't. I still talk to my sister and she's been dead fifty-five years."

Mike lifted his head and met Stuart's gaze with a smile. "Mavis helped me sort out the programmes on the washing machine and I swear she reminds me about our children's birthdays."

"Sandra is intent on mapping out my future. But she doesn't always get hold of the right end of the stick."

Mike laughed and clapped him on the back affectionately. "Thank you. You've made me feel normal for the first time since Mavis died."

Stuart grinned. He was still feeling warm inside when he got home and the house didn't seem quite so forlorn. Later,

Jayne phoned. Lillian was better today and it was a *Vera* night — she could come round, if he liked. Yes, he definitely liked.

"It's different here," Jayne said, as soon as she was in the lounge. "Something's changed."

"Perhaps I've moved a cushion or straightened a picture."

"No, it's something in the atmosphere. Is Florence in?"

"No."

"Those fluffy slippers with the dogs' heads weren't by the door. Are you sure she isn't upstairs?"

"She's not here." He looked at his feet. It was no big deal that a lodger had decided to move out.

"She's gone, hasn't she? Moved out." Jayne's smile filled the whole of her face and then she wiped it away. "Why didn't you tell me?"

"Didn't have chance. She only told me this morning and then went."

Jayne clasped both his hands. "So from now on we have the place to ourselves?"

"Unless I advertise for someone else."

"Don't." Jayne's grin returned, the tiny laughter lines around her eyes crinkling. "It feels like we're teenagers again with one set of parents away. It's awkward at mine because of Mum and it was awkward here because of Florence. But now it's just you and me. Wine and romance for the next . . ." Jayne looked at her watch. "Almost two hours. You have got wine in the fridge, haven't you?"

She was looking at him expectantly, her eyes playful and a coy smile on her lips. Suddenly the message got through. Jayne hadn't lost any of her forwardness. The loss of his lodger flew from his mind and nerves rushed in. His hand trembled as he poured the wine and there was a clink as the bottle nudged the glass. He breathed and raised the bottle a little higher. His heart was pounding. Something in the way Jayne looked at him had taken him back nearly forty years to the night they'd both lost their virginity.

He placed two glasses of chilled white wine on the coffee table. He'd have liked them to be in a posh hotel with coasters and little bowls of nuts. Instead, this shabby piece of wood, which bore the marks of hundreds of coaster-less coffee mugs from down the years, would have to do.

Jayne took a sip of wine. "I'm assuming you feel the same as me." Her eyes were teasing and questioning.

What was the right answer? Was it a trick? Could he phone a friend? Did he have a friend? "Yes. Probably."

"I don't want to risk things on 'probably'."

"Definitely." He hoped he was gauging her correctly. She was wearing jeans and a floppy blouse but he remembered the smooth shape of her body in the leggings as she showed him the yoga moves by the quarry. Definitely, the answer was definitely.

She looked at him and smiled. If this was an old film, Stuart would move both their glasses out of the way. Then he'd lean over and kiss her on the lips. A long, slow kiss, building with urgency. Their bodies would press closer and their hands begin to explore. Then the camera would pan out and away. If this was a recent film, they'd tear each other's clothes off and be at it like rabbits on the sofa. Stuart preferred the old-fashioned way.

Jayne looked at him over the rim of her glass. "I feel we're still those naive teenagers, wondering how, when, what it will be like. Desperate for the opportunity but scared to death as well."

He took her hand, grateful for her honesty. Her expression was the same as four decades earlier when they'd finally got the space and privacy. Vulnerable.

"I . . ." He wanted to tell her that he felt worse now than back then. Back then he'd known he'd been the first and she'd had no comparison. Now she had the experience and he had nothing. "It's a long time since I . . ."

"I thought it probably was." She smiled and looked as though he'd just bolstered her confidence by making himself more vulnerable. "It's a while for me too but it's supposed to be like riding a bike."

"I'm good at that — shall I get the Lycra out?" It was a feeble joke but they both laughed and the atmosphere eased. He finished his wine in two gulps.

"Do you need another? Dutch courage?" she asked.

"No. I need to remember the moves in case I ever need to do it again." These pathetic attempts at humour were coming without conscious thought.

Jayne led the way upstairs. Stuart wished he'd changed the bed and tidied up. That hotel of his imagination would've had a four-poster and a roaring fire and a deluxe ensuite. Instead they were in a tired brown room with a heap of clothes on the only chair and dust on top of the chest of drawers.

They kissed for a long time standing up before he felt Jayne's hands on his shirt buttons. He reciprocated until they were both in their underwear. Her black bra and pants were trimmed with scarlet ribbon. He remembered Florence's large pants hanging on the shower screen. Did Jayne always dress like this or was it for his benefit, in case the opportunity should arise? Despite her slim build she had more curves than the skinny teenager who'd captured his heart before. Curves were good.

Hardly able to breathe and with great desire, he started to touch her. She gave a little moan as his fingers found their way inside her bra. She was right. It was like riding a bike. It was like the exhilarating downhill freewheel when the senses were open to input from all sides. And, like cycling, the sex left him satisfied. Very satisfied indeed.

It was Jayne who remembered first. She sat bolt upright and looked at her watch. "*Vera* finished fifteen minutes ago."

They both leaped out of bed and for a second looked embarrassed at their nakedness. Then they were scrabbling for their discarded clothes.

"I'll come with you." He didn't want her to have to cope with anything alone ever again.

When they opened Stuart's front door, Lillian was standing like a pale ghost on the gravel. Her figure visible from the light of the streetlamp. She had bare feet. Stuart put his shoes on and then carefully lifted Lillian's feet, one foot at a time, into his slippers while Jayne helped her to keep her balance.

"You said you'd be here," Lillian said. "I came to tell you, I've made cocoa for all three of us."

"That's good, Mum."

In the kitchen they found three mugs, each half full of lukewarm brown liquid and a trail of cocoa powder and milk spills along the surfaces. Jayne cleared up and Stuart made fresh cocoa.

"I hope you two get married," Lillian said as the three of them sat on the lounge sofa sipping their rich chocolatey drinks. "I'm going to be quite a burden to Jayne on her own."

"We'll manage, we're a team now." Jayne put down her drink and placed her left arm around her mother's shoulders and used her right to squeeze Stuart's hand. He squeezed back. The future was suddenly looking bright enough for sunglasses.

CHAPTER TWENTY-NINE

After that, Stuart and Jayne saw each other every evening. Sometimes she brought Lillian round too and Stuart cooked for them all.

"She's so much better when all three of us are together," Jayne said. "It helps that she's known you for such a long time. She's not good with strangers anymore. The day centre suits her because there's a couple of ladies there she was at school with, but one day a week isn't enough. I'm going to have to get someone to pop in once a day when I'm at work. I leave her lunch ready, but sometimes she forgets about it or eats something completely inappropriate — yesterday it was a full packet of digestives."

Even though it wasn't a question, Jayne seemed to be looking towards him for the solution. Stuart opened his mouth to offer to help. He had the time and it wouldn't be much effort.

Stop! Remember what Lillian said about wanting you to help Jayne find a care provider and not to sacrifice your own lives at her expense. Is offering your help the right thing to do? Wouldn't Lillian want you to suggest a better solution?

Since his conversation with William, Sandra's voice had changed again. It had become less strident and less sarcastic. It was moving towards his own way of speaking and thinking.

"That's a good idea. Getting a carer."

Jayne frowned. "But Mum won't like a stranger in the house."

"It would only be a stranger the first time."

"I'll give it a bit longer and see how she gets on. But if you get a minute after William's lunchtime visit . . ."

"As you say, let's see how it goes." Being noncommittal was a struggle. He wanted to say 'yes' to see the relief on Jayne's face, plus it was silly to pay for a carer when he was only next door. And, with no Florence bubbling brightly around the house during the day, he'd be glad of the distraction. The flatness of the house without her still dismayed him each time he returned from William's. He kept hoping she'd reappear but she'd not even responded to his texted requests for a forwarding address.

There was a charity shop near William's house and, one morning, when Stuart was getting back in his car after a breakfast visit, he noticed a woman trundling a basket of DVDs out onto the pavement in the early autumn sunshine. She saw him looking.

"Not a fan of *Vera* are you? We've just had a donation of what must be every episode ever made. They're not easy to shift now that everyone's got Netflix."

"I'll take them all."

When he presented the pile of plastic cases to the old lady, Jayne caught his eye, a half-suppressed smile playing around her lips. She'd got the message. They developed a regular routine of Jayne settling her mother down with a DVD in the early evening and then scooting over to Stuart's. They set an alarm for just under two hours later to avoid a repeat of the bare-feet-on-gravel episode.

"I feel guilty," Jayne said on the third evening. "Gradually she's going to get worse. She'll be able to do less and less. By sitting her in front of the TV, I'm wasting what quality time she has left. Surely I should be doing something more stimulating with her?"

There was a frown line across his girlfriend's forehead and anguish in her eyes. Stuart didn't know whether to reassure her or suggest they both go and attempt a game of cards with Lillian. He kept remembering the earnest way Lillian had spoken to him about not wanting to destroy her daughter's life.

"It's not my decision, but Lillian came to talk to me the day after your birthday. She was emphatic that she didn't want her condition to destroy your life."

"Are you sure?"

He nodded and a little bit of the fun came back into Jayne's expression.

After that, Stuart always made sure that his bedroom was clean, bought flowers for the chest of drawers and a bright new duvet cover. He invested in new boxers and threw out the old threadbare pairs. There was always wine in the fridge and sometimes chocolates too. They didn't always have sex. Sometimes they just cuddled, talked and enjoyed being cosy together. The evenings were starting to get darker and it was good to be able to close the curtains on the world. Everything was more comfortable now that physical barrier between them had been demolished.

Life took on a steady routine of Jayne and Lillian and William and cycling, spoiled only by the absence of Florence's brightness. Stuart wanted to ask Jayne's advice on how to tell Florence that she would be welcome if she wanted to return but, even in his gaucheness, he realised it might not be an appropriate question to ask his girlfriend.

* * *

One evening Jayne filled in some of the gaps of her past.

"For most of the time my marriage was OK," Jayne told him. "It was never a passion to set the world on fire but we were both ready to tie the knot at the same time. It was what a lot of our group that didn't go away to university did."

She paused just long enough for Stuart to feel relieved that Carl had been no stud and then to pick up the reproach directed at him.

"I always planned to come back here. I needed a degree to make a good life for us. I did come back. But you didn't wait."

Attaboy! Don't let her put all the blame on you.

Jayne gave a wave of her hand. "We've already talked about why I didn't wait. It's water under the bridge now. After a few years of trying, Carl and I realised children weren't going to happen. I got the all-clear but his macho ego got in the way of medical checks on him. That's when he started gambling. With hindsight, it might have been his way of coping with the attack on his manhood. His addiction to the horses meant we never had any money. I hated the insecure, hand-to-mouth lifestyle. But despite that I stayed with him until he started playing away."

"I will never do that." Stuart kissed her slowly, wanting to take away her years of hurt.

Jayne responded deliciously, making his toes curl, before continuing. "And then we got divorced and that's all there is to tell. What about you?"

"Can I ask you a question first?" Only now did he feel confident enough to broach the subject. "What about recent dating? There was a man in an Audi?"

Jayne flushed. "That was before you and me . . . He . . . he didn't understand about Mum. He wanted to sweep me off my feet and for a little while I was blinded by his money and the secure financial lifestyle he offered. But my circumstances don't allow for knights in shining armour. You know what it's like to constantly have to put someone else's life before your own. Unlike you, he couldn't understand that. That's why you and I are such a good match and the fact that we have a history and get on well and, somehow, we just fit together. Having you back in my life makes me feel that I've finally reached where I want to be. I'm whole again."

She cuddled closer to him and put her head on his shoulder.

It felt good, very good, to be wanted — but if Lillian didn't exist, would Audi man have triumphed? Would Stuart's own star dim if Jayne decided to put Lillian in a care home? Perhaps then they wouldn't be such a good match in Jayne's eyes. It wasn't a thought he wanted to pursue.

"What about you?" Jayne repeated her question.

"There were two or three girls at university. After you'd taken up with Carl. And a brief thing with a Dutch girl in Paris when I went inter-railing. But since then, nothing."

"Life is changing for the better for both of us now." She snuggled even closer to him.

Again, that wonderful feeling of warmth and being wanted flowed through Stuart. Audi man didn't matter. Stuart had won fair lady. He gently kissed her and then inclined his head towards the stairs. "I think we've just got time before *Vera*'s latest case is solved."

* * *

When Jayne wasn't there, the atmosphere in the house reverted to the heavy emptiness of Eric's last years, despite the glow that Stuart carried within him. The silence was more absolute than being home alone when Florence had lived there. Stuart pondered this phenomenon and hoped, that wherever she was, Florence was happy. She'd never returned to collect Tibby; that both worried and pleased him.

The cat had eventually cottoned onto the idea of weeing outside and, after a lot of scrubbing and carpet shampoo, the unpleasant smells in the house had gone. Tibby's habit of winding herself around his legs while purring like a jet engine had remained and Stuart liked the comfort this brought.

But he worried that his ex-lodger might be out there alone, still grieving for her daughter. He'd now texted a few times about Tibby's progress and left several voicemails to tell her some post had arrived. When she responded to any of these, he'd promised himself he'd keep the conversation going by telling her she was welcome to return at any time. But there'd been no response.

Jayne wanted the cat taken to a rescue centre. "Florence has gone for good. She's probably got her hands on the tortoise diamonds and is living the life of Riley somewhere. The cat can't come when you move in with us. Mum might trip over it or catch some feline disease."

"Move in with you?" He hadn't been expecting that.

Jayne flushed. "Sorry. I assumed . . . I thought we . . ."

Stuart couldn't form his lips into the right words. He was flooded with happiness at being wanted but panic-stricken at the prospect of another sudden life change.

"In less than six months you'll have nowhere to live and we're in a relationship . . . It seemed obvious that you'd move in with us. Did you have other plans?"

"No." Plans needed money.

"You'd be around in the day to keep an eye on Mum. She'd be so happy as well as me — it would mean no strangers in the house confusing her."

"Oh." This needed digesting. He'd be part of a real family. There wouldn't be the loneliness of caring for Dad because Jayne would be there every evening. They'd do things together. It would be like now, only better. He couldn't understand why her suggestion felt like a pillow being placed over his face.

Jayne gave him a hug. "Mum will be over the moon; she likes you. And she keeps on at me about a wedding."

"Was that a proposal? Sorry, I . . ." Stuart's world had suddenly become turbo-charged.

"Not exactly." She frowned. "That's your job. But Mum will need to know a wedding is on the horizon if we're going to share a bed."

"I see."

"You can move in as soon as — no need to wait until the cloth is pulled from beneath you."

Jayne was pushing the pillow down on him.

Sandra latched on to his unease. *It's OK to take it slowly. There are months before you have to get out of the house.*

"And this isn't just about what's convenient for Mum." Emotion was brimming in Jayne's voice as she spoke. "I love you, Stuart Borefield, with my heart and my body. I understand now that I've loved you all my life."

After years of life in the slow lane, Jayne was moving too fast for Stuart. He couldn't sprint to the finish line at her speed. He thought he loved her but how could you know for sure? She was looking at him expectantly and his words came out garbled. "I'm not going to make things easy for Robert and George. I'll stay here until my time is up." He squeezed her hand. "And being with you is fantastic."

Jayne seemed disappointed but didn't press the subject.

After that, the house felt even more like a deflated balloon. Stuart was simply marking time until he handed over the family home to his brothers, using the weeks and months as a window to get used to the idea of living next door.

This isn't good for you, bro. Bright new future — remember.

Stuart did remember but he didn't know what to do about it. He spent more time in the library but sitting alone reading didn't improve anything. He wondered about applying for a supermarket job but that would mean no more visits to William, and he'd grown fond of the old man.

"Back again?" The librarian spoke to him as she shelved books on the large-print romance carousel that Stuart was browsing in the hope of finding something to stimulate Lillian to read. "Could you do me a favour?"

Stuart nodded.

"The toddlers are arriving for story time but I'm a staff member down. Could you direct them into the children's section and let them know I'll be with them as soon as possible?"

There was a handful of two- and three-year-olds making a disturbance amongst the local history shelves. Stuart pointed the way to the brightly decorated children's section and sat down on a too-low, lime-green plastic settee to wait for the librarian to take over. The children's mothers huddled together in conversation. Stuart thought of the witches at the beginning of *Macbeth*. Their offspring walked over settees, pulled books willy-nilly from the shelves and stared at Stuart. The teacher within him started to rise but was immediately squashed by the fear of being accused of interfering, or of something even worse. A small boy decided that a red armchair made a good trampoline. A girl strayed, unnoticed by her mother, towards the adults' shelves and started moving books from shelf to floor.

Stuart coughed loudly. One of the mums looked from him to the children and back again and frowned. Stuart suddenly got the message: the parents thought he was in charge of story time. He began to panic. The librarian was nowhere in sight.

Breathe, bro.

He had choices. Tell the parents to take charge of their children and risk being bad-mouthed or simply walk away and let the library be destroyed or . . .

Stuart picked up the nearest picture book. There were very few words per page; it wouldn't take long to read. The noise from the youngsters was growing and other readers were beginning to glare at him as though the growing mayhem was his fault. He couldn't bear that everything wasn't as it should be. Stuart liked order and planning. When things weren't happening as they should, he needed to bring back that order. A handful of toddlers couldn't be worse than a class of teenagers. Could they?

His hand trembled and tried to focus on the children, not the parents who were eying him critically. "Whoever sits quietly on the floor first for story time will get to choose the second book."

For a moment there was silence. Children and parents looked at him. Nobody moved. Then a small boy sat down clutching a copy of *The Very Hungry Caterpillar*.

"Who are you?" A girl sat on the lime-green plastic beside him and put her thumb in her mouth.

Stuart looked around for authority or at least a nod of permission. The librarian was deep in conversation at the information desk. This was his decision. It felt like he needed to cough. He swallowed hard. He cleared his throat and swallowed again.

"I am the storyteller. The magic storyteller." He had their attention. There was sweat under his arms and he had to clear his throat to stop the cough taking over. He made himself believe that he was no longer grey Stuart Borefield and instead he was actually the magic storyteller.

"Once upon a time there was little girl called Red Riding Hood." He turned the book around so the children on the floor could see the picture of the blonde-haired girl in a red cloak. He made himself read slowly and with emphasis. He tried to put pauses in the right place like the professionals narrating short stories on Radio 4. It felt like the story was taking forever. He glanced to the back of the audience; the expressions on the parents' faces had softened. There was a satisfying sense of order in the library once more. Then it was the last page. He consciously put the brakes on to avoid dashing pell-mell through the last bit. And then finally, "The End."

"Now this one!" The small boy pushed the caterpillar book under his nose.

Stuart took some breaths. The magic storyteller had done it once so he could do it again. Grey Stuart Borefield was watching somewhere in the wings, amazed at the ability of his alter ego.

"Let's begin," the storyteller began. The children were rapt with attention in a way Stuart's classes of teenagers never had been. The magic storyteller was generating a kind of respect and even power that Stuart hadn't felt for a long time. He continued the story of the caterpillar and the multitude of foods he ate.

There was a pile of five finished books at his side when he became aware of the mothers trying to encourage the children back to their feet.

"That was fantastic." The librarian gave him a little round of applause and the children joined in.

"Would you fancy doing this on a regular basis? As a volunteer? It would really help us out."

"I . . ." It took a moment to reorientate himself back into his true identity. "Was I *really* OK?" The time had flown by. Stuart had been as immersed in the stories as the children.

"More than OK!" The librarian grinned and the last mother to leave gave him a thumbs-up. "There's some paperwork of course, but if you're interested. . ."

It felt as though someone had pinned a medal of achievement on his chest and he'd grown a couple of inches. "Yes, I think I would like to do it again."

* * *

Stuart's weeks began to gain some structure. It was the dawn of a future that might become bright enough. Thursday mornings meant story time and every day he checked on Lillian immediately after his lunchtime visit to William. There was still no contact from Florence but without knowing where she was, it was impossible to do more than keep sending the odd text with a photo of Tibby.

Checking on Lillian had become a habit despite what he knew of her wishes; it seemed the least he could do if he was eventually going to be part of the family. Besides, he liked the old lady's company. He made her a cup of tea and a sandwich. She was appreciative of his time and, mostly, was capable of sensible, if repetitive, conversation with the odd spark of the lady he'd grown up knowing as 'Aunty'.

One afternoon she talked a lot about Jayne and her regret at having had only one child. "She has to carry the burden of me alone. And because she's no children and no husband, she's got no one else to lean on. Have I ruined her life because I didn't give her brothers and sisters?"

"No. Of course not. I have two brothers but they've been of no use to me."

"I don't want Jayne to have the same empty life you had. Don't let that happen, will you?"

For a while, Lillian gazed silently over Stuart's shoulder at nothing. Then she smiled and spoke brightly. "You didn't take me shopping."

"What?"

"With the money from the computer to buy Jayne's birthday present."

He couldn't burst Lillian's bubble by explaining the birthday had gone and he'd forgotten about the shopping trip. "I'll take you soon."

CHAPTER THIRTY

Stuart cycled every day now, except Thursdays when he was at the library. It was a safety valve to the indecision building inside him. Between his breakfast and lunchtime visits to William and Lillian there was just time to pedal the fifteen miles to the quarry.

He'd sit by the edge of the water enjoying the late October sunshine and drinking hot milky coffee from his flask. It was the best place to find peace. Modern life had forgotten about the quarry. There was no traffic noise. No sirens. Mostly there was no other people, just the calling of birds and silence. Stuart became part of that silence, able to watch rabbits feeding for a full five minutes before they sensed he was there and disappeared into the undergrowth and invisible burrows.

Once he'd heard the persistent knocking of a woodpecker but when he tried to follow the sound the bird disappeared. From that he learned that the best antidote to twenty-first-century life was simply to sit still and absorb the atmosphere. He'd discovered a dryish spot for the damp, dismal days that heralded the arrival of autumn. A large holly bush had developed a dimple, creating a tiny cave-like shelter that kept off the worst of the wind and rain. Even in the bad weather, visiting the quarry was a tonic for Stuart's spirits. The rain made the air feel extra fresh, clean and new.

When his time was up, Stuart let himself go as fast as he dared on the downhill sweep towards home and his next set of caring visits.

Tibby became more demanding. Launching herself into his lap as soon as he sat down. Refusing to use the cat flap if Stuart was there to get up and open the door. Becoming picky over food and refusing everything but premium brands. Perhaps she sensed her time in his home might be nearly up. All of this made Stuart's mind wander increasingly to Florence and, specifically, what to do about Tibby, if and when he moved next door.

He discovered that Double Berry Black had a website and the website had a picture of Florence in her stage outfit. She looked younger but just as full of enthusiasm and energy. A greasy mark developed on the laptop screen where he ran his finger over her face. He read the biographies of all the band members and learned that Jim was the drummer. It had never occurred to Stuart that she was still seeing her husband so regularly. The biography also said Jim worked on the production line in a local biscuit factory, backing up the little information Florence had volunteered about him. He wondered if they were reunited now. How could they remain separated if they played in a band together every night? This thought worried him even though it was none of his business.

He dragged his mind away from what Florence might or might not be doing. He had to focus on his new life with Jayne and Lillian, his role at the library and his job with William. Part of that new life meant rehoming Tibby. He took a photo of the cat curled contentedly in sleep on the sofa and sent it to Florence. She'd ignored all his other messages but maybe this one would remind her that she couldn't simply forget her responsibilities. He pondered for a long while over the words to go with the image; he wanted to get the tone light but caring in the way a friend might.

Tibby enjoying her sojourn chez Stuart. But all good things must come to an end and the brothers are waiting in the wings.

He checked his phone several times after pressing 'send' but there was no response. Perhaps his pathetic attempt at French had bamboozled her. He resent the picture with a simpler message: *Tibby will need a new home soon. Please?* He almost added a series of Xs in typical Florence-style but decided that would make him appear too forward, considering Florence's self-imposed absence.

Still no reply.

To distract himself, he texted Jayne at work and told her he was taking her mother on a shopping trip. She responded immediately with a row of smiley faces. At least someone was taking notice of his messages. He drove Lillian to the out-of-town shopping centre and gave her twenty pounds of his own money to spend on Jayne.

"Perfume," Lillian declared and they went into Boots.

Stuart loitered some distance away to give Lillian the illusion she was managing this on her own. After some time, she returned to him holding the twenty-pound note and looking crestfallen. "It's not enough."

He wanted to give her more. Jayne deserved a decent present from her mother. But he knew that even a few pounds more would mean the direct debit for the council tax would send him into the red and the mire of bank and interest charges.

"What about chocolates?"

"Are you sad, Stuart?" Lillian asked as they walked through the mall to a specialist chocolate shop.

"Sad?"

"That wasted life. I keep thinking about Jayne. How many years of her life might be lost if she insists on caring for me? Surely it's better to go in a home and let our children lead their lives? Or is there a case for euthanasia? If we were animals we'd probably be put to sleep."

"Jayne loves you. She hates the idea of putting you in a home."

"But I've tried to tell her that's what I want. Or I think I've told her."

"Is it what you really want?"

Lillian was walking slowly, one arm on Stuart's. Now she stopped and turned towards him. Her face said it was an effort to keep her concentration on their conversation. "It's not what I want *for me* but it is what I want *for Jayne*. I want her to be able to enjoy her life while she still can. Even at my age, you always put your children first."

"I don't know what to say."

"You don't have to say anything. Just be a sounding board. I tried to talk to Jayne but she wouldn't listen. At least I think that's what I did."

As soon as they entered the chocolate shop, Lillian's attention was diverted by an assistant in a white coat giving out free samples. Her feet picked up speed and Stuart was pulled along in her wake.

"Would you like to try today's speciality? White chocolate strawberry cup."

"Yes, we would. Thank you." Lillian picked up two chocolates and pushed one into Stuart's hand. "Do you have a chair? I'm feeling a bit faint."

Two chairs appeared and they sat down.

"If you're not well, I can take you home," Stuart said.

"I'm perfectly well," Lillian muttered through a mouthful of chocolate, "but don't tell them that."

The other customers were giving them sidelong glances. Stuart focused on making his chocolate last. When it was completely gone, he turned to Lillian. "I think you should buy a box for Jayne and then we'll leave."

"Not yet. Watch."

Another assistant approached them with two mugs and a plate on a tray. "This might help revive you. It's from our new hot-chocolate range and the biscuits coordinate rather nicely." She produced a small table from an alcove and put the tray down.

Lillian smiled knowingly at Stuart and passed him a mug.

"Have you done this before?" he whispered.

"Let's just say it's worked in other establishments."

"Now we've got a seat and refreshments we can go back to our earlier conversation. Do you think Jayne is worried about the financial aspect of me going in a home?"

"It's possible. But I think she genuinely wants what's best for you."

"And that is the conundrum. I might want to stay at home under her care but will that still be best for me if I start mithering and worrying about the impact that's having on her? Or worse, I might not even notice the impact it's having on her."

"Are you feeling better?" A badge on the white coat indicated this was the store manager. She was carrying a stack of large boxes towards an empty shelf.

"Much better, thank you. Oh! Is one of those for me? How kind."

"Er . . . yes, with our compliments."

Lillian threw Stuart a superior smile and they stood up to leave. Stuart felt a sugar rush spring in his step as they walked back towards the car. "I don't believe you just did that. Those boxes were fifty pounds each."

"If you don't ask, you don't get. And you can have your twenty pounds back. I know you can't really afford it."

"Mummy! It's the magic storyteller!"

Stuart felt a tug on the back of his jacket. A small boy from the story-time group was looking up at him.

"I'm so sorry." A young woman in jeans and a leather jacket took hold of the small boy's hand. "But you are excellent at keeping the children absorbed. He's always so excited on a Thursday."

Stuart felt himself grin with pleasure. He ruffled the boy's hair. "Thank you. Those sessions do me good too. I think it's the opportunity to escape into a world of imagination."

Lillian dozed during the drive back and Stuart reflected on the pleasure that little bit of praise had given him. How much nicer the world would be if we always let people know when they'd done well. At home Stuart helped Lillian out of the car and then had to remind her that she was supposed to give the chocolates to Jayne as a belated birthday present.

"Does she like chocolates? I can't remember."

* * *

The calendar on Stuart's phone reminded him it was speakers' club night. He should have deleted the recurring entries when he'd realised it wasn't for him and was about to do so, when he remembered the small boy and his enthusiasm for the magic storyteller. If he sat quietly at the back of the room and enjoyed all those who spoke more eloquently than he did, he might absorb some tips that he could use at the library without being forced to speak at the club. John wouldn't be expecting him and would, hopefully, be too busy organising the speakers who were on the programme to notice and pick on Stuart in the audience. Before he could get cold feet, he drove to the Red Lion.

As usual, the main speakers were impressive with their use of humour, audience rapport and the confident way they paused and let silence fill the room. At the interval, he allowed himself half a pint of bitter and listened to the discussion about the upcoming national speech contest. Then it was time for Topics.

"Please welcome to the lectern, Stuart, speaking to the topic . . . The Future."

He'd forgotten that everyone was expected to contribute to this part of the evening. Suddenly his heart was thumping, his cheeks were burning, his mind was blank and applause was propelling him to the front of the room.

"Topics' Chair, speakers and guests," he began.

Twenty pairs of eyes were watching him and he had nothing to say about The Future. He groped around in the darkness of his mind.

"The future . . . it means different things to all of us." He tried to squash the panic, to formulate his thoughts and to say something sensible. Then he reached for his magic-storyteller persona — speaking was easier if it wasn't Stuart Borefield standing in front of all these people. The magic storyteller didn't have a problem with audiences. "To me it means . . . trying new things. Not repeating the joyless things that got me this far." Ideas slotted into place. "It's too easy to sit in a rut. It's too easy to fear change. It's too easy to sit in the shadows and not push forward. But where is the pleasure and satisfaction in that?"

There was the click of a light switch and he saw the green bulb at the back of the room light up, indicating he'd been speaking for one minute and forty-five seconds. He took a few breaths and tried not to panic about filling the full three minutes. He was in control.

"I hate coming here."

There was a whisper of laughter. He smiled at the audience and felt his shoulders relax a tiny bit.

"But fear makes me grow. I get nervous when the toddlers arrive for my story-time group but afterwards I feel good. I'm terrified of the first Sunday of next year because I'll be leading a group of cyclists."

Then a sudden realisation came to him. "But if I was given the option of not doing any of these things, I wouldn't take it." He paused and let his eyes sweep the audience. The red light came on, indicating it was time to wind up. "I want my future to be challenging and full of new things. But I also want friends, old and new, by my side. Otherwise, what is the point?"

Applause. He sat down, heart pounding, cheeks burning and legs shaky. At that first meeting, John had told him that Topics didn't have to be based on the truth so Stuart had spoken off the top of his head, not thinking through the veracity and implications of his words. That's what had made him fluent — and his words had ended up being the truth.

* * *

"Is she still talking to you?" William asked at lunchtime the next day.

"Who?" Stuart's mind was on Florence and her lack of response to his message. He wondered if it was personal.

"Sandra. Your imaginary sister."

"She's not imaginary, she did exist."

Does exist. Not 'did exist'. Don't consign me to history like some dusty artefact.

"You know what I mean — her imaginary voice in your head."

He could say 'no' and end the conversation. "In a reduced way."

"Less often?"

"Less off the wall. She talks a bit more like me."

"That sounds good."

"Maybe. How's Andrea?" Stuart didn't want to leave a silence for William to fill with more questions.

The old man looked down and his fingers started to work the bottom ribbing of his woollen jumper. He glanced up again to speak and his eyes seemed extra bright. "The same. She still phones every Sunday evening. She still doesn't visit except on high days and holidays."

"So the argument is forgotten."

"Not forgotten. It's the elephant in the room. We don't go near it."

"That's a shame." Stuart placed a hand on the old man's shoulder. "I hope you can find a way through."

"I doubt that. Andrea's been used to everything falling into her lap her whole life. But I believe good fortune must be earned."

This was a riddle too far for Stuart; there was too much of his own life swirling in his head without taking on William's relationship with his daughter.

"I best be off."

"Lillian?"

"Yes, she needs feeding as well."

"Your relationship with Jayne doesn't mean you have to look after her mother."

William's words felt like a criticism. "Whatever I'm doing for Lillian, I'm doing because I want to."

* * *

There was still no response from Florence to the picture of Tibby. This ongoing silence was making Stuart increasingly worried about Florence's wellbeing. Shirley's death had affected her badly. Maybe she wasn't coping. Maybe she needed a friend.

Stuart pulled up the website of Double Berry Black and checked the details of their next gig. Tonight. The only way to stop worrying about Florence was to see her alive, well, happy and doing what she enjoyed best. And give her a chance to reclaim Tibby before the animal went to a rescue centre.

He scratched the cat under the chin. She looked at him with grateful eyes and licked his hand with a tongue like wet sandpaper. When Tibby was gone there'd be no point in sitting out the last five months here, alone. He would hand the keys to Robert and George, and take up Jayne's offer of moving next door. This feeling of living in a temporary, indecisive interlude would be gone. He'd be living where he was appreciated instead of in a gloomy house too big for one person.

But first he had to see Florence. Just making that decision made Stuart feel better.

Don't you think that Florence would have contacted you if she had any interest in Tibby's future?

"Stop creating obstacles, Sandra. I have to do this for my own peace of mind."

Before nerves and doubt crept in, he entered his credit card number and clicked 'confirm order' on the screen. The

PDF of a gig ticket dropped into his inbox and he printed it out on a sheet of A4. He rang Jayne immediately to stop himself overthinking and doing none of it.

"I won't be in tonight," he said.

"Oh?"

"I'm going out."

"I guessed that when you said you weren't going to be in. Where are you going?"

He paused.

People in solid relationships don't keep secrets.

"I'm going to one of Florence's concerts." His words came out too quickly. "Just to make sure it's OK to rehome Tibby before we . . ." He let the future drift away.

"Can't you text her?"

"She doesn't respond. We parted on bad terms." He hadn't told Jayne that her story about tortoise smuggling had triggered everything.

"I could come with you?" A dash of hope lightened Jayne's voice. "It would be nice to have a night out."

"I'll be gone more than two hours. *Vera* won't stretch that far." It was wrong to feel relieved she couldn't go with him.

Interesting feelings, bro.

Silently, he replied, "Thank you for the observation, Sandra, but this isn't a night out for pleasure. It's more of a business meeting and Jayne's presence plus the need to get home for Lillian might sidetrack me."

"This won't become a habit, will it?" Jayne asked. "Like the website?"

"What?" He'd never mentioned looking at Florence's picture online.

"The other day, you said I could use your laptop to check my email while you cooked."

Stuart felt uncomfortable. "You checked my browsing history?" Was that normal in a relationship?

"Accidentally."

On purpose.

He and Jayne shouldn't have secrets. It didn't matter.

But it does matter, doesn't it? You're feeling spied on, aren't you?

"Tonight is a one-off attempt to talk to Florence and give her a chance to reclaim Tibby before you, Lillian and me start our life together."

"OK." Her voice was resigned. "I'll see you tomorrow night, though? And you will call in on Mum during the day?"

"Yes and yes."

"I do love you, Stuart. I'm sorry if I'm giving you the third degree but I hate the thought of losing you again."

Her voice pulled at his heart. "You won't lose me. This is something I have to do."

After Stuart put the phone down, a strange combination of freedom, anticipation and exhilaration crept over him. His last concert had been as a student. This wouldn't be the same, of course. He wasn't going to see proper pop stars in a big arena, but there would be foot-tapping and singing and, even alone, he would be part of communal enjoyment and good feeling. He smiled and turned his mind to the practicalities.

What did people wear to concerts? Florence liked his navy chinos and that shirt in a slightly lighter shade of blue.

CHAPTER THIRTY-ONE

The venue was a working men's club. Double Berry Black were due to play at 9 p.m. and Stuart arrived just before. The young girl on the door smiled when he unfolded his A4 ticket. Stuart cringed — everyone else had the ticket on their phone.

Oh dear. But slow and steady does the job. You've made it to the concert, haven't you?

The hall was set out with tables, mostly at least part-occupied. Rather than sit with strangers, Stuart got a cola from the bar and found a wall to lean against at the back of the room. The band's gear was already set up on the stage and the largest drum was emblazoned with *Double Berry Black* in red-and-black lettering. Stuart tried to imagine how Florence's husband might look on the drums: an ageing rocker with a T-shirt stretched tight over a beer belly or well-toned, well-groomed and well-dressed?

Conversation ebbed and flowed around him like the buzz of insects. Stuart pulled out his phone and pretended to be in demand. He scrolled through the sent text messages that Florence had chosen to ignore.

If they'd fallen out so badly that she wouldn't even reassure him she was still alive, what was he doing here? Any normal person would accept the friendship was beyond repair, rehome the cat and move on. Clinging on to the wreckage labelled Stuart as a Billy No-Mates.

Except he did have mates. He had Jayne and Lillian. He had William. He had his role at the library. He had his cycling-club buddies. Life was becoming fuller than it had ever been. He didn't actually need Florence. He went to the bar for another cola and returned to his wall space as the lights dimmed and a figure bounded out into the pool of light on stage.

Stuart stared at her. She was too far away to see the detail of her face but he recognised the outline of her body, emphasised by a white-and-gold close-fitting catsuit that shimmered whenever she moved. She was curvy but lithe. Her voice filled the auditorium as it had once filled his kitchen. After a solo verse, the other band members bounced on to the stage, encouraging audience applause with energetic, enthusiastic hand movements. People responded with shouts and foot-stamping. The sentiment of the crowd made Stuart feel warm inside, a sort of reflected glory.

Like the rest of the band, Jim was dressed in white and gold. The cymbals hid his torso but, even from the back of the room, it was obvious his arms and face weren't carrying flab. His expression was animated and constantly glancing towards his wife. Every few minutes Florence smiled in the drummer's direction. They were definitely back together.

The band's set was an hour long. A high-energy, all-encompassing hour. The crowd loved them and it was obvious the band loved the crowd. It was impossible not to get carried away in the music-induced euphoria. People were now standing rather than sitting at the tables. They were swaying and clapping. Movements grew bigger and very soon the audience was warmed up enough to be actually dancing.

As he leaned against the wall Stuart felt his toes begin to tap and his shoulders move from side to side. The urge to properly lose himself in the music grew. He glanced sideways; the man next to him was absorbed in his pint and phone. Everyone else was focused on the performance.

Stuart took a step away from the wall and began to transfer his weight from foot to foot. His arms went forwards and back. Memories of discos from his youth flooded back. His torso was moving and he felt his lips curl into a smile. A sort of happiness grew in his chest. He was kind of dancing and he liked the feeling.

The track faded out and applause filled the room. Stuart glanced backwards. The man had put his pint down. He gave Stuart a double-thumbs-up and a look of enthusiastic approval. Stuart couldn't judge whether this stranger was making fun of him or offering genuine encouragement. The curtains of self-doubt swished closed. The next song had started but Stuart leaned back against the wall and didn't meet the other man's eyes. He didn't attempt to dance again.

Finally Double Berry Black tried to leave the stage. The audience wouldn't let them go. They were on their feet shouting for more. After a moment's hesitation and a glance to his left, Stuart raised his arms above his head and clapped too.

Florence walked to the front of the stage, gesturing with her hands for quiet. Gradually, the crowd obeyed and Florence began to reprise the most popular song. It started quietly.

"She's knock-out, that lead singer, isn't she?" The man standing next to Stuart raised his pint glass and gestured at the stage. "The rumour is that she's split up from her husband. He's the one on the drums. Someone said she's got a new man but he's never been seen."

A new man. He hadn't expected that. Not so soon and not with everything else going on in her life and not with the way she kept looking at Jim. The sound and the beat of the encore song was growing. Jim brought it up to a crescendo with a dramatic drum roll. Did he know about the new man? Did he care? The combined noise of band and audience was deafening. Everyone was up on their feet. Stuart's foot tapped discreetly. Now the man next to him was slurring the lyrics as if he were on the stage.

In Stuart's head the noise receded, drowned by thoughts of Florence with a new man. She deserved to be loved, after all the affection and kindness she had freely dispensed. He tried to imagine her going home to this new man. Did they dance around the kitchen? Did he love Slowcoach? Perhaps he drove her to gigs and picked her up afterwards.

Stuart became aware of applause, like the thunderous bangs of a battlefield. Then there was a gradual reduction in volume and the lights brightened. A scrum surrounded the bar and he was forced to relinquish the safety of his patch of wall. Florence's face filled his mind. Her beaming smile, her bobbed platinum hair gone slightly skew-whiff with the energy of the performance, a sheen of sweat across her forehead picked up by the lights and the visible energy bouncing from her. He couldn't go home without seeing her face to face. Without asking her about Tibby.

Seeing her face to face. I agree that's the important thing, isn't it? Making sure there are no loose ends.

"Exactly. No loose ends," Stuart muttered under his breath. "And she can't ignore me if we're face to face like she can a text message. If her grandchildren are expecting to have their cat back, I can't take it to a rescue centre."

Enjoy!

After a protracted elbow battle, Stuart reached the bar. He didn't want a third cola but it was a small price to pay for information about Florence. He put his glass on the bar. "Where do the band make their exit?"

"What?" The barman frowned; the place was still noisy with conversation.

"Is there a stage door? I need to speak to one of the singers."

"You're after Florence, aren't you? Join the back of the queue, mate. She's no spring chicken but in the sex-appeal ratings she's up there." He raised one hand above his forehead.

Stuart didn't like that all these men were ogling his . . . Stuart's mind paused to frame the right word.

'Ex-lodger' is the word you should be using.

"I know. I know."

The barman gave him his change. "They usually park their van around the back. They'll be loading up for the next twenty minutes or so."

"Thanks."

Stuart abandoned his drink on an empty table and went outside. He'd parked at the front of the club but the car park continued around the side and rear of the building. Following the barman's directions, he found a white transit with its lights on and rear door open. Two men in jeans and dark fleeces were carrying bits of drum kit from an entrance at the side of the club to the van. The silhouette of a woman emerged from the doorway with a small suitcase on wheels and a large shopping bag. As she moved into the light of the open doors of the van, her black-and-white fake-fur jacket became visible above the curves of her bottom, accentuated by dark leggings.

Stuart's heart leaped but his feet had forgotten how to move forwards. His brain panicked about what to say to her. He stayed hidden in the shadows. The drum kit was stowed. The two men exchanged words that weren't loud enough to carry. They were both slim. One of them, Stuart couldn't tell if it was Jim or the other one, nodded towards Florence. She returned a thumbs-up sign and closed the door of the building. The loud thud and clunk of wood and metal reached Stuart. The man, who was possibly Jim, went over to Florence and gave her a hug. A long hug. Stuart took a step backwards, deeper into the cover of the building. The barman had got it wrong. There was no 'new' man — Florence was back with her husband. Stuart half ran back to his car. He couldn't take the humiliation of being discovered lurking around his ex-lodger. Tibby's future would have to be sorted some other way.

Once in the car he barely paused at the car-park exit to check for traffic. Florence would recognise his registration. She would know he was there for her.

Coward! Exactly how important are these loose ends and moving into your new life next door?

"You know how important the future is to me. You also know I'm more tortoise than hare. Stop prodding me forwards too fast."

* * *

"You wasted a whole evening when we could've been together, plus the cost of a ticket, and you still didn't get this cat thing sorted out?" Jayne didn't look happy. "Is it that on some level, you want to keep the connection with Florence?"

"Of course not." There was no point in striving for a connection with someone who didn't want to know you, however much you wanted to know them.

Tibby was sitting on the floor in front of them, staring at the occupied sofa. She crouched, ready to leap onto Stuart's lap. Stuart moved his hands to make space for her. He liked the comforting warmth of her weight and the soporific effect of her purring.

"No." Jayne spoke sharply to the cat and then draped herself over Stuart's lap. She looked up at him. "Sometimes you've got to be cruel to be kind. Don't let that animal get attached to you. It will make taking it to the rescue centre more difficult."

"I was thinking . . ." He'd been doing internet research and had discovered some people with dementia showed decreased levels of anxiety and agitation when they had an animal to care for. Stuart was sure Lillian would benefit.

"I've been thinking too," Jayne interrupted. "I know you want to sit out your last five months here to avoid giving George and Robert an easy ride. But that's cutting off your nose to spite your face. Life will be so much easier if you move in with us now. Mum will have your company for most of the day. I won't have to crawl out of your bed after two hours to go home. I hate doing that — it makes me feel like a dirty secret. I want to spend the whole night in close physical contact with the man I love. With the only man I have ever properly loved. We could even think about a granny-flat extension on the back of the house, using the money from the sale of my flat. It's still sitting in the bank. That way we'd have the privacy to be a proper couple — that's what I really want from our relationship. I hate all this backwards and forwards between different houses. I just want us to be together!"

"Oh." The depth of Jayne's feelings for him was obvious and Stuart wasn't sure he could match it.

"What's not to like?"

Stuart was pedalling madly around his brain trying to determine why his heart wasn't full of joy at this idea. There were no concrete reasons against and lots of sensible reasons in favour. He tried to conjure up Sandra for help, but she'd gone AWOL. "It's a bit sudden."

"No, it's not. We've talked about it before." She spoke as though explaining something to a child for the umpteenth time. "Without the aggro of running backwards and forwards between our two houses, I'll be more relaxed with increased energy for you." She pushed herself up from her sprawled position and kissed him on the lips. A demanding kiss that wouldn't be refused. He gave into it and his body remembered why it adored being with Jayne.

Later, when their *Vera* slot was almost up, Jayne pulled her clothes back on. "You will phone Robert and George tomorrow, won't you? And the cat place? And start packing your stuff? Just your personal stuff. There's no room at ours for all this . . ." She extended her arms to include the general house contents. "Check for anything of value but then let a house-clearance firm deal with the rest. Please do it. For me."

Stuart made a noncommittal movement of his head, which seemed to satisfy her.

When she'd gone, he sat up late, thinking. He had a future with the girl he'd loved passionately as a teenager; she'd become the woman he was loving again in middle-age. They shared a similar outlook on life. They were good together. She loved him deeply. Most people didn't get a second chance like this. His bright horizon was within touching distance. At eighteen, Jayne had slipped through his fingers. He shouldn't let her slip away again.

So why the hesitation, bro?

"I'm not hesitating. I'm thinking. Moving in with Jayne ticks all the boxes."

Love isn't a series of tick boxes. It's an ethereal emotion.

"I know that and I don't want her to slip away again."

So?

"So, I'll work out how to return Tibby and then I'll move next door."

CHAPTER THIRTY-TWO

Stuart overslept and was late for his first visit of the day to William. Unusually, the old man wasn't sitting up and waiting to be transferred to the commode. Stuart found him still under the quilt, dozing.

"William? Are you OK?"

The old man rolled from his side to his back and opened bleary eyes. "I didn't sleep. Crisis of conscience. Suddenly had doubts about whether I'm doing the right thing by Andrea. I don't want to leave this world with regrets."

"Do you want to talk about it?" Stuart opened the curtains.

"No." William blinked in the sunlight.

"It's a lovely day out there — crisp and autumnal."

"The seasons carry on, regardless of our own mess. The sun rises. The sun sets. The birds sing."

"And we get too much rain."

"Nay, lad. Rain, like the love of a good woman, is essential." The old man eased himself up into a sitting position. "Talking of good women, have you heard anything from Florence?"

Stuart told him about the concert.

"I don't understand. Why didn't you have the nerve to speak to her?"

William was charging into an area that Stuart didn't understand himself. Nobody in their right mind was too scared to talk to their ex-lodger. Perhaps he wasn't actually in his right mind.

"You must be dying for a wee."

"In a minute." The old man flapped a hand. "Let's bottom this Florence thing out first."

"There's nothing more to say. I didn't speak to her and she won't respond to my messages. The business with Tibby is holding things up. Jayne wants me to move in with her and Lillian as soon as possible." He helped William onto the commode and disappeared to make breakfast before William could dig any further.

Why are you worried about him digging?

Porridge, toast, tea. Porridge, toast, tea. Stuart cycled the words in his mind until they drowned out his sister.

William didn't speak again until he'd been dressed and was sitting in the chair with his breakfast. "Is Jayne still adamant about not putting her mother in a home?"

"She thinks her mother will have a better quality of life surrounded by those she knows and loves. There's a lot to be said for that. And for Jayne not having to live with the guilt that she palmed her mother off on someone else."

"But the life of the person doing the caring suffers. Dementia only gets worse. Trust me, I was a doctor. Lillian will deteriorate physically as well as mentally. The only unknown is how quickly."

"Jayne wants to do the right thing by her mother. The three of us will be comfortable together." Stuart turned his back and busied himself with William's notes on his phone.

After a while William coughed and Stuart had to face his client again.

William waved a piece of toast at him. "I still don't understand why you were scared to talk to Florence. And by the way, you're too young to be using words like 'comfortable'. You should be looking to get outside your comfort zone, not nestle further into it."

"Reading to those kids is outside my comfort zone. Speakers' club is outside my comfort zone."

"Exactly. They have added new dimensions to your life and made you feel better. You need more of that."

William's preachy attitude was annoying him. "You should be an agony uncle. Talking about my life has brightened you up. You're almost back to normal. Do you feel better?"

"Go see Florence again. And don't bottle it this time."

"Let's change the subject. Tell me about your crisis of conscience. I can be a good listener."

William waved a hand. "Boring. Put sugar in this tea, will you? I need something to pep me up. And then go do something for yourself. Something challenging with no women involved."

Stuart was angry when he left William's. The old man had wound him up with his prying, preachy attitude. There was only one way to get rid of the aggression.

Aha! The hill. Good choice, bro. Conquer the hill and grab a confidence boost.

Stuart winced as he caught the skin under his chin with the helmet clasp. He wasn't after a 'comfortable' life — he was still on course for a bright future *and* he was up for challenges along the way. Since his father died, he'd almost tripled his weekly mileage on the bike and now the time was right to show the hill that had floored him in the long-distance ride who was boss.

He took a circuitous route to the start of the hill, warming his muscles and letting the calming greenness of the countryside focus his mind. There was an end-of-autumn chill in the air but that only served to sharpen his muscles and his resolve. There was an old Henry Ford quote he'd seen on social media: *Think you can, think you can't; either way you'll be right.*

"I think I can!"

Attaboy!

His legs were fresher than after the long-distance Audax ride he'd done at Easter and for the first quarter of the climb he had the momentum from the approach on his side. It felt good. A flock of geese passed noisily overhead in a 'V' shape. Teamwork got those birds where they needed to be; Stuart had only himself to rely on. But he could do it! His thigh muscles hit the demand for power and he gradually took the bike down the gears as he rose further up the hill. It became a battle to keep his legs pumping at the same rhythm and he raised himself from the saddle. The crest of the hill was fifty yards away. He had this in his pocket. Not many men his age would attempt any sort of fitness challenge. And definitely not this hill. He grinned. This would show William he wasn't after a comfortable life.

Thwack. His front wheel took a sudden dive. His arms jolted painfully. There was a struggle to balance and then a flash of blackness and bright lights. Sunshine and birdsong made him blink. Wetness was creeping on his neck and crawling down his back. He was shoulder first in a ditch.

Stuart eased himself to a seated position and twisted his arm behind to touch the skin below his hairline. Ditch water, with an odour of decay and death. A couple of cars went past. The thump-thump from their wheels made him look more closely at the tarmac. If potholes had personalities, this one would have worn a sly grin and a wink.

You took your eye off the road, bro.

Stuart thumped the ground in frustration. His front wheel was bent and he had to walk home, dropping the bike in for repair on his way. With no time to change, he made William's lunchtime visit in his damp Lycra. The old man's amusement made Stuart even more determined to show that he was in charge of his own bright future.

This time a definite line would be drawn under the custody of Tibby so that he could devote his attention to Jayne. She deserved it after all the patience she'd shown him. He went online again. There were tickets left for that evening's concert at a small theatre. Jayne wasn't pleased at another absence but things would be better once he'd closed the door on all this.

"This has to be the last time," Jayne said. "It's like you're stalking her."

* * *

Stuart arrived at the venue early and walked around the building to make sure he knew where the stage door was. Parked close beside the back entrance was the white van. He recognised the registration plate. His heart thumped. Florence was in the theatre and in a couple of hours he'd be speaking to her. Deep breaths. It wasn't normal to get nervous about discussing a cat.

According to leaflets in the foyer, the theatre was owned and run by volunteers, principally to stage amateur productions but occasionally they booked outsiders as money-spinners and to help raise the theatre's profile. Stuart fumbled with his spectacles and phone, finally managing to bring up his e-ticket for validation.

"You're shaking," said the young usher, in bow tie and suit. "Are you all right?"

"Fine. Just been rushing to get here." Stuart tried to smile confidently.

The tiny bar was doing good business and the homemade cakes on the tea stall were almost gone. Stuart paid for a cup of tea in a paper cup and a fairy cake topped with white icing and a cherry. Juggling them was an issue and his still-shaking hand slopped hot tea onto his wrist. Wincing, he found a window ledge to use as a table. He'd barely swallowed the last bit of tea when a five-minute warning was given for the start of the performance.

This time the show started differently. The curtains went back to reveal the whole band on stage and they immediately launched into one of the best-known Blackberries hits. The first part of the song was drowned out by applause.

Stuart focused on the two female singers. He couldn't see in detail because, again, he was near the back of the auditorium. They were taking it in turns to sing verses of the song but neither voice was right. Both lacked Florence's high energy. He strained his eyes. The body shapes weren't right either. They were too skinny, with angles instead of curves. Neither was Florence.

Stuart went cold and stood up to get a better look. Maybe Florence was elsewhere on stage. Somebody pressed on his shoulder and made him jump. He turned around.

"Please sit down. We can't see." It was an angry-looking woman.

Stuart apologised and sat down. There was no Florence. The tension built across his shoulder blades and his stomach clenched. She must be ill. He imagined her, pale-faced, in a hospital bed, all her energy and enthusiasm extinguished. He wanted to go to her, care for her, reignite her bright flame. A fighting spirit grew in his chest. As soon as the show finished, he'd race to the stage door and demand to know where she was. Perhaps he could write a message to pass on to her. He felt his pockets, no paper and no pen.

Despite his preoccupation, the familiarity of the Blackberries' music took hold of his body. Without conscious thought, his toes and fingers were tapping out the rhythm and his head was going from side to side. Around him seats were emptying and the side and central aisles were filling. Nobody was taking any notice of anyone else. Nobody here knew him. He wanted to dance but the thought of pushing past the remaining seated people in his row made Stuart tremble.

Bright new future. Life is for living. Make the most of the time you have. How many more clichés do I need to spout? I never went to a disco. You need to dance for me as well.

She was right, and what was the worst that could happen? He tried to make eye contact as he apologised to those still seated but in the darkness it was impossible. Then he was in the aisle and the music took him. At first he was painfully aware of how he must look: a middle-aged man with jerky limb movements that didn't match the beat of the music. Then he shut his eyes and imagined Florence dancing in front of him. He mirrored her movements and the tension across his back and in his stomach subsided. Now he understood why some people actively sought out dancing as a pastime. With a sudden surge of confidence, he wondered if he might become one of them.

You are one cool bro!

His sister had a talent for exaggeration but Stuart couldn't deny feeling a spark of pride in his dance moves.

At the end of the set there was the same standing ovation, even though Florence was missing. Stuart's anxiety descended again. He wanted time to slow down, but eventually the audience tired of clapping and the curtain fell. Stuart pushed his way through packed conversations in the overheated lobby into the cool air outside. The stage door was still closed. Before his fighting spirit could flee, Stuart positioned himself between the door and the van.

A few minutes later the door was flung open hard so that it rebounded off the wall. Jim was coming out backwards. He and the other male singer were balancing a large part of the drum kit between them. Stuart let them place it in the van before he stepped forward.

"What have you done with Florence?" The words shot out abruptly.

"What?" Jim was frowning.

"Where is she?" He'd spoken too sharply but his anxiety had been growing ever since Florence hadn't appeared on stage. Now his concern was at an almost uncontrollable peak.

"Who are you?" Jim's voice now held a hint of aggression. "We called the police on the last stalker and I can do the same now."

Florence *had* been stalked; the thought cut at Stuart's heart. And he remembered Jayne's accusation. Perhaps he was just one of a string of men bowled over by Florence.

Bowled over?

"I didn't mean it like that, Sandra. Go away."

"I'm waiting. Tell me who you are."

Jim's attitude and Sandra's comment stole his bravado. "I am . . . was . . . her landlord. I've got her cat, Tibby."

Jim's expression relaxed slightly. "I put the cat flap in while you were out."

"That's sort of why I'm here. I can't keep the cat much longer. I'm moving in with my girlfriend and she doesn't want Tibby. So I need Florence to take her away."

"She's gone down to London to sort the grandkids out." Jim paused. The defiant frown left his face and his voice softened. "They lost their mother."

Stuart nodded, his heart aching as he remembered Florence's reaction to her daughter's death. "No problem. It's the wrong time to hassle her. If you could just mention Tibby . . ."

"The kiddies love that cat." Jim's head disappeared into the back of the van. Stuart couldn't see his face but the catch in the drummer's voice was obvious.

The antagonism had evaporated. Stuart stepped forward and put a hand on Florence's husband's shoulder. "No problem. I can hang on to Tibby for a bit longer."

Nothing had been resolved but it felt better than drawing a big thick line. He'd done the only thing a friend could do.

CHAPTER THIRTY-THREE

Stuart was having lunch with Lillian the next day when Jayne made a surprise appearance.

"Hello, Mum." She kissed the old lady on the cheek and helped herself to a bite of one of her cheese sandwiches.

"What are you doing here, love? Stuart and I were just wondering whether to open a tin of peaches for pudding." Stuart caught the smile Lillian threw at him. It was immensely satisfying to add pleasure to the long, uniform days of old age.

He jumped up and squeezed Jayne's hand. "I'll make you a sandwich first. Have you got long?"

Jayne followed him into the kitchen. "About twenty minutes. I'm on my lunch hour and the traffic's heavy."

There was just enough cheese left for a third sandwich.

"Kiss me!" She took the knife from his hand and put it on the chopping board. "Properly."

Her kiss was determined and demanding, as though she wanted something from him that she couldn't put into words. She held him tight and he gladly reciprocated. He wanted some peaceful normality after a sleepless night spent worrying about Florence.

"I'll help you with those peaches." Lillian was suddenly beside them with an empty sandwich plate in her hand. "Oh. Sorry. I'm interrupting."

"Mum!"

"I said sorry. But it is nice to see young love. Can I expect to have to buy a new hat soon?" She winked at Stuart and went back towards the lounge.

Jayne looked at him expectantly.

"What?" Her expression was difficult to read.

"I came home because I wanted to know how you got on with Florence last night. When is she going to collect the cat so we can get on with the rest of our lives?"

"I spoke to her husband. She's down in London with the grandchildren. I need to hang on to Tibby for a bit longer."

A shadow settled on Jayne's face for a few seconds and then her expression brightened. "You could still move in and just nip back to feed the cat. And send Florence an ultimatum, in writing. I can draft you a letter. A legal letter."

"I . . ." There was no argument against Jayne's idea. He should be happy. Stuart desperately wanted that happiness to run through him and put a smile on his face. It didn't.

"We could even . . . This isn't my job and I don't want to spoil it if you've got something planned but we're not spring chickens . . ."

There was a silence. Stuart knew the words she wanted him to say. The knowledge started a whirlwind in his mind. She looked vulnerable. He wanted the same thing. Eventually. There was hope in her eyes. Life was so much better when there was someone to share it. She'd helped him back to life over the last seven months. He liked her. No, he loved her. They fitted together. Jayne deserved happiness. He'd grown up emotionally over the last few months and now he was man enough to do this. There was no reason why they couldn't have a bright new future together.

He put a finger over her lips. "Don't take the words out of my mouth."

She smiled. Her eyes sparkled.

Stuart went down on one knee. "Jayne, please will you do me the honour of becoming my wife?"

"Yes! Yes! Yes!" She jumped around the room with excitement.

Stuart levered himself back to standing with the aid of a kitchen chair, amazed and flattered that he could have this effect on someone. Jayne enveloped him in a hug and then took him by the hand and they went into the lounge.

"Have you got my peaches?"

"No, Mum. Something far, far better than that. You tell her, Stuart."

"Lillian, Jayne has agreed to marry me." As he said the words, his gaze went past Lillian and to the lounge windows, which looked onto the road and gave a partial view of his own drive. A faded orange Panda was pulling up on the drive. His heart rose and then sank.

"Oh, Stuart! I'm so pleased you'll be living here with us. You two should never have split up in the first place. Can I see the ring?"

Jayne and Lillian were looking at him expectantly and Florence was getting out of her car. Even from this distance, his ex-lodger's movements looked deflated. Jayne was squeezing his hand. She and her mother were waiting for a reply. He remembered Florence no longer had a key.

"We need to go shopping." With an effort he switched his gaze back to the room. "Jayne's going to be wearing this ring for a long time so I want her to have something she really loves."

Jayne turned towards him, holding both his hands and kissed him deeply. A rap on the window interrupted them.

"I thought you said she was in London." The smile and happiness were gone from Jayne's face. "Please give her the cat now."

* * *

Florence wasn't alone. She had Slowcoach in his box of straw and two pale, thin children. Stuart didn't have pop or squash or whatever youngsters drank and, having devoured his entire stock of chocolate digestives, they were staring disgustedly at the glasses of milk in front of them. Milk given to him by Lillian when Jayne had gone back to work.

"Where's Tibby? Gran said we were coming to stay with Tibby," said the boy. He was the taller of the two and Florence had introduced him as Shayne. Two words from the boy's statement stood out. The first was 'Gran'. Stuart couldn't think of anyone less like his idea of a typical grandmother than Florence.. His grandmothers hadn't sung with bands or dressed with such flamboyance. The second word was 'Stay'. The children knew more about what Florence had in mind than he did.

"Go outside and look for Tibby in the garden," Florence urged.

The glasses of milk were abandoned as the children rushed out shouting for the cat.

"Jacob and his new partner are returning to South Africa. She's from there as well."

"Can't he take his children with him?"

"There were some problems." Florence spoke slowly and seemed unwilling to elaborate.

"So they'll be living with you and Jim?" Stuart tried not to imagine Florence, Jim and the children as a cosy family.

"Jim and I aren't together. You know that."

"But when you left here, I thought . . ."

"I went to stay with a girlfriend. She doesn't have room to swing a cat. Never mind two children."

Stuart's relief wasn't logical. What did it matter to him whether Florence was back with Jim or somewhere else? He didn't know what to say so he said nothing.

"I was hoping we could stay here. Temporarily. Of course I'll pay more rent because there are more of us."

"I've just proposed to Jayne. We're going to get married."

Florence reset her features within a couple of seconds but Stuart had already seen her shock.

"Congratulations. That's what you need — the love of a good woman." Her voice didn't quite reach the level of warmth he would've expected.

"You're the first person I've told."

"Let me give you a tip." Florence had regained some of her composure and was staring at him earnestly. "Next time, inject more joy into your voice. At the moment it sounds like you're indifferent to the prospect of marriage."

"Of course I'm not indifferent. I've waited a long time for this second chance."

Only the shouts of the children playing outside broke the silence between them. When Stuart had allowed himself to imagine the possibility of Florence's return, it hadn't been like this. He'd looked forward to her energy and bounce, her singing and enthusiasm, and the way she softly bullied him out of his comfort zone.

"Done any karaoke yet?" she said, as if reading his mind.

"What do you think? I can't go to one of those places alone."

"I suppose not. Look, this is awkward and especially now you're engaged and everything. But please can me and the kids stay here for a while?"

Jayne's face was large in Stuart's mind. He had obligations now. He was going to be a married man.

"What about Jim?"

"I don't love Jim anymore." She stared straight at him. "If I go back there, it gives both him and the children false hope."

Stuart needed someone to tell him what to do. He wanted Florence and the children to stay. He wanted them to stay more than was right for a man who should be in the first flush of engagement to another woman.

Sandra was silent on the issue, drowned out in his mind by Jayne. Jayne didn't lack compassion or love; he'd seen both those emotions in her. But Jayne wasn't fond of Florence. Stuart didn't understand why but she wouldn't be happy if Florence stayed. Robert and George wouldn't approve of children tearing round the house — they had the potential to cause more damage than Tibby.

"Shayne and Eunice will be good. I promise."

Stuart looked at his watch. Nearly five o'clock. They wouldn't be able to find anywhere else to stay today and he was due at William's.

"You can stay tonight. But after that . . . I'm not sure."

Florence nodded. Stuart fetched two camp beds from the loft. They hadn't been used since his nephews were small. He left Florence wrestling with them in the limited space of the smallest bedroom, the one that had been his father's study. He went to give William his tea.

CHAPTER THIRTY-FOUR

William was dozing again when he arrived. Stuart felt a stab of unease; this wasn't usual. Television, radio or a book were usual. He gently woke the old man, wondering if he should call a doctor. He picked up a book that had slipped from William's lap to the floor. Then he stood back for a moment and judged the older man's pale face.

"What you staring at?" The words came out as a loud whisper. William coughed and then spoke in a louder, stronger voice. "Nothing wrong with me that caffeine and sugar won't fix."

He was right. A mug of coffee and a chocolate biscuit seemed to revive the old man and he looked more alert.

"Shall I get the doctor to call?"

"No. Don't bother anyone. I'm not ill, just a bit tired. We all have bad days, don't we? Tell me about you. What have you been doing this afternoon?"

Had everything that had happened with Jayne and Florence been since his midday visit to William?

"Spit it out. Has the delectable Florence returned?"

"Yes." Stuart paused. "And there's other news."

William rubbed the palms of his hands together as if looking forward to a big revelation. Stuart poured two more mugs of coffee and related the afternoon's events.

"Your life's never dull, is it?"

"Jayne's over the moon and she deserves that excitement. But, for some reason, she sees Florence as a rival. So, should I let Florence and her grandchildren stay? I don't want Jayne upset."

William drained his mug. Stuart waited for wise words. None came. "I can't make Florence and her grandchildren homeless."

"What does Sandra say?"

Stuart looked down, wishing he'd never revealed the dead sister who talked to him. Now he didn't know whether her voice was an actual phenomenon or the imagination of a lonely boy and a friendless man. Either way, Sandra wouldn't speak. "She hasn't commented on this situation."

"Sandra's realised that you've grown up enough in the last few months to make your own decisions. Make them wisely."

Stuart floundered. He didn't like decisions — usually, somewhere along the line, someone got hurt. "I don't want to rock the boat. Jayne and I are comfortable together. When I asked Jayne to marry me, she was ecstatic."

"And Florence?"

"It's a business relationship. She needs somewhere to live and I need the money."

"And she's offering to pay more for the children to stay on camp beds in the spare room?"

"Yes."

"There's your answer. Nothing has changed between you and Florence, therefore continue the business arrangement."

"But Jayne doesn't like her."

"Do you like the clients at Jayne's solicitor's office? Do you like her colleagues or her boss?"

"I don't know them. But it doesn't matter whether I like them or not. It's just her work."

"Exactly. And Florence is your 'work'."

* * *

The noise of loud canned laughter battered Stuart's ears when he opened his front door. Eunice and Shayne, dressed in pyjamas, were on the sofa watching a game show which seemed to involve adults in brightly coloured outfits racing around and pouring buckets of shaving foam over each other. Florence came out of the kitchen with two mugs of hot chocolate and almost collided with him in the hallway. They both looked down at the slops of brown liquid that had escaped the cups.

"I'll fetch a cloth." Their identical words crashed against each other. For a second their eyes met and then Stuart had to look away. This new, returned Florence was different, more vulnerable and less of a confident performer.

He signalled she should continue into the lounge. With a damp cloth he rubbed at the stain. The marks were of no great consequence on the worn hall carpet; whoever bought this place would throw it away. The volume of the television went down and the conversation of his three guests became audible.

"Drink up quickly. Mr Borefield is back, so it's time to be quiet and creep upstairs to bed like little mice."

"Can Tibby come with us?" the little girl asked.

Through the open door, Stuart could see the cat stretched out on Eunice's lap, no doubt purring and making her feel loved and warm inside.

"Best not. We don't want Tibby to get shut in anywhere upstairs and have an accident."

"But—"

"Sshh!" Florence stopped the little girl from protesting.

Stuart retreated to the kitchen and a few minutes later the children and their grandmother went upstairs. The phone made him jump.

"Why is she still there? And who are the children? Mum says they were running round the garden earlier."

The catch in Jayne's voice made him feel guilty. He tried to think how to soften the blow and let her know that he still loved her.

She didn't give him time before charging on. "At lunchtime I get engaged. I go back to work, explain to my colleagues why I'm late and they rush out to buy flowers and cake. They've even given me a bottle of sparkling wine to bring home and drink with you tonight. It doesn't look like there's going to be much chance of a romantic evening, does it?"

"I'm really sorry, Jayne." How could something so important go so horribly wrong?

"Are you calling the whole thing off?"

"No! I didn't know Florence was coming back. I didn't know they'd be homeless."

"Send them to the council."

"I can't do that. They might end up somewhere awful."

"So what's going to happen?"

"They're going to stay here until things get sorted out."

Jayne ended the call. Stuart felt like a baddie.

"Thank you."

He turned. Florence was standing in the kitchen doorway. Her eyes were wet with tears.

"I'm sorry, I heard you on the phone. Thank you for letting us stay."

She stepped into the room and he moved towards her. Somehow they ended up in an awkward embrace. The transfer of electricity between them was immediate and unexpected. Stuart had learned enough over the past few months to know that hugging Florence shouldn't feel like this. Especially now he was engaged to Jayne. He moved away and looked at the floor.

"It's the least I can do. I don't want the three of you sleeping on a park bench. Tibby wouldn't be very impressed at such living conditions." He tried to force lightness into the last sentence but it sounded more like someone in pain.

Florence laughed anyway. "Jim told me you were looking for me last night. He thought you were a stalker."

"I only wanted to know what to do with . . ." He gestured at the cat who'd just walked into the room, her tail held high and making little vibrating movements as she wound herself around Stuart's legs wanting food. "I'll be moving in with Jayne soon and I can't keep her then."

"Of course." Florence was suddenly businesslike. "I'll talk to the council tomorrow and, as a last resort, we could squash in with Jim. It'd be a tight squeeze but we don't have any plans to swing Tibby."

"What?"

"It was a joke. I was trying to say that at Jim's there won't be room to swing a cat." For a moment Florence looked like her old exuberant self and then her face dropped.

"Why didn't you answer any of my texts?" Stuart suddenly remembered the way he'd been stonewalled.

"Anger at first. About Slowcoach. Then I realised I'd overreacted and I didn't know how to apologise." She looked away from him. "Then delaying tactics — I had no home for Tibby. Confusion about the children and their future. It hasn't been a good time for me. I didn't have the headspace for everything."

Stuart squeezed her hand. "It doesn't matter."

CHAPTER THIRTY-FIVE

The council put Florence on a housing list but wouldn't act immediately because she had a roof over her head for the short term. The local school agreed to take Eunice and Shayne. Despite Stuart's offers to babysit, Florence didn't return to the band because she wanted to be around for the children in the evenings.

"They've lost all the stability they ever had. *I* can't neglect them as well."

Living with youngsters was unchartered territory. Stuart kept out of their way as much as possible, not wanting to impose on their family unit or influence their activities. But he couldn't get used to sitting down and finding a painful piece of his old Lego digging its way into his butt cheek. Or finding half-empty glasses of squash abandoned on random surfaces around the house. When he picked these glasses up there'd be a momentary resistance from the glue of spilled cordial, which left a sticky circle ready to attach itself to whatever book or paper Stuart placed there next. He had to acclimatise to the constant television blare of the multi-coloured cartoons that Eunice and Shayne devoured.

One day he came back from William's with a headache. The old man still wasn't on top form and Stuart had been trying to persuade him to allow the doctor to visit. But William had refused, putting forward the argument that sometimes you just knew when your life had run its course and, as an ex-GP, he was adamant that he knew better than most.

"I don't want to stay alive for the sake of it. Quality is better than quantity and I've had some good quality in my life."

The William problem made Stuart knock on Lillian's door when he got back.

"Stuart! How lovely but Jayne's not back from work yet."

He was in luck — his old neighbour was on the ball today. "It's you that I want to see."

"Ooh!" Lillian's smile grew and she gestured him inside.

"I don't know what to do about William. There's something not right with him but he won't let me call a doctor."

"Is it serious?"

"It's not an emergency, just a general air of malaise and tiredness. He doesn't want me to bother anyone. He says he's had his share of life."

"I can understand that."

"Really?" Stuart sat forward in his chair.

"Things wear out, usually at different rates. Sometimes it's the mind." The old lady smiled ruefully. "Sometimes it's our legs or our eyes or our ears. If we're lucky, we cope with what's missing and our quality of life remains. If we're unlucky, what's left feels like mere existence. Take your William. His brain is sharp but physically he's dependent on others and that must be constantly frustrating. He knows that no doctor can improve his situation, only prolong it."

"But isn't staying alive what we all want? Surely it's instinctive to want to keep a grip on life?"

Lillian smiled. "I'm glad that's how you feel, Stuart, but in thirty years you might have a different view. Days spent alone in the same four walls are endless. They merge into one long black corridor and it's a one-way corridor with no U-turns allowed."

"Do you think depression is William's problem?"

"Possibly that's part of it." The old lady spoke more slowly now and a frown was crawling across her forehead as though she was struggling to keep her concentration.

"Do you think I should report it to my boss?" Stuart spoke quickly before he lost her.

Lillian fiddled with her cardigan. "Interference. It's not always good." She paused and then her face lit up. "Interference — that doesn't happen with the television anymore, does it? It used to spoil the picture. Things weren't how they were supposed to be." Lillian smiled at him triumphantly. "Everything went all fuzzy and you had to hit the television. Hard." She slapped her thigh for emphasis.

Stuart smiled and patted her hand. That sentence, "Things weren't how they were supposed to be", repeated in his head as he walked to his own house. Nature knew how things were supposed to be and when man interfered, things got warped. Did William want his life to follow nature's plan rather than be controlled by the medicine and pills he'd spent his life prescribing for other people?

Stuart's head felt like the knot in tug of war, as he tried to decide the best path of action. The blare from the television as he opened the front door was the last straw. He marched straight into the lounge and turned it off.

"I can't stand that noise," he said. "I can't hear myself think. Haven't you got homework to do?" He regretted the words as soon as they shot from his mouth.

Eunice and Shayne shrank back into the sofa cushions, their eyes wide and their mouths making a little O shape. Florence came in, bringing the smell of shepherd's pie with her.

"What have you done to upset Mr Borefield?" Florence's voice was angrier than his own.

The children seemed to have lost the power of speech.

"It wasn't them, it was me." He sat down and put his head in his hands. "The television noise is wearing me down. Perhaps you could do something else?"

"You could play outside until tea's ready." Florence was casting him anxious glances. "Let's give Mr Borefield some peace."

"It's raining." Shayne's voice was whiney. "And my wellies got left behind at Dad's."

"Grandma said you're a story-maker, Mr Borefield." Eunice looked at him with bold eyes. "She says you're in charge of stories at the library and that one day, if we're good, you'll tell a story just for us."

Florence mouthed, "I'm sorry." All Stuart's ingenuity had been used settling the library toddlers that morning. William weighed on his shoulders. Jayne nagged about his lodgers. Stuart's head pounded. There were no children's books in the house for stories.

"Drawing!" Stuart said. "You could do some drawing."

"We don't have paper and pens here, Mr Borefield," Eunice said. "There wasn't room in the packing for our toys."

"Please don't keep calling me Mr Borefield. It makes me sound like my father." He looked at Florence. "Is it OK if they call me Uncle Stuart?"

A wave of relief passed over Florence's face and she nodded.

The easy option would be to blend into the sofa and say they could have the television on again. But that wasn't right. He remembered his own childhood. So much pleading to be allowed to tag along with his big brothers and then being left behind as they sprinted away from him at the first street corner. The misery of his mother's death. He had that tragedy in common with these youngsters. He remembered those dark days when he'd been left to his own devices for long periods, his brothers were young adults and his father had been preoccupied. What was it he'd really longed for at that time?

Attention. Someone to pay attention to him. Lillian had tried but, being only a neighbour and with her own family, she was limited in what she could do.

"Let's go to the supermarket while your grandmother finishes cooking tea. We'll buy some drawing stuff."

The children looked at each other and a flash of excitement passed between them. Then they looked hopefully at Florence.

"Are you sure you don't mind?" She was looking at him.

"We're going to be living together for a while, I think we should get to know each other a little."

There was a flurry of coats and shoes and orders from Florence that they must be as good as gold and remember their manners.

The supermarket didn't have the range of drawing things that Stuart would've liked but he let them each choose what they wanted. At the till he paid for two carrier bags so they could each carry their own new treasures. After tea they were allowed to draw one picture each before bed and Stuart learned a new diplomacy skill: the art of praising a child's drawing while at the same time teasing out the subject of the picture. In tandem with Florence, he managed to discover that Shayne had drawn a picture of Stuart's car with the sun glistening on its roof and Eunice's portrait showed Stuart bending down to stroke Tibby.

"You are both fantastic artists," Stuart said, feeling strangely warm inside that both children should want to do pictures focusing around him.

Jayne wasn't happy when he spoke in glowing terms about the children the next day. Lillian watched the conversation between them and then spoke quietly to Stuart when Jayne was in the kitchen.

"She still hurts from not having her own babies. I may be a bit doolally at times but I can recognise pain in my own daughter. She hasn't said it in so many words but she sees you living at such close quarters with another woman as a threat. Now that woman comes with grandchildren, something she can never offer you, she feels even more threatened."

Stuart suddenly realised how little he had truly considered Jayne's feelings and felt ashamed. When she came back in the room, he took her hands.

"Can you have Monday off work and we'll go ring shopping? I don't want you going around with a bare left hand any longer."

His fiancée's face lit up, giving him the same warm feeling as the children's drawings.

The tiny diamond took a significant chunk of Stuart's savings, but the look of happiness on Jayne's face made it worth every penny. Fleetingly, he wondered how life would've turned out if Carl hadn't snatched her away and he and Jayne had married thirty years ago. Would they be cooing over their own grandchildren now?

With the ring on her finger and excitement buzzing, they booked the registry office for the 31 March, the date that Stuart would lose the right to his brothers' house.

"Only four and a half months away!" Jayne gave a little joyful jump when they were back outside in the sharp November sunshine.

Lillian insisted on giving them a lump sum to pay for the wedding.

"Call it an advance on my will," she said. "I know you're as poor as a church mouse, Stuart, and Jayne's capital from her bedsit is a safety net for the future. This money is my gift to both of you. But Jayne will have to get it out of the computer."

"Mum doesn't have as much money as she thinks," Jayne told him later. "I'll draw some money from my savings but please let her keep her dignity and think she's paid."

Stuart nodded and tried not to feel that his dignity had been stripped away by his fiancée paying for the wedding. "I'll pay you back," he promised. "Veronica's pleased with me, so I'm a hopeful for a pay rise."

They arranged a small reception in a local restaurant for family, a couple of Jayne's work colleagues and a few mutual school acquaintances. It would be tactless to suggest inviting Florence, and William wouldn't be able to make the excursion.

CHAPTER THIRTY-SIX

Gradually Eunice and Shayne lost their pale, wan appearance. Despite the December weather they ran about in the garden and spent time with both Florence and Stuart at the swings in the park. On Saturday mornings, all four of them went to the playground together.

"Going to the park again today?" William asked over his porridge one Saturday morning.

Stuart nodded as he put the duster around the room.

"I thought so. The whistling gives it away."

Stuart hadn't realised he was whistling. He went silent.

"Don't stop. It cheers my day up. And there's little else positive in my life now."

Stuart's mood lowered in sympathy but when he was in the kitchen washing the cereal bowl and mug, he started thinking about the morning to come and the whistling was an unconscious by-product.

"Have a go down the slide for me," William said as Stuart was leaving. "I wish I still had the boundless energy of a child instead of this constant lethargy."

"How about I phone the surgery and get a doctor to call?" Over the past weeks William's spark hadn't returned, and he often seemed in discomfort as Stuart helped him onto the commode and when he moved his limbs to gently wash him. Interference couldn't be a completely bad thing if it made the old man more comfortable.

The old man waved a hand. "I've had my fair share of life. No point spending money to prolong it artificially. Better that effort is put into a kiddie or a young person with a life in front of them. I know how strapped for cash the NHS is."

Stuart worried over whether he should call a doctor anyway or if he should talk it over with Veronica. But most days, before he could dissect the dilemma in too much detail, his own life reached out and dragged him in. And Saturday mornings were the best example of that.

On arrival at Stuart's house, Shayne had been a quiet, self-effacing child with wide eyes that followed Stuart around the room with a combination of curiosity and fear. But as Shayne sat on a swing now, all trace of caution disappeared.

"Higher, Uncle Stuart! Push me higher!"

By the end of the morning, Stuart's arms and shoulders would ache from the effort of continuous pushing.

"I'm flying!" Shayne would call. "I'm flying like a bird!"

In the meantime, Eunice would be up the ladder to the slide and then shooting down its shiny metallic surface. On each outing she'd start off feet first and then, after a few confidence-building goes, she'd turn around and come down head first.

Despite the winter weather, the four of them would finish the morning buying ice creams with strawberry sauce and chocolate flakes from the little kiosk. There was great contentment in walking home with a cone in his hand and the milky, sweet taste of ice cream on his tongue, with Florence at his side telling him about her plans to visit the job centre now the children were on an even keel, and Eunice and Shayne ducking and diving between them, their dirty hands and faces smeared with chocolate and red sauce. Sometimes Florence would turn to look at him, a look that got right inside his soul and made him want to keep her there. When that happened, his heart soared, his toes curled within his shoes and he felt lucky to be able to share in this family, even if only on a temporary basis. They had both avoided any further electrically charged hugs.

Saturday afternoons were a slow descent into reality. Florence took the children to see Jim, their grandfather — the other adult male in the life of the little family. She was negotiating with the council for a new home. In less than four months, their home with Stuart would be gone and he would be married to someone else.

Saturday afternoons were an opportunity for him and Jayne to do their planning.

"I've bought the dress," she told him a couple of weeks before Christmas. "Antique cream lace. Ballerina length. I think I'm too old for the long white meringue."

"Don't tell him all the details," Lillian said. "It's bad luck."

Stuart put his hands over his ears, mimicking the 'Hear No Evil' monkey. To him, ballerina length meant a tutu sticking out in a neat little circle around the hips. He doubted that was the sort of outfit Jayne intended but he asked no further questions.

"Have you got your suit?"

"Suit?"

"The suit you're going to get married in. Have you bought it?"

Stuart hadn't thought of buying anything new. The suit he'd worn as an usher for both his brothers' weddings still fitted him and had plenty of wear left in it.

"I was hoping you'd come with me to choose it." She'd be disappointed if he admitted he hadn't thought of buying new.

"That's bad luck as well. I can't risk it. And you'll need a best man. At my age I can get away without an entourage of bridesmaids but you have to have a best man. What about one of your brothers?"

He'd assumed getting married would be simple, but now Jayne was producing all these complications, as though in order to win her hand, he had to pass certain tests. He suddenly thought how nice it would be to have Shayne and Eunice involved in the wedding. Shayne looking after the ring and acting as best man and Eunice dressed like a princess to act as bridesmaid. It would do both of them the world of good and send their confidence sky-high. But he couldn't suggest this.

"Is a best man a legal necessity?"

"It's not a legal thing but it is sort of expected. And we do want to do this properly, don't we?"

Lillian's eyes were flitting between the two of them. "I think Stuart's not totally in favour," she pronounced.

Stuart tensed. The old lady might be struggling in some areas of her life but she was amazingly good at picking up on hidden messages.

"No, I am in favour. Now I know what's expected, I'll get a new suit and a best man. After all, I'm only going to get married once, aren't I?"

Jayne leaned forward and kissed him on the cheek. "I told you Stuart was a keeper, didn't I, Mum?"

The old lady smiled but didn't look convinced.

Stuart phoned his eldest brother, Robert, that evening, to ask him to be best man. In the absence of close friends, it was the only option but he didn't have chance to make his request before Robert bounced in with an announcement of his own.

"I'm glad you've phoned, kiddo. George and I have been talking and we think it's best to get the house on the market ASAP in January. That way we might have a buyer ready to complete when you vacate at the end of March. No point in letting these things drag on, is there?"

"Oh!" The wind had been sucked from Stuart's sails and his news was relegated to the Any Other Business part of the conversation — the part of the agenda where Stuart was always placed.

"Obviously, we'll give you warning before the men with their clipboards and tape measures arrive, but I thought a heads-up now would mean no nasty surprises and a ship-shape house. Might be worth you getting a window cleaner in and tidying the garden. All the stuff that creates that vital first impression — as they say, you never get a second chance with first impressions, do you?" Robert chortled and Stuart could sense the conversation was coming to an end.

"There was something I wanted to ask you." Nerves suddenly constricted his throat. "Would you be my best man? Please." He kicked himself for adding the 'please', it made him sound desperate.

"Best man! Cindy! Kiddo is getting married!"

Stuart cringed as he listened to footsteps and muffled voices. He wished he'd suffered Jayne's wrath and got married without a best man.

"Congratulations!" Cindy's voice shouted a little way from the phone. "I really am genuinely pleased for you."

"I'd be delighted." Robert's voice cut over his wife's. "Who's the victim — I mean, lucky lady?"

"Jayne, from next door."

"Wonderful. A second bite of the cherry, if you get my drift."

Stuart forced the conversation to a close by giving the date and time. At least Jayne would be happy now.

The next morning's club ride was bitterly cold and it was a smaller than usual turnout. Guiltily Stuart realised he was glad Mike wasn't there. Mike always wanted a progress report on how Jayne was doing with Mavis's old bike and Stuart always had to give a fudged reply. The truth was that Jayne showed no interest in improving her cycling ability or anything else that was even slightly outside her comfort zone.

Following her birthday, they'd had one more trip to the quarry but the weather had turned showery and she'd insisted they cut it short. After that, combining their individual time off work with the day-centre session made it difficult to get out during the week, and at weekends Jayne wouldn't leave Lillian. Stuart suspected that time could have been engineered if Jayne had really wanted.

Today he chatted with Jennifer and some of the others and at the café stop, they wrapped their hands around warm mugs of hot chocolate and nibbled on hunks of bread pudding. Jennifer was one of the better ride leaders, always finding a new lane to explore or a different way of avoiding the busier roads. She seemed to be aware if someone was struggling and slowed the pace accordingly. With only a couple of weeks until his turn to lead, Stuart was apprehensive.

"Just be you," Jennifer said when he asked her for advice as they waited for the stragglers to leave the café. "You always make newcomers welcome and encourage anyone who's tired. You're a natural."

It was difficult to take confidence from mere words. It would be a relief when that first ride was under his belt with no mishaps. After the coffee break in the warmth, it was hard to get limbs moving again and there was a lot of foot-stamping and exaggerated shivering as they prepared to set off on the homeward route.

Stuart had a shopping trip planned for when he got back, one that couldn't be put off any longer. The build-up to Christmas was usually a non-event. He'd buy bed socks and pyjamas for his father and choose himself a couple of books, which Eric would inscribe with the year and wrap with precision. Last year, Stuart had had to cut the paper and sticky tape to assist with the operation of wrapping his own presents. But this year contained the excitement of youngsters plus the difficult job of buying for three women. After the failure of the bike idea, he'd decided thinking outside the box was too risky and he picked a department-store perfume counter at random for Florence and Jayne, and asked advice from an immaculate woman in a white overall.

"What are the ages of the ladies? And do you know what type of perfume they favour? Spicy, floral, light or heavy?"

He hadn't realised buying scent was so complicated. "They're both mid-fifties and I don't know what they like."

"Hmmm." The woman frowned at Stuart as though he'd failed an important test. "This is our bestseller." She sprayed perfume on what looked like an ice-lolly stick and handed it to Stuart to smell.

It smelled like perfume. He tried to imagine the smell on Florence and Jayne. He couldn't see how it could be construed as 'wrong'.

"That one is on special offer at the moment. If you buy the largest size of perfume, you'll get the matching body lotion free."

Stuart digested the information. His carer's wage plus Florence's rent (he hadn't taken the extra money she'd offered for the children's presence) didn't leave much money to splash around and this way they'd each get two parcels to unwrap.

"I'll have two, please." The saleswoman smiled, revealing very white teeth, unfortunately marked with a splodge of lipstick.

Stuart pushed his debit card into the mouth of the machine and tried to ignore the exorbitant amount it was demanding for bottles of nice-smelling water. For Lillian, he followed Jayne's instructions and bought a specific pale blue nightdress from Marks and Spencer. He felt conspicuous — it was his first time in a lingerie department — but he also felt proud to be moving into the real world.

Florence had been pleased when he'd told her he wanted to buy something for the children. She'd shown him two lists created with laborious handwriting and containing spelling mistakes. The present of a dictionary had crossed his mind, but he'd realised that wouldn't go down well. Just as it hadn't gone down well with him when the gaily wrapped present had been handed to him at age seven by his father.

"Choose something that fits how much you want to spend," Florence had instructed.

How long is a piece of string? How much did Florence think he should spend? He didn't want to appear mean but there was no money tree in the back garden. On principal, he avoided anything electronic or screen-based, choosing a Barbie Doggy Daycare set and an Action Man helicopter, on the basis that he and Sandra would probably have liked those as youngsters.

Stuart managed to keep his mouth shut when he saw the children's advent calendars contained cheap chocolates rather than Christmas images. But the Elf on the Shelf thing tested him to the brink. Florence explained that the elf kept an eye on the children and reported any wrongdoing back to Father Christmas. Each day, Florence made the elf pop up in a different part of the house to carry out his spying duties. Shayne and Eunice kept reminding Stuart about the red-suited toy's eagle eyes and Stuart hated the feeling of being watched.

* * *

On Christmas Eve, the children were hyper with excitement. Stuart loved that this was happening under his roof. Unusually, Florence was harassed.

"I've got mince pies and a trifle to make and I can't do it with these two under my feet." She looked at Stuart. "You were a teacher, you know about children. Can't you occupy them for a couple of hours? Teach them something useful?"

Stuart shook his head and started to back away, his hands raised defensively. "No, sorry. Teenagers were my thing. And I wouldn't have tried to teach them geography on Christmas Eve. Definitely not."

"Please?" Florence flicked a strand of hair from her eye and left a blob of flour on her nose. "Or read them a story?"

"What's geography? What's geography? What's geography?" Shayne was pogoing in front of Stuart.

Eunice dipped her finger in the jar of mincemeat, licked it and then dug further into the jar.

"Please?" Florence removed the jar.

"Geography! Geography! Geography!" The children turned the word into a football chant.

"OK." This wasn't going to work.

"Thank you. Thank you. Now shoo! Out of the kitchen!"

Stuart cranked up the rusty part of his brain labelled geography topics. Water cycle, deserts, rainforests, volcanos and earthquakes. With no textbooks or teaching resources, it was an impossible challenge. The children bounced on the settee still chanting. "Geography! Geography!"

Eric's old globe was on the sideboard. Stuart picked it up. "Geography is about the whole world." He spoke slowly, trying to gain time for an idea to percolate in his mind. "Who is travelling across the whole world tonight?"

The children frowned at him. Stuart was back in front of a class of thirteen-year-olds asking the easiest of questions but getting nothing back.

"Geography! Geography!" Shayne had started bouncing and chanting again.

Then Eunice's eyes lit up. "Father Christmas!"

Shayne stared at his sister. "Not true! He's coming from the North Pole. Not around the whole of the gigantic world."

Stuart picked up the globe. "You are right, Shayne. He is coming from the North Pole, which is here. But Eunice is right too, because Father Christmas has to go to all the countries in the world to deliver presents to all the children."

Now he had their attention. The next challenge was to keep it.

"He has a special route which starts here, in the Pacific Ocean."

"What's the Pacific?"

There were only seconds to answer Shayne's question or risk the boy winding himself up with excitement again.

"It's the biggest and deepest of all the oceans on the planet." Keep the answers simple.

"Too deep to swim?" Eunice asked.

Stuart nodded. "Unless you stay right near the beach."

"Where does Father Christmas go after that?"

Stuart stared at the globe and tried to dredge up fun knowledge about somewhere else.

Shayne started bouncing again. "Does he go to Australia to see the kangaroos?"

"He does exactly that." Thank you, Shayne. "Do you know what other animals live in Australia?"

A conversation about koala bears and poisonous spiders followed. Stuart was enjoying himself now. It was too long since he'd been challenged on his knowledge and his ability to make learning interesting. Eunice and Shayne were like sponges compared to the stonewalling he'd received from some of his teenaged classes. Was he too old to become a primary school teacher? A wave of unexpected excitement for the future washed over him.

In no particular geographical order, they moved on to Father Christmas delivering presents to the lions of Africa and the tigers of India. He would have to sharpen up on his lesson planning.

Later, Florence joined them and geography was abandoned. The children could no longer sit still and they talked endlessly about which items from their list they thought Santa would bring. A few nights earlier, Stuart had helped Florence wrap a stack of stocking presents and hide them in the loft.

"Jacob and Jim both gave me money to help with the cost," she said. "Otherwise it would've been a very meagre Christmas and it would've been difficult at school for them when everyone's comparing presents. They've had a tough life and I don't want them to suffer more than is absolutely necessary."

There was pure love in Florence's eyes and at that point, without thinking, Stuart had leaned over and given her a hug. The electricity was still there. She tensed and pulled back first.

"Be careful what you're doing, Stuart," she said lightly and gave him a gentle punch on the arm. "You're engaged to be married. What will your fiancée think if you go around touching other women?"

"I wasn't touching, I was only . . ."

"Let's keep our relationship as it is. I can't cope with complications at the moment."

Florence's reaction shouldn't have mattered. But it did.

CHAPTER THIRTY-SEVEN

Christmas morning started at five thirty a.m., before Stuart's alarm clock. Noise and squeals sounded from downstairs. Excitement raced through him and he grabbed his dressing gown and slippers.

The lounge was a sea of paper and Florence looked at him apologetically. He grinned and shook his head at her. This was like all the Christmases he'd never had. His older brothers had ensured the Santa Claus myth hadn't lingered long for him and his mother's premature death had meant there had been no one to wave a magic wand over the season. Now he wanted to dive into all the detritus and be a boy again.

"I want to see everything that Santa's brought," Stuart said. "But first I'm going to make special Christmas coffees for your gran and me."

Maybe Florence read the longing in his expression. "No. I'll make the coffee and you get stuck in."

He smiled at her and mouthed the word, "Brandy." He sat down on the floor and the children were all over him, fighting to be the first to show off their spoils. Afterwards, he sat on the sofa next to Florence, enjoying his caffeine with a kick and the chocolate coins that Eunice and Shayne were handing around from the net bags Santa had brought.

The hands on the clock were moving too fast. At 6.45 a.m. he'd have to race through the shower and get dressed in order to get to William.

"Mistletoe!" Eunice leaned over the back of the sofa and dangled a plastic piece of mistletoe in front of them. "My teacher says that people kiss under the mistletoe. You can kiss if you want to."

He did want to but didn't dare turn his head. Kissing Florence wasn't the right thing to do. She didn't want it and he was engaged to someone else. The tension was awkward and then Stuart stood up.

"No time. I'm going to be late for William and he needs a Happy Christmas as well."

* * *

"Happy Christmas, William!"

The figure in the bed rolled over and began to stretch with a groan. The old man wasn't right. Stuart helped him into a sitting position and then onto the commode.

"I think we should get the doctor in."

"Not today. Don't spoil anyone's Christmas. Andrea will be here at lunchtime and then I'll be right as rain."

"Are you sure?"

"All I need is a mug of tea and some of your lovely porridge with extra golden syrup. You always get the temperature just right now."

"I make a good breakfast, but it doesn't work miracles."

As William drank the tea he brightened up and after a few spoons of hot cereal he was ready for conversation. Stuart told him about Florence and the children and their excitement.

"You're glowing, Stuart."

"Childish excitement. It's contagious." Stuart didn't meet the old man's eye.

William scraped his spoon around the edge of the bowl and Stuart was satisfied that his client had perked up enough to not require a doctor. Florence hovered in his mind and he pushed her away; he had Christmas Day with Jayne to look forward to plus his wedding day — the gateway to that bright new future.

"You best be off to your fiancée then and I'll see you tomorrow. Andrea will make sure I'm OK before she leaves this evening."

The children were putting coats on and hauling a black bag into the boot of the Panda.

"I need to get to Jim's and start on the dinner." Florence was carrying mince pies and the trifle out to the car.

"And we're going to show Granddad our presents." Shayne patted the bin bag.

"And I'm taking the mistletoe." Eunice held up the green plastic twig. "Granddad likes to kiss Grandma."

The seed of disappointment in Stuart's stomach grew another layer. Florence had turned her back to fiddle with the key in the car door.

"Have a good time." He forced a grin and waved at the children.

"We might stay over. So I can have a glass of wine." Now she was looking at him.

He nodded. "No problem. I'll feed Tibby." From the corner of his eye, Stuart saw Florence nudge each of the children.

"Thank you for the Barbie," said Eunice. "I like the little dogs."

"Thank you for the helicopter." Shayne produced it from behind his back and ran down the drive pretending it was flying.

"I'm saving my parcel to open after dinner," Florence said. "There's one for you on the kitchen table."

At that moment there was a knock on glass from next door. Jayne was gesticulating.

"We'd better go." Florence shooed the children into the car.

Stuart gave a thumbs-up sign to his fiancée and went indoors to collect presents. There were two parcels from

Florence on the kitchen table, both book-shaped. He decided the day might go more smoothly if he left them where they were and opened them later, on his own. When he could savour them.

The rest of Christmas Day was quiet. He and Jayne cooked dinner together at her house. Lillian ate heartily and talked a lot about the relatives that would be arriving for tea. Jayne pointed out, under her breath to Stuart, that these people were all deceased. After the King's speech they opened presents. Stuart was relieved when Jayne immediately sprayed herself with the perfume.

"Good perfume is my favourite luxury," she said. "But I can never justify buying it for myself."

Lillian tried to put the nightdress on top of her scarlet Christmas jumper until Jayne rescued it. Stuart received five pairs of socks marked with an 'S' from Lillian, but obviously chosen by Jayne, and a shirt and tie from Jayne herself.

"I thought you could keep them for the wedding."

"What about all that bad luck stuff?"

Jayne shrugged. "I didn't know which was the greater risk, the bad luck or you turning up in a polo shirt."

"Mistletoe!" Lillian positioned a real piece of the plant above her daughter's head and Stuart kissed his fiancée slowly and gently. She smiled at him and he held her close.

Later, when Lillian was in bed, they snuggled up on the sofa with glasses of Baileys and a box of Quality Street. It felt like a safe, comfortable place to be; the best ending to Christmas Day he'd ever had. Except for the wandering thought about what Florence was doing.

CHAPTER THIRTY-EIGHT

On Boxing Day morning, Stuart hammered the alarm into silence and lay back for a minute. No noise. The house was empty again. He wished Florence and the children were there. Jim's house was small. Where was Florence sleeping? He pushed the thought from his mind; it was none of his business.

In the kitchen, the two parcels were still waiting for him. He'd looked at them last night. Opening them had felt traitorous to Jayne. It shouldn't feel this way. Florence had no romantic interest in him; she'd given the presents to him as a friend not a lover. He should open them and text her. It would be rude not to. He made mule-kick coffee.

The first book made him smile: *Fiendishly Difficult Cryptic Crosswords*. He opened the front cover, hoping for an inscription with a typical Florence comment, but the pages were pristine. The second book had a picture of man on the cover with greying hair and the beginnings of a paunch. There was a huge rucksack on his back and a map in his hand. It was called *Grown-Up Gap Years*. This time she had written something. It was on a piece of paper slotted in between the pages. *I bought this ages ago, before you made things official with Jayne, when you were still looking for that bright future. Perhaps now it's something you can do together? Best wishes, Florence.*

Stuart had to blink a couple of time. Florence had put thought into these presents. She hadn't just walked up to a beauty counter and bought two of the first thing offered. He ran his fingers over the cover of the travel book and flicked through the pages. The chapter headings made him excited for what could be. Sharing a journey like this would be the perfect start to married life. But then he remembered Lillian and put the book back on the table.

William would be waiting. He dropped bread into the toaster and got the marmalade out. He hoped Andrea had given her father a day to remember, something to eject him from the mysterious lethargy that plagued him.

"So how was it?" he called as he let himself in and took his coat off.

Silence.

"Must have been good if you're still asleep. What did Santa bring?"

He walked into the back room and immediately noticed there was no hump in the bed and no William in the chair.

"William!" The old man wasn't mobile enough to get anywhere else in the house but still Stuart checked all the rooms. He even went upstairs where it was chilly, disused and dusty. There was no sign of the old man. He managed to unlock and open the swollen back door that was rarely used except when the man came to mow the lawn in the summer. He walked the perimeter of the garden but found nothing.

Stuart began to panic. How could a frail old man disappear into thin air? He'd often imagined the scenario of arriving at the house and finding William unconscious or even cold with death. But he'd never foreseen him just not being here. He should phone someone. The police? Veronica? Andrea was here yesterday and she was his next of kin. There was a list of phone numbers taped to the top of the bedside cabinet where the cordless phone sat in the charging unit. There was both a landline and a mobile number for Andrea. This early in the morning, Stuart tried the landline.

It was answered on the second ring. "Hello?"

"Hello, Andrea. My name is Stuart Borefield. I'm your dad's carer. I don't want to alarm you but I've just arrived for my morning call and he's not here."

"Stuart. He mentioned you a lot." There was an edge to her voice.

"Did you see him yesterday? Do you know where he is?"

"He collapsed. I called an ambulance. I'm about to go back to the hospital now."

Stuart closed his eyes for a second, feeling overwhelmed by guilt. "I'm sorry. He'd been out of sorts but he wouldn't let me call a doctor. What's wrong with him?"

"They need to do tests but with it being Christmas, the right people aren't available. It's serious though." There was a catch in her voice as she said the last words.

"Can I see him?"

There was a silence before Andrea replied. "Meet me at the Infirmary, Ward Nine, at noon. You could sit with him and feed him his lunch while I get something to eat. The nurses are always busy."

"He feeds himself."

"Not anymore."

Stuart sat for a few minutes surveying the four walls that had become the extent of William's life. Guilt gnawed at the edges of his mind. Then he carefully locked the house and replaced the key in the small safe next to the front door.

Jayne pulled a face when Stuart told her that they couldn't spend the whole day together. "It's not as if he's family."

"I'm sorry but I've grown fond of him. Seeing a familiar face might do him good. Think how you'd feel if it was Lillian." He'd only be gone an hour or two. Jayne and Lillian would survive but William might not.

"It's not the same thing at all. I wanted to have Boxing Day with my fiancé instead of another day with my mother who's expecting her dead cousins to turn up for mince pies and mulled wine at any moment. *I* need support too."

* * *

Andrea didn't say much when he arrived, just introduced herself, shook his hand and went off in search of the canteen. William was propped up on pillows with his eyes closed. There was a drip of clear liquid connected to his arm.

"William, it's Stuart. Can you hear me?"

"Yes." The old man's voice was like tissue paper and he didn't open his eyes.

"How are you feeling?"

"I can see light at the end of the tunnel. It's not too far away."

There was a lump in Stuart's throat. He touched the hand lying on top of the bedclothes. It was cool and still.

"Before I say goodbye . . ."

Stuart had to lean closer to hear him properly.

"One last piece of advice."

There was a long silence but Stuart didn't dare fill it with reassuring platitudes in case he talked over William's faded words.

"Don't choose the comfortable life."

Stuart closed his eyes, trying to infer exactly what the old man meant and not liking his conclusion.

"Comfortable turns into a rut." William was speaking slowly, as though he was choosing each word for economy and effectiveness. "You deserve better."

"I've got some soup for William." A young girl in pink scrubs pushed a trolley alongside Stuart. "Would you like to help him eat or shall I?"

"I . . ." Stuart found there were tears in his eyes. He blew his nose. "I'd like to do it."

The girl adjusted the bed to make William more upright. "Your son's going to feed you, William. Can you open your eyes?"

"I'm not his—"

"William? Can you hear me?" There was a hint of panic in her voice and she pressed the buzzer on the bed next to William's hand. Then she turned to Stuart with an apologetic look. "If you're not family I think you'd better leave. You can call later for an update."

* * *

It was a long afternoon with Jayne and Lillian. He tried to be bright and enjoy the games of rummy and snap when Lillian's concentration waned, but his mind was with the old man. He ate Quality Street under sufferance of being branded anti-social but refused more Baileys in case he needed to drive to the hospital again.

His phone vibrated and Andrea's name came up on the display as he was laying out a buffet tea of cold turkey, pickles and bread rolls.

"I thought I better let you know. Dad passed away thirty minutes ago. He never regained consciousness."

Stuart gripped the back of the nearest kitchen chair and then sat down on it.

"I . . . I'm really sorry to hear that." What were the right words? What would he have liked people to say or do when his father died? "Shall I come over? Do you have someone with you?"

"Thanks, but everything's under control."

"You'll let me know about the funeral?"

"Yes. I'd better go, more people to phone."

Jayne and Lillian ate the lion's share of the tea. Stuart sat between them as they watched a re-run of the original *Charlie and the Chocolate Factory*. Lillian occasionally gave his hand a squeeze. Jayne appeared not to register that he was upset and focused completely on the film.

"I wonder what's happened to all those Oompa Loompas?" she said.

"Dead, probably." If it hadn't been Boxing Day he'd have gone home and set up his cycle turbo trainer in the garage. He needed to do something to work through the stress that had been building in him all day. "Shall we go for a walk?"

"It's dark." Both women looked at him as though he'd suggested a trip to the moon.

"I'm sorry. I'm a bit uptight. I need to do something. I'll call you tomorrow."

He cycled, stationary in the garage with the door open so he'd know immediately when Florence returned. When the orange Panda finally crunched over the gravel, it felt like a weight had been lifted. He showered, helped get the children to bed and then he told Florence about William. She put a hand on his back while he had a little cry.

"I've got it out of proportion, I know. It was only work but he was, well, a friend."

"You've seen him three times a day for months. You're entitled to be upset."

"I feel guilty."

"It wasn't your fault he wouldn't see a doctor."

"Not just that." Stuart blew his nose and looked Florence in the eye. "I didn't cry properly when Dad died. It's like William meant more to me than Dad."

Florence held his shoulders. "Grief isn't logical, Stuart. Crying doesn't mean you're grieving more. It just means you're grieving differently."

Stuart took some breaths and managed a smile. "Thanks."

They sat in silence for a few minutes and then Florence described how the stay at Jim's had gone better than expected, considering their marital differences.

"There was just one embarrassing thing. The kids kept chasing us with that dratted plastic mistletoe. Jim seemed to quite like it but I had to keep dodging out of the way. Didn't want any of them getting the idea that reconciliation was a possibility."

Stuart went to bed feeling that there were still some positives in life.

CHAPTER THIRTY-NINE

Before Christmas, Stuart had arranged for another of Veronica's carers to do William's breakfast visit the first Sunday in January. As things had turned out, there'd been no need. Stuart lay in bed, waiting for the alarm to go off and thinking about the old man. William would've been keen for him to be successful leading his first group ride. Jayne didn't seem to grasp its importance or understand his need to take on new challenges like this.

"Why do you create all this stress and aggravation for yourself when we could just have a quiet morning at home together?" she'd said when he'd expressed his anxiety.

He tried to explain about building a bright new future but she looked as puzzled as if he'd just said he was going to shape-shift into a unicorn.

The previous evening he'd checked his bike over and made sure he'd got his phone and water bottle ready, plus tools in case anyone was unprepared for a puncture or other minor mishap. Now he got out of bed slowly and took deep breaths, trying to relax away the nerves. It didn't work — they decided to sit in a hard ball in his stomach. Breakfast was difficult to eat but in a couple of hours he'd be glad of the energy.

The turnout was good and he shouted for order over the melange of New Year greetings and Christmas news. After a couple of attempts at raising his voice, everyone got the message that it was time to depart. Most of the other leaders on the rota downloaded their routes onto GPS devices, which then conveniently sat on their handlebars. Stuart didn't yet have the finances and was forced to work the old-fashioned way with a map in a plastic case. The traffic was light with few people out yet — they were still within the Christmas holiday period — and the group made good progress. He was grateful to Jennifer for offering to be a backstop in case he didn't notice anyone failing to keep up with the speed. As they stopped at each junction he glanced backwards and was rewarded with her wave. At the top of all hills, he waited for the stragglers. It also gave him time to take in the views. The height made him feel on top of the world as he looked down on miniature farms, toy trains and a patchwork of fields still in their winter slumber. It put his 'problems' into perspective — in the grand scheme of things he was just a very tiny cog.

"You're doing good," Jennifer whispered as they queued for coffee and slabs of Christmas cake in the café at the mid-point. "But the hard bit is yet to come."

"What?" Stuart went cold, trying to think what he might have forgotten.

Jennifer laughed. "Getting everybody out of the warmth back into that chilly wind!"

Then Mike sat next to him. Stuart tried to think up a new excuse why Jayne wasn't cycling and wondered if he should offer to give the bike back. Despite his best efforts, it was obvious that his fiancée had no interest in travelling on two wheels. But before Mike could speak there was a tap on Stuart's shoulder and he was plunged into answering questions about the route home. From the corner of his eye, he saw Mike's frown and resolved to return Mavis's bike. He didn't like the responsibility for giving it a loving home and generating glowing reports about its use and wellbeing. It was a generous gift but had too many strings attached and Stuart risked tangling them. He'd talk to Mike about returning it. But not today. Today he had to keep all the balls in the air until the ride was safely over.

The closer they got to home, the lighter Stuart felt. The last mile felt as though he was flying, even though he kept the pace steady, mindful that people would be tired. At the end, a couple of the men shook hands and thanked him.

Jennifer gave him a grin and a peck on the cheek. "It'll be less traumatic next time!"

Stuart rode slowly home feeling as though another bridge towards his brighter future had been crossed. He could do this. He could actually interact with the real world without mishap. He could be accepted for who he was.

"You look like a cat who's got the cream," Lillian said when he went round later, and Stuart suddenly realised that his facial muscles were aching from a grin that didn't want to go away.

* * *

A few days' later, three estate agents came to value the house at hourly intervals. Stuart got it organised for the morning Florence had a job-centre appointment immediately after the hairdresser's. He didn't want her upset or reminded about the fact that there were less than three months remaining for her and the children in the house.

It was difficult watching each of the agents, two men and one woman, in their cheap jackets and scuffed shoes, nose through the decades of his life. Excluding his student days, this had been his only home. The large rooms and high ceilings got universal approval, the word tired was bounced around the kitchen and bathroom and 'has potential' won the prize for the most uttered phrase. Each agent promised to get back to George and Robert directly with their valuations and marketing plans. Stuart tried to nod and smile as though all of this was of absolutely no consequence to him.

When he shut the front door on the last jacket, which had a loose thread pulled across the shoulders, he leaned against the wood for a few seconds and then slid down and sat on the doormat. It felt as though the whole of his personal history had been examined and found wanting. And he and Florence were going to have to prepare the children for yet another change of home. He only stood up when he heard his phone beep in the kitchen. Andrea had sent him a text with arrangements for William's funeral in three days' time.

"Do you want me to come with you? Moral support?" Florence asked later.

It was a tempting offer and Stuart knew William would have approved. Jayne would be working . . . but he couldn't betray his fiancée in that way.

"Thanks for the offer but I'll be fine on my own."

* * *

On the morning of the funeral, the estate agent appointed by Robert and George called to arrange a viewing. The potential purchaser was insisting he had to visit the house that day, preferably ASAP.

"He's lost three houses due to being pipped at the post," the agent explained. "Now he's kicking up a fuss if he doesn't get first dibs at the new properties on our books."

Stuart managed to delay the viewing until after the funeral, when Florence would be out, collecting the children from school and taking them to a playdate. He hadn't yet plucked up the courage to tell her the estate agents had been round, never mind that the house was on the market. After some negotiation, the agent had agreed not to stick a sign outside the house until Stuart had given the go ahead.

All the subterfuge meant Stuart arrived at the crematorium in a bit of a lather and not fully focused on saying goodbye to his old friend. He sat at the back of the chapel, closed his eyes, took a few deep breaths and remembered. His relationship with William had left him so much to be grateful for. Visiting the old man three times a day had forced a structure into his life at a time when he'd been directionless. Those visits hadn't felt like work, they'd been like calling on a friend for a chat and wise counsel. Stuart smiled — maybe the counsel hadn't always been that wise; they hadn't always seen eye to eye over the women in his life.

As he took another deep breath, the anodyne background music switched to the opening bars of Elgar's *Nimrod*. Stuart opened his eyes, expecting the chapel to have filled but, aside from the first two rows, the seats were almost empty. It reminded him of his father's funeral ten months earlier and the sad fact that the longer you live, the fewer people will attend to say goodbye.

He assumed Andrea would give the eulogy. She was in the front row on the left of the chapel dressed in a black skirt suit. When she'd turned round, her eyes were hidden by a small piece of netting on the front of her hat. But she didn't stand to speak about her father or to do a reading. She occasionally dabbed beneath the netting as a celebrant spoke warmly, but without real fluency, of William. It was obvious he was regurgitating what he'd been told of the life of a man he'd never known. That made Stuart even sadder.

At the end of the ceremony, the curtains closed to the familiar tune of 'Amazing Grace'. Then the celebrant announced everyone was welcome to the wake at a local restaurant. Stuart looked at his watch and realised that he needed to leave now in order to get home before the house viewer arrived. If William was watching from above, Stuart felt sure he would forgive him.

Florence had already left for the school when he got home. He scooted around the house plumping cushions and hiding toys. He started a pot of coffee brewing, hoping to create an enticing smell to override any odours so familiar that Stuart no longer noticed them. The appointed viewing time came and went. Stuart paced up and down in front of the lounge window, watching for a car. Nothing. He phoned the agent.

"Ah! Didn't your wife mention it? There was a confusion over times and the purchaser came at two o'clock rather than four o'clock."

Stuart groaned and sat down on the bottom chair.

"Mr Savile loved the place. He likes the potential. He phoned me straight after. Said your wife gave him tea and biscuits and he's put in an offer." The agent paused. "But, as you know, I'm not allowed to discuss that with you. Your brothers are considering it as we speak."

"I see." Poor Florence. It hadn't been supposed to happen like this. She wouldn't be happy, having a strange man turn up out of the blue to poke around the place she called home.

"Strange that your wife didn't tell you."

"She's not my wife and she was out when I got back."

"Oh. In the meantime, I'll let you know if we get any more requests for viewings. By the way, is it OK if we get the sign up now?"

"What? Yes. It's OK." The damage was done. "Thank you."

An hour later, the house erupted into life as Eunice and Shayne burst into the hallway and Florence's voice followed, urging them to take off their shoes and hang up their coats. For once Stuart was the one to turn on the television for the children and leave them in the lounge with squash and biscuits. He gestured Florence into the kitchen and closed the door.

"I am so sorry. That Mr Savile should never have come when you were here."

Florence frowned. "I think that makes it worse, don't you? Why are you trying to hide that the house is up for sale? I'm not stupid, I do remember your time here is limited."

"I was worried about the effect the upheaval would have on the children."

"So you were going to keep it a secret and then spring it on us just before moving day? That would hardly help matters, would it?"

"I'm sorry." Stuart was out of his depth. Weighing up the effect of his actions on others or working out what was best for them was a skill he hadn't yet grasped. "I got it wrong. I'm sorry."

Florence sat down on one of the hard chairs and put her head in her hands. There was a quiver across her shoulders and a barely discernible sniff. He pulled another chair up alongside her and tentatively stroked her back.

"I'm worried about the upheaval too." Her voice was muffled. "It's the first thing I think about in the morning and the last thing I think about at night. Those kids have been through enough. But unless the council comes up trumps, I don't know what we're going to do." The shaking of her shoulders became more marked.

Stuart was desperate to hold her close. When Florence had first arrived on his doorstep, he'd pre-judged her as some showy, brash airhead. Over the months he'd come to realise that her flamboyance and extraversion brought colour and fun. And that underneath she was more vulnerable, caring and thoughtful than many 'ordinary people'. He felt privileged to be in her orbit.

His arm, resting on her back, was tense with anticipation. He thought fleetingly of Jayne's disapproval. She wouldn't like him comforting Florence with a hug, even though Florence had made it plain she wanted nothing but platonic friendship with Stuart.

Florence was fumbling in her pocket for a tissue. The familiar sound of a cartoon chase was muffled by the closed kitchen door. Playing the part of his usual grey self, Stuart felt helpless. Bugger it. Sandra had become increasingly silent but he knew exactly what she'd be exhorting now. Florence deserved the same empathetic treatment she had shown him when he'd been in distress.

Stuart stretched his arm around Florence's shoulders and pulled her close. Her head turned towards him and he gently brushed away the hair that had fallen over her eyes. She looked at him, her cheeks wet with tears and smudges of makeup escaping into the creases of her eyes and lips. Stuart didn't stop to analyse or prejudge his next movement. He leaned in and kissed her on the lips. For a split second he felt her tense and then she relaxed. Stuart felt warmed and tantalised. Inside his slippers, his toes curled. He felt Florence shift her position so that she could wrap her arms around him. Who needed mistletoe?

There was a crash as the kitchen door flew open and the exaggerated noise of a helicopter filled the room. The moment was gone. Shayne was skidding across the vinyl in his socks, Christmas toy held up high, making engine noises. Eunice was staring at them as though they'd each turned into one of the multicoloured unicorns she left scattered across the lounge floor. Her expression was one of maternal concern. "I thought you two didn't do kissing?"

"We don't." Florence stood up and headed for the freezer. "Who wants fish fingers for tea?"

"Me!" Shayne started cheering as though he was on the football terraces.

"Stuart?"

He shook his head. His brain seemed to have lost the power of forming words and transmitting them to his tongue. Or perhaps it was his tongue that had gone on strike, in order to savour the specialness of what had just happened.

"Can I tell Granddad that you kissed Stuart?" Eunice's eyes were darting between the two adults.

"Kissing's soppy." Shayne landed the helicopter in the exact centre of the kitchen table. "It's for girls."

"Best not tell Granddad." Florence dumped a bag of frozen chips onto the work surface next to the fish fingers. "Kissing is a private thing." She looked over at Stuart, catching his eye as she next spoke. "And it was a mistake. I won't be kissing Stuart again."

The rosy glow within Stuart sputtered and died beneath the cold water of her words.

"I already explained to you that Stuart is going to marry Jayne, who lives next door. When you're going to be married you can't kiss other people."

"Pooh! Jayne doesn't like us." Eunice disappeared into the lounge and came back with a unicorn and a tiny pink plastic hairbrush. She started to brush the plastic animal's mane.

Stuart looked at Florence, trying to make his expression into a question mark. She misinterpreted the question, perhaps on purpose. "The children don't like it when she calls over the fence for them to be quiet."

It would be wise to leave the room now. He should go for a walk, clear his head before he went next door to eat with Jayne and Lillian. But he didn't move. He watched the other three eat fish fingers, chips and beans. The children were a non-stop fountain of chatter about school, Tibby, unicorns and helicopters. It seemed hardly possible that they were the same pale, silent, timid youngsters who'd arrived on his doorstep after losing their mother. Whoever said kids were resilient was absolutely right.

Eventually Jayne rang to summon him and Stuart left with a reluctant wave to the little family.

CHAPTER FORTY

Veronica called Stuart into the office of the Primo Care Agency for a chat.

"I'm going to put you onto our bank of carers," she said, "standing in when someone's off sick or on holiday. You'll get a broad range of experience then. I think that's what you're missing. It doesn't do to get too close to a particular client."

"So I won't get regular hours?"

"No."

Jayne was going to hate this. She liked to know where he'd be and when. Plus it was now their routine that he be available to check on Lillian.

"I'd prefer a setup something like I had with William."

"That's . . . not possible at the moment."

She wasn't giving him the full story.

"What about all those times you wanted me to work more hours and take on another client?"

"I wasn't going to say because there's no proof or anything but . . ." Veronica looked down at the desk. "William's daughter thinks you may have influenced him about changing his will."

"I did no such thing! Yes, his solicitor visited cand yes, Andrea wasn't happy about something. But we never talked about the contents of his will."

"I believe you but I have to take any allegation seriously. Andrea has no proof. I've spoken to William's solicitor and he says that William was definitely of sound mind and there was no indication of any pressure on the old man. So no further action will be taken. However, it's important that the agency is seen to be doing the right thing."

"So I'm made to suffer for something I didn't do?"

"Call it getting off lightly, Stuart. I could've let you go."

Veronica gave him the name and address of a lady who needed a lunchtime visit the following day while her regular carer was at a hospital appointment with her own mother. Stuart had a final attempt at protesting but Veronica stood up and shooed him out as though he was an annoying bluebottle. Stuart wondered which charity might have received part of Andrea's inheritance. He hoped they'd be suitably grateful.

In the car, the primary school teacher idea flickered again. The geography lesson with Shayne and Eunice had had the advantage of Father Christmas on his travels and only two pupils, no syllabus, no paperwork, no league tables. But he'd got a kick from it. When the children in the library hung on his every word, it was magic. Imagine the high from holding the attention of thirty young pupils. And a primary school teacher's salary would mean he wouldn't be dependent on Jayne and would be able to eventually give her back the money for the wedding.

Florence looked serious when he got home. Since the kiss they'd avoided being alone together. When one of them walked into a room, the other would walk out, unless the children were there. Now the children were at school. Florence hadn't found work and Stuart's days, apart from Thursday at the library, had become a blur of nothingness since William's death.

"Things to do upstairs," he muttered. He'd been reading the *Gap Year* book and trying to work out the best time for putting the idea to Jayne.

"Wait!" She touched his arm.

He flinched and stepped away from her.

"This isn't working anymore," she said. "Things have changed between us."

He wanted to argue that everything was absolutely fine. But it wasn't.

"I'm happy to do more singing and dancing, if that helps?" Stuart had never learned to crack a joke and the corners of Florence's mouth hardly twitched. He adopted a more serious tone. "In the end I was quite enjoying it, you know. But after your Shirley died, it didn't seem the right thing to suggest."

"No. And maybe that's my fault. I've had to stop acting like a star-struck teenager and become a proper grandmother."

"Watch out the wolf doesn't come along and gobble you up!" Stuart bared his teeth.

"Stop it. This is serious. Why the comedian act when you've never so much as laughed at one of the children's knock-knock jokes before?"

"Self-preservation?" He hadn't meant to be so honest, hadn't even realised that was what he was doing until the word was out there.

They sat down in separate armchairs in the lounge. Stuart told her about his chat with Veronica and the feeling that the little structure his life had was leaking away. As he spoke his phone pinged — Robert telling him they'd accepted Mr Savile's offer on the house and were aiming for completion on 31 March. He read the message aloud to Florence.

"That ties everything up then," she said, with a tightness to her voice. "The thirty-first will be a busy day for you, what with the wedding and everything."

Stuart nodded, suddenly remembering he was supposed to be booking hotel rooms for his brothers.

"What I wanted to say." Florence looked at him, making sure she had his attention before continuing. "I think it's best if the children and I leave now. Eunice keeps asking me if kissing means you have to marry someone." She looked down at the floor and spoke quickly. "She says that she wants you and me to get married. I told her that's impossible because you're going to marry Jayne and I'm still married to her grandfather."

"That doesn't mean you have to leave."

Florence held her right hand up like a police stop signal. "It will be difficult for you to pack the house up with all our stuff around. You'll be wanting to sell off what furniture you can. I suspect Jayne won't have room for it. If we stay, it won't be good for the children to see their home disappearing from under them."

In Stuart's mind, the next few weeks were turning black. "Where will you go?"

"Jim's. With two children and no income there's no other option until the council do something. At least Eunice and Shayne are familiar with the house and they love Jim. It's a tight squeeze but we'll manage."

The mention of Jim felt like a stab to the heart. "What about Tibby?"

"After a lot of persuasion and emotional blackmail on my part, he's agreed that Tibby can come too."

"Butter her paws to make sure he doesn't run back here."

"What?"

Stuart shook his head. "Old wives' tale. Ignore me." He felt as though he was standing on the edge of a precipice. All that would come out of his mouth was absolute rubbish. "When are you going?"

"As soon as I collect the children from school. The car's packed."

Stuart suddenly realised the lack of unicorns and Lego in the lounge and a quick glance showed the coat hooks in the hall were empty except for his own jackets. He was being pushed to arm's length by those who'd kept him sane and functioning. He could make himself look weak by pleading or he could stand up tall and let her go.

"Don't be a stranger this time," he said. "Keep in touch."

"I do appreciate what you've done for us. Not every landlord would've been so understanding."

Landlord. Was that all that she thought of him as?

"Best wishes to you and Jayne for a long and happy marriage." She was holding her hand out. He took it and swallowed hard when a little tingle of electricity travelled up his arm.

"I'm going to take our stuff over to Jim's now so that I can do some unpacking and make the place feel like home before collecting the children."

Stuart stood at the front door until the orange Panda disappeared from sight.

Jayne smiled when he told her the news about Florence later that day but was slightly less happy when he told her about his new haphazard working hours.

"Mum and I depend on you now, don't we, Mum?"

Lillian nodded as she twiddled with a knitted square on her lap, rolling it into a tube and then trying to press it flat with her fingers.

"I'm sure you'll find a way of making it work, Stuart." Jayne paused and now her eyes began to sparkle. "But the positive news is, that with Florence gone, you don't have to stay next door and play landlord. You could move in this very evening."

Lillian nodded and smiled. Stuart patted the old lady's hands.

Jayne stood up. "Go home and pack an overnight bag. You can sort the rest of your stuff out tomorrow. I'll go and clear space for you in my wardrobe. Isn't it exciting! We're going to be a proper couple at last!" She almost skipped from the room and her footsteps on the stairs were quick.

"A proper couple at last." Lillian raised her head to speak again, then smiled, nodded and looked down at her twiddling square.

He should be happy but felt like he'd been cornered. Two women had cast him aside today but now two more were welcoming him with open arms. It should balance the scales. It didn't. It made him feel like things were even more out of kilter.

"Off you go, Stuart!" Jayne's voice trilled down the stairs. Everything was good in her world now and he ought to keep it that way. He kissed Lillian on the cheek and went home.

He put a change of clothes into a holdall along with his toilet bag and shaver. The *Gap Year* book went in, just in case the opportunity presented itself. He hesitated over the pyjamas. It was winter; he hated feeling cold at night. But didn't most men sleep naked? He and Jayne had spent several evenings in bed during Florence's absences but they'd never actually slept together. Would she expect him naked or were pyjamas acceptable?

He sat down on the bed and tried to bring some logic back to his thoughts. He was getting this out of proportion. He was panicking over nothing. The pyjama problem was a symptom of the shock at Jayne's sudden instruction to move in.

He gave up packing and wandered downstairs into the lounge, expecting to find Tibby in the middle of the settee and amenable to a tickle under the chin and some thinking out loud. She wasn't there. She'd gone off in the cat basket with Florence. She'd taken the cardboard box from the garage containing the hibernating Slowcoach as well. Florence. There was an ache in his heart that shouldn't be there. Combined with the loss of William and his rapidly shrinking job, it felt like his whole life was disintegrating.

He couldn't face moving in with Jayne tonight. He texted her: *Can you put* Vera *on the TV? We need to talk.*

CHAPTER FORTY-ONE

She was at his front door within minutes, fear plastered across her face.

"What's the matter?"

He ushered her into the lounge where he'd already poured two glasses of wine. There was no easy way of saying this. He had to be direct.

"I can't move in with you."

Jayne's face froze in an expression of pain. "What do you mean?"

"I can't move in with you." He didn't know how to soften the blow, instead he squeezed her hand.

"Are you saying you don't want us to get married?" She pulled her hand away and took a large gulp of wine, as though preparing herself for the worst.

"No, I'm not saying that. Moving in just doesn't feel right for me at the moment." He was trying to choose his words carefully. They shouldn't sound like an excuse; Jayne could be quick to misunderstand. "If we start living together now, what is the point of us getting married? I want our wedding to be the start of a new life together, not just the continuation of something we started out of convenience some weeks earlier."

Jayne drank more wine. "You're making the wedding sound special." She'd got the point but still sounded suspicious. "Are you sure this isn't some clever way of giving me the brush-off?"

"No. Yes. Our wedding will be special, whatever the circumstances. But it will mean much more to me if we don't live together until we are married."

She smiled. "I understand and I like the sentiment. But does that mean we can't . . ." She undid the first few buttons of his shirt and then leaned in to kiss him.

It was impossible to stop the comparison. Impossible to stop Florence's face hovering. He tried hard to make it passionate. He held Jayne close, pressed against the warmth of her body. But now there was a comparison and Jayne was found wanting.

"Something's wrong. You're all tense."

"I'm a bit under the weather. I stopped for a prawn sandwich when I was out cycling yesterday and I think it must have been a bit dodgy."

Jayne shuffled a little away from him on the settee.

"It's probably best if I have an early night and get it out of my system." He needed Jayne to go. He was confused and afraid of saying the wrong thing that might actually turn out to be the right thing. Where were Sandra and William when you needed them?

"Phone me if you need help?"

Stuart nodded and listened for the front door closing.

* * *

Life became haphazard. Veronica had work for him most days but Stuart never knew until the night before what time he would be required and where he would have to go. The clients were often hostile when they discovered their usual carer was off. Most of them were ladies who weren't used to being washed by a man but he did his best to preserve their dignity. It was refreshing to visit the occasional man who was pleased at the prospect of exchanging football gossip and Stuart tried to keep up with all the local teams so he could provide proper conversation, which was what most of his clients wanted above all.

As the days turned into weeks, it became easier to slot Florence into a box in his memory marked 'Not To Be Opened' and to focus on Jayne and the wedding. He rediscovered his mojo and made sure his fiancée knew he found her attractive.

Then Florence phoned. Stuart was immediately on his guard. Florence assured him everything was fine. The children were well, Tibby had settled without the help of greasy paws and she'd got work in the local supermarket.

"Actually, it's Shayne who begged me to phone. He wants to ask you something. I tried to dissuade him but you know how kids can wear you down when they go on and on about something."

Stuart didn't know. "Oh?"

There were muffled voices and clattering as the phone was handed over.

"Uncle Stuart? It's Shayne."

"Yes."

"Please can I have my birthday party at your house? Granddad doesn't have enough room. He says I can only invite five people but I want all the boys in my class to come."

Stuart hesitated.

"You can say no, if you want." Florence's voice sounded from somewhere behind Shayne. "I explained you needed to keep the house clean and tidy because you're moving."

"We won't make a mess. I promise."

When had there last been a party in this house? There'd been the odd sedate family gathering at Christmas when his brothers' children had either been banished into the cold or amused with electronic games. He tried to remember parties from his childhood and drew a blank. Words from William and Sandra about grabbing a bright new future came back to him. In his mind Jayne frowned at this 'out of their comfort zone' suggestion and the brothers winced.

"Yes. I'm honoured that you've asked me." Then Stuart had to raise his voice above the cheering. "But I will need help. Lots of help. I don't know what happens at children's parties."

There were suddenly three voices talking at once at the other end of the phone and Stuart could decipher none of it. Then Florence rose in volume. "I'll call you back later when I have a plan. It will be 28 February."

Stuart marked the date on the calendar and felt suddenly brighter. The routine was going to be broken by something out of the ordinary, something involving Florence. But the box marked 'Not To Be Opened' must remain closed for reasons of sanity.

Jayne listed all the problems involved with hosting the party. From food stains on the carpets, to broken windows and parents suing when their offspring fell down the stairs.

"Neither of us have any experience of children," she said. "Fifteen boys will wreck the joint and Robert and George will force you to make good the damage. Let Florence hire a church hall or take them to a burger joint or something."

"No. Shayne asked me himself. I can't let him down. You don't have to be involved."

"Of course I have to be involved. I'm your fiancée. Even though it means wasting a whole day of my weekend when I've been working and looking after Mum all week."

If that was a dig at Stuart's meagre part-time work compared to her full-time, much better job, he didn't rise to it. Instead he tried to placate her.

"Your support is most welcome. Thank you. And of course Lillian is expected as well."

* * *

Florence arrived early on the morning of the party to prepare all the food, move furniture and make the house as little-boy-proof as possible. She gave Stuart the job of filling party bags.

Apparently, every child had to go home with a bag of goodies. The small plastic bags were printed with images of pirates and the skull and cross bones. The contents consisted of a myriad of sweets, plastic dinosaurs, a whistle and a fake gold medal on a ribbon. Most of it would be discarded by tomorrow but the little boy inside him felt the excitement this trash would bring.

When the bags were filled, he buttered bread and then removed all breakable objects from the downstairs of the house. It was grey outside but Stuart put out a couple of footballs he'd bought for the occasion and then couldn't resist dribbling one around the edge of the lawn. His skills were rusty and he and the ball ended up in a flower bed. He eased it back onto the grass and looked forward to a swarm of small boys chasing around and imagining themselves Premier League players.

In the kitchen Florence was spreading buttercream generously over a chocolate cake, seven candles in holders shaped like racing cars on the table next to her. Her tongue poked halfway from her mouth in concentration. As the day and the preparations moved on, the tension in Florence's stance increased. Surprising since she'd never seemed to suffer from stage fright or nerves. Eventually she spoke.

"I'm so scared this will all go horribly wrong and leave your house a wreck. I should never have let Shayne ask you."

"It's going to be great!" Stuart's excitement was bubbling more than he'd expected. "This house needs a burst of life. It's been dowdy and boring for too long. Like its inhabitant."

Florence smiled at him. "You do yourself an injustice. At another time I might—"

The doorbell cut into her words and she went silent. For a second neither of them moved. Florence with indecision on her face and Stuart hoping she'd finish what she was about to say. The doorbell rang again. Florence obeyed its demand.

It was the man with the bouncy castle, swiftly followed by Jim with Eunice and a version of Shayne that Stuart had never seen before. He was wearing a brand-new football strip, bouncing instead of walking, and talking madly about the afternoon to come. Then Jayne and Lillian arrived. Jayne was frowning as she stepped through the front door. Lillian was grinning and holding a brightly wrapped parcel. Shayne grabbed it almost before it was offered and tore at the paper to reveal an Action Man colouring book and a set of pens.

"Thank you." His grin spoke louder than his words.

After that everything happened at once. Small boy after small boy was deposited at the front door with parents yelling their thanks for being able to disappear home to a couple of hours of peace. Stuart opened the French doors and shooed the boys onto the giant inflatable to wear themselves out. Jayne acted as health and safety, ensuring that all shoes were removed before bouncing. Eunice helped Florence finish preparing the food and Jim set himself up as a goalie for those who didn't want to jump. Stuart stood next to Lillian and watched the somersaults, star jumps and play fights.

The whole event was something that had never happened at this house in Stuart's lifetime. Maybe when Robert and George were young, small boys and birthdays were still enough of a novelty to warrant a party, but by the time it was Stuart's turn, sons were routine and the much-wanted daughter was dead.

Don't blame me for something over which I had no control. I did actually fight to stay alive.

It was an effort now to conjure up Sandra's voice. More and more these days, his thoughts were totally his own.

He became aware of Florence calling him into the kitchen. Worried that a loose cannon of a boy might catapult off the inflatable and accidentally floor Lillian, he guided the old lady into the house with him.

"How's it going?" Anxiety was all over Florence's face. "Anything broken? Bones or furniture?"

"Everything's absolutely fine." He touched Florence on the arm to reassure her and then remembered Lillian was watching and removed his hand. "Don't worry."

"Tell me if I've forgotten anything, food-wise? Shall I pour the orange squash?"

"Yes, pour. And everything looks great."

"Can I call them in?" Eunice had started bouncing up and down now.

Stuart gave her the thumbs-up and then the gannets landed. Jayne, Lillian and Jim stood to one side while Florence and Stuart kept everyone plied with sandwiches, pizza slices and sausage rolls followed by chocolate biscuits in a myriad of shapes. When everyone looked sated, Florence gave the nod. Jim started filming on his phone, Stuart lit the seven candles, Shayne was placed in front of the cake and Lillian started the singing of 'Happy Birthday'. Stuart tried to remember such a crowd around him and a cake, but the memory eluded him.

"Happy Birthday, dear Shayne, Happy Birthday to you!"

The singing finished and Shayne took a massive breath, filling his cheeks with air until he looked like a hamster. And then he blew. Moving his head slowly around the cake to ensure that he caught all the candles.

"Three cheers for Shayne!" Stuart called. "Hip hip . . ."

"Hooray!"

Across the room from him, Lillian's face was alight with childish joy and she waved her arms in the air as though she was at a football match. Next to her, Jayne was fighting a frown.

Afterwards, when the cake had been cut and wrapped in pirate serviettes and each boy despatched with the correct parent, Stuart made coffee and served up the remainder of the cake to the adults. Shayne and Eunice bickered gently over the pile of presents that Eunice wanted to investigate but Shayne wanted to keep for himself.

Florence looked pale and tired, but she was smiling. "Nothing got damaged."

"You were brilliant." Stuart smiled at her.

"Three cheers for Florence!" Lillian said.

The children started hip-hipping and Jayne frowned again.

It was dusk outside but the bouncy castle was still there, waiting to be deflated and collected.

"I think we should go," said Jayne.

This time Lillian frowned. "Those weren't invented when I was a little. Do you think I could . . ."

"No." Jayne was standing up, motioning towards the hallway.

"Just for a minute."

"You'll break a leg, Mother. And then where would you be?"

"Not much worse off than I am now."

Florence and Jim were watching the exchange without offering an opinion. Stuart could see his own longing reflected in the eyes of his mother-in-law-to-be. He'd never bounced on a giant inflatable either. If he kept hold of Lillian, perhaps she'd be safe. He imagined the joy on her face. But Jayne was her next of kin, she was in charge and she'd hate him if he went against her. But, maybe, he actually knew better than Jayne in this case. He had more experience of caring for older people. He knew that the quality of those final years was of at least equal importance to the quantity of years.

"I'd like to try it out too," he said slowly. "Lillian, perhaps we could hold each other up?"

"I'm game if you are?" She sparkled.

Jayne bristled but said nothing.

Stuart offered his arm to Lillian and they went out of the French doors. He bent down and removed his own shoes and Lillian's. The grass was damp and cold through his socks. Jayne had followed them, hovering.

Lillian had to go onto her knees to climb onto the castle. Stuart stayed close behind her so that she couldn't slip back off. They both crawled into the centre of the inflatable, beneath the rain canopy and well away from the edge. He was surprised how agile the old lady was and wondered if this was the pay-out from the years of yoga classes that she'd attended in a younger life. She was smiling at him.

"Let's try standing up," he suggested, slowly becoming upright himself and finding his balance. It felt like standing on a listing ship with a deck that was soft and sank a little with each foot movement. He bent so that Lillian could hold both of his arms as he brought her up into a standing position.

They stood, connected like ballroom dancers about to steam their way to victory in *Strictly*. Her arms were thin between his fingers and he was suddenly aware of her frailty and the recklessness of bringing her onto the castle. He could suggest they'd done enough and should dismount gracefully but he wanted this joy and youth to remain on her face and in her mind for as long as possible.

"You be the driver." He raised his voice over the hiss of the machinery keeping the castle inflated. "I'll walk backwards. You set the speed and tell me if I'm about to bump into something."

She grinned. Relishing the opportunity to control a tiny part of the life that was left to her. She was leaning forward, all her weight on him as she experimentally shuffled each foot in turn. It was like bearing the burden of an angel. He moved his feet backwards carefully over the undulating canvas. If he went over, both Lillian and his future would go down with him. Jayne wouldn't marry the man who injured her mother.

"Watch out!" Lillian's words were snatched at by the inflatable's hiss.

Stuart glanced over his shoulder, the wall of the castle was inches from his back. He turned slowly, arms still outstretched and concentration fully focused. Their movements were far removed from the boys throwing themselves around but their own personal joys in the moment were greater. Together, synchronised, smiling, they managed a small circuit of the inner castle. Then the applause showered.

He hadn't noticed the others come outside. Jim was filming, Florence was clapping and Shayne and Eunice were being held back by Jayne. This time he was grateful for her caution — two children bounding onto the castle would have knocked him and Lillian off balance, like a bowling ball against skittles.

"Sit down," he said to Lillian.

She sat down and shuffled on her bottom to the edge of the inflatable where Jim caught her and helped her with her shoes.

Stuart walked to the front door with Jayne and Lillian.

"I've had a lovely time," Lillian said. "You and Florence worked like Trojans. You're good together. I can see why my Jayne is worried."

Jayne's face was stone and she said nothing.

Stuart tried to defuse the situation by leaning over and kissing his fiancée. She turned her head slightly and he caught only her cheek.

CHAPTER FORTY-TWO

In the days after the party, Jayne was cool towards him but Lillian made it her job to sing his praises. Florence called to the house once with a bottle of wine and a note from Shayne, written in a laborious hand and accompanied by a picture in smudged felt-tip entitled *My Bouncy Castle Party*. Stuart was grateful for the title and Florence's visit but she refused to come over the doorstep, insisting she was in a hurry to be elsewhere.

The fallout from the party wasn't what he'd expected. He'd agreed to the idea mostly because he'd wanted fun in the house, but also because it would please Florence, and he'd hoped Jayne would be won over in all the merriment. The event had succeeded in very temporarily enlivening his home but had failed on both the other counts. Florence seemed to be rapidly loosening the strings of their friendship and he was having to work hard to regain Jayne's favour, despite Lillian's constant comparisons between him and a knight in shining armour.

"Jayne, this one is such a keeper," she would say. "He's a prince among men."

Stuart would try to catch Jayne's eye and then look heavenward as if to say he knew that Lillian was exaggerating. But Jayne wouldn't give him the comfort and confidence of that silent communication. He realised that she had intuited the hazy connection between Florence and himself, even though it was unspoken, unacted upon — apart from the kiss that should never have happened — and definitely not practical under both their circumstances and probably wouldn't work in the long term even if it was.

Veronica was finding him plenty of stand-in carer work and, despite the haphazard hours, he liked having a purpose back to his days and a reason to rush about. The postman arrived one lunchtime as he was heading out to see an elderly lady who needed a hot meal and a spot of housework.

"Can you sign for this, please?" He handed Stuart a long white envelope and pushed a computer tablet in front of him "Just signing with your finger tip is fine."

Stuart glanced briefly at the letter as he flung it onto the passenger seat of the car. It was embossed with the name of a local solicitor's office but he was late and it would have to wait. He stayed longer than necessary with the old lady; she had a wealth of tales about the cats who criss-crossed her garden and gave her company during the long hours alone. It seemed rude to walk out when he had nowhere else to immediately be.

He remembered the letter when he'd put a toad-in-the-hole in the oven at Jayne's and he rushed out to the car for it. His fiancée arrived home from work just as he was easing his finger under the flap of the thick envelope.

"Looks interesting," she said.

The sheet of paper he pulled from the envelope matched it in thickness and quality. The contents of the letter made him sit down. He read it again to make sure he'd fully understood what it said and that it was actually addressed to him.

"Well?" Jayne was standing over him. "What is it?"

"William's left me some money in his will."

"Wow. How much?"

"Two hundred thousand pounds."

Jayne sat down as well. "That is significant," she said slowly. "We could move to a bigger house. Or extend here to create a granny flat and go on a world cruise."

The words washed over Stuart. He was thinking about Andrea and the way she and William had fallen out, about the visit of William's solicitor, about the way Andrea had been cool towards him on the phone and at the hospital. His meeting with Veronica was starting to make sense. Stuart didn't like the way the pieces were falling into place. He didn't want to take money that had caused a family rift. He had no idea of the total value of William's estate, nor how much Andrea herself had inherited, but she must have been left with very little. This was like blood money and he wanted no part of it.

"I can't take it."

"Of course you can."

"This should've gone to his daughter but for some reason, after he met me, he decided to deprive her of it. That's not fair. I'll tell the solicitor that William can't have been of sound mind when he changed his wishes." He wondered if Veronica already knew what he'd inherited. This would be another black mark against his name.

Jayne took the letter from him. "You will not. Things have a way of working themselves out. This compensates for missing out in your father's will. This money means we can push the boat out for the wedding. Have a bigger do. It's short notice but not impossible."

Stuart was still thinking about Andrea. However they looked on the windfall, it wouldn't make it any more acceptable.

"I've never had so much money," Jayne continued. "There were no luxuries with Carl and you don't earn . . . I'm going to phone to see if they've got late availability at the Hilton." Jayne was on a roll now. "And we could afford for Mum to have a short spell in a residential home while we have a proper honeymoon. Where's hot and sunny at the beginning of April? Somewhere we could relax by the pool all day."

Rein her in, bro. This is getting out of hand.

It was a shock to have Sandra back and he flinched. He looked at Jayne, her face alight with enthusiasm for the first time since before Shayne's party. She had the same excited expression as when he'd proposed. He didn't want to be the pin that burst her bubble. He also didn't want to be a figure of a hate in Andrea's mind.

"You told me it was toad-in-the-hole for tea." Lillian stood in the doorway, an accusing look on her face.

"Mum!" Jayne took off her work jacket and gave her mother a hug. "Stuart has come into money and our wedding is going upmarket."

The old lady frowned. The cogs of her concentration were visible in the expression. "But it's still toad-in-the-hole?" she asked eventually. "With ketchup and gravy?"

"It's still toad-in-the-hole, Lillian," Stuart said. "Sit down, I'm dishing up now."

"If we have a bigger venue, I need a more of a statement dress. Something that will make people look."

"Doesn't everyone look at the bride anyway?" Stuart helped Lillian with the ketchup bottle.

Don't get drawn in or she'll think that you agree to the wedding upgrade. Do you want to waste money on flashy nuptials? Do you actually want *to spend two weeks slumped on a sunbed turning into a well-cooked lobster?*

Sandra's time spent AWOL seemed to have knocked some sense into her. She'd found a way of finding the thoughts hiding in the shadows of Stuart's own mind and plonking them down centre stage so he was forced to confront them. A large part of him wanted to gift Jayne her big wedding happiness but, aside from the initial satisfaction of pleasing someone, the long-term benefit was nil.

And Andrea will eat at your conscience. Her potentially penniless plight will stop you from sleeping.

Florence wouldn't need a statement dress. She'd feel totally confident just being herself.

The thought came from nowhere. It had the feel of Sandra but lacked her imperious edge. Stuart looked at Jayne. She was smiling at him with a forkful of sausage and Yorkshire pudding on its way to her mouth. She didn't know he was comparing her, unfavourably, to another woman. A woman who didn't want him. This sudden realisation that

Florence ranked higher in his mind than his fiancée made Stuart push the rest of his food to one side.

Was it wrong to marry your second-best choice? If you got along all right then surely a 'good enough' Miss Right was acceptable? There wasn't any other option if your first choice wasn't interested.

Jayne disappeared while he was washing up and bounced back into the room ten minutes later, coming up behind him and nuzzling his neck in a most unlike-Jayne gesture.

"Success!" she said. "The Hilton are holding their Wigmore Wing for us. We can go and look at it tomorrow. They do a sit-down meal for one hundred guests. Five courses, each one served with a sommelier-suggested wine. And the Green Dale. That posh residential home at the top end of town can take Mum for a fortnight. All we need to do is choose our sunshine destination. When we're back home as Mr and Mrs, I'll get plans drawn up for a granny annexe on the back of the house. The garden's long enough to take it and it will add value in the long term. And give us more privacy." She nuzzled him again.

Stuart felt like a fox cornered by hounds. Nowhere else to run. He must speak now or be flattened by juggernaut Jayne.

"No."

"No what?"

Stuart was aware the tea towel in his hand had taken on the role of Lillian's twiddling squares. When he looked down, it had become a long damp worm in his fingers.

"No, we can't do anything until I've spoken to William's solicitors."

"He wanted you to have the money."

"I can't take it until I know Andrea hasn't been left in need."

Jayne shook her head. The evening became a litany of things they could do together and with Lillian if Stuart would only accept the money. Stuart refused to be persuaded. Other thoughts were exposing themselves in his mind. Thoughts that he'd previously stamped on. Thoughts he needed to acknowledge before events swept him away.

CHAPTER FORTY-THREE

That night Stuart slept fitfully. William's will was having a bigger impact than the old man would've anticipated. It had triggered Jayne's vision of a perfect future where money was no object. A future that energised her voice and lit up her face. When Stuart thought of the future, he didn't see that same vision. Jayne's vision was a more elaborate version of the present with a few luxury holidays thrown into the mix. It was a future without challenges, a future without proper travel or participation in different cultures, a future without learning or experiences. In Stuart's eyes it was a malnourished future to tag on to the malnourished life he'd led so far.

Previously he'd been happy to settle for a future curtailed by their joint finances, Lillian's condition and the continued need to work for a living. But Jayne's projections for a perfect future, where such curtailments were minimal, didn't reach high enough to match his. It was now obvious that, even without William's money, Stuart would be striving for different experiences outside of the status quo that satisfied his fiancée.

In the morning he arranged a meeting for the following day with the solicitor named on the thick, headed paper. Then he changed into his Lycra and made sandwiches and a flask of coffee. Lillian was at the day centre and Veronica had pushed no work his way. He was free to think his way through the mess in his head. But before he did his thinking, he needed to prove something to himself.

"Think you can, think you can't; either way you'll be right."

It was a matter of mental focus as well as physical endurance. Now he knew why top athletes had psychological training. Last time he'd jumped the gun, thought he'd had it in the bag and had stopped panning the road in front for obstacles.

He rode steadily to the foot of the hill, feeling his muscles warm and become more mobile. With the sharp incline in sight, he began building his momentum. He forced himself to ignore the views and the peace and the soothing sights of nature.

There was tension across his back. Suddenly this hill was much more than a physical challenge. It was a metaphor for the rest of his life. To live well he needed to feel well in his own skin. To feel well in his own skin demanded confidence. To get that confidence he needed to succeed in this hill climb. He needed to build on his success at story time and his tentative visits to speakers' club. As the momentum diminished, he forced his legs to pump. The gear changes were smooth. He didn't look towards the crest, only at the road in front of him. His quads began to object and there was no longer enough downward thrust into the pedals. Already in the lowest gear, he stood on the pedals. He was aware of his heart, his lungs and his grip on the handlebars. Ahead he spotted the pothole that had thrown him before. He glanced over his shoulder, ready to move nearer to the middle of the road and smoother tarmac. A lorry was about to overtake him. There was nowhere to go. If he slowed his speed to move out after the lorry passed, he'd wobble and fall. If he continued, the pothole would throw him again.

At the last minute, Stuart saw the way and turned the handle bars slightly to the left, towards the narrow strip of compacted mud between the pothole and the ditch. As the lorry disappeared over the hill, Stuart pulled back out onto the tarmac.

"Yes!" He whooped and started the exhilarating swoop down the other side.

Now he released his thoughts towards that bright new future. Should he stay in the comfortable cocoon with Jayne and experience the same old, same old, regardless of money or opportunity? Or, break free for the precarious life of a butterfly, which, without William's money, might leave him homeless on a park bench? A life that would require self-reliance and determination. For it to be the right decision, he had to make it before he knew whether or not he could ethically keep the money.

There would be no third chance with Jayne. If he rejected her now, she would never speak to him again. He would be alone. His brothers would be Christmas-cards-only after the house sale. Jayne was all he had. It would be a brave man that turned her down.

As he raced towards the bottom of the hill, the wind in his face made his eyes water. The prospect of no Jayne and living alone in a squalid bedsit with only the daily company of Veronica's clients weighed heavy, like a *Groundhog-Day* re-run of the decades spent caring for his father, only in worse living conditions. In contrast, the prospect of Jayne's warm bed, companionship and the simple presence of other human beings was pleasant.

Pleasant wasn't enough. He could do better than that. The direction he should take was still hazy but the first steps were becoming clearer and he was going to take them. Hope for that butterfly emerging from its cocoon rose as he hit the flat road, plans forming at pace in his head.

He peeled himself out of the Lycra and showered. His stomach growled and churned. Once the decision was made, he hadn't wanted to stop for the sandwiches and coffee in his pannier. What he was about to do to his fiancée was unforgivable. It made him the lowest of the low. Was it worse or better than proceeding with a 'good enough' marriage that might have made her happy? Impossible to know. The knot in his stomach still wouldn't allow food. Jayne was due to come round with the seating plan that evening, possibly with it upgraded to Hilton standard and a fresh wave of ideas, excitement and sparkly eyes. His resolve must not crumble under her enthusiasm. He must not let her follow her passion. He had to tell her before the conversation got that far. He had to find the right words and place the blame where it belonged: on himself.

"Brochures!" Jayne walked into the kitchen and placed a pile of glossy publications on the table. She sorted them into three small piles. "Firstly, everything I could lay my hands on at the Hilton about their wedding service and," she paused and grinned at him, "their honeymoon suite for our wedding night. Secondly, exotic honeymoon destinations offering sun and sea. Finally, information from Green Dale about their respite care. I think I've covered all bases. Where do you want to start? I've canned the seating plan until we know exactly which room at the Hilton we prefer. They've got two vacant on our date."

"Let's take a step back, Jayne."

"Why?" She was oblivious to what he was about to say.

"Getting married isn't about hotels and guests and posh holidays. It goes far, far deeper than that."

She was looking at him as though he'd just stepped from a UFO. Her mouth was slightly open.

"It's about spending the rest of our lives together and we have to decide whether that is the very best thing for the two of us." Stuart tightly clasped his hands so they didn't shake. "Do we share the same vision of our future?"

There was a frown of incomprehension across her forehead. "When you proposed and I accepted, I thought we'd both decided that was the very best course of action for the two of us." She glanced down at the ring on her left hand.

"At that point my hopes for the future didn't extend beyond keeping a roof over my head. Now I realise that I've got over two decades of living to catch up on — even if that means gambling with the security of that roof."

"What do you mean?" Her voice shook slightly as though a slow realisation was seeping through her. He wanted to backtrack and protect her from all the doubts seething in his mind.

Sometimes you have to be cruel to be kind.

He blessed Sandra for being right behind him on this. She had stopped him capitulating.

Stuart took hold of both Jayne's hands. "This year, since Dad died, has been a journey of self-discovery for me. I've had to learn about real life and what I want for me. About how I can grab enough life now to make up for all those years in the shadow of a sickbed. It's taken me many months but now I know I want my freedom. I want to travel the world unencumbered by responsibilities. I can't go straight from caring for Dad to being responsible for the happiness of anyone else."

"I'm not marrying you to get myself a carer for Mum! We can research homes or respite care or . . . I've no intention of taking advantage of your good nature."

He squeezed her hands. "I know. But if we're married. If you come travelling with me, then I'll be responsible for your happiness. And I really do want you to be happy, so I'd be forming plans around your needs and wants. You wouldn't be happy living in a hostel or out of a rucksack or not seeing Lillian for eighteen months."

"I could wait for you to come back."

"No. We tried a long-distance relationship when we were eighteen. Remember? And it didn't work."

Tears formed in the corners of Jayne's eyes and Stuart felt dampness in his own lashes too.

"Does this mean the wedding is off?" Her voice was mixed with the beginnings of a sob and her expression began to crumble. "I was worried I might lose you to Florence but it never occurred to me you'd prefer living rough in some foreign country to the two of us being cosy together here. Especially now that you've got William's money and we could travel together in luxury."

"I haven't accepted the money yet. It will probably turn out to be unfair for me to take it. And if I do take it, it will be my nest egg for when I decide to return."

"I have my pride. I won't argue about this with you. I know when I'm not wanted." Jayne stood up, tugged off the engagement ring, placed it on the table in front of Stuart and walked out.

Stuart sat for a long time with his head in his hands. He regretted the pain he'd inflicted on Jayne. But it would have been far worse for both of them if he'd gone ahead with the wedding.

It had grown dark outside and inside. The only light was a faint orange glow from a street lamp.

He put the diamond ring on top of the *Gap Year* book and stared at them for a long time. Then he put the ring in his change jar and began to read the book.

CHAPTER FORTY-FOUR

Florence arrived at the café door at the same time as Stuart, having come from the other direction. He handed her a bunch of daffodils and she beamed. Then she grabbed a table while Stuart queued for lattes and, because cake suited all occasions, a hunk of chocolate brownie and a slice of red velvet cake.

"Lovely flowers, thanks." Florence took the knife and cut both cakes in half, sharing them equally.

Stuart smiled, not trusting his voice.

Florence talked about the children and how she enjoyed the supermarket job because she got to talk to lots of different people. "I miss performing, though. Especially when I see Jim go out every night. There's something about applause. The more you have, the more you want. It's like an addiction."

The words he wanted to say were sticking in his throat. He wanted Florence to know the important thing that had taken him too long to learn. The thing that she'd helped him realise. The new path would be full of blind bends, humpbacked bridges and punctures from perilous potholes but that was the joy of being alive; you could never be certain about what was going to happen next. The hardest thing had been getting himself to the start of this path.

"How about you?" Florence paused, took a sip of latte and looked at him. "Not long to go until you're a married man. I bet Jayne's fizzing with excitement?"

Stuart swallowed, trying to get rid of the tightness in his throat. He couldn't be sure whether the lump was nerves about the future or his unremitting guilt at betraying his ex-fiancée. "We're not getting married."

Shock landed on Florence's face. She put her latte glass down heavily and brown liquid slopped from the top of it.

"I finally realised that we don't want the same things from life."

Florence's eyes were wide.

"You helped me realise that an ordinary life isn't enough. I need to experience the extraordinary."

"I helped you realise that?"

"With the dancing."

She was watching his face. He wanted to know what she was thinking.

"And the singing."

She cocked her head on one side.

"I miss all of that." The words were out and the sky hadn't fallen in. "I miss trying to make you listen to the news. I miss trying to persuade you that politics is a necessary evil."

She was focused on him but silent. Not helping him out. He ploughed on. "You were fun to live with. You are fun. And when we kissed." He paused, desperate to find the right words so that he didn't come across as a dirty old man or as an over-embellished romantic novel. "We only did it that one time but it was good."

"Good?"

He wanted to say life-affirming, toe-curling, heart-warming. "More than good."

Florence picked up the tall glass coffee mug. The surface of the brown liquid rippled in response to the shaking of her hand. The silence pulsated with tension. Stuart took a mouthful of coffee and looked away. He'd meant to just say goodbye and thank you, but, somehow, he'd got himself stuck in an awkward quagmire of feelings.

"So what will you do now?"

"Travel. A working holiday." He pulled the *Gap Year* book from his backpack. "A couple of months here, a couple of months there until I feel ready to settle back here. I might look into primary school teaching. The exact plans are a work in progress."

"But you will come back?" She was staring into his eyes and his stomach flipped.

"Yes."

She smiled.

"What will you do?" he asked.

"I have responsibilities. Baggage. Little people who will be relying on me for years to come. I've had my turn at freedom and excitement. Now I want to be there for my grandchildren."

"And as they get settled and a bit older?" Stuart barely knew what he was saying. Florence's eyes wouldn't leave his.

"It will be a game of wait and see."

He nodded.

"I like you, Stuart. I'd even go as far as to say I love you."

A grin broke over his face. It reflected foolishly back at him from the window against Florence's back. He wanted to leap on the table and shout what she'd just said. But he was Stuart Borefield and he didn't do things like that. Instead, he leaned over the table and kissed her full on the lips. Slowly. There was the sound of clapping and they pulled sheepishly apart. Three teenagers in the coffee queue gave them a thumbs-up sign.

"I love you too." He touched her face. "You have made me so happy."

"Why?"

"I thought I'd imagined it all. I thought it was wishful thinking. I thought the years alone with Dad meant I'd lost the ability to read other people."

"Slow down! I'm not ready for a relationship. Not with you, not with anyone. And you've got a lot of living to do before settling down. Bright new future, remember?" She leaned over the table and stroked his cheek. "We might never be ready for each other. At least, not at the same time. For now we are both free agents. Open to whatever experiences and people come our way — be it a Dutch girl at the Eiffel Tower or a reconciliation with Jim."

She was pulling on the brakes. He swallowed the lump in his throat. She loved him. He hadn't misread the situation. Perhaps she would still love him when he came back.

Florence looked at her watch. "I have to go. School run."

He took a breath. It was the final scene in a movie. He wrapped the uneaten cakes in a serviette, handed it to Florence and tried to speak in a normal voice. "For Eunice and Shayne from Uncle Stuart."

He walked her to her car and waved her off. Then he found a bench on which to compose himself before his next appointment.

"I only have ten minutes." The solicitor looked at his watch. "What was your question? Mr Rutherford's will was quite straightforward, there were no grey areas."

"My bequest was . . . unexpected. I'm not family. Before I accept it, I want to be sure that his daughter Andrea is well provided for and that no one else was missed out." Stuart's heart thumped. This was the first time he'd had a sizeable chunk of money to call his own. He glanced down and saw his hands were shaking.

The solicitor was examining a sheet of paper in front of him. "The money left to you represented one tenth of the total estate and the rest of the estate went to his daughter, Andrea."

Stuart let out a low whistle. He'd never imagined William had been sitting on such a fortune. "Thank you, that's all I needed to know."

The March sunshine had broken through when he got outside and there was a rainbow arching over the office block at the end of the street. Stuart felt a sudden rush of wellbeing in his heart. Everything was going to work out all right. He grinned at the multicoloured arch and mouthed a silent thank you. His future held just the right degree of brightness.

CHAPTER FORTY-FIVE

The house-clearance team had been in the week before the buyers completed on the house. Everything went bar a camp bed, the cooker, fridge and a rickety table from the shed. Stuart lived like an upmarket squatter for those last few days while he made the final preparations for his trip.

Mike had been round to collect Mavis's bike. Apparently his daughter had persuaded him to try internet dating and he'd met a lady who'd expressed a wish to have a go at cycling. He'd also offered to store Stuart's bike until his return.

William's money had been invested as a nest egg for whenever that return might be. He'd emptied his savings account to buy the initial flights. He'd sold the car to cover expenditure on the first leg of the trip. Veronica's contacts in Australia, New Zealand, Canada and Florida had been happy to promise temporary work in their care homes, subject to a couple of weeks' notice about his arrival.

The *Gap Year* book was well-thumbed and annotated. A brand new and extremely large rucksack was packed and tablet purchased, as it was more travel-friendly than lugging a laptop about.

He was dumping yet more accumulated rubbish in the wheelie bin when he heard his name.

"Stuart!" It was a loud stage whisper from the open lounge window of next door. Lillian beckoned him over. "I wanted you to know. You made the right decision. Jayne doesn't see it exactly that way at the moment. But she is interviewing for a private carer — she's finally realised she can't do it all alone. So that's progress."

Stuart opened his mouth to speak but Lillian silenced him. "I need to finish before I forget the words and wonder why your head is leaning inside my window. I want you to have this." She handed him a slip of dark brown paper with gold lettering. "It's the menu from that posh, free box of chocolates we got for Jayne. Always remember me as FUN. Not as the dribbling moron I will have become by the time you return."

There was a lump in his throat. He kissed her papery cheek. Then she pushed him away as Jayne's voice called from the hall. The menu still smelled of chocolate. He remembered the mugs of rich, sweet liquid and the joy mixed with triumph on Lillian's face as they'd sipped them. The folded paper went in an inner pocket of his rucksack.

Robert, George, Cindy and Theresa arrived early on completion day, having used the hotel bookings originally made for the wedding. Robert had been put out when told his services as best man would no longer be needed. He'd muttered something about suits and dresses having already been purchased and that Borefield men didn't jilt women at the altar. The words had slid over Stuart like scrambled eggs on Teflon; after the hash he'd made of his life, he was past caring.

Robert marched into the hall with an envelope in his hand. "Some woman was about to post this through the letterbox. I saved her the trouble."

The handwriting matched the note in the book that had become his bible. Stuart's heart hammered and his hands trembled as he attempted to open the envelope. He turned to face the wall, in an attempt to get some privacy from his brothers and sisters-in-law who were marching around the echoing, empty house checking for any family heirlooms that might have been forgotten.

It was a 'Bon Voyage' card. Stuart took a breath. He hadn't been in touch with Florence since their coffee date. Inside it read:

To Stuart,
Happy travels!
From Florence, Shayne, Eunice, Tibby and Slowcoach.

The children had written their own names and drawn paw prints under the animals' names.

George was shouting something about checking the loft and loading the remaining bits of furniture into the cars to go to the tip. Stuart pushed the card into his rucksack before Robert propelled him up the stairs to check the loft. Satisfied it was empty, three trips to the dump got rid of everything else.

Then, for the last time, the three men stood in the kitchen of the house they'd grown up in. For a moment none of them spoke. Stuart tried to remember his mother cooking but it was too long ago. He wondered how life might have been different if they'd had a sister to bind the siblings more tightly. It's impossible to imagine something you'd never known. But now was his chance to level the balance of power between him and his brothers, whom Lillian had once described as 'more like ugly sisters'. Cinderella Stuart was no more.

Robert offered Stuart his hand. "All the best, kiddo."

Stuart left Robert's hand hanging awkwardly in mid-air. George patted Stuart awkwardly on the back. "Have a good trip and send us a postcard or two."

"No." The firmness in Stuart's voice surprised even himself. "I won't waste another second of my life thinking about either of you. Finally, after fifty-six years I have learned that blood is NOT thicker than water." He paused and four pairs of shocked eyes stared at him. "Over the last twelve months I've been given much love plus bucketfuls of encouragement to reach for a bright new future. None of it from family members. I've also had ultimatums, put-downs and meanness — all of it from my closest blood relatives."

His brothers' faces were flushed and frowning, mouths partly open as though they wanted to speak but couldn't find the words.

"I rest my case. Blood is NOT thicker than water. Do not expect a postcard or any other communication."

No one responded, except Cindy, Robert's wife, who followed Stuart out of the kitchen as he went to retrieve his rucksack.

She gave him a hug. "You deserve this freedom," she whispered. "If I'm totally honest, I'm envious. Be free for me, too."

Stuart hugged her back, unable to find the words to respond to her final comment.

"The station?" George was in the hallway wearing a bitter expression and his voice was tight.

"No, thanks. My taxi's just arrived."

As he went out to the waiting car, there was a movement in the window next door. A brief wave and then the person was gone. Whether it was Jayne or Lillian he couldn't be sure.

* * *

Heathrow. Bustle, noise, smart shops, departure boards, cafés, seasoned travellers and Stuart. Everyone seemed to be with someone. Everyone knew the drill. Everyone was relaxed. Only Stuart positioned himself directly in front of the board of lights, endlessly checking when the gate for the flight opened. First long-haul flight. First flight for decades. He was anxious about the connecting planes in Frankfurt and Singapore before he even set foot in Sydney and attempted to navigate himself to his accommodation and then tackled a week of sightseeing before starting work for three months. His nerves were on edge and he was doubting the logic behind his decision to travel. But it was now or never.

The lights on the departure board rearranged themselves into a new order and a smattering of people began to move.

His stomach lurched. The gate was open. Then there was more waiting while the ground crew set themselves up for boarding. Nearly time to switch off his phone.

Thanks for the card and for coming into my life.
En route to Australia.

He pressed 'send' and stood up to join the queue that was forming. Florence's reply arrived just before he turned the phone off.

When you come back we might be ready for each other. Enjoy!
XXX

THE END

THE CHOC LIT STORY

Established in 2009, Choc Lit is an independent, award-winning publisher dedicated to creating a delicious selection of quality women's fiction.

We have won 18 awards, including Publisher of the Year and the Romantic Novel of the Year, and have been shortlisted for countless others.

All our novels are selected by genuine readers. We are proud to publish talented first-time authors, as well as established writers whose books we love introducing to a new generation of readers.

In 2023, we became a Joffe Books company. Best known for publishing a wide range of commercial fiction, Joffe Books has its roots in women's fiction. Today it is one of the largest independent publishers in the UK.

We love to hear from you, so please email us about absolutely anything bookish at choc-lit@joffebooks.com

If you want to hear about all our bargain new releases, join our mailing list: www.choc-lit.com

Milton Keynes UK
Ingram Content Group UK Ltd.
UKHW041036110224
437582UK00005B/305